Moon Shadow

JOE BARFIELD

CreateSpace Publishing

Moon Shadow

Copyright © 2015 Joe Barfield

All rights reserved.

No part of this book may be used or reproduced by any means, graphic, electronic, or mechanical, including photocopying, recording, taping or by any information storage retrieval system without the written permission of the publisher except in the case of brief quotations embodied in critical articles and reviews.

ISBN-13: 978-1511901314

DEDICATION

To the men who risked their lives in air combat and to those who survived their ordeals. And to what I believe to be the best propeller driven aircraft ever made, the North American P-51 Mustang. And to the memory of the nineteen-year-old pilot, John Magee, who lost his life in the Battle of Britain. He left us with these few words I shall never forget:

High Flight

Oh, I have slipped the surly bonds of earth
And danced the skies on laughter-silvered wings;
Sunward I've climbed, and joined the tumbling mirth
Of sun-split clouds—and done a hundred things
You have not dreamed of—wheeled and soared and swung
High in the sunlit silence. Hov'ring there,
I've chased the shouting wind along, and flung
My eager craft through footless halls of air.
Up, up the long, delirious burning blue,
I've topped the windswept heights with easy grace
Where never lark, or even eagle flew.
And, while with silent, lifting mind I've trod
The high untrespassed sanctity of space,
Put out my hand, and touched the face of God.

For those who believe this story is impossible, forget not David and Goliath, the Trojan Horse and the heroic action of men throughout history who have conquered insurmountable odds.

Recall the words of one of the first and maybe greatest fighter pilots of all time:

"It is not the machine but the man who flies the machine." Captain Manfred von Richthofen, the legendary Red Baron

MOON SHADOW
TABLE OF CONTENTS

	Acknowledgments	i
	Introduction	1
1	The Duck and the Hawk Talk	3
2	The Girl and the Dutchman	15
3	Birth and Death	26
4	Tribute to an Old Warrior	49
5	The Mustang Flies	58
6	The Devil's Angels	68
7	On a Wing and a Prayer	80
8	The Abduction and the Fury	100
9	"Angel Eyes"	114
10	Illusions of Truth	120
11	Wings of Death	129
12	Picnic	148
13	Torture	155
14	The Hero	166
15	To Find a Blackbird	176
16	When Moon Shadows Falls	195
17	The Untold Secret	203
18	Intrepid Specter	209
	Glossary	218
	Reasons For the Collapse of the Roman Empire	220
	National Debt, the Deficit, and Spending	222
	Comments from the Author	229
	Excerpt From *Moon Shadow the Legend* (Book 1)	233
	Excerpt From *Moon Shadow's Revenge* (Book 3)	237
	Other Books Available by the Author	239
	About the Author	248

ACKNOWLEDGMENTS

To John Hadfield; the wild adventure began in Kansas City.
And lets not forget **"Thunder Bunny"**

"The technical aspect of Moon Shadow is well covered, making what the P-51 Mustang accomplishes even more believable. A wonderful and thrilling adventure."
-**Pat Moran**, the first American pilot to fly the Russian Mig 29 and Sukhoi 27

America will never be destroyed from the outside. If we falter and lose our freedoms, it will be because we destroyed ourselves. –Abraham Lincoln

From the beginning of time, every empire has collapsed. There have been no exceptions. — The Author

Tolerance is the last virtue of a dying society. – Aristotle

I predict a black day for the United States. -- Osama bin Laden

SPECIAL THANKS TO:

"David and Goliath"
Cover art by
Dan Zoernig, who wishes to extend special thanks to his daughter Emily and his nephew Zachary for their invaluable help in producing the model aircraft used in this illustration. www.danzoernig.com

"SR-71 Blackbird"
Cover art by
John Bedke
http://www.laughingcatsstudio.com

"Blackbird Up and Away"
Philip Alexander
www.rb-29.net (click on Art Gallery)

My editor, Karen Gordon, and Dan Zoernig for his wonderful cover idea.
To my son Beau, daughter Becky and wife Lucia I want to thank for the wonderful adventures that have led to so many novel ideas. To John Hadfield and the long drives from Kansas where the idea for Moon Shadow originated in 1987.

Introduction

The Middle-Eastern brotherhood and numerous countries from South America, calling themselves the "Coalition," had joined together and managed something people said could never be accomplished. After all America was favored by God; this was also true for Sodom and Gomorrah at one time. The mightiest empire had been invaded and virtually defeated but it was not the power of the invading forces that accomplished such an impossible task. It was more a self-inflicted defeat. First and foremost you must have a standing army to defend and defeat invading forces. Hundreds of America's best military leaders had been replaced with incompetent officers that had no faith and no God. To add to the military incompetence was borne the financial destruction of what had been the most feared and technologically advanced military force in history. America's military was more like welfare, being paid for nothing, capable of nothing and accomplishing nothing. The year before the invasion America was on the verge of bankruptcy but instead of cutting their entitlements they cut more than ninety percent of the military sending them home. Those that remained fought a war not to protect their country and the oath they had sworn but rather to spy and expose their fellow soldiers. Christians were considered terrorists and traitors. Few that remained believed in God or Country. Before the invasion began America's military was really non-existent. Without America's President the Coalition would never have succeeded with the invasion. In reality America had lost the war before it began.

Many things had led to the demise of America but the one thing that could be pointed to as the leading factor was the President of the United States of America followed closely with America's Congress.

America had been invaded but it was not so much invaded as destroyed from within through the greed and corruption of liberals and conservatives alike. Although have claimed to be conservative and the other half liberal they were neither. Government did everything they wanted with the exception of one thing and that was what they were elected to do; represent the people. Moral, government and financial decay had destroyed the greatest country in history; the United States of America. Her fate had been sealed when the government became financially insolvent and was unable to pay the military. The military walked home leaving only a handful of people to defend America. Even though small, poorly equipped and with few leaders it was easy to take over where no army existed. The illegal aliens crossing into America daily had shown the invaders America' Achilles Heel. It had been easy to convince the Spanish speaking people to join the invasion. Few it was that were found who only spoke English.

The invasion was swift and what military remnants that remained had been pushed up to the northern states. Complete defeat had been delayed when a harsh and severe winter set in. All the Coalition did was wait for winter to end so they could finish America.

The President had been executed and not by the Coalition. Angry Americans called the Minute Men had marched upon his residence and hung him and his wife, with a bold sign stuck beneath his feet that read, "This is the execution for the treason they committed to the United States of America."

Alaska had already separated and become an independent country breaking all ties with America. Washington State, Idaho, Utah Montana and Wyoming had signed a peace agreement with the Coalition to cease all hostilities.

The winter had slowed the Coalition but the Texans had stopped them. The Coalition had taken all of the military bases but had run into an army of about four million hostile angry citizens that knew how to hunt and how to kill They were young old and female of which about half were marksmen and well-armed. The Coalition sent out marksmen with night vision. Many returned taking out the Texans they sought but most never returned. The Texans victorious. Soon they found each other joined and created formidable groups against the Coalition. Groups of militia and former military banded together to stop the Coalition. They never were strong enough to defeat the Coalition but they were enough to force a critical delay on the Coalitions advance.

One such group comprised of some of America's best pilots had escaped the initial attack and tried to regroup in a remote area of Texas known as the Hill Country. With no weapons and no aircraft they made no plans to attack the Coalition. They concentrated on more immediate problems to find water, then food, and if possible shelter. They had no means to fight a war. Their thoughts were on how to survive the next day. They made camp on the Frio River, slept in their cars and waited. For what they waited they had no idea but they had survived…so far.

Chapter 1
THE DUCK AND THE HAWK TALK

    The Frio River's crystal clear, cold waters continued to flow unaware of the events changing history. Could the river speak, it would have told of men from Mexico crossing its flowing rivers over 175 years earlier. Gallant men at a tiny mission in San Antonio called the *Alamo* stalled the advance for thirteen days. Eventually those invaders lost. But the river told none of this to the strange array of men and women not prepared to defend themselves and so unlike their ancestors before them, nearly two centuries before. These people were pilots and military personnel, not rough and tough frontiersmen. They were not survivalists, but to survive they would need to adapt and learn quickly, for their very lives would depend on it.

    From the main road the group turned off and skirted the winding Frio River. The narrow path was wide enough for the vehicles to follow. For a mile they continued north along the river. The terrain continued to change and when it seemed like they could go no farther they still continued on.

    Finally they came out into an opening that was like an amphitheater and fairly level. It was open to the river and about four feet above the fast running cold water. On the other side a cliff rose vertically over forty feet. The wet slope revealed numerous springs running down the timeless limestone cliff and into the river. The area was lined with water oaks that perpetually held their green foliage. Numerous cypress trees lined the banks. Mesquite trees filled the area and provided excellent wood for cooking fires and providing warmth for the people now hiding from American invaders. The spot was an excellent place to wait, and far enough away from the main road that they could safely stay there without anyone detecting them. The site was suitable for a prolonged stay.

While everyone worked on setting up camp, Robby continued his effort to establish contact on the short-wave radio with anyone who would respond. While the women gathered wood, the men started setting up tents.

Deberg, Marix, and James continued to devour Lindy with their eyes and almost stumbled over her in their efforts to help. Although Warren enjoyed watching Lindy, he helped set up camp, as he knew the situation demanded. He and Pickett were busy erecting tents.

Mulholland found a small steel pipe and a sledgehammer while unloading the tents. He looked at the items and then across the river at the cliff and gradually an idea came to him.

Blackman started a small fire and immediately Sunday retrieved what she needed to start a pot of coffee and some hot chocolate. James moved into action, took a large plastic bucket to the river, filled it with water, and brought it to Sunday. Krysti helped with the efforts to make the warm drinks. Sunday dished a pot of water from the bucket and put it on the rock-lined fire with a steel grill cover to boil it for the coffee and chocolate.

When James scooped a cup of water from the bucket and started to drink, Krysti motioned him to stop. "I wouldn't do that."

Dropping the cup from his mouth he said, "Why? It's just spring water."

"Yes and no," she said. "That's the mistake many people make. The water you are about to drink has been running down the river for miles. All the animals around here drink from the river and many times relieve themselves in the same water."

Looking at the cup James mumbled, "Ohhh." He poured the water on the ground.

"And God forbid that there is a ranch upstream with cattle or pigs," Krysti noted.

Moving into the area Marix asked, "Why is that?"

Finishing the erection of a large tent, the usually quiet Blackman said, "Because those animals carry diseases that kill people."

For a moment the hammering from across the river distracted everyone. Facing the cliff Mulholland pounded away on the steel pipe, driving it slowly into the limestone. Another plastic bucket lay near his feet. When he had the pipe firmly embedded at a point where water had been flowing from a crack, he hung the bucket near the end of the pipe. A few moments later clear, fresh spring water started to trickle into the container.

"Kipp, you are a dear," screamed Sunday.

With a big grin Mulholland said, "That should solve our water problems."

Everyone returned to his or her respective jobs trying to make the campsite more livable. Soon the smoking mesquite and sweetness of the chocolate and the aroma of coffee gradually relaxed the tense group, and for a while the knowledge of a war seemed far, far away.

The Grays pulled a tent from the back of their luxurious SUV and set it up quickly. If a tent could be called fancy their tent would have been called that. They set up lounge chairs and a table and started their own personal gas stove and made tea. They didn't help anyone else.

Before darkness settled in, the camp had been set up and a campfire crackled, giving light to their darkening surroundings.

Soon they had all gathered around the fire. Even the Grays joined them. It didn't appear that Stephan Gray knew anything about roughing it or camping out. Most of them stared quietly into the flames.

Still the unanswered questions haunted everyone in the small group. Speculation as to who the attackers were became as varied as the people in the camp. How was it accomplished? Who were the leaders? How far had they penetrated? Could they escape? They seemed so detached and far away from the attack and the action. If everything was true, could Beau find Tracy and could he find them? Some doubted he would succeed, two hoped he would fail, but Ruben and those who knew Beau had no doubt he would accomplish his personal mission and return with Tracy.

Slowly the evening wore on. They settled into their makeshift camp quite comfortably. Krysti and Justin kept a personal watch for Beau and his brothers. Every time they thought they heard something, their eyes would search the trail expecting all four men to emerge with the news they could leave and return home. No one noticed Lindy and Deberg missing from the camp.

The only distraction was Garrett and Schmitt working on the short wave radio. Garrett gave a special emergency frequency to Schmitt: a frequency to be used should a situation like this ever occur. Soon Schmitt had the radio crackling. Garrett never dreamed the frequency would ever be used. Schmitt started broadcasting a special coded sequence and soon he received a response. Eventually they stopped transmitting and joined the others around the fire.

Garrett asked Stephan Gray, "What do you do for a living?"

"Greenpeace. My wife and I are environmentalists."

Sully looked at the Cadillac SUV. "Didn't know there was so much money in saving the environment."

"No there isn't," he half chuckled. "My family is wealthy from oil lease royalties."

"I didn't think they were too environmentally correct," laughed Ruben.

The crimson color on his face could be seen even in the light of the fire.

Gray's wife said, "We know, that's why we're against it now."

Stephan said, "That was a long time ago. As my wife said, we're against it now."

"Take the money and run," quipped Ruben.

"Shouldn't ya be driving a Volkswagen, mate?" Kipp asked.

Quickly Sully added, "Yeah, Al Gore is just like you. In fact I think he drives the same Escalade."

Trying to change the subject Garrett asked, "So what were you doing so far away from Houston?"

Stephan responded, "A place in Austin was slaughtering animals for hides and furs. We organized a protest to stop them from selling the furs."

Garrett regretted the question. Sully smirked.

In the darkness it was obvious that Joan was shaking. The night was already cool and it was rapidly getting colder.

"Do any of you have a couple of extra jackets?"

The Indian Blackman was quick to respond. "Yes," he said and went to one of the trucks bringing back three heavy jackets. He gave them to Stephan Gray.

Gray looked at the jackets almost in disgust and snapped, "What are these?"

Turning to the man, Blackman squatted by the fire and void of emotion said, "Leather jackets. They will keep you warm."

With a laugh Kipp said, "You know mate—animal skins."

Ruben chuckled, Sully laughed, and Sunday had to hide her smile. Krysti shook her head and even Marix managed a slight grin, while James nodded but kept a watchful eye out for Deberg who he knew was with Lindy. Justin kept poking a stick into the fire.

Shocked at the jackets, Stephan said, "We can't wear these."

Blackman walked over and took the coats. "Then stay close to your family when you sleep tonight because it will be cold." He spread the jackets over a log near the fire. "When you need them they will be here."

"We can't wear animal skins," said Joan.

The tension could have been cut with a knife. The Grays quickly retired to their tents, where, in a vain effort, they tried to keep warm. Not long after they disappeared into their tents Deberg returned. Lindy followed a few minutes later. James was quick to get her attention. Before any noticed Lindy and James had disappeared from the camp. Pickett shook his head at Deberg and he grinned back.

It was Sully who first expressed the thought that was on everybody's mind. "How could something like this happen?"

Deberg, Pick, and Sunday shook their heads while Kipp and Warren nodded.

Blackman said, "Wolf."

They all looked over at him. Sully and Ruben seemed confused. Pick, Warren, and Deberg were confused as well, although it did not show on their faces.

Waving his hands in the air, Ruben asked, "Could you maybe use a few more words so the rest of us could understand?"

"The government."

Again Ruben asked, "Maybe you could expand on that also."

Blackman said, "Since the 9/11 incident in New York, all the presidents cry wolf to get their popularity up with the people."

Shaking his head, Pick understood. "Cried wolf so many times the people quit listening."

"Yes," said Blackman.

"Well, the economy sure didn't help," said Deberg.

"So when do you think this started?" Sully asked.

"Kennedy, in the sixties," said Warren.

Ruben quipped, "Reagan. All that money he spent."

"Bush added to that," Pick noted.

"Which Bush?" snipped Sully. "The father or the son trying to finish what the father started?"

"What about Clinton?" Deberg asked more than he said.

"Aye, mates, it was the second Bush," said Kipp. "He wanted to blow up every Middle Eastern country."

"What difference does it make now?" asked Marix.

"Gives us somebody to burn in effigy," said Ruben.

"They were all to blame," said Krysti.

"True," said Ruben.

"Something else that bothered me about Bush after 9/11 was how he protected all of those CEOs that destroyed the American economy. I lost everything I had in the stock market," said Deberg, the anger in his voice evident.

"Ditto."

"Yeah."

"Me too."

"No kidding."

Ruben quipped, "Yeah, the CEOs of America! Now there was a real group of terrorists."

"Did any of them ever go to jail?" Pick asked.

Sully groaned. "I don't think so."

Warren noted, "If Bush had come down as hard on the CEOs as he did Afghanistan and Iraq, I'd have probably still been able to retire."

"Looked more like Bush was protecting the CEOs," said Deberg.

"When you look back it makes you wonder whose side he was on," said Sully.

"You might say that with Bush in office," said Ruben, who then laughed out loud, "we got Bush-whacked."

Warren and Kipp laughed, while Pick and Sully chuckled. Sunday, Deberg, and Krysti only nodded their agreement.

"Shoulda nuked the Middle East back then," said Sully.

"Or controlled the politicians," Sunday interjected.

Krysti sighed, "As easy as controlling the CEO's."

Pick said "If you look up the definition of traitor and treason, most of the CEOs of America fit into that category."

"I coulda destroyed the Middle East without firing a shot," said Ruben.

Everyone turned to look at Ruben. Sully asked, "How, send them all of our CEOs?"

Deberg laughed. "No, send all of our politicians."

A few of them chuckled at Deberg's words. Some of the others laughed out loud.

"Actually the solution was simple," said Ruben. "No war. All we had to do was send them Fords, Chevys, Sony, MacDonalds, DVDs and CDs."

Marix asked, "What would that do?"

"Well," said Ruben, "When you saw kids walking down the streets of Baghdad with a baseball cap sideways, a headset on, and they were doing Michael Jackson's *Moonwalk*, you would have known then that we had defeated them."

A few of them chuckled; Deberg and Sully laughed.

About the same time Deberg, Sully, and Pick stood and Sully said it first. "I'm turning in."

Deberg and Pick chimed in, "Me too."

"See everyone in the morning," Pick added.

As they walked slowly to their respective tents, Marix made a friendly helpful move on Krysti that became more amorous and serious as the night wore on. The tension and pressure made her pull away. Slowly the others retired to their respective tents. Only Warren, Blackman, and Kipp remained. Soon only Blackman waited on watch.

Beau and his brothers failed to return that night.

* * *

Dawn brought no change. All four Gex brothers had failed to reappear. Blackman pointed out to Kipp that the three jackets were missing. It looked like an animal skin was okay when you got too cold. Marix continued to put pressure on Krysti.

Coming out of their tents and toward the fire and smell of coffee were the Grays. Nothing was said about the leather jackets they wore.

Slaving over the fire, Krysti and Sunday prepared breakfast of sausage, bacon, and eggs. Finished with their meal, Ruben, Blackman, and Kipp washed their plates in the river. The three environmentalists looked to the two women with hungry eyes. Deberg offered them coffee.

"Any Sweet and Low?" asked Joan.

Sully laughed. "Afraid not."

In an effort to please the Grays, Krysti brought two plates filled with food. Joan and Stephan took the plates and stared at the meat and eggs.

Stephan shook his head. "Sorry, we don't eat animal flesh."

Already exhausted from cooking and with what was more like a reaction to a disobedient child, Sunday literally jumped to her feet, marched over to the unappreciative pair, and jerked the plates away from them. She gave one to Deberg and the other to Sully who had been waiting patiently. Krysti was stunned to silence. The others had turned to watch Sunday in action. Those washing dishes in the river had stopped and were walking over.

"What are we going to eat?" Joan almost demanded.

Sunday turned to Deberg and Sully and said, "Do you mind?" Before they could respond she had taken a biscuit off each plate and shoved one into Stephan's hand and the other into Joan's. "This is it. Unless you want to go pick berries or onions."

As Sunday stormed back to the fire, no one made a move or a sound. Not even the Grays. When she reached the fire she turned her head toward them. "You should know that I cooked those biscuits with animal fat." She turned back to the fire and continued cooking. The camp remained tense and silent. The Grays, minus Lindy, returned to their tent.

Timidly, Lindy approached the fire. "Mrs. Alonzo?"

Sunday and Krysti turned to the girl. Sunday said, "Yes."

"I'm not like my parents. Can I eat?"

Sunday smiled, the tension gone. "Sure, Sugar." She filled the plate and gave it to the young woman.

Soon the camp was busy with activity. Schmitt and Garrett continued with the radio trying to find broadcasts with information they could use. The camp became more settled. Even the Grays came out and walked about the campsite, taking time to relax near the river. The morning episode had already been forgotten.

Just a little after lunch Schmitt made contact. Garrett hurried over to listen to the transmissions and authenticate the codes. They exchanged a series of signals before the communications continued. First, they asked their location.

"Eighty miles from San Antonio," said Schmitt.

"Where?" After Schmitt repeated the location the radio operator said, "You're about 600 miles behind enemy lines." The answer destroyed what little hope the small band had for a quick rescue or escape.

The commander took over for the radio operator and gave the small group details of the invasion. The invaders sent three strategically placed airliners on courses set for Los Angeles, New Orleans, and Washington D.C. The red alert had been sounded and all available aircraft became airborne. The strategy had worked. When the jets intercepted the airliners, the pilots of the planes indicated radio problems. They were pursued for an hour, then the pilots unexpectedly bailed out of their craft. Fifteen precious minutes passed before the decision to destroy the airliners could be rendered. Fear that others might be on board caused the delay. With this accomplished, the jets, low on fuel, returned to their bases. While this happened the invaders sent a blanket of jets across the border of Mexico and the waters between Cuba and Florida. The thousands of jets managed to stay below radar detection. The masterpiece of the operation was sending passenger jets along. They also had the schedules of all commercial airlines. More than twenty passenger jets were shot from the skies or sabotaged at the airports and replaced with exact counterfeits, filled with armed troops. They landed throughout the southern part of the United States unmolested and untouched.

The commander explained how the jets scrambled for the three decoy airliners had no chance. Although armed, they were outnumbered and out of fuel. The returning jets had limited airtime remaining and the ones on the ground were sitting ducks, of which most were unarmed. Somehow a few pilots managed to escape north with their aircraft. The invaders had a firm hold on the southern half of the United States. Winter gripped the north, and he said the biggest problem now was that supplies of gas and oil were not readily available. All the oil storage facilities were located in the south, and the Coalition controlled them. Over the past decades environmentalists had been able to eliminate oil and gas storage and drilling, and now the northern part of America had no oil and no gas.

"It will be a long time before we can push them out. Even if we could regain control of the U.S., it would be years before we could drive the last of them out. They have a stronger hold than you can imagine," said General Waddle.

The voice sounded familiar to Garrett. "Duck?"

The response was slow in coming. "Hawk?"

Hawk, the name Garrett used in Vietnam. The officer on the other end was Garrett's old friend, Chuck Waddle—the same officer who had been present at Beau's civilian review board.

"Hell, I was afraid you were either dead or a prisoner in Del Rio. They've taken over all the bases in Texas," said Waddle.

"All?" mumbled Garrett obviously stunned.

"You're in the middle of all this crap." Waddle paused as though hiding something, and then he added, "The president and vice president are dead." Both ends of the short wave were silent as Garrett and his group absorbed the news.

"The president," mumbled Robby.

"How?" Garrett asked.

Sounding distraught, Waddle managed to say, "A commercial airliner crashed into the Orange Bowl Stadium killing the vice president. The President was taking a two-week vacation in Tahoe. It was a bloodbath. His Secret Service did their best but they were overwhelmed. The President and his wife were hung in the front yard for all to see. They even hung a sign around his neck that said 'Last of the Czars.' We haven't found his children."

"Is the Speaker of the House in charge?"

There was a moment of silence before Waddle continued. "She was in Las Vegas with a hundred of her followers. They were caught and killed at a private airport, while trying to escape."

The information stunned Garrett, "How did the invaders do that?"

"THEY didn't," said Waddle. "A group of Americans, out for what they called justice, executed nearly every member of her group. A former military officer saw it all but was unable to stop them. The assassins called themselves the Minutemen. Shot all of her followers and hung her from the roof of the hanger with a sign saying, "Justice For Her Treason."

"Damn," said Garrett. "What about Congress?"

The groan could be heard over the microphone. "You really don't know anything, do you?"

"What do you mean?" Garrett asked.

"Most of the members of Congress have been killed. Along with our wealthier business leaders. Especially those bailed out by Bush and Obama."

"Americans?"

"That's right. The few we caught said it was justice for the treason Congress committed to the citizens of the United States. Only a few members of Congress remain, and that's only because they were with the military when the executions started."

Shock filled Garrett's face. "I can't believe it."

"I know what you mean. We still can't believe it."

"From what we can tell twenty-nine Congressmen survived. Those were men strongly against the government. The Minutemen call them Patriots."

"So who's running the country?"

"The military until we can regain a semblance of control."

"This is a nightmare."

"Yes it is," said Waddle. Then he added, "It's small consolation but tell Commander Gex he was dead nuts on the money. The information he uncovered in Lebanon was right. Those bastards did it. They've formed a line from Los Angeles across southern Oklahoma over to Florida. We're forming a defensive line from Detroit to Washington, D.C. Let me tell you those crazy bastards have some balls. In order to use those commercial airliners the way they did without detection, they had to have flown them five hundred feet or less above the ground. An ingenious scheme that paid off and may have cost us our country."

When they heard the news most were shocked. The Grays were horrified.

Like the others, Krysti heard and was stunned. The startling truth was almost like being punched in the face. The president dead, the country at war, and the man she had unexpectedly become so attracted to was the same man she had read about—the same man who they said had killed children. Iran and Egypt had filed a grievance with the U.S. to have him extradited so he could stand trial for murder. How could it be this gentle man? Her stomach was twisted in knots as she absorbed the information. She wanted the truth to go away. She wanted someone to tell her it wasn't so, that this man couldn't be the same. The man she had come to . . . to love! No! She could love no such man. She refused to cry.

Instantly visions of her parents filled her mind. She worried about her father and hoped they were safe in the river house near El Paso. An emptiness overwhelmed Krysti. She felt alone as visions of her parents, sister, and home in El Paso continued to fill her mind. With those reflections came new fears. Still, she could not comprehend the awful truth or the extent of the living nightmare. The United States had been invaded!

Sunday started to cry and Ruben tried to console her. Some thought Krysti's silence to be born of fear and shock at the news of the current events. All listened as the conversation continued.

"What about the carriers? Why don't you attack?" asked Garrett.

"Not that easy, Hawk. The invaders control the military bases. Prisoners are being held there. We can't use nuclear weapons."

"Nuclear weapons?" Garrett repeated. All of those that could hear gasped and continued to listen. Some even whispered in stunned disbelief and horror.

Waddle responded. "It was contemplated and even discussed. A few small detonations at some of their key strongholds was thought to be a very real viable option. It is no longer a consideration."

"What about our forces in the Middle East? When they return that should help?"

"I guess you don't know anything." There was a long silence before General Waddle continued. "It now appears the situation between Israel and Egypt was fabricated. In fact, most of the Arab nations were in on it. Once we were set in the Persian Gulf and the troops off loaded, they waited for the precise time of the invasion here and launched a nighttime attack there. Their leaders sent more than a million civilians to mob our troops. They had nothing but sticks, knives, and farm tools. For all intents and purposes they seemed like refugees and that's what the troops thought until it was too late.

"Behind them came 500,000 crack troops." He paused before he continued. "We estimate we killed more than one million of their people but we lost over 400,000 of our men—all dead in a couple of hours. Those that survived are retreating to Israel but they haven't made it yet."

"The naval fleet?" asked Garrett almost afraid of the obvious answer.

"Gone!" The Duck lamented. "Our naval fleet was dealt a crushing blow. It came so quick and fast. While their people attacked our troops, they sent hundreds of small Cessna-like aircraft at ground level for our ships. Each was loaded with enough explosives to take out a carrier. We didn't have a chance. Those crazy bastards made suicide dives into the carriers. One sunk and three inoperable. Our air service, what remains of it, either escaped north or were captured. We're almost defenseless. If they had used aircraft and missiles, we could have detected them. But no, they hit us with the one thing we could not find. Those small planes were almost skipping across the water. They sacrificed their lives and destroyed almost all of our ships. A few managed to send radio messages about the battle. When they tried to limp away, the United Arab Air Forces finished them off."

"What should we do?"

"Take evasive action. Keep in contact and wait. In case you don't know, you're in a real hot spot with no way out."

"We'll contact you when we can."

"Funny, all the gun control this country has passed actually helped the invaders. We've intercepted some of their transmissions and it seems they didn't anticipate armed citizens. They met some resistance they hadn't expected in Texas, Arkansas, and Louisiana. They intended to split the U.S. right through Texas to the Great Lakes. They do control the Texas bases, but it seems the natives of Texas have taken to shooting them at nighttime.

And those damn Cajun boys stopped them cold when they tried to cross the swamps. It stalled the drive and has given us time to regroup."

Marix grabbed the microphone and interrupted. "You've got to get us out of here! Now!"

"Well, now, that's just fine but . . . hey, who is that?" asked the Duck.

Garrett jerked the microphone away from Marix and motioned for Blackman and Warren to restrain him. "Sorry, Duck, got an over-zealous pilot just itching to get into action again."

"Well, you just tell him there isn't a damn thing he can do. A man can squash a hornet but God help you if the whole nest attacks you. They out number us at least fifteen to one. The jets may not be as good as ours, but they surprised our ass and there just aren't many left. They also captured a lot of our jets. We're way outnumbered and now we have to fight the ones they managed to capture. Thank God for the Canadians and their help 'cause we're in a lot of trouble. Only thing saving us is them trying to find enough fuel to finish their drive and the severe winter up here. The refineries in Corpus and Houston, near as we can tell, are being set to produce fuel that will bring them to the final part of their plans."

"We better get off the airwaves."

"Now, if we could get those good ol' Texas boys to increase their numbers by about a thousand times over and attack in sniper fashion, maybe it would give us enough time to create a counterattack of our own. It's a good thing the weapons laws didn't move fast in Texas. Those guys have really hurt the invasions advance. Good luck, Hawk." The radio went dead and the Duck was gone.

Ted Garrett whipped around to face Marix who was still being restrained. "Listen, Marix," said Garrett, pressing a finger firmly against his chest. "You will control yourself from now on. Don't ever do that unless you have permission. I still command this group."

For an instant, Marix appeared ready to hit Garrett, but with Blackman and Warren restraining him he refrained and forced control. "Yes Sir. I apologize for my actions."

His answer, under the current circumstances, satisfied Admiral Garrett. He nodded to Blackman and Warren and they released him. Marix pulled away and moved to the other side of the camp to console Krysti.

"I didn't know who Beau was," Krysti said while silently she thought, *I cared for him so much.*

Mike put his arms around her and hugged her to him. "There, there, Krysti. You had no way of knowing. I knew, but it wasn't my place. It would have been wrong for me to tell you. I was concerned about you and what would happen when you learned the truth. I was only hoping he would be gone before you found out. He has such a bad reputation with women. The things he does with them, using them then discarding them as if they were old furniture. I was afraid he would do that to you. I'm just grateful you found out before something happened."

"I'm so sorry, Michael. I thought he was so kind and brave. He was so gentle . . . I . . . I was wrong," said Krysti, but all she could think about was Beau and her feelings toward him.

"I don't know how to tell you this—Beau is a coward," said Marix, feeling smug in the control he so swiftly regained. He wondered how Beau could ever find them. Common sense told Marix it would be impossible for Gex to track them. This was the chance to win over Krysti permanently. "He won't come back, he's afraid." Then just in case Beau did make it back he added, "We'll only see him if he was unable to save himself."

Marix felt her body tremble, and he knew he had succeeded. He raised her head and kissed her hard on the lips and she responded. Satisfied for the moment, he was determined to take advantage of the present opportunity and have Krysti for the night.

To Krysti, Michael was so kind, so generous, but for some reason she didn't have the same secure feelings in his arms as she had in Beau's. This she excused to the whimsical and the current situation and the war in which they found themselves involved. She was foolish to care so much for Beau. Coward, she thought. She should have known when he left with his brothers. But for some reason her mind returned to a bar and a man called Haun and she became confused.

Krysti was lonely, scared, and sad. James and Marix had told her the truth. Beau was not going to return. A tremendous desire for attention and to be touched filled her being so reluctantly she stayed with Marix.

Three men stood beside the fire, stunned at the position fate had given them. Larry James, Barry Pickett, and Fred Deberg mulled over the problems. Across the campsite and near her parents' tent, Lindy tried to decide which man she would sneak away with for her own personal fun and pleasure.

Pick assumed their present situation was just a challenge put before him by God. Cozmo was angry at the government and politicians for having let the situation occur. And James was whining about his bad luck in getting into this situation.

"I tell ya what. We need to figure out how to get away from here," James said pointing to Ruben and Tang who were unloading one of the pick-ups. "We got a chink, a greaser, and an Indian. We're in a lot of trouble."

"They're part of us," said Pickett, agitated at James's words.

"They're American pilots just like the rest of us," Deberg challenged.

"Not the chink," he interjected. Both men mumbled and walked away from the cowering figure near the fire.

"Hey Mr. James," said Tang. He was carrying water. "You want drink?" He still found it hard to break the habit of calling people Mister.

"No," came the ungrateful reply. He cast a furtive glance about the campsite. The Indian was gone and so was Mulholland. Great, the only ones who could help were gone, he thought. Also, he noticed one of the Jeeps missing. What Larry James failed to notice, as had the others, was a pair of eyes watching curiously from the other side of the river.

From the darkness, Mulholland kept his eyes trained on the campsite as he casually ate a sandwich. He had found tracks and they were recent. Someone had been watching them. From the cover of the brush, he wondered who had been so close to their camp and where Blackman had taken the Jeep.

Chapter 2
THE GIRL AND THE DUTCHMAN

A quiet chill cloaked the campsite, while the aroma of coffee filled the air. Krysti was cold and stiff but the smell of coffee was pleasant and calming. She stuck her head out from beneath the cover of the tent but could not see the fire. The sun was just rising over the hills but darkness still held the campsite.

Neither the thermal underwear nor Marix, who had rolled away during the night, could keep the chill away from her. She sat up and reached with her feet to find the missing bottoms of her thermal underwear, then slipped them on. She stared at Michael and thought she should touch him or thank him but she couldn't. Wrapping a blanket about her, Krysti checked on Justin who lay in a tent with Fitz.

A lone figure knelt beside the fire, but the shadows from the semi gloom and the bright flames she stared into made it impossible to recognize the person. When she was ten feet behind the figure, he asked, "Want some coffee, Krysti?"

"Beau?" she asked, but she already knew it was him before she asked. She was excited, happy, and relieved but her heart was heavy. "How did you know it was me?"

"The way you walk. Short, soft steps. I know how Sunday walks. The men are different."

"I didn't think you were coming back," Krysti said rather coldly.

The tone in her voice caught Beau off guard. "I told you I'd come back. We had problems eluding the invaders. Had to hide out yesterday," he said, handing her the coffee she readily accepted.

"Thank you," Krysti said tartly. "Did you accomplish what you set out to do?"

He pointed to Tracy asleep, cozily wrapped in a sleeping bag. "Her husband was killed."

"I'm sorry." Krysti in her anger had forgotten about the others. The invasion was becoming more real with the knowledge Tracy's husband was dead. For the first time the war had touched them. "Is this the way it's going to be? Just a bunch of killing?"

"I hope not. But there's not much we can do, is there?"

"You can kill them," Krysti said rather bluntly.

Beau turned his head to her and sighed. Sadness filled his eyes. "You know about me?"

"Did you kill those children?"

"They say I did. What do you think?" Beau asked, refusing to deny the murder of children. To argue his point was futile; she would have to trust him. He would not defend himself.

Now Krysti knew. "I should go." She stood and retreated to her tent where she dressed so she could help Tracy. Her heart was filled with sadness, her jaws ached, and something seemed to stick in her throat. Her mind was confused as she questioned the actions of the man she had come to care for in a far greater way than even she imagined. Faintly she remembered Justin and Garrett saying he would return. But that was only natural, because they both liked him. Mostly she remembered Marix's words that Beau would only return if he could not escape. He had saved Tracy and returned. Was he a murderer and a coward? But why had he come back?

Beau said nothing, while the hurt inside deepened. Krysti meant more to him than he let himself believe. The thought of the children he may have killed still haunted him. Would the accusations never end, even from those he most cared about?

Blackman walked to the opposite side of the fire from Beau and bent near with his palms stretched toward the flames.

"She doesn't understand war. But she will soon. Why don't you tell her your side of the story?" Blackman asked. Beau didn't answer. "She likes you," said Blackman.

"What is the story, Dean? What is it? Even I don't know," Beau snapped, confused and angry at Krysti's actions. "She's better off with Mike."

"No she isn't. She'd be safer sleeping with a rattler," Blackman stated simply, which was a lot from a man who was normally quiet and kept his opinions to himself.

"Who are those new people?" Beau asked.

"The Grays. Environmentalists. But harmless and helpless."

"I didn't thank ya for taking the Jeep and waiting for me and my brothers. I'm glad you were there."

"I have a feeling you could have found us anyway. I just made it happen sooner."

Kipp strolled over and immediately told Beau and Dean about what he had found. Someone had been watching them. They all agreed to keep it quiet. From then on they would keep watch farther from the camp so they would have time to warn everyone. All three were sure if someone intended to do something it would be when they so desired, because whoever was watching them was good and they were cautious.

* * *

A week after they made camp on the Frio River things were still calm and unreal. The tension with the Grays had eased. Stephan and Joan wore leather jackets and ate whatever breakfast was prepared. They had a very hard time coping with the demands and expectations that they perform menial jobs like washing clothes, dishes, and gathering water and wild berries and onions. These were tasks below their level in society regardless of what society might have become with the invasion. The invasion. How unreal it still seemed to all but those few who knew.

Everyone in camp knew about Lindy and her antics with James, Deberg, and it seemed even Pickett. The only ones that didn't know were her parents. Krysti hoped her son could be added to the list of those who didn't know what was going on with the girl.

What no one knew about was the occasional liaison between Lindy and Marix. He had been cautious and careful. The other three men had preferred their secret meetings at night. But this was something others always managed to notice. During the day everyone was out and about, so no one noticed when Lindy and Marix would meet.

None of the others, especially Krysti, knew that Marix was meeting with Lindy. Only three knew his secret. Blackman knew because of the signs along the trails where they tried to hide, but he said nothing. The same signs spoke to Beau and Kipp, and they suspected what Blackman already knew. But those three watched for signs along the trails revealing intruders and not people in their camp meeting secretly.

One night found Krysti, Sunday, and Joan clustered around the fire. Joan had made them tea. They sipped on their drinks and talked. Lindy slept in her tent, gathering energy for her evening meeting with James.

"This seems so unreal," said Krysti.

With a nod Sunday said, "Yes it does."

Joan sighed. "Stephan and I are thinking of returning to Houston."

"I said it felt unreal. Don't do anything foolish until we know."

"I know you're right but I need to get Lindy back in school. She's a straight A student and next year she will be a junior."

Sunday and Krysti almost choked as they did the math in their minds.

"And after starting a year before most students she will be so far ahead of the others."

This time Sunday did choke on her tea.

"You all right?" Joan asked.

Again Sunday coughed and tried to clear her throat.

Words failed Krysti. She did manage, "Yes, school is important."

Joan appeared so relaxed and almost happy. "You two have been so kind to me. I'm sorry for all the trouble we have been."

"You haven't been any trouble," said Sunday.

"Sunday is right," said Krysti.

"Thank you for everything." Joan stood. "I'm going to sleep. Enjoy my tea."

They nodded, and Joan returned to her tent.

Quietly, Krysti and Sunday sipped their tea and watched the fire.

"About eighteen," blurted Sunday.

"What?"

"Eighteen. The age you were thinking you were when you graduated from high school," said Sunday.

"Yes, eighteen or nineteen. And you were thinking fourteen or fifteen," Krysti noted.

Taking a long slow sip of her tea Sunday said, "Yes I was. Fourteen or fifteen was how old I would have been if I were a sophomore who had started school a year earlier than most."

"Fifteen at the most."

They turned their heads and locked eyes with each other.

"Should we tell the men?" Sunday asked.

"And what do we tell them? That we know about their indiscretion. And what is that? We are assuming something we know nothing about."

"So what do we do?" Sunday asked.

"We have enough problems as it is right now. I don't have an answer for this one."

"Neither do I."

*　*　*

Three weeks had passed and the small group was still camped at the same site. The intruder continued to pop up around the camp but they still didn't know who it was. One morning when they awoke, breakfast was almost finished when Lindy, tired and exhausted, stumbled from her tent.

"Get your parents so they can eat," Sunday grumbled.

"They're gone," said Lindy, almost casually.

"You need to find them so they can eat," said Krysti.

Dramatically and with her hands on her hips she retorted, "No, they're really gone. Back to Houston."

Both women dropped what they were doing and turned to Lindy.

In unison Krysti and Sunday almost screamed, "What?" "They said they would be back for me when they found out things were okay."

When they saw the SUV was gone they dropped everything. Krysti and Sunday went to find Garrett, Beau, Blackman, and Kipp and tell them what had happened. The Grays were gone and they had left their daughter behind.

It wasn't long before Sunday found the men. After she told them what the Grays had done she returned to make breakfast.

"Hey, mate, this isn't good," said Kipp.

"You thinking what I'm thinking?" Beau asked.

"We might need to move the camp," said Kipp.

"Good point," said Beau. "If someone captured them they could lead them back here."

"I've watched the Grays. I don't think they will be able to find us again," said Blackman.

"Is it worth the risk?" Beau asked.

"I don't think we should stir things up," said Kipp.

Blackman nodded in agreement. "We need to post guards on the main road. Be careful and keep watch."

All three men nodded in agreement.

* * *

A month had passed and a February chill hung in the air. The intruder had been detected four more times and each time "she" had taken up a different position to spy on them. Except for the last, which was the same as the first.

Dean was convinced the intruder was a woman. The foot size and the way she walked revealed that much. Beau concurred.

Kipp was determined to catch the "lass." Each time they tried to follow her trail they lost it in the rock. She had spied on them once every week and Kipp thought he had detected a pattern in her arrivals.

The month had created tension in the group. The factions had separated with some wanting to move on, some afraid, others demanding they stay put. The occasional contact with Waddle proved a move on their part would be futile. Beau's brothers went out on daily excursions but they found nothing. Krysti became closer to Marix while drifting away from Beau. Only Ruben and Sunday appeared to enjoy the month together.

Another day was about to begin. The sun had not risen and Kipp was gone from the camp. Both Kipp and Dean suspected this was the morning of the next encounter with the spy. Dean was a distant guard.

Soon the camp came alive with activity and it wasn't long before the smell of coffee, bacon, and biscuits drifted across the campsite. Mike and

Larry whined about the conditions and the cold, but few listened to their complaints.

While making biscuits, Sunday heard the two men moan and she became angry. "If you lie around doing nothing, you'll remain cold."

The comment silenced both men and brought a chuckle from Ruben and Beau and what could be called a slight smile from Dean.

Deberg came out from his tent wrapped in a blanket and rubbing his sleep-filled eyes. "Well, I guess there won't be many single women around anymore."

Near the fire Krysti talked to Tracy, who had come out of her self-induced depression. Occasionally she would burst out crying over her husband, which was understandable for anyone who had lost a loved one, whether it was during war or peace.

Slowly, Lindy had become an asset, helping with the cooking and becoming friends with Tracy. Both Sunday and Krysti accepted Lindy as a great benefit to the camp and tried to overlook her midnight indiscretions. Every day Lindy expected her parents to return but with each passing day her hopes dwindled. All were accounted for except Mulholland and no one knew where he was.

Suddenly, a woman's angry screams pierced the quiet camp. It came from the far end, near the river and a thick clump of brush and mesquite. Casually, Mulholland strolled into the camp, holding a struggling woman beneath his arm.

He had the most pleasant grin on his face when he said, "G'day, mates. Look at the lady I found watching us." He dropped the woman unceremoniously before them. "Hey lass, how's about some coffee or maybe a little tea?"

She scrambled to her feet screaming and savagely pounding Mulholland on the chest. "I don't drink tea!"

"Impetuous lass, ya are," Mulholland said as he grabbed her hands and shook his head.

Garrett tried to calm her down. "We're officers in the United States Navy. We mean you no harm."

This seemed to have a calming effect. "You don't have uniforms." She acted suspicious. "And there isn't any ocean around here."

"We had to discard the uniforms. We are pilots for the Navy."

"Aye, lass, we fly."

"My names Donna," she said, and pointing at Mulholland added, "He's not American."

"Aye, lass, I'm from Australia."

Kipp's smile and answer seemed to relax her. "You're pilots?"

Garrett nodded his head. "That's right. It's a case of being at the right place at the wrong time."

"If you're pilots, my uncle should talk to you."

"Who is your uncle?" queried Beau.

"John Hadfield."

The conversation continued and they learned the woman was Donna Lee. She was tall and strong with long, straight blond hair hanging below her shoulders. She agreed to take a few of them so they could talk to her uncle. Ted, Beau, Dean, Ruben, and Kipp went to meet him.

Kipp instantly took a fancy to the wild woman he found. "The lass has spirit," he said.

* * *

Nestled high on the hill, not far from the river, was a small rustic log cabin wedged among tall, thick oaks. Donna led them straight to the front door and knocked. There was no answer. She knocked again. "Daddy John," she yelled.

A steel plate, in the center of the heavy solid wood door, slid open, revealing a face on the other side. "Go away Donna and take your friends. There's a war a brewing and I don't aim to have any strangers around here."

Beau stepped up to the opening. "Sir, we need a place. There are more of us, more than you can handle here. We're pilots and when we find a way to return, we'll leave." He shook his head. "Personally, if I were you, I'd send us away. You're safer without us."

"What's your name?" he asked.

"Beau Gex."

"Gex . . . Gex." Suddenly, Hadfield's eyes opened wide in recognition. "You're the one that gave them Iraqis and Syrians all that shit! Right? We need an army of boys like you."

Beau was amazed at Hadfield's ability to pronounce his name correctly, and for a moment thought it would be better to lie and say no so his friends could find shelter. Before he could answer, the door pulled inward and before them stood a pudgy, slightly balding man with a gleam in his eyes and a double-barreled sawed off shotgun in one hand. Older than he first appeared, he had short-cropped, thinning, reddish gray hair but there was a lively bounce to his stride.

"Beau Gex! Well, I'll be damned, I never thought I'd . . . hell, I'm sure glad to meet a man who knows when it's time to kick some ass. Now, ya'll come on in, I can take care of ya," Daddy John said excitedly. "Maybe with your help we can kick their butts."

Beau took a deep breath and sighed. "I'm afraid our little party will be more trouble than help."

"Nonsense! Come on in!"

Donna, who was now friendlier with Kipp, whispered in his ear, "Daddy John never takes to anyone like that. You're very lucky."

Mulholland kept a watchful eye on her. "Aye, this is my lucky day." Smiling straight at her, he detected a slight blush.

Daddy John told them about another house he built into the cliff along the river only a mile from the cabin. "There's enough room there for everyone," Hadfield said. "Come, I'll show you."

As they walked to his home in the cliff, he constantly got sidetracked, returning to Beau and wanting to hear more of his story. Soon Hadfield was rambling about his past and how he had invested in oil after the Korean War. He had become wealthy and spent a fortune on his hobbies. Although he told them about his past, he never got specific about his other interests.

They walked around boulders, mesquite, brush, and rugged overhangs but almost continually downhill until they came on a rock outcropping about thirty feet above the Frio River. To the right a rather steep but easy trail continued on down to the flowing water. To the left it appeared the trail stopped. Across the river was a sheer cliff more than 200 feet high. The cliff across the river had huge pockets where millions of years of the running river had eaten away the limestone.

Hadfield went to the left around a boulder, then down two large rocks that were more like steep but very wide steps. The river had curled its way along the jagged rocks from the onset of time. In places, the land was almost level with the river, while in others small canyons skirted its cold running spring waters. Daddy John led them into what was no more than a canyon and at first appeared inaccessible, but in reality was rather easy to follow. He made it appear easy. They all trailed behind the spry old man. Beau was just behind him. Bringing up the back but not too far behind came Kipp and Donna.

"Daddy John, you going to show them your toys?" Donna yelled up her uncle.

"No," Hadfield snapped. He stopped and glared at her. "I don't want to bother these gentlemen with what I have and I don't want you to say any more about it." The statement was cold and silenced her. It was evident she would say no more on the subject of Daddy John's toys.

He continued with his story of how at the age of sixteen he was one of the youngest pilots to fly over Korea the last year of the war. During the latter stages of the Korean War, he flew three missions and reluctantly admitted to being shot down all three times. "If I'd of had a P-51 Mustang, it wouldn't have happened. Those F-86 Sabres just couldn't cut it."

"Why a Mustang and not a jet?" Beau asked.

"The Sabre wasn't as maneuverable as the Mustang. It might have been slower but it could turn on a dime and—"

Garrett's eyes grew big. "You're the Dutchman. The Dutchman was shot down three times and each time he escaped and rejoined his unit, only to be shot down again. Right?"

Daddy John reflected for a moment and with a far off look in his eyes remembered. "Haven't been called the Dutchman in thirty years. Yep, that was me, the Dutchman."

"Dutchman? Why the Dutchman?" Kipp asked.

"Because he was always in *Dutch* with his commanding officer," Garrett responded.

"Dutch?" asked Kipp.

Daddy John laughed. "Just another word for trouble."

For a few moments, Garrett and the Dutchman reminisced about the different wars in which each had served.

Beau interrupted the reunion. "We need to return to the others. Mr. Hadfield doesn't have the accommodations for our people."

"Oh, but I do. Please, you must call me Daddy John," he said with a sly smile. "Maybe one day you will see my toys. Come, I'll show you where you and your friends will stay."

Beau nodded to the old man and wondered about the "toys."

Daddy John led them along a winding path and toward the Frio River. The path wound its way along the river becoming steep and narrow, rough and rocky. There was no discernible path and it was more a process of memory. What appeared like a four-foot rock sticking out with an overhang about five foot above seemed inaccessible, but Daddy John bent under the overhang and continued along the path. The overhang was deceiving and only about a foot wide. The trail wound around a few more boulders then up about a half dozen easy steps that wrapped around another large rock.

Gradually, it opened to a cavern sculptured from eons of churning water. Recessed in the cliff, a modern structure resembling an old Indian cliff dwelling came into view: a cliff house made from concrete block and fitted with heavy wood doors and glass windows—something the Indians never had. The modern cliff dwelling almost took everyone's breath away.

Daddy John laughed. "Everyone can stay here and it can easily be guarded from there." He pointed back up the trail from where they had come to what was a natural lookout point.

From the ledge, a 50-foot vertical drop went almost directly into the Frio River and also provided a breathtaking view in both directions. The cavern was more than forty feet high, where the rock continued another sixty feet vertically to the top, and not too far from that point was the cabin where they had met Hadfield. To the north the canyons opened up and provided a view for almost a mile. Across the river was a matching cliff that completely hid the dwelling. After they had paused a moment to take in the view, Daddy John motioned them to follow him into the modern day cliff dwelling.

Beau and Kipp stopped ten feet from the entrance to the house while the others entered. They could not see down the river in either direction and the cliff across concealed them in the other direction. They turned to each other and nodded.

"No one will be able to see us here," said Kipp.

Beau nodded. "And it will be easily defended."

Kipp shook his head in agreement. They both took another look around and then went into the cliff dwelling with the others.

The concrete block wall was covered with oversized glass windows and provided light and an unobstructed view across the canyon. Inside the dwelling was a natural floor of stone, leveled through time and generously covered with a display of animal skins. The walls dividing the interior rooms were rough-cut cedar and filled the space with a pleasant aroma. Rough-hewn logs of pine and oak formed the staircase and railings leading to a second floor that was open to the enormous gathering area below.

The living area was divided into four distinct areas. One included a section of raised flooring surrounded with cut cedar railing and an oversized antique oak table with huge claw feet. A fireplace constructed of bleached river rock with a mantle cut from a large oaken beam was in the center. The two other areas were like individual sitting rooms. The large first floor living area complemented an enormous kitchen to satisfy any cook's dreams. A bedroom-size storage room off the kitchen was filled to capacity with enough canned goods and dry foods to last a dozen people for a year. Also on the first floor were four rooms and two complete bathrooms. Donna and Daddy John occupied two of the rooms.

For water, Daddy John had tapped a deep spring. A mechanical pump led to a 500-gallon storage tank just outside and above the dwelling to create a gravity flow. Once the tank was filled, the fresh spring water would last for weeks. A sewer system led to the base of the cliff and a septic tank drained to a level area a quarter mile from the time worn cavern where a septic field lay hidden.

"All the comforts of home," said Daddy John.

Beau pointed at the fireplace. "That will almost be useless when the invaders start stalking around here."

Again Daddy John grinned slyly. "The cabin where you found me is directly overhead. I had a hole for the flue drilled through the rock before I built the cabin. The fireplace has a double flue. Everyone will think the smoke will be coming from the cabin. Most times I even start a little fire up there when I want to use this fireplace."

"Drilled through the rock?" Ruben asked.

"Yep. It was very expensive and took a few drill bits."

"How did you manage this?" asked Garrett.

Daddy John shrugged his shoulders. "You can do anything with money. I did this fifteen years ago. Got tired of dreaming about it and decided to do it."

"Kinda reminds me of Colorado and those cliff dwellings," said Ruben, as he snapped his fingers trying to recall the name. "The, uhh—"

"Mesa Verde," said Blackman.

"Figured an Indian would know," said Beau.

"A regular Cliff Palace!" beamed Ruben.

"Aye mate, a Cliff Palace."

"I like that," said Daddy John. "Cliff Palace."

Garrett hated to intrude on the man. "I will understand if you say no, but can we set up our camp here?"

"Contrary, I would be offended if you didn't stay." He watched the other men he knew to be pilots—pilots that might figure into his future plans. "Besides, some of you can help me complete my dream." Daddy John eyed Beau when he made the statement.

Everyone assumed the dream had something to do with the massive structure in the cliff. But his dream was vastly different from the stationary cliff dwelling. He had a dream of adventure: an adventure wilder and deadlier than a normal man could imagine. These men, or more accurately this man, Beau Gex, would one day fulfill his dream. Only Donna knew of her uncle's wild and passionate desire. And she had promised not to tell.

Chapter 3
LIFE AND DEATH

Two weeks had passed since the strange group came upon their savior Daddy John and the place they affectionately called, "Cliff Palace." As the season turned unusually cold and rainy, sometimes freezing rain restricted them to their new residence. With all the comforts of home and Daddy John's large library of books to keep them occupied, the war seemed far away and even non-existent, if not for the occasional contact with Waddle. The only one not happy with the books was James who wanted to watch video movies.

The attitude of the group had changed immensely. Living inside the cliff house provided a sense of security to the little band of travelers, and offered them a home-like atmosphere at a time when home and security were commodities not likely to be found. A war was going on all around them but they seemed so far removed from reality in Cliff Palace where a semblance of normalcy prevailed, even if everything wasn't normal.

Although the stone path to their haven was well hidden and virtually undetectable, it would be deadly to become apathetic; something they all knew well. The unreal peace and security could not deny the death and danger beyond the canyon walls. Permanent sentinels on the mesa were a necessity to protect and save their lives. The men rotated shifts to the top of the cliff, which provided them a view for miles. They must be ready. There was no peace—only war.

Friction between Marix and Beau continued and became obvious to the others. A few noticed the strained relationship with Krysti and Beau. She avoided dealing with him, doing so only when it became necessary.

The only other casualties appeared to be Sully and Tracy. Sully had withdrawn into himself, not talking to anyone. He believed his wife, Natasha, to be killed when her airliner was replaced with one of the invader's duplicates. He slept constantly and was interested in nothing.

Tracy secluded herself since the death of her husband, Gene. Beau and Ted worked continually to bring her spirits up, but the only one even partially successful was Krysti, who demanded Tracy's help.

Depression in some of the others like Deberg, Pickett, James, Marix, Schmitt, Warren, Tang, and Fitzhenry became more obvious with the passing days, as they slept later and quit the simple daily tasks like shaving and washing their hair.

Garrett tried to change some of this when he forced Schmitt to go with him to make periodic contact with the Duck. Soon the others started taking turns making radio contact. Sully waited impatiently but still had no word about Natasha.

Fearing the radio transmissions might be located, they used two vehicles and traveled at least ten miles before establishing contact, which would make it more difficult for the invaders to pinpoint their location.

The vehicles were hidden at a safe distance from Cliff Palace. Soon Kipp, Dean, Ruben, Beau, and his brothers took turns venturing to Hondo checking for signs of the invasion's advance into the area. Beau's brothers ventured into another world—their world. Each day they would take a sortie farther to see what they could learn. Fuel was no problem with the large fuel tank stored near the log cabin where they originally met. Daddy John had thought of almost everything, but each time out they still tried to refuel, using abandoned cars or finding empty gas stations before they returned from each of their trips. Beau's brothers never used Daddy John's fuel, instead always managing to find their own.

At the women's urging, the men spent the first week attaching a solar water heater to the water line—the one thing Daddy John failed to finish. A cold shower was just fine with him.

When the system became operational, the women rejoiced and cooked a meal of enormous proportions. Later in the week Daddy John complained that since the water heater started working, three times as much water was being used.

Sunday teased with him. "But aren't we nicer to be around now?"

The comment brought a nod from Daddy John and he cocked one eyebrow. "I guess if the women are happy, I shouldn't complain."

The accommodations of Cliff Palace worked perfectly with its abundance of rooms. Ruben and Sunday retained one, while Krysti and Justin stayed in another. Fitzhenry and Warren roomed together, Mulholland and Pickett in one, and Marix and James had a room next to Krysti. Rooming together were Deberg and Blackman, a most unlikely pair. Ted Garrett roomed with Beau while Schmitt and Chin Tang shared accommodations. All stayed on the second floor except Beau and Ted, who occupied a room on the first floor. Tracy and Lindy shared a room.

Deberg had pulled away from Lindy. He had surmised her age through their occasional conversations. Lindy divided her meetings between those at night with James and special secret ones occasionally during the day with Marix. Relieved and thinking the rendezvous with the men had ended, Krysti and Sunday no longer had reason to suspect her or her activities. Only Tracy had a faint idea, and that was because she was Lindy's roommate.

The only remaining room on the second floor was saved for Jack, Brook, and Danny, but the three brothers never stayed in it, preferring instead to camp outside the small fortress. They made a few trips to Hondo where they scavenged mufflers to silence the noise on their dune buggies. The end result were two virtually silent all-terrain vehicles. They also painted their bright red buggies with a dull camouflage earth-tone pattern. With each new day, they wandered farther from Cliff Palace and were gone longer and longer. One night they failed to return.

On that night, Beau stood his solitary vigil for his brothers. Cliff Palace was dark but the infinite stars made the sky bright. Unable to sleep, Krysti walked to the living area hoping to tire. From the railing, she watched Beau wait for his brothers. She knew he felt the same anguish she felt not knowing about her parents in El Paso. Sometimes the pain of not knowing was more than she could stand. She was overcome with compassion for him and wanted to talk, but was confused with the shocking reality of war, denial it happened, and the truth about the man before her. Was he really the ruthless killer she heard so much about? Why didn't he defend himself?

* * *

The next day was no different from the others, except it was unusually warm for mid-February. The day before had been overcast and cold. Early in the morning, Beau and Blackman disappeared from Cliff Palace.

Everyone was busy at small, predetermined chores. Most of the men were making an effort to shave and clean up. For the women, keeping Cliff Palace in order was a natural. The work really helped Tracy become more adjusted and they all gained confidence in Lindy. Some detected something between Tracy and Fitz. When he was around Tracy, he acted more like he had two left feet. The interest Donna showered upon Kipp was almost funny. Still no one suspected Lindy and James of their secret meetings. Of course all the women enjoyed spending time helping Sunday during her pregnancy, as did Ruben. The counting of weeks for the baby to be born had now turned into days. Krysti had told Sunday everything was progressing normally and she saw no signs whatsoever of a problem with the birth of her child.

With Beau gone, Mike seized the opportunity to make another advance on Krysti and invited her to spend the day on the river. If she would organize the meal, he would bring a bottle of wine he pilfered from the now deserted town of Hondo. The prospect of a change in routine actually excited Krysti, and it would provide her an opportunity to break free of the problems and a chance to get away with her son.

The thought of Justin tagging along did not set well with Mike or with what he had in mind for the finishing touch to the excursion. Reluctantly, he accepted her terms. They had not gone far before Mike found a suitable spot on the river where they spread a blanket beneath a large cypress shading the cold running Frio River. The water ran thirty feet deep in places, and large boulders jutted from the middle of the river. Both sides of the river were lined with oaks and cypress.

After they finished lunch, Mike convinced Justin pieces of arrowheads were in the area and if he looked very carefully, he would surely find some. Marix didn't believe there were any arrowheads but it would keep Justin away for some time. And time was something Marix wanted: time without Justin.

"The Karankawas Ruben told us about?" Justin asked excitedly.

"Those Indians don't really exist," said Mike.

"Wrong," interjected Krysti. "The Karankawas were a real Indian tribe." Marix did a slow burn and although he showed no outward change, the one thing he hated almost more than any other was to be corrected.

"Will I find arrowheads?"

"Maybe," said Krysti.

After Justin disappeared, Mike brought out the bottle of wine and poured two generous portions soon followed with two more servings. Mike tried to kiss Krysti but she pushed him away.

"What's the matter?" Marix asked rather scornfully. "Before we came to Cliff Palace I was good enough. You'd do more than give me a kiss. What is it, Gex?"

"That's not it, Michael. There are more appropriate places. Justin is near; besides, I came to enjoy the river and the warm weather. I want to relax and forget."

"Forget what? Beau?" Marix snipped.

Justin interrupted with a discovery he excitedly rushed to share with his mother. "Hey Mom, look! I found an arrowhead."

"It's just a piece of flint," snapped Mike.

The tone Marix used bothered her, but she looked at the rock. She was not sure what it was. "I don't know, honey. Maybe Daddy John would know."

"Yeah, Daddy John would know. Hey, Mom, can I go swimming?"

She threw him a towel. "Be careful, it's cold."

"It's not that cold. Beau swims in here every day."

"How do you know?" quizzed his mother.

"I go with him. Beau said there's nutin' to be afraid of except moccasins and rattlers."

"Snakes?" The surprise in Mike's voice brought a smile from Krysti and a giggle from Justin.

"Yep. Beau says it's too cool for them. Mike, did you know a water moccasin can bite ya under water?" Mike's startled eyes brought another giggle from the boy.

"I don't want you to spend too much time with Beau," said Krysti.

"Why? He knows how to hunt and fish and do everything."

"Those things are not important if you are to get ahead. An education is necessary in today's world," said Mike.

"What world?" Justin asked, but for that, Mike had no answer.

Krysti couldn't help but wonder at the truth of her son's words. What was important in this world in which they now found themselves? She wondered if Michael had a true grasp of their situation. Beau was teaching Justin all the practical things. Her little boy was growing up and she didn't want him to.

With Justin's interference temporarily stopping Mike's advances, Mike and Krysti talked about their past and hopes for the future while Justin braved the river for a cold swim.

For a while Krysti and Michael talked, but he continued to make advances so she politely ended their conversation. She asked Michael to find Justin while she gathered the blanket and basket.

Mike walked to the river and he soon found the boy who was preparing to swing into the river from a rope hanging from a branch high in a cypress.

"Don't swing on that, it's too dangerous," Marix ordered.

"Why not?"

"You're not old enough."

"Why don't you?"

"Because I'm a grownup and don't do those things anymore."

"If I can't and you can't, who can? Who put the rope here?"

"You ask too many stupid questions."

Neither Justin nor Marix noticed Krysti approach but she saw and heard them. She did not appreciate Michael's attitude.

"Come on Justin, it's time to return," said Krysti.

Krysti and Mike walked along in silence, while Justin jumped about, oblivious to his mother or Mike. For every step they took, Justin took four, and all in different directions.

All of a sudden Marix spotted a snake directly in their path. Startled by the creature on the stone trail, Mike screamed a warning. "Watch out, a snake!" He pulled the unfamiliar revolver from the awkward holster dangling from his hip and pointed.

Directly in front of them, Krysti and Justin saw a snake, a large snake, with dark markings, stretched across the two-foot wide path. It didn't move.

"No," screamed Justin.

He could not be heard over the roar of the pistol as Mike fired four times, knocking dust into the air with each shot. When he stopped, the snake lay still.

"That was stupid," snapped Krysti. "You scared the hell out of me."

"The snake was poisonous, it could have bitten us," said Mike. "I hate snakes."

"It wasn't even moving and we had enough room to avoid it," said Krysti. She was taken aback when Justin picked it up. He held the body in one hand and gently pinched the head between his thumb and finger with the other while he scrutinized the reptile.

"Justin, put it down," she ordered.

"Yes, it's poisonous," Marix added.

Justin laughed. "Mike, you can leave your gun at Cliff Palace. It's a king snake and he's alive. You missed him. He's just confused because the weather's changing."

Justin jumped nimbly from the path, placed the snake safely under some brush, and then returned to his mother. Marix was now thoroughly embarrassed at both his ignorance of snakes and his poor marksmanship.

"How do you know it's not poisonous?" asked Mike.

"Because Beau taught me. Beau also said you better hit what you're aiming at on the first try. You might not get another chance," Justin said, as though they all knew.

"Snakes are dangerous," snapped Marix.

With a shrug Justin responded. "No they aren't. They eat rats, mice, and insects. Beau showed me." Now Mike was beginning to hate Gex more even when he wasn't around.

When they resumed the walk, Justin said, "Lucky for the king snake you're a bad shot."

"I may not be a good shot with a pistol but it's different when I'm in a jet," Marix said smugly.

"Gee, I hope you're not in a jet the next time we go to the river. You sure would make a mess with those guns. I bet even you could hit the snake then," said Justin in all seriousness.

The humor was not lost on Krysti as she failed to restrain a laugh. During their return Krysti wondered how much time Beau actually spent with her son. With the setting sun, they arrived at Cliff Palace. To Mike's chagrin, the story of the snake spread much too quickly.

* * *

Less than a mile outside of Hondo, down a steep ravine covered thick with oak trees, Beau and Blackman investigated an abandoned vehicle. It was covered with dirt and had been deserted for some time. A fancy SUV made by Cadillac. Beau held the door open and peered in at the driver's seat. He shook his head and frowned. Behind him Dean stood with his arms folded.

"I thought you should see this."

"Yeah. Thanks," said Beau. "I'm sure it belongs to the Grays."

"It's theirs."

Curiously, Beau rubbed the expensive brown leather seat covered with reddish brown stains.

"Someone was hurt."

Dean nodded.

Nothing was in the back seat. The SUV was empty. No other signs of violence were evident. Beau shut the door and turned to Dean.

"Looks like it was driven down here. Can't tell if they did it on purpose or not. Maybe fell asleep. I don't like the blood but it doesn't appear that anyone was shot."

Again Dean nodded. "Could have killed Stephan and taken his wife."

"They could have had a problem, got another car and are just fine."

"Maybe," said Dean with a less than positive attitude. "If so why didn't they come back?"

"I don't know. But this isn't enough to tell us what happened to them."

"You saw the body I showed you on the edge of town."

"Yeah, but the animals have destroyed it. Nothing but bones and a skull. No telling if it was a man or a woman. Could have been somebody from Hondo. We wouldn't know if it was them unless we were forensic experts. I'm just not that good," said Beau.

"You saw the hole in the skull. I'm not a forensics expert either but that was a bullet hole. And whoever it was they were executed. I just thought you should see this."

Visions of Sarah Lipton, Washington, and the men in the pickup trucks filled Beau's mind. He could still see and hear her begging for her life. He was sure the remains Dean had shown him, whomever they had belonged to, had once been someone who also begged for his or her life.

Disgusted with what they had found Beau said, "You're right about the skull. But we will never know who it was. It could be one of the Grays then again it might not. For now I don't want to destroy whatever hope Lindy is clinging to. It is something she needs. She needs to think her parents will be returning. I don't want the others to know about this."

Shaking his head, Dean said, "I understand."

* * *

Late in the evening after everyone fell asleep, Krysti heard voices coming from the cliff overlooking the Frio. She recognized one of the voices. It was Beau. She could not hear what they were saying so she crept down the stairs.

"Soldiers are all over. They'll stop you," Beau pleaded with his brothers.

"Yeah, there are a lot of soldiers," said Jack, "but from what we've seen they stick to the main highways. We don't. We wanna go back to West Texas and Big Rock. The cabin is there and we know the area. Besides, they can't catch us. Come with us."

"Can't. I have to stay."

"You might owe Ted and Ruben or Tracy something but you don't owe anybody else," said Jack.

"Krysti," Brook snickered. "The love bug's done bit him."

Beau frowned at Brook. "I have my reasons. I'm staying."

Slowly, Krysti moved closer so she could hear the men talk.

"You don't need to stay, Beau," said Jack.

"I've seen Kipp and Blackman. They can take care of this group," Brook said.

"Contrary to what you think, even Ruben can make it without you," said Jack.

Thin lips reflected Beau's smile. "Why don't you three stay with us; we could use you."

Danny said, "You don't need us and we want to go back to the Rio."

"Jack?" Beau almost pleaded.

Kicking at the dirt with his boot, Jack mumbled, "Sorry Beau, we've gotta go. I need some answers. I want to check out where Natasha's plane crashed. I need to make sure. I just can't believe she's dead."

Beau could remember how Jack had secretly been in love with Natasha since the day they met, but he had always been sure to hide that love from her and Sully. "You always loved her, didn't you?"

The flush was apparent in Jack's face when he caught Beau's eyes with his. Brook gave Jack a playful push from his right and immediately Danny did the same from the left.

Still red in the face, Jack said, "I guess it doesn't matter now. She always thought I was a best friend. She loves Sully. As long as she loves him, I'd never do anything." Jack sighed. "I'll always be her friend."

Jack didn't say he loved Natasha but all three brothers nodded their understanding even though Beau's question was never answered.

"I need to find her and put it to rest," said Jack.

Beau again nodded.

"When ya decide you've had enough, you know where we'll be," said Jack.

They exchanged farewells. A moment later the three brothers walked slowly down the narrow trail. Beau watched until they disappeared from sight. He turned to go back into Cliff Palace.

"Beau," said Krysti as she stepped from the shadows.

"Krysti?"

She moved closer to his side. "Aren't you worried about your brothers with those troops out there?"

"No. They won't catch them. They travel fast and light. Besides, if the enemy is real lucky, they won't run into them," he said as he gazed into her eyes. "I've been wanting to talk to you."

They stared silently at each other for a moment, each wanting to say something but both refusing to let words heal the hurt.

Krysti said, "Don't say anything. We should just remain friends. There are things I need time to think over."

"This is war," Beau snapped. "It's not a picnic."

"Maybe, but I have to deal with it in my own way and my own time. I'm sorry."

"So be it," Beau said, then turned to stare into the starlit sky.

Darkness hid the confusion and sadness in Krysti's eyes as she walked slowly to her room. Her mind was filled with so many questions. She worried about her family in El Paso. What would become of Justin? But her thoughts always returned to the man she had walked away from on the cliff.

She had failed to sense the heaviness in Beau's heart. His thoughts were filled only of her. He stood alone for what seemed an eternity, before he too turned in for the night.

* * *

The building gave all the protection Juan Ortega promised, with an excellent view of the Gulf. All of this went unnoticed while Ortega and Sharafan talked.

Not far from them two of Sharafan's men relaxed. Both Aziz and al-Majid enjoyed the deadly work they had accomplished while in America. Now they were attached to Sharafan to protect him and to do his bidding, and as always the orders they received they enjoyed with sadistic pleasure.

"You said you had instructions as to the American refugees?" Ortega asked.

"Yes," said Sharafan nodding his head. "I have talked to Navarro and we believe it would be best to let the Americans go unmolested. Let them return to the America of the North. You see they will only bring us trouble.

We have kept the important people who refused to help as prisoners and those that have promised to help are a blessing from Allah."

With a shrug of his shoulders Ortega said, "Then why not kill the other Americans; they can only come back and create problems in the future."

Sharafan nodded. "Not true. Those that flee are too old or too young or worthless. The America of the North has no food but they will try to help the refugees. And the refugees will be unprepared to cope with the winter as they travel north while those who make it will only deplete the remaining resources the Americans have. They will become a parasite to their own country. Those that make it will be greeted with the disease we planted."

"Ahhh," said Ortega with one slow nod of his head. A grin lit up his face. "They will be more beneficial to us alive than dead."

"Precisely," said Sharafan, rubbing his hands together. He became solemn. "Now go and send Zahir in when you leave."

A moment later Ortega was gone. Rasht Sharafan waited impatiently. Across the room the door opened and Zahir entered.

Sharafan paused and turned to him. "Well?"

Rigidly Zahir stood at attention. "Nothing, sir. We have found nothing."

"His home? Relatives?"

"His niece and brothers are gone. You have accomplished so much. We have broken the United States. Even now we are slowly moving north. You have achieved such a great victory. Sir, give up this quest. The one you hunt may already be dead," Zahir pleaded.

"Never!" Sharafan snapped. His mood took an abrupt change and a smile creased his face. "Relax Tahar. I have thought much on this. Beau Gex is not dead; he has more lives than a cat."

Sharafan walked to a map spread on a table and motioned for Zahir. He pointed to San Antonio. "We know his group signed in here." Then he touched Del Rio. "They never arrived here." He pointed to Hondo. "This is where we found those two jets. I believe Beau Gex was one of those pilots."

He made a sweeping elliptical arc around Hondo. "I know they are here. Find them!"

* * *

When Sunday went into labor, Ruben was of no help to anyone, least of all Krysti. She had everything under control, with Donna assisting in the delivery. Early in the evening, a small baby boy was born. Sunday christened him Paul but all the men called him "Little Ruben." It made Sunday angry and she would snap at them when they called her son by the nickname. The only exception was Beau, when he inadvertently used the reference. He was not scolded, but he was the only one.

Everyone celebrated the birth, drinking Daddy John's homemade brew of wine. Ruben wanted to celebrate with his best friend and after much toasting and drinking to the new life, Ruben and Beau walked from Cliff Palace to stare down at the river.

"What do ya think of the little one?" Ruben asked. He stuck his finger in the drink and swirled the ice. Daddy John concocted a strange looking drink and said it was better than wine. Ruben sucked the end of his finger. "Isn't Little Ruben something?"

"Don't let Sunday hear ya," said Beau taking a sip of his drink.

Ruben had a smile that filled his face. He shook his head. "My son. Can you believe it?"

"Ya did a fine job, Ruben. I'm happy for you and Sunday and I'm glad you have a son." They stood on the edge of the cliff above the tranquil Frio River. "If it wasn't for what we know, I'd swear nothing had ever happened. We sure don't feel the war here."

"Umm," said Ruben after taking a swig of the potent solution. "Daddy John doesn't mess around when he makes his liquor."

Beau held his glass high. "Here's to your son. May he have continued peace at Cliff Palace. To your son's birth. To the new life."

"Amen."

* * *

A brisk breeze blew in from the north, making the air cold and dry. A "Texas Norther" had moved south across Texas and nature had stripped all but the evergreens.

In good spirits, Kipp, Beau, Tang, Ruben, and Dean went on another trip beyond Hondo to make contact with Duck Waddle. They were equipped with enough armaments for a small war. During the drive, the men's conversation still managed a return to Marix and the snake—a topic that never grew old.

Still testing the area, they went beyond Hondo. With each passing day they knew the enemy came closer but there were still no signs of the invaders. The two Jeeps pulled off the main road where they would not be visible if anyone passed. Before radio contact could be established, they heard men on motorcycles approaching in the distance. They took cover and waited.

Hidden to the side of the road, the five men watched from the safety of the brush. Mulholland pointed to the dirty unshaven figure straddling the lead motorcycle. The hulking mass of Haun, from the misadventure at Shanghai Pete's, led the procession. Behind him trailed his two friends, a half dozen more cycles, and a pick-up. The deadly and vicious group moved along the road uncontested.

Hidden in the trees the five men failed to see the two helpless women bound and gagged in the bed of the truck. Renegade bands of Americans like Haun brought more fear than the invaders.

"They can't harm us," said Ruben.

Haun and his men brought only death and destruction. Soon their presence would come to haunt Beau and others in their group.

The motorcycles and the truck passed, and slowly disappeared in the distance.

A few minutes later, the radio ready, they contacted Duck Waddle. The Duck said aerial battles continued, with neither side making any noticeable advancement. Harrier jets near Dallas had caught the enemy unaware and had done quite a bit of damage. In the process the Harriers managed to escape to Canada. Beau was sure Scott Walker and his men had accomplished their task. His only wish was to be one of those doing the damage to the enemy.

Then the Duck added some unwelcome news. A week earlier, in an effort to reach peace with the invading Coalition, Alaska had declared their state an independent nation and broken ties with the United States. When the Coalition agreed to peace with Alaska, they were beseeched for peace by the northern half of California, stretching to a point approximately fifty miles south of San Francisco. Joining in with California were Washington, Oregon, Idaho, Wyoming, Montana, the northern half of Nevada, and a portion of Utah just south of Salt Lake City. The eight former states of the United States also declared their own independence and called themselves Western America. They were near a peace settlement with the invaders.

The information brought the small group to a new low. The United States was coming apart.

Before the Duck finished, he added some information regarding the invaders. A Syrian pilot in Texas was collecting kills at an alarming rate: a pilot called *Cobra*.

Beau was only slightly surprised at the information. He had thought all along that Cobra was in Texas. The only problem was he had no way of getting revenge. If only he had the chance to fight him.

The Duck told them of other enemy aces: Wings of Death, El Lobo, and Tiburon. As near as intelligence could figure, some Asian countries and most of South America had managed to unite for one concentrated effort to break the back of the United States. The amnesty law passed in 2008 when another 500,000 illegal aliens sought citizenship was the turning point. No one questioned the amnesty, thus enabling thousands of crack South American troops to be placed in strategic locations throughout the southern part of the United States. The language barrier helped the invading troops convince thousands of Spanish speaking Americans to join their side in the belief they fought for their new adopted country. The remaining American troops were outnumbered.

Disheartening was the fact that money for the invasion came in billions of dollars of unsupervised loans. For years the unpaid loans were used to buy jets and war materials from other countries. Thinking the jets obsolete, the United States sold them for pennies on the dollar and had even given away thousands of F-4 Phantoms, F-104s, and F-86 Sabres in the hopes of buying foreign cooperation within the United Nations. With the loans, foreign countries had bought Migs and French Mirages and promised friendship. The enormous and irresponsible financial decisions of America's lawmakers and bankers had brought the country to the edge of destruction. The skies of the United States were filled with invaders, something never before achieved in history. And ironically the invasion was financed with the aid of the United States through loans that were never repaid.

Duck said, "It was like giving a man a gun and then asking him to shoot you."

The new information disgusted the men even more. On the return trip, they stopped in Hondo to eat. They pulled the two Jeeps beneath the shade of the oaks in front of the city hall.

Beau took a moment to walk behind the building and down a few stores. He found his old Corvette covered with dust. He climbed inside, found the key under the mat and tried to start the car. No response came from the dead battery. Once a valuable collector's item, it now served no useful purpose in this time of war. Only a material possession, it was still one more thing taken from him. Reflecting on how things had once been saddened him deeply. Gradually smiling to himself, he thought how wonderful it would be to speed along a highway, get pulled over by a Department of Public Safety officer, and be given a simple ticket. He sighed and returned to the liquor store where the other four waited.

They pulled out a lunch basket, passed around the sandwiches, and ate while standing at the rear of the two Jeeps.

Chin Tang spread a blanket and dismantled his M-1. All the men except Beau were equipped with M-1s previously taken from Hondo. Beau continued to carry the lever action 30.30 his father had given him. With blinding speed, Chin took the M-1 apart and reassembled it.

"Hey, mate, that was faster than a Kangaroo rat race."

Chin stood and bowed to the men. "Chin loves America. You are my friends. I am very happy here."

As they walked down the deserted main street of Hondo, the men talked about the invasion and the possibility of escaping from occupied territory. Both sides of the streets were close together and lined with two-story buildings filled with all types of stores and an old-fashioned sidewalk a few feet above the street.

They all carried their rifles except Beau, who for some reason opted to take the quiet, deadly crossbow. They passed an empty liquor store then stopped and peered into a vacant department store filled only with silent mannequins. The peaceful, serene setting put the five men in a situation for which they were neither prepared nor ready.

Quietly an infrared dot crept across Chin's face, centering on his chest over his heart.

"Chin!" yelled Beau and Kipp simultaneously.

They shouted a warning but it came too late! There was a sickening thud as a small crimson hole opened in the chest of the small Chinese man who called America home. An invisible force threw him violently against the stone wall of the store. Tang fell heavily onto the concrete sidewalk lining the street. His shirt was torn from his back revealing a gaping hole. Innards were strewn across the wall against which he had been thrown and steam rose from the hole in his back. Chin Tang was dead.

Before their friend hit the ground, Beau grabbed Ruben's shirt and jerked him along when he dove through the window.

Kipp jumped through another window, shattering the glass and sending it in all directions. He crashed to the glass-strewn floor next to Ruben and Beau.

Dean reacted swiftly, throwing himself against the store's wood door, knocking it from the hinges. He did two rolls, cocked the M-1 as he moved, and came to a kneeling position with the rifle ready. Likewise did Kipp.

Beau pulled Ruben across the floor with his crossbow ready in his left hand. Behind them, two more vicious thuds landed harmlessly against the same stone wall, barely missing the quick thinking men.

"What the hell was that?" asked Ruben, his head so deep in shards of glass his chin was cut and bleeding. But he didn't try to rise. Instead he continued to lie on his stomach.

"Snipers!" said Beau, the surprise apparent in his voice. Beau dragged Ruben to the back of the store, and pulled him to his feet. With great control Beau filled the crossbow with a steel shaft. Next, he slipped the plastic cover from each end of the scope mounted on the bow, followed with a reflex check to the .357 magnum clinging to his side and the two knives. Beau was ready.

Instinctively, Blackman and Mulholland moved to opposite walls of the store, perpendicular to the street, and checked their rifles. They slid slowly up the walls, scanning outside the building for signs of the snipers.

"How many?" Beau asked, moving his eyes from Mulholland to Blackman.

"Three, maybe more," suggested Blackman.

"Four," said Mulholland.

"One shot," said Blackman.

Kipp and Beau knew what Blackman meant. If they were to succeed, they would have possibly one shot. One chance, no more.

Blackman felt for the large knife strapped to his waist. He called it a knife: Ruben called it a sword. Actually, it was a cross between a knife and a sword. The blade extended twelve inches from the four-inch handle. Then again it seemed small on Blackman. It was a knife that would have made Jim Bowie proud.

The snipers came with high-powered rifles equipped with infrared scopes. For accuracy, they would be using bolt action. The men knew this and wondered how many lay in wait. Somewhere in the buildings along the main street, hidden from their view, the snipers waited.

Ruben watched as Beau, Kipp, and Dean prepared to find the killers. Beau pointed in the direction of the shots. Mulholland nodded but Blackman pointed off to another area where he thought he had seen movement. The three men decided to spread out; Ruben would be the diversion. He would fire his M-1 while they escaped out the back of the store.

First, Beau took a dressed mannequin, bent it in a kneeling position, and wrapped a cord around it. He motioned to Blackman on the other side of the store and threw him one end of the rope.

"Drag it across the store," Beau said.

Blackman pulled on the cord and Beau slowly let it out on his end, making the mannequin move so it appeared to be crawling near the window.

Three silent thuds blasted the inanimate figure. Both men released the cord and backed away from the window. All were in agreement; there were four snipers. Three fired but they all knew one stayed ready for safety.

Beau gave instructions to Ruben. "I want you to go to the corner of the store and fire your rifle in their direction to create a diversion so we can go out the back and find them. Don't let them see you, just shoot the rifle."

Wide-eyed Ruben responded. "Don't worry. I'm not about to let them see me."

Cautiously, Ruben crawled to the front of the store while the other three waited at the back. He slid up the wall, held the M-1 so it pointed out the window, aimed in the general direction of the deadly intruders, and fired until the rifle was empty. He turned to watch his friends but they were already gone. He reloaded.

Silence reigned for what seemed an eternity. Suddenly a blast from an M-1 echoed down the deserted street of Hondo. A body plummeted from a building across the street, coming to a sickening crunch on the sidewalk below. Again, a hush hung over the area. The chilling quiet of death.

Blackman crept silently behind another one of the snipers. A powerful hand covered the shooter's mouth, almost breaking his neck. Silently, the long, deadly knife did the rest, as Blackman slid it effortlessly between the ribs through the heart and out through his chest. The last thing the sniper saw was the blade protruding from his chest. With a wicked jerk, Blackman shoved the knife down the rib cage splitting the chest cavity in half.

Beau found another sniper crouching on top of a three-story red brick Victorian office building. Both sighted the scopes on each other at the same instant. Beau reacted first and let the small steel shaft fly silently toward its target.

The sniper could not believe what he saw and his hesitation cost him his life. Startled and somewhat curious, his fingers reacted in slow motion, as he tried to squeeze off a shot from his rifle. The small shaft shattered the front glass of the scope, exiting the rear and entering the shooter's right eye, going completely through the brain and emerging from the back of his skull.

Like a rag doll, his limp body rolled over the side of the building, crashed through a second floor decorative balcony, and snapped to a stop six feet above the ground when his leg caught between two steel rods of the red and white awning. The rifle still hung from the shaft embedded in his brain.

Beau didn't take time to watch; he knew the man was dead. He ran out the back of the building, behind four more stores, and entered the rear of the fifth building, loading the crossbow as he ran. Slowly, he approached the front of the windowless store with his weapon loaded and ready. Across the street, at a slight angle less than thirty yards away, stood the last sniper, hiding behind a doorway and drawing a deadly bead on Mulholland who crawled unsuspecting toward him. Beau sent another silent steel shaft on its mission. The final sniper cried out in pain as the steel shaft caught him between the wrist and the elbow, embedding itself deep in the ornate wood door where he stood. He dropped his rifle.

"Two," yelled Beau.

Then came the word "One" from Blackman and Mulholland.

"Over here," said Beau. Slowly Mulholland and Blackman moved toward him. "Ruben!" yelled Beau.

Cautiously, Ruben stepped from the doorway, glanced both ways, and scanned the rooftops like a kid crossing the street for the first time, still unsure. He stepped out then jumped back. Satisfied, he moved to where the others waited.

Beau was already half way back to Ruben when a flash in the distance caught his eye. He jumped and readied his crossbow just as Ruben walked up.

"What are you doing?" Ruben asked.

"I thought I saw a flash, possibly another sniper." Beau pointed. "About a half mile away."

This brought about an immediate response from Ruben who burst out laughing.

Puzzled, Beau asked, "What's so funny?"

"You," laughed Ruben uncontrollably. "If there is a sniper, he's half a mile away, and you expect to do something with that," he said pointing to the crossbow. "You're good but not that good. And if there was a sniper you and I would already be dead." He turned and faced the direction Beau had pointed then stretched out his arms in a manner of, "come and get me if you can."

Even Beau started to laugh. "I guess you're right. Let's talk to our prisoner."

As they walked away, Beau cupped a hand over his eyes and checked one more time in the direction he had seen the flash.

* * *

The crosshairs of the scope were lined up on Beau when he unexpectedly peered in the direction of the sniper.

Bravo glanced from the scope to Pepe then he said, "Turn sideways, Pepe, he sees you." Pepe turned.

"I told you not to wear shiny objects. Throw away that knife you found."

Again Bravo scoped in on his target but this time on Ruben as he waved his arms. The actions brought a slight smile to Bravo. Pepe threw away the shiny knife.

Now the crosshairs were lined up over Beau's heart again as he and Ruben walked away. Bravo saw as Beau again checked in their direction. Again Bravo smiled. "You know I'm here. You are good." He lowered his rifle.

"Aren't you going to kill them?" Pepe asked.

"No."

"But they killed the other four that were with us."

"Those four liked to kill everything. They got themselves killed and this had nothing to do with our mission."

"So we aren't going to kill them?"

"No, we are to kill military personnel and break any supply lines we find. Those are just men trying to survive."

"But they are too good. We should kill them."

"Yes they are good, Pepe, but we want to defeat the United States. We don't want to kill everybody here."

"Oh."

* * *

The sniper was screaming out in Spanish when Ruben and Beau arrived.

"What's he saying," Beau asked.

Ruben shrugged his shoulders and his face reddened. "I don't know. I don't speak Spanish."

Beau's jaw dropped. "Ya gotta be shitin' me."

"Nope."

"Sunday does, and you don't?"

"Yeah. What the hell, I don't speak Spanish," Ruben said with a wave of his arms. For some strange reason on that field of battle littered with the bodies of four dead men, three men found a reason to laugh.

Neither Blackman nor the sniper joined in.

The sniper pursed his lips and said in Arabic, "Allahu Akbar!"

"Well he's not from the out-back, I can tell from his accent," said Mulholland.

The hair on Beau's neck stood up. "That's Arabic. He said, God is Great."

Ruben shrugged. "That's true. God is great."

"Not the way he said it," snapped Beau.

The sniper looked at Beau and snarled in English, "You know Arabic?"

Eyeing the prisoner suspiciously, Beau said, "Enough to know when I'm in trouble."

Abruptly, the sniper brought them back to reality. "You Americans are crazy. You will take me prisoner. When I escape, I will kill you. You Americans are too soft. Now you must take me prisoner." With his last words he laughed at them.

He stopped laughing and terror filled his eyes when Blackman stepped forward and whispered something in his ear. The sniper had time but for a brief glimpse of the blade, as Blackman held it before his eyes just before he plunged it into the man's heart. Blackman moved too swiftly for anyone to act.

"Dean!" yelled Beau, grabbing at Blackman's arm.

The dead sniper hung limply on the door. Blackman pushed him away. "Would you have taken him prisoner?"

"Yes."

"Now you won't have to worry about him escaping," said Dean calmly. "Let's get Chin."

"You can't . . . we can't let this happen to us," Beau mumbled under his breath.

"Ask Chin. The snipers had no intention of taking prisoners, neither should we." Blackman held out his hands. "Do what you must. The others are safe."

Beau shook his head and pushed Blackman's arms down. Ruben and Mulholland were too stunned to speak. They loaded the snipers in one of the Jeeps, and hid their bodies just outside of town where the animals would take care of them before they could be found.

The four men returned, and pulled both Jeeps in front of the liquor store next to where Chin lay. Carefully, they wrapped their dead friend in a tarp and loaded him in the vehicle. As the sun set, Blackman and Mulholland sat on the curb directly in front of the once lucrative liquor store where the picture window was broken and the door ajar.

"Come on, mates, I think it's time for a drink," said Mulholland, swinging the door open. The others went in, scrounged around the debris and managed to find a drink from what remained. When they each found something to their liking, they returned to the street.

On the floor, Beau had found a quarter, picked it up, and headed for the street where he leaned against a parking meter next to the Jeep. He slid the coin into the meter and twisted the handle, making the red violation flag promptly disappear. He chugged his drink, then tossed his bottle back into the liquor store where the shattering glass broke the silence.

"Hell, I'll probably never get to do that again," Beau mused.

"Right on," yelled Ruben, swinging his drink in the air. "Here's to running the next red light we see."

Beau laughed and went in search of another drink in the liquor store. They were all sitting on the curb like small schoolboys waiting for something to do when Beau returned with five bottles. He gave the other three a bottle and deposited the rest in the back of the Jeep.

"Welcome to Texas. Here, have a man's drink."

"Hey, mate, this 'ere bottle has a bloody bug in it," said Mulholland, half-choking.

"It's a worm, Kipp," said Ruben.

"What do ya do with the little beggar?" Mulholland asked.

"You eat it," said Beau, tilting the bottle straight up until the contents disappeared.

He grinned at Mulholland, flashing the captured worm between two rows of white teeth. Beau closed his mouth, swallowed the slimy creature, and then wiped his mouth off with the back of his sleeve. Moving to the Jeep he grabbed another bottle and popped the top of the glass on the door.

"I want to make a toast," said Beau. The others stood and followed Beau to the door of the Jeep where they held their drinks in mid-air. "To an American—to Chin!"

"Chin!" they all chorused, while staring at the back of the vehicle where the small body of their friend lay carefully wrapped. The first death within their small group. Silently they raised their drinks. They returned to the curb in front of Hondo's only liquor store and continued to drink. They talked more freely than any time since the strange events of the invasion started.

Loosened with the alcohol, Ruben asked Dean, "Hey, what the hell did you say to that guy? He was scared shitless."

Dean took another swig. "I told him what he said was true, only I wasn't an American. I was a Choctaw Indian, he had trespassed on my land, and he was going to die."

Kipp and Ruben chuckled at the words.

Then Dean turned to Beau. "I've heard a lot about you. Tell me what really happened."

With the liquor freeing his inhibition, Beau popped another bottle and told them about his wife and son, how he joined the Israeli Air Force, and the story of Cobra and the invasion.

"Some story," said Mulholland, then added, "The hardest thing to believe is the part about an invasion." They all started laughing.

"Dean, why are you here?" asked Beau.

"Because they say I murdered two men. They never found the bodies."

"Did you do it?" asked Ruben.

Dean took a swig of his drink. "It doesn't matter; they'll never find the bodies."

Then he proceeded to tell them how his family lived on a reservation near Eufala, Oklahoma, and how his mother had given him the name of "Dove." When he graduated from high school, his family went to Eufala to celebrate. He went with his father for his first drink, while his mother and sister went shopping. The women never returned and their bodies were found a week later floating in the lake bordering Eufala.

The murderers were found and brought to trial. The two men had records of previous Indian harassment. They abducted the two women but things got out of control when one of the men hit Blackman's mother, killing her. They took the body and Blackman's sister to a remote place in the hills, where they repeatedly raped the young girl before they killed her. Then, the killers deposited both bodies in the lake.

The men were found guilty and given life imprisonment. But four months after the trial, the men were released from prison on a technicality. One month after their release the two men celebrated and went on a camping trip. They were in the foothills twenty miles west of Eufala when they mysteriously disappeared, without a trace.

Blackman was held in jail with no bond. The bodies were never found, and he was released with a promise he'd join the service and leave Oklahoma.

"Hell, what happened to them?" asked Ruben. "Do you know?"

"Yes, I know," said Blackman, pleased at the memory of their demise. "I trailed them into the mountains and when they fell asleep, I charged into their camp in full Choctaw dress, hollering at the top of my lungs the great Choctaw war cry. When I told them they were about to die, they chased me in the dark. The mountains are honeycombed with caverns." Blackman took another swig and laughed. "They didn't see the hole they fell into. No one will ever find them. They were blind and helpless. Now, they are dead. They belong to the Dove. I simply led them to the place where they would die."

"Damn, they just stepped into the hole!" said Ruben.

Blackman only shrugged his shoulders. "When your time comes . . . it comes."

"That may be fine for you to say but when your time is up. I don't want to be standing next to you," Ruben said pointedly.

"A bloody way to die, in the dark, afraid of yer own shadow," said Mulholland shaking his head. "My story has nothing on you. I was in the ground forces in Thailand back when bloody hell was breaking loose in China. Some Cambodian Red Chinese jets strafed us. They shot one of me mates while he sat in his jet on the runway. I pulled him from the cockpit and strapped myself in. Decided I'd kill some of the bloody bastards."

"How long had ya been flying?" Beau asked.

"Never had."

"Come on, how'd ya know how to get it off the ground?" asked Ruben.

"Well, me mate had showed me all the levers, and how they worked. So it was up and away."

"Don't tell me you shot any of them down," said Blackman.

"Are ye kiddin', mate? Hell, I had my damn hands full."

"How'd ya get down?" asked Ruben.

"Crashed, of course."

"You didn't get hurt?" asked Beau.

"Didn't get hurt? Hell, mate, I was in traction for two months and in the hospital for six months. Some officer decides if I want to fly that bad, I should be sent to flight school. So here I am."

"Boy, that took guts," said Ruben.

"It was bloody stupid," said Mulholland, shaking his head. Then as an afterthought, "Donna sure is a pretty lass."

"What?" the other three responded.

"Donna," he repeated. "Very pretty, don't yuh think?"

They all nodded their approval and continued to drink. They made a final toast to Chin, then pulled their weary bodies from the streets of Hondo, and readied for the return trip. When Beau returned to the liquor store to find more drinks for the men at Cliff Palace, he spotted boxes of candy and among them, a familiar box. It was filled with Three Musketeers candy bars.

Already half-drunk with the liquor, he stuffed the box under his arm and mumbled, "He's gonna kill me for this." He returned to the Jeep, and unobserved, placed the box under his seat.

Mulholland asked Beau directly, "Why don't you take Krysti away from the Baron?"

"'Cause, he's a wimp," snapped Ruben.

"I saw ya in the bar that night against those three bullies. You're no wimp," said Mulholland. "Besides, I think the lady likes ya."

"She's better off without the likes of me," said Beau. "She sure is a sweet thing." With the drinks, his tongue loosened and he admitted, "Damn, I really like her."

Ruben started his engine and yelled to Dean driving the other Jeep. "Now ya'll be careful, 'cause we don't want to go and get any DWIs." All the men laughed and waved their drinks in the air. "You know how bad it'll be on our insurance rates."

When Ruben finished, they started their insane, wobbly return to Cliff Palace, and miraculously arrived undetected.

* * *

The next morning found the solemn group standing around the grave of Chin Tang, while Admiral Garrett said a few words of respect for the man who called America home. He gave a short ceremony over the grave of their first fallen comrade.

The mood was subdued the rest of the day. Everyone stayed close to Cliff Palace, except for Beau. After the funeral, he disappeared and didn't return until dark, and then he secluded himself from the rest. In the evening, he just stood at the edge of the cliff peering into the distance.

During his absence, Larry James took sadistic pleasure in tormenting Krysti. He found her alone and started to put his plan in action, as he was sure it would help him get into the good graces of Marix.

"The guy has some blood lust."

"What?" Krysti asked, confused. She had been prepared to talk to Beau and apologize for her unfair treatment of him.

"You know they killed the snipers?"

"Yes."

"But I bet you didn't know Beau murdered the one they captured," said Larry. He had heard Blackman talk about how Beau wouldn't kill the prisoner so he did.

"I can't believe it."

"It's true."

Krysti rushed off in a huff to have that question and other doubts burning inside her heart answered. Promptly, she sought out Ruben and Sunday. She found Ruben first.

"Is it true one of the snipers was murdered?" Krysti asked.

"Well, not exactly," said Ruben stumbling over his words, remembering what Blackman had done.

With Ruben's hesitation Krysti reasoned what Larry said was true, making her believe Beau committed the act, just like Larry said.

"Never mind. That's all I wanted to know."

What she learned only backed Larry's accusation. Now he justified all her fears. Hurt and bewildered, she rushed to her room where she fell across her bed and burst into tears. The false information only tormented her, adding to her misery. For a moment, she thought about confronting Beau with the story. She knew he had many things on his mind, including the death of Chin and concerns for the safety of their group. Still, she thought it was no reason to murder someone.

Later in the evening Krysti grew restless and paced about the living area. Beau stood on the edge of the cliff, silhouetted against the night sky. She ventured to the door and could hear him speak as he aimed his voice to the heavens.

"Don't take any more—let us be. Take care of them, and watch over Krysti and Justin. They don't need to see what men can do to each other," Beau said.

Alone, he stood in the dark silence of the night. He failed to notice the shadow disappear into a room at the top of the stairs. In the room, she tried unsuccessfully to deny her true feelings for the man, letting the facts of his actions confuse her emotions. This was war, she reminded herself, and yet what he did was wrong. So very wrong, she thought, and again she cried. She loved him.

Chapter 4
TRIBUTE TO AN OLD WARRIOR

Three weeks had passed since a sniper killed Chin Tang. Trees and bushes were budding, but a late March chill still hung in the night air. The days and nights had been quiet.

Ruben and Sunday had been extremely happy with the baby. Tracy had made great strides with Fitz's help, but Sully had become more withdrawn. Krysti had stayed away from Beau during the time since Tang's death. She had even spent a few intimate nights with Marix. It was still the same with him; all he offered her was a faraway look from empty eyes. He didn't seem to want to touch her. She hated having given herself to him.

Ironically, the little wild thing Lindy had become a pillar of support for Sunday and Krysti. Most of that was probably because of her desire for a mother. Lindy confided everything to those two women. Almost everything. She told them nothing about James or Marix.

Robby, Fitz, and BJ were drawn into a late night argument over the ignorance of the computer age. Soon Beau, Ruben, and Ted were drawn in. Daddy John listened intently.

"Kids can't add without a calculator," snapped Robby. "The day this country runs outa those small batteries, our future is sunk."

"Might be already," lamented Ruben. "I don't even have a calculator."

"Forget the computers and jet age," said Beau. "If I could find a crop duster right now, I'd fill it with rocks and then I'd take this war to them."

Daddy John became excited at Beau's words. The men continued to argue about the war, planes, computers, and the invasion. Daddy John joined in but waited patiently. When the group split up and Beau walked away, Daddy John followed him closely.

A moment later, he casually pulled Beau to the side, away from the others and asked, "Would you really fight them if you had a plane?"

"Hell yes. Better to die fightin' than to wait for it to come to me. It's just a question of time before they find us."

Bubbling with excitement, he motioned to Beau. "I want to show you something. Come with me."

Five minutes later, they were walking along a dark narrow path near the river. They walked for nearly a mile and all the while Daddy John chattered incessantly.

"When John Wayne died we lost the last American hero. Reagan and Bush started America's coffin. Damn, I liked the first George Bush, but he was so busy with foreign policy he forgot America. Democrats and Republicans, Liberal or Conservative, I never saw any difference. Those two damn goobers in 1999, Clinton and Gingritch, claiming to do the best for America. Why Gingritch had to hide and not Clinton I'll never understand. Every time Gingritch opened his mouth it was like he slapped himself. And Hillary. Clinton's wife kept doing it to America; just bend over and we'll poke ya again. I knew the people of America were too stupid to help themselves when they elected her Senator of New York, and she never even lived there. And Bush's son, George W., I thought he was aiming for dictator of the world. There was only one view and it was his. He was worse than the McCarthyism era and communist witch hunts of the fifties. Yep Democrats and Republicans. That bin Laden might have killed a lot of Americans, but the Democrats and Republicans stood at each end of America's coffin and drove in the final nail. Oh, history will blame the last president, but those people put us in a hole I knew we couldn't get out of.

"Boy I swear, this country should've started hangin' all those politicians back when Reagan was elected. Damn, and you could've tossed in all the judges and attorneys, because they didn't do a damn thing but make it worse. Should've known everything was gonna go to hell in a handbag when we elected an actor. I saw the Savings and Loan crap before it happened. Those sons-a-bitches destroyed this country. Republicans and Democrats kept doing the same thing and expected some Goddamn miracle to pop-up and cure all. Want some money for a new program? Hell, we'll just print some more money and tax the people. Then there were the accountants and CEOs of America that put that damn coffin in the ground. They really had some honor and integrity, huh?" But Daddy John didn't wait for an answer as he continued to lambaste America's political structure.

"Damn corporate accountants seemed to forget that two plus two was four and not a billion. America's CEOs and accountants were enough to give an attorney a good name. Should've elected Nader in 2000. Welfare for the wealthy? What a crock. They needed to be put in jail, not given any money. Too late now, besides, we'd have been broke on our butts in another year," he declared.

Beau laughed.

"What's so funny?"

Beau shook his head and sighed. "You sound like me."

"Should've dropped the A-bomb on Congress when they were in session and saved America," Daddy John moaned.

Again Beau laughed. "You'd only gotten half of them. If you wanted to get them all, you'd have to do it at the conventions or inaugurations and not when they were supposed to be working."

This time Daddy John laughed. "Oh, I like your style."

"I can see the bumper sticker now: *Save America—Nuke Washington, D.C.*" Beau's face was solemn. "But like you said, it's too late. We have more important things to worry about now."

Daddy John nodded. "Old Nader never even had a chance in 2000, with the media never even letting him say a word. That just proves what I had said for years. Democrats and Republicans controlled the media. Anyway, Nader sure pinpointed the problems. Had the Democrats and Republicans running scared for a while. Should've elected Perot in '92, when the country still had time."

Daddy John continued, with no argument from Beau, on the stupidity of the politicians and the downfall of the country—a country that no longer existed, as they knew it. "And Obama! Nothing but a communist. Shoulda hung that boy like Saddam Hussein. He and those czars destroyed America single handedly. I'd of given ten million to see what that lying bastard was hiding in College. Probably really a foreign student. He was as worthless at teats on a boar hog." Daddy John shook his head. "I'll bet if we checked the election we'd find a lot of dead people voted and Romney really won the election."

"Hey, no argument from me," said Beau.

The trail wound up a steep incline and opened to a flat mesa over 300 yards long. At the end rose a vertical fifty-foot rock barrier, forming a small box canyon. Tall oaks grew around warehouses on each side, completely obscuring them unless someone stood on the mesa. Beau had walked along the same cliff but never seen the structures. They were completely hidden from above.

What caught his attention was the size of the structures and the doors to the warehouses. The large rolling doors were the same kind used to house the crop duster he had flown years before. Did this eccentric old man actually have a plane, he wondered? The buildings could have housed a half dozen or more with ease. The mesa was flat enough and long enough for a plane to take off and land.

A delighted gleam lit Daddy John's eyes as he neared one of the large doors. It was as though he were a kid showing his friend a secret hideout. He bent over an enclosed generator and pushed the starter button. The small motor jumped to life.

"This is the only power I have down here," he said apologetically.

"Do you really have a crop duster in there?" asked Beau doubtfully.

"Oh, more than that, much more than that!" Daddy John chuckled excitedly. He pushed the large door open just enough to allow them access. "You'll see now." He stepped into the dark warehouse and flipped a switch to the overhead fluorescent lights.

Before them was a fighter plane from World War II. The sleek lines were those of the P-51D Mustang, probably the best propeller fighter ever flown—the most advanced prop driven aircraft of World War II, boasting a full teardrop canopy like those used in modern jets. The Mustang was a much smaller craft than the jets to which Beau and his men were accustomed. With no electronics, the Mustang was controlled only with mechanical gauges and was much closer to the size of his old crop duster: small, but nimble and quick.

The P-51 Mustang was finished in black satin, trimmed in gold. The black was neither glossy nor flat in color. Glistening in the light, it appeared as though the plane had never been flown. As Beau walked past the old World War II relic, the overhead lights cast a moving sheen on the dark metallic skin giving the effect of movement, making it appear to be alive, moving, watching Beau's inspection with eager anticipation.

"She's beautiful," he murmured.

The mischievous old man stood with his arms crossed in front of his chest. A smile lit his face. "Son, this is not a jet. It's not the king of the sky, nor is it the biplane you requested. She's much, much more."

"I can't fight them with this."

"That's what they said to David when he faced Goliath. All ya gotta do is throw the first stone."

"If I did fly it, I'd need ammunition, bombs, a flight suit, and God knows what else," said Beau.

With his words barely finished, Daddy John grabbed his arm and led him deeper into the warehouse. The red hair stood out against the enthusiasm he radiated.

"I'm sure a prayer would help. As far as the other things . . . well, I have them! I've had these planes for over thirty years. Bought the one you saw from a South American gentleman. Cost me $2000." As Daddy John flipped switches to lights in the rest of the long warehouse, he paused and watched Beau. "Did ya know our own government sold over 1000 of the P-51s to countries in South America for one dollar each? Now that's a crime. Sometimes I think they oughta hang the politicians up by their balls."

The words were almost lost on Beau. He saw other planes: another black P-51 Mustang, two British Spitfires, a P-38 Lightning and an old P-40 Warhawk painted with the Flying Tigers emblem. All were in prime condition and appeared to be in combat readiness. One stall had rows of ammunition and machine gun belts loaded with deadly projectiles, missiles, and dozens of reserve fuel tanks for the P-51 Mustang. A dozen bombs lined the floor ready for the P-38 and P-40.

"Where the hell did you get the arsenal?"

"Same South American gentleman. The U.S. sold him two train cars full of parts, ammunition, old fuel tanks, and spent cartridges. I don't know why, but for the last twenty years I've loaded the empty shells, probably twenty a day. It was just a hobby but it was important they be exactly as they were. Everything works: the guns, the bombs, and the rockets. These planes and the ones in the other warehouse are combat ready."

"You have more?"

"Yep. In the other warehouse are more of the same. But this one," said Daddy John pointing to the one he first showed Beau, "she's my pride and joy. A P-51D, the best Mustang, in my opinion." They moved closer to the black and gold aircraft. "This one has a fine history. One of the first to shoot down a jet in World War II, over the English Channel, she downed a ME-262 German jet. Shot down at least a dozen V-1 rockets aimed for London. And she was one of the first to destroy a Mig in Korea. What was her fate for her heroics? Sold to a foreign country for a dollar."

"That's hard to believe."

"There's a lot of things politicians do that's hard to believe. But this time they got caught with their pants down and playing with themselves to boot."

For a moment, Beau recalled his meeting with the civilian review board when he tried to explain about the invasion. "Well, maybe not that hard to believe."

"Damn right. Hell, look at the mess they got us in now. Well, anyway, this damn country gets a hero and just puts her out to pasture. I wasn't about to let it happen to this one," Daddy John said with emotion.

Beau ran his hand over the sleek black fuselage. The touch of cold steel aroused a warm, glowing, feeling inside him. This was like coming home. He couldn't wait to climb into the fighter.

"May I?" Beau asked, pointing to the cockpit.

"My pleasure," said Daddy John, climbing on the wing beside him.

Once inside Beau slid down into the cushion-filled natural aluminum seat. The cushion was where the parachute would normally rest in flight. He checked the mechanical controls and the gauges. Simple and easy. Unlike the dozens of computer gauges and electronic gadgets filling modern day jets. Just put in the gas, start her up, and fly away. Almost as easy to operate as his old crop duster. The stick felt tight and the controls responded to his touch. Beau reached back and pulled at the clear teardrop canopy and moved it effortlessly along the steel runners. The bubble canopy provided an unhindered 360-degree view.

Daddy John's eyes sparkled with excitement.

"She wouldn't stand a chance," said Beau.

"Not so," said Daddy John. "A man once said, *It's not the fighter that wins, but the man who flies the fighter.* You've got the experience and you're a natural. If what I've heard and read about you is only partially true, then you were born to fly! Ever seen a mockingbird and a cat? Hit and run. Drive them crazy. Peck and run, be a thorn in their side. Drive those damn invaders batty."

"I'd need a flight suit for the G-forces."

Daddy John pointed across the room to a half dozen crates containing flight suits. "I've got them. Not the best, mind ya, but at least a dozen bladder suits. All ya gotta do is pick one out. They did the trick in the war, no reason they can't handle what you can dish out."

"Should've guessed."

"But this lady may be different."

"What do you mean?"

"I followed racing for years so she's got the latest technology. She's got a special supercharger with water injection and a sensor to adjust the magneto to prevent detonation. Has a Merlin engine. You know, like the magician? Never hurts to have a little bit of magic on your side.

"The record for a prop is 550 mph held by one of these. This lady can do better. The wings have been trimmed for less air resistance and the edges replaced with carbon fibers. I've replaced the six 50-caliber machine guns with four 20-millimeter MK 12 cannons from some old discarded A-4D Skyhawks."

"More surplus you scrounged?"

"You got it. You've seen the waste in the military. If you're under budget, then throw something away, burn it or bury it. Keep buyin' till you've spent your money, otherwise ya get your money cut. Got the cannons from friends in the military. Perfectly good, just more military throwaways! All my planes have twenty-millimeter cannons built into them. Makes for more kill power. Better to have a three-quarter inch bullet than the old half incher. Those 20-millimeter cannons will bring down the biggest jets."

"I don't know, Daddy John," said Beau wondering if the insanity of it might just make the crazy scheme work.

"The jets have gotten too sophisticated. This lady is simple and sure. Son, this is a fine lady. She'll respond and obey better than any woman you ever touched. She's soft as a rose, strong as a lion, and as deadly as a shark," Daddy John beamed. "If jets are King of the sky, then she's the Queen." His laugh echoed through the warehouse. "And son, if you ever played chess you know the power of the Queen."

"I wonder how she'll do against the jets."

"Treat her right and she'll bring ya home." After a moment's thought he added, "When it comes to fightin' and givin' them hell . . . well, she's the Devil's Angel."

"We need fuel. I suppose you have that figured out?"

"Of course. The planes can all be run on regular, if necessary. I have plenty of fuel in storage tanks. I have a chemical additive to keep the fuel from breaking down into varnish."

"Now, if I just had a fire bomb," Beau mumbled.

"Problem solved. I have dozens of spare fuel tanks. All I need to do is attach it to the Mustang, fill the tank with fuel, and add some detergent. Hell, the gas just turns to jelly and you have napalm. That'll do the trick, I guarantee it. Everything for a hunerd yards will burn to a crisp."

Daddy John motioned for Beau to follow him to a gallant and beautiful silver aircraft. "This here one is a real performer. If there is one plane equal to the P-51, it's this one. The Supermarine Seafire 47. You've heard it called the Spitfire. This has four-.303 Browning machine-guns and two 20-millimeter cannons. This was the first plane to ever shoot down a jet-powered aircraft. The Rolls Royce Griffon engine generates over 2,000 horsepower. When she's running full force, she purrs like a kitten. None better except the Mustang, which is my personal preference. Sure a lot of Englishmen would disagree with me, so pick one and give them hell."

"The Mustang, no doubt about it."

"I thought ya would."

"Let me think on it." Beau turned and faced Daddy John. "The whole idea is crazy. No, it's more like suicidal. I've got about as good a chance of succeeding as I would winning the Indy 500 with my brothers' dune buggies."

Daddy John said, "You're kinda right, but it's more like taking an Indy race car to the dunes and getting it to chase your dune buggy through the hills and sand." He made a gesture pointing straight up with his finger. "You're not going up there to fight them; you're gonna make them come after you down here on your terms where you will be their equal.

"With all of this," Daddy John said, waving his arm toward the weapons he had collected, "you have something the enemy doesn't—you will have surprise on your side. They won't expect ya. And they won't be prepared."

"Kinda like they did us," Beau mused.

"Yep. Time to give them a taste of their own medicine," said Daddy John.

Daddy John's comparison seemed logical. Maybe there was a chance of it working. For a moment Beau sat in silence and pondered the consequences. Maybe even his own death. Then Daddy John asked, "Say, it's none of my business but how the hell did you lose your finger?"

A glance to his right hand, and in an instant Beau was back in the room half way around the world as Cobra, Rasht Sharafan, took deadly delight in stealing the digit. General Waddle had mentioned Cobra's name over the radio. Maybe if he flew, he could find—

The cold blue eyes turned on Daddy John. "You've got a deal. Can you be ready tomorrow night?"

"Yep."

"Don't tell anyone."

They shook hands on the arrangement. Daddy John asked again, "The hand, what happened? Wasn't that from when you went down in an Israeli jet?"

Glancing at the finger again, Beau turned to him and said, "Yes."

Beau surveyed the equipment, flight suit, and parachute. Everything was in order. The power was cut, and they returned to Cliff Palace. The deadly mission was less than twenty-four hours away.

Many thoughts rushed through Beau's mind as he walked to his room. Was Cobra in the area? The odds were slim but he hoped to run into Sharafan just one more time and make up for what he failed to do the last time they met. Revenge would be sweet in coming.

For a moment his mind returned to reality. What chance did he have against men with jets? He would know tomorrow night.

Upon his return to Cliff Palace, Beau found he was alone. Everyone had turned in for the night. His mind raced with the thoughts of his mission. Sitting on the couch he leaned back and tried to relax but his mind would not turn off, and his thoughts now were not about the mission. He thought about Krysti and wanted to talk to her. He dismissed the notion; it would be better for her if he avoided her. For some reason, he could see Rasht Sharafan preparing to tell him the second secret while he was being tortured. Would he find Cobra? Would he learn the untold secret? His future was uncertain to say the least, and most likely it was a short one.

* * *

Machine guns continued firing under the orders of Rasht Sharafan, and in the distance Beau could see a woman and a small boy riddled with the deadly gunfire. He watched helplessly as they fell to the sandy beach. Now the enemy had him and he was being shaken.

"No!" Beau yelled, swiftly lurching erect on the couch, eyes open wide. Ruben shook Beau's arm trying to wake him from his dream.

"Quiet," he whispered, holding a single finger to his lips. "You're having a nightmare."

The night was cool and dry but Beau was perspiring profusely. "How'd ya know I was having a nightmare?" Beau asked, trying to breathe normally again.

"I couldn't sleep and came down for a drink and heard ya. What the hell are you doing sleeping on the couch instead of in your room?"

Beau shook his head. "I was just sitting here and must have dozed off. Did I wake anybody?"

"No, I don't think so. Was it the dream with Becky and Shawn?" Ruben asked.

Puzzled and confused Beau said, "Yes and no."

"What do you mean?"

"It was the same dream only," Beau paused before he finished, "it wasn't Becky and Shawn—it was Krysti and Justin!"

Chapter 5
THE MUSTANG FLIES

The next morning was quiet and rather subdued, not much different than any other since Tang's death. Donna and Kipp had become inseparable and spent the early hours on the river. In the kitchen, Daddy John was unusually excited and whistling for no apparent reason. Beyond the sanctity of Cliff Palace, the March weather was dry and cold.

"Your uncle seems a mite happy, eh?" Kipp asked as they walked up the trail and then followed another path to the river.

She frowned and said, "He's up to no good. I know he's scheming something. I just don't know what it is. Unless. . . . no, he couldn't be . . ."

"Be what?"

"Nothing. I just had a wild thought. Forget it. It's not important."

Together, they continued to the river. Kipp threw a flat stone, skimming it across the water until it bounced onto the farthest bank. They walked across a barrier of rocks while laughing and teasing each other. A short climb and a quick jump over a ravine put them beneath a large cypress. Donna slipped but Kipp caught her hand and pulled her to him. A soothing quiet prevailed over the river as they peered into each other's eyes. For a moment Kipp smothered Donna's anxious lips with kisses. When they returned to Cliff Palace, no one seemed to notice their unusually happy spirits—except Daddy John, who wondered what they were up to.

Standing behind Sunday with his arms wrapped around her from her backside, Ruben teased her and patted her now flat stomach. When Beau approached, Ruben stopped and asked, "What ya got planned tonight? Another wild night on the town?"

Beau was caught off guard. "What do you mean?"

"Well, I just thought you might be going to town to catch a movie or something," Ruben said mischievously.

"Ruben that's mean," said Sunday. Then she asked Beau, "Why don't you talk to Krysti? I think you both should talk to each other."

"It's better this way. Besides, I have plans and it's best she not be concerned with me."

"Stubborn fool," groaned Sunday.

Ruben laughed at his friend. "What kinda plans? You intend to take the invaders on alone?"

The question again caught Beau unprepared. "Of course not. How would I do it?"

"I know you. You'd find a way."

Beau felt awkward. "Hey, I gotta ask Daddy John something. I'll be back later."

Abruptly Beau turned to search him out. As he was making his way to where he would be working on the plane, Justin tagged along and begged Beau to go with him to find more quail or doves. At the moment he had more important matters to contemplate.

Reluctantly, Beau agreed, but first he said he had to find Daddy John. When he found him he sent Justin on ahead with the promise he would catch up after he finished talking. When Justin was gone the two men discussed the plans and decided Daddy John would prepare the plane and Beau would rendezvous with him in the warehouse at 1800 hours.

As they parted, Beau could have sworn Daddy John said, "I'll have them ready."

* * *

A strange noise attracted Beau first. He had heard a fox in search of food before, but whatever the small animal was after was big. That was very unusual as a fox only hunted small prey like birds. Then he saw Justin trying to ward off the predator with a stick. The boy circled the small mesquite defensively as though protecting some unseen treasure. When the fox saw Beau approach, it was too much. The animal turned and quickly scampered into the underbrush.

Justin was all excited as he ran to Beau, grabbed his arm, and pulled him quickly towards the tree he had been defending. "Look what I found!" he gasped.

Beneath the mesquite was a tattered and torn bird nest. Five hatchlings lay near. Two were partially devoured, obviously from attacks by the fox. The third was dead, but two were still alive and one of those looked to be injured. Only a few feet away lay a torn and tattered mockingbird. The small female had defended her brood valiantly, in the end even giving her life to protect her young. The mate was nowhere to be seen and Beau correctly surmised he had also given his life to the protection of its young.

Gently Justin touched the two survivors. Bending down, Beau checked the two young mockingbirds. The eyes were still closed but they chirped vigorously, pleading for food from parents that were never to return.

"Can we keep them?" Justin pleaded. A slight smile creased Beau's face and he could remember the first birds he had brought to his mother when he was a small child.

"Sure," he said. He started to take off his T-shirt. "Be careful and put them back in their nest."

Carefully, Justin tried to push the nest back to its original shape and then, gently, he placed the two orphans back in their home.

"I thought they had babies in the summer."

Beau put his shirt on the rocks. "Some, but most birds will start nesting in spring. Justin I want you to put the nest in the center of the shirt."

"Okay. Beau, I know I have seen nests in the summer?"

"That's right. Blue jays, mockingbirds, and many others will start nesting in the spring but continue to make nests with more young: at least two broods and as many as four each year. Being this early is just a sign that nesting is good and they might have had as many as four new ones this year."

"Wow! I didn't know that."

"Most people don't."

Justin did as Beau said and placed the nest with the two small mockingbirds in the center and then folded the four corners across to protect the birds from the spring chill that still hung in the air. With great care he picked up the small package and carried it proudly back to Cliff Palace.

* * *

The two small birds took everyone's thoughts away from the current dangerous situation. Animals throughout time have had that calming effect on people, and it was no different there—except for a few people.

"We need to feed them as soon as possible," said Beau.

"I'll make up something with a little milk, honey, and bread," Daddy John offered.

"I have a box in my room we can put them in," said Krysti.

Donna said, "I have an eyedropper we can use to feed them."

Both Justin and Lindy doted on the two small birds. Even the men showed a little interest and curiosity towards the new tenants of Cliff Palace. All that is except for James. He thought the whole thing was stupid and it would have been better to let the birds stay with the fox.

"These are mockingbirds," Justin beamed. "They are the state bird of Texas." Krysti and Beau smiled.

Beau said, "Legend is when Texas picked a state bird they chose the mockingbird because it would fight to protect its home, even giving its life if needed, just like the Texan's that gave their lives for independence."

"Shoulda left them for the fox," snipped James, who thought his comment was funny. Nobody laughed. Krysti frowned at him, while Kipp shook his head, and Blackman just stared at the small man. Ruben and Sunday snorted their displeasure.

"That's not very nice," snapped Lindy.

"Yeah," Justin responded.

"They're gonna die anyway," said James.

With the bird food in hand and Donna following, Daddy John said, "If you have nothing nice to say best you say nothing." Then he made a point to shove his way in and push James away. A slight smile creased Blackman's face. Others grunted their agreement with Daddy John.

As though presenting an award, the elder man took the small bowl of food along with two eyedroppers Donna had supplied and gave them to Justin. "These two young birds are now your responsibility. You are now their mother and father." Simply, Justin beamed. Krysti wiped a tear from her eye. Kipp, Sully, Pick, and Warren smiled.

"Can I help?" Lindy almost begged.

"Sure," said Justin. He gave her an eyedropper. "Be careful." Lindy nodded. Justin picked up one of the small mockingbirds and started to feed it and Lindy did the same with the other.

"You have a name for them yet?" Fitzhenry asked.

Justin looked to Ruben and Beau and then grinned. "Yep. Champ and Buddy."

"How'd you pick those names?" Ruben queried. Before Justin responded, Beau had an idea as to where the names had come from.

"You always call Beau *Buddy* and Beau always calls me *Champ*," said Justin.

Most of those standing around either nodded or chuckled at the remark. Krysti wiped another tear away. Beau and Blackman nodded, because they both knew Justin was aware of far more than most people suspected.

"Aye, mate, and which one they be?"

Justin looked at both the helpless birds now dependent upon him for survival. "The strong one is Champ, and the sick one is his Buddy."

Krysti turned away to remove another tear from one of her eyes.

* * *

The appointed hour arrived and Beau slipped away from Cliff Palace. On the cliff he almost walked right into Krysti. He stopped.

They both shuffled about uncomfortably, neither wanting to stay, and neither wanting to leave.

"Krysti. I want to thank you for helping Tracy."

"I'm just glad I was able to get her to respond," Krysti said. She wanted to ask him questions; she wanted to tell him she missed him but she didn't.

"Today with the birds. That was sweet what you did with Justin."

"I think I enjoyed it as much as he did. Well, I best be going. If you need me, let me know. I'll be there," said Beau.

Krysti wanted to tell him she needed him now. She just wished what she had learned about him were untrue. If only James had never told her. If only she had never learned the truth.

"Where are you going?" she asked.

Again, he hesitated. "To help Daddy John. Then I'll be back." Beau turned, leaving Krysti standing alone on the cliff.

Minutes later, Beau had traveled the distance and scaled the narrow trail leading to the mesa where he knew Daddy John and the lone P-51 Mustang awaited him.

When he topped the mesa, he saw Daddy John preparing not one P-51, but two. Both of the black Mustangs had been rolled from their hangars. Daddy John was not alone. Beside him, with a grin spreading from ear to ear, stood Robby Schmitt, wiping grease from his hands.

"Daddy John, you didn't need to fix both planes," said Beau not understanding why he prepared them both.

"No problem. Didn't take much more time. They're both loaded and ready to go."

"Now this is a real fighter," said Schmitt.

Beau was concerned Daddy John had enlisted the aid of Robby when he asked him to keep it a secret. "Why did you get Robby to help?"

"Well, he said the two of you would need Robby to check them out."

Beau caught the word this time. "He?"

"Well, yes," said Daddy John rather confused. "He said it was too dangerous to go alone, so you'd both fly out tonight."

"Who did?" asked Beau. But no sooner did he ask the question then it was answered from behind.

"My buddy!" said Ruben. "Gonna go off without me and have all the fun? What kinda friend are you?"

Spinning about, Beau confronted Ruben, who was already outfitted in a bladder suit. The flight suit prevented blood in the body from pooling in the legs and making the pilot pass out due to the G-forces exerted during tight maneuvers.

"How'd you know?" Beau asked.

Ruben couldn't restrain a laugh. "You talked about a few other things during that dream last night."

"Well, it doesn't matter, you can't go."

"Says who? You better get your bladder suit, I'm ready," said Ruben admiring his own. "Isn't this the damnedest thing ya ever saw?"

"I thought he was supposed to go with you," said Daddy John.

"Damn straight," said Ruben.

"You don't know the aircraft."

"Wrong. I've been going over it most of the day." Then Ruben said, "I figured Robby could help. And the answer to what you're thinking is no, I didn't tell anyone else and no, I didn't tell Sunday."

Ruben was right; those were the exact questions Beau was about to ask him. "Sorry, I can't let you go."

"Well, old buddy, then you'll be killing me, 'cause when ya leave I'm gonna follow ya," said Ruben shrugging his shoulders and shaking his head. "And ya know how I hate to drive in the dark alone."

"Damn you. You could get killed when we attack."

"And what makes you bulletproof?" snickered Ruben.

"Daddy John, do you have radios in the planes?" Beau asked, turning toward him to confirm the questions.

"Well, I got a CB in each one. They should do the trick for ya," said Daddy John with reluctance.

Beau rubbed his face with his hand. "Okay, you can go. But I want you to stay close and do as I say. Understand?"

"Roger that," said Ruben. He took a few steps, bent over, and picked up another bladder suit. "I think this one will fit ya." Ruben walked to Beau and handed him the flight suit and the helmet. "Especially the helmet; it's oversized."

Beau couldn't repress a small grin. "We'll be skimming the treetops and there won't be much light out tonight, so you stay on my tail."

"I'll be as close as your breath. Hell, this is just like the crop dusting."

"Except it's not daytime, we won't be able to see, and these bugs will shoot back. You've gotten yourself into a mess of shit now." Ruben knew otherwise. As long as he stayed close to Beau, he'd be all right.

The four men checked the gear one final time. The guns were loaded, the tanks full, and a reserve tank was mixed with detergent creating napalm. While they made the checks, Beau explained to Ruben his intent to fly to Lackland Air Base in San Antonio. They would hit, dump the tanks on the parked jets, and run.

"Ya know if these things had a radar?" mumbled Schmitt in deep thought and rubbing the thick beard he had grown since the invasion.

"Sorry, Robby, it seems like we gotta fly by the seats of our pants on this one," mused Ruben.

"Yeah, communications, radar, chaff for heat-seeking missiles. It might work."

"What the hell are you talking about?" Beau asked.

"Nothing, just thinking," said Schmitt.

Beau and Ruben climbed into the Mustangs and checked the radios. Both planes were equipped with electric starters. The engines sputtered and coughed, then came to life.

Ruben's voice boomed over the old CBs Robby had wired into their helmets. "Sorry, but I'm gonna need to abort this flight."

"Why?" asked Beau.

"See, I knew you'd miss me."

"What's the problem?" Beau repeated.

"There's no barf bag," said Ruben. The radios were silent and nobody could hear both men laugh inside their cockpits.

"Mongoose to Moon Shadow, it's a check here. Ready for takeoff?"

In his best imitation of the *Star Trek* character Scotty, Ruben said, "Aye Cap'n, let's go in search of the Klingons."

Beau nodded. Yes, Ruben was right; it was almost like old times. Only this time, it was far more likely they would not return. And yet he was beginning to wonder how they could lose.

Both planes taxied to the boxed end of the small canyon, increased the rpm's of their fighters and rumbled down the flat stone runway, dropped slightly as they fell from the edge of the cliff, then soared upward.

The time had come to take the battle to the invaders.

* * *

In Cliff Palace, everyone heard the engines. The men scrambled to the edge of the cliff in time to see two large, black shadowy objects move through the dark sky at tree level.

"Hell, its two old planes," said Mulholland.

"He did it!" said Donna excitedly.

"Damn, it's Beau and Ruben!" exclaimed BJ with a touch of regret in his voice. "They found some planes and didn't take me."

"Oh no," moaned Sunday.

Confused as to how the two could be in planes of any kind, Krysti turned and asked Sunday, "Beau and Ruben?"

"Those crazy bastards are going to get killed," mumbled Marix, rather overjoyed at the thought.

"Sunday, it's okay, they'll come back," said Krysti, trying to comfort her.

But Sunday laughed at Krysti. "If that's Beau, then they'll return."

* * *

The night sky was overcast and there was no Moon, which added to the difficulty of the seemingly impossible mission: two World War II vintage airplanes making a short historic journey to a full-fledged air base to inflict as much damage and chaos as they were capable of doing. For the moment Beau and Ruben concentrated on the terrain surrounding them. Before they could fight they had to survive the flight. Both men flew through, around, and occasionally over the ridges of the tall rocky hills between them and their destination in San Antonio—Lackland Air Force Base.

What could they hope to gain? The invaders came in such concentrations that they had achieved what no one had done since the War of 1812: Invaders had set foot on American soil. Even more important, they now controlled a large portion of the United States. The Coalition had taken the American forces completely and totally unprepared.

Who could expect to succeed where one of the mightiest armed forces had failed? The invaders had accomplished their task: total surprise with massive numbers. They did something no enemy had ever done. They controlled American skies.

Now two antique warplanes held a small ray of hope that they could be as big a surprise to that same formidable force.

"Mongoose, can't we just follow a highway and quit hopping over these damn canyons and mountains?"

"Sorry. The highways probably have troops that could warn the surrounding bases. We'd be located and destroyed in no time. I'm afraid this is our only alternative," said Beau, noticing legitimate concern on the part of his wingman.

"Damn! I almost hit those trees," snapped Ruben, pulling back on the stick. He narrowly missed a group of large oaks lining a ridge. "I don't think we're gonna make it. They'll find us."

Beau detected a trace of fear in his old friend. "Mongoose to Moon Shadow, in a few minutes we'll come out on a flat area. Hang in there 'cause we'll need to stick within fifty feet of the ground."

"Roger, Mongoose. What are we gonna do, cut the grass with our props?" asked Ruben, the tone of his voice returning to normal.

"Moon Shadow, listen and stay close to me. We must not be detected if we are to succeed. If they can do it, so can we. Remember when that German kid flew a Cessna and landed in Moscow Square? And the Cessna that almost hit the White House when Clinton was in office? Well, we're about to do the same thing. Unlike them we know what we're doing."

"Are you sure?"

"I'm sure. They have warning systems in operation, but they expect to be assaulted from the north with jets. They won't expect us. I repeat—they will not be ready for us!"

"Roger Mongoose. You don't mind if I cross my fingers anyway?"

They cleared the last ridge, dropped low, and sped perilously close to the ground.

"Moon Shadow, I want you to drop back about a thousand yards. I'll light them up, you drop the tank. Then we'll make one more pass. Disable the jets and try to make the runways inoperable."

"Roger."

The lights of Lackland were now visible. It was then Ruben noticed Beau pulling away. Over the rough terrain, they had kept their air speed low to maneuver around the obstacles. Now in the open, they increased to 400 mph.

The base was clearly visible and enough lights lit the runways for Beau to perform his task. He shoved the throttle forward and the P-51 Mustang responded to his touch. He crossed the perimeter of Lackland at an altitude of 400 feet. Jets lined the runways and were easy targets. He could hear the alarms even from his cockpit. Pilots on the ground scrambled to their jets. Toward those planes he cut a path, opening up with all four of the newly installed 20-millimeter cannons. The armament responded with deadly accuracy. He pulled the stick back and prepared for another run when it abruptly became bright as day—a moment which was followed with a thunderous roar. Ruben had dropped his load.

"EEEhhhaaa! It's the Fourth of July. Looks like we got our asses in more trouble Mongoose. San Antonio has an ordinance against fireworks in the city limits."

"Roger, nice work. Make the last pass. Hit and run," said Beau. "Get the movers, we don't want them to come after us."

Beau came out of his loop almost ninety degrees to the left of where he made his initial run. Lightning quick his mind had memorized the runways on the first pass, anticipated Ruben flying past, and returned on the only probable direction the enemy would become airborne. He guessed accurately because as he completed his loop, he spied an F-16 Viper and one F-14 Turkey just making their turn to the runway—ready for takeoff! He could see the flames from the jets as they accelerated, only seconds from being airborne. In that split second, he lined the P-51 on the two birds, crossed his fingers and fired two HVAR rockets, at the same time firing his guns. Beau wondered if the work Daddy John did would be successful. His guns had worked and so had Ruben's napalm bomb. The first rocket missed, but as though in answer to his questions, the second rocket found its mark just as the lead F-16 lifted from the runway. The Viper exploded into a horrendous ball of flame that arched through the air and then rolled on the ground for a hundred yards. The F-14 helpless at his speed and with 20-millimeter holes in his tanks crashed viciously into the wall of flame. The F-14 exploded, sending shrapnel skyward like a modern day fireworks display.

"Bingo!" screamed Ruben over the old CB. "Never thought I'd like to see a Turkey and a Viper burn. What a beautiful sight."

Beau half smiled then concentrated on a row of formidable jets. Once within range, he released his reserve fuel tank filled with napalm. Again, the night sky lit to a bright orange brilliance. Curiosity made him do a slow barrel roll to view their handiwork. All runways were out of commission and twenty-five percent of the aircraft were destroyed or on fire.

Once he cleared Lackland, he nosed earthward and maintained an altitude of less than fifty feet. "Moon Shadow, do you have a read on me?"

"More than that, Mongoose, I'm closing in on your ass. Did you see the shit we just did?" said Ruben, laughing as he spoke.

"We threw our first stone," said Beau. The reference to David and Goliath was lost on Ruben in his excitement.

"Man, we kicked the shit out of them. Did you see the napalm? It was a regular Fourth of July. And—"

"Moon Shadow, maintain radio silence." The air speed had picked up to 500 mph.

"Roger," Ruben answered. "Say, can you find your way back?"

"Yes." With the answer, Ruben relaxed and relished the moment and the victory they accomplished.

When they reached the hills, they dropped the air speed. Cutting, weaving, and winding in and among the close-knit hills seemed easier on the return trip. The mission was accomplished without a flaw or a hitch.

In the excitement of the fight, Beau gave little attention to the bird he flew. Now, his thoughts were on the wondrous little machine that responded to every request he initiated and had done them all effortlessly. What was the P-51 Mustang actually capable of?

Soon, he would discover all she could do.

Chapter 6
THE DEVIL'S ANGELS

When Ruben and Beau brought their aircraft to a safe landing, they were surprised at the activity on the once secluded and quiet mesa. Everyone stood in the safety of the hangars when they landed, but the excitement was obvious when they swarmed the two black aircraft.

Sunday poked Krysti in the ribs and jumped for joy. "See, I told you they would return." When Ruben crawled from the cockpit of the P-51 Mustang, she charged the plane.

Tracy and Justin were the first to greet Beau. Krysti stood at a distance but was no less impressed with the actions of the two gallant crusaders. The only two who seemed unimpressed were James and Marix who were curious more than anything else. To them, it was of little concern whether or not either man returned. In fact, they might have rejoiced had Beau failed to come back. Lindy didn't really understand, but she too was caught up in the enthusiasm.

BJ and Sully approached Beau. The exploits of the two pilots excited Sully; it made Beau feel good to see him come around.

"You son-of-a-bitch!" shouted BJ. "And you didn't even invite me along." Both embraced.

"Wasn't sure if it would work," said Beau, "so I thought I'd try it out first. We caught them with their pants down."

Ted stood in front of him. "I want you to know that was a stupid thing to do, going up against jets with nothing but old planes." Then he broke a smile. "Glad you're back."

Behind them stood Daddy John with his legs spread wide, arms folded across his chest, a grin on his face, and a twinkle in his eyes. When he spied Beau, he gave a thumbs up sign, which Beau returned with a nod and a grin.

"Daddy John," yelled Beau. "We threw the first stone. The *Devil's Angels* came through." Daddy John said nothing; he just nodded his head knowingly.

With Sunday under his arm and grease streaking his face, Ruben moved toward Beau. "Hell, we kicked their asses! Sully, BJ, we just blew the shit out of Lackland. And ya should've seen Beau," said Ruben waving his arms and describing what had happened. "He makes this big loop then goes straight for a Viper and a Turkey, fires his rockets and blows them to smithereens."

A hand touched Beau on the arm and he turned to face Krysti. "I'm glad you made it back safe," said Krysti.

"Krysti, can I talk to you?" he pleaded.

She shook her head. "Maybe later. Give me time." For a moment, she reconsidered and hesitated. She was about to accept Beau's offer when Marix approached from the side, coming between the two. He put his arm around her shoulder.

"Are you all right?" Marix asked her. Then, in a controlled voice aimed at Beau, he added, "That wasn't too smart a thing to try."

"A man's gotta do what he's gotta do." Beau's words pierced through Marix. "What would you do? Stay here with the women?"

Krysti felt Michael stiffen. "No," she pleaded.

"One day, she won't be here to defend you," Marix hissed. "An F-16 and an F-14? In that?" Marix shook his head in disbelief, and pointed to the black and gold P-51. "You expect us to believe your yarn? That old plane would have a hard enough time just taking off," he snickered. Then he took Krysti's arm and led her away.

Beau restrained himself while Justin mumbled, "I don't like him."

Beau slapped the kid on the shoulder. "Forget it, Champ. He's not worth it."

Justin turned to Beau. "One day, Mike's gonna make you mad, and he's gonna be in real trouble. I can tell."

The boy's words surprised Beau and he knelt beside him. "Don't worry about Mike. Tell you what, why don't we go fishing tomorrow?"

The response was immediate. "Oh boy! You bet."

"Then you get some sleep," Beau ordered. Justin turned to do as he was told, but Beau's words halted him. "You haven't told your mom about the rabbits and armadillos?"

"Shoot, no," said Justin. "Mom's a girl; she wouldn't understand. See you in the morning, Beau."

"Goodnight, Justin."

Beau turned to leave, but BJ, leading Kipp, Ruben, Cozmo, Fitz, Dean, Pick, Sully, and James, confronted him. Reluctantly, James joined but only because the others had decided to challenge Beau with their demands.

Warren made a wide sweep of the mesa with his arms. "We've taken a vote and decided we would prefer to fight in these than to wait here and maybe be killed by troops like the snipers you ran into. At least in the air, we know what we're doing. There are enough planes and armament for all of us. We can all work in shifts making ammunition and whatever else is necessary for our missions."

"You can't; it would be suicide," said Beau.

"It's too late. We're all going to be a part of this team," Warren countered. Reluctantly Beau conceded. That night ten men, without Marix, discussed their plans for another assault. Behind them stood Daddy John, Robby, Donna, and Tracy listening as the men made plans.

Only Robby had heard the words "Devil's Angels" when Daddy John had mumbled them. Robby had an idea that would help them all.

Schmitt turned to him. "Is there a place around here like a Radio Shack? I need some electronics, wires, radios, and other things like flares and aluminum foil."

"There's a place in Hondo, kinda off the beaten path. Maybe some of the stuff you need might still be there."

Schmitt noted, "I think I can give your *Devil's Angels* a fighting chance."

* * *

Lackland Air Base was still ablaze when advisors reached the scene. The stories they described were of Americans accomplishing a sneak attack with a half dozen jets. The troops were helpless to defend. Only two jets had managed to get to a runway, but American jets destroyed them as they swooped down for the kill. The F-16 and F-14 didn't have a chance.

Five men arrived just as the sun was rising. They had come to inspect the effects of the raid: one from Argentina, Sergio Quintana; another from Iran, Azad Mustaq; and the third, a vicious man with no patience. He had helped coordinate the invasion of the United States. Now, he was in control of the middle section of Texas. The third man was Rasht Sharafan, known to those who flew with him as Cobra. With him were Aziz and al-Majid ready to do his bidding.

Sharafan was angry. His carefully laid out defenses had been penetrated. He was confused as to how the Americans had accomplished such a feat. During the invasion his men had managed to capture ten of the prized F-16s. Now, they had only nine. He had many questions. Why did they only hit one base and why had the base been so far behind the line his forces now occupied?

When each man approached and told his story of countless jets, Sharafan called him a liar. He pointed out the jets were not detected on radar. He also noted the absurdity of such an invasion—the size they described, taking place without being detected. After inspecting the site, he came to the conclusion based on the firepower used to destroy his aircraft, it could have been accomplished with as few as two jets.

However unrealistic it sounded, only an old man who refueled the jets made any sense to Sharafan. He told of two planes with propellers coming mysteriously from the darkness, flying as though demon possessed. Then, just as quickly, they disappeared. They had done all the destruction and created all the confusion. The old man waved his hands as he told how one plane came for the F-16 and F-14 and fired rockets, destroying them on the runway.

The story was impossible to comprehend; how could old planes accomplish so much damage? Sharafan's mind searched for an answer.

Beau Gex was to have been in Laughlin. Sharafan led the raid to that destination personally so he could find Gex and finish what he had failed to do the first time they confronted each other. Sharafan could think of no other man capable of doing so much with so little. The attack must surely be the work of the one called Mongoose. Beau Gex was a formidable foe that must be destroyed. Sharafan would take personal charge of the search and demise of his enemy.

*　*　*

The morning after the raid, Cliff Palace bubbled with excitement. Enthusiasm made a quantum leap among the members of the small band. The weather only helped buoy their spirits with temperatures in the low seventies and the skies cloudless and blue. A slight breeze came from the north. The air was crisp and dry.

They contacted Duck Waddle to pass on the news of the successful attack, but he already knew and kept asking where they found the jets. Again and again, they tried to explain how a team of two P-51s destroyed the modern day jets.

"You mean like World War II P-51s?" Waddle asked. When his question was confirmed, he still found it hard to believe. "Impossible," he said.

Finally after they convinced him their story was true, he told them to continue what they were doing, whatever it was, because it had created an enormous amount of confusion in the enemy. He added a bit of bad news. A late winter storm had halted the Coalition's advance, but had also made it difficult on the remnants of the United States forces.

More devastating news came from New York where tens of thousands had died from anthrax and smallpox. Also hundreds of thousands of refugees were pouring north daily. The onslaught of American refugees had created chaos. There was a shortage of food, and people were dying on the road of hunger and/or exposure.

After things had settled down, Robby and Daddy John disappeared from Cliff Palace for the day saying they were going to scavenge things for radios.

The women went about their assigned chores with renewed vigor. Even with her extra load of the newborn baby, Paul, Sunday helped organize them. Before the men could start flying, Krysti demanded they take physicals to see if the stress from the previous three months had any adverse effects or had changed them in any detrimental way. Tracy, being an artist and specializing at one time in cartoons and caricatures for her college newspaper, volunteered to paint a picture on the side of each plane. Her work reflected the names of each pilot.

During the activity, Krysti caught Justin about to leave Cliff Palace. "I've noticed you leaving quite often the last few weeks, young man. Where have you been going?"

"I've been hunting for rabbits and things. I'm going fishing now."

"With who?"

"Beau. He's a real good shot with the crossbow. He even let me shoot it, and I got an armadillo."

"You just kill those animals?"

"No. We eat them too. Beau taught me how to clean and cook them. The rabbit tastes just like chicken. And I can make a fire without matches!"

At first, Krysti was appalled. Her small son was running the hills with a man she believed might be dangerous. Although in her heart she knew otherwise, her fear and love for Beau only seemed to confuse her. Deep inside, she knew Justin was safe, but a lifetime of civilization prevailed.

"I don't want you to go with him anymore. You need to be around a more educated man like Michael. Think of your future and school," Krysti said, as though their current situation didn't exist and everything was as it used to be.

"I don't like Mike," Justin said with a sneer on his lips. "He can't even take care of himself. Remember the snake? I like Beau. He's the nicest man I've ever met." Then, half pleading with his mother he said, "Mom, Beau's taught me all kinds of neat things. There are a whole bunch of plants and animals I can eat, and they grow all over. Mike can't find his way to the river. I want you to talk to Beau. I thought you liked him. If you don't, tell me why. You always give me a second chance. Why don't you give him one? You'll really like him, if you give him a chance."

"Oh Justin," Krysti said, her throat tightening.

"I'll quit seeing Beau if you can tell me where I'm going to go to school."

Krysti paused and peered straight into her son's eyes. Slowly, she looked to his feet and saw he wore only tennis shoes. When the ordeal began nearly three months earlier, he was almost an inch shorter than Krysti. Her little boy was growing up too fast.

Almost in shock but more in bewilderment, Krysti answered, "You win, Justin. Let Beau teach you what he knows. I'll teach you everything else I can."

Justin hugged his mother, excited in the knowledge he could still see his friend. "Thanks Mom." Then he turned back to her. His eyes sparkled. "I'm sorry you like Mike 'cause Beau is just about the nicest person in the world."

With those words, he turned and walked away, leaving his mother alone. "I know," she mumbled. She noticed Justin now called her "Mom" and no longer "Mommy." He was growing up, and nothing she did or said could delay it. Even in his hug, she could feel his muscles hard and strong.

Justin would always be her little boy. Now her son spent time with this man whose past experiences weighed heavy on her mind and heart. She started to weaken and thought of talking to Beau.

An hour later, with fishing gear in hand, Beau and Justin sneaked away from the others and made their way to the part in the river where Justin had seen the swing. They set up their equipment and fished. Soon Justin snared a small perch, and Beau showed him how to grasp the mouth of the fish and wiggle the hook free.

For the first time in a month, Beau relaxed. The lack of a breeze made the day feel warmer than it actually was, so he threw his towel over a rock, removed his shirt, and lay against the large boulder to absorb the rays of the sun while Justin enthusiastically threw the fishing line back in the river.

"How's your mom?" asked Beau.

"She's okay, but she spends too much time with Mike. I don't like him."

Beau was unable to suppress a smile. His exact sentiments. "Well, you have to back your mother, in whatever she does."

"Do you like my mom?"

"Yes. I like her very much."

"I thought she liked you too. What happened?"

"There were things I've done in the past that people say I was wrong in doing. Your mom knows this and doesn't like it."

"If you didn't do it on purpose, don't you get another chance?"

"I hope so, but not everybody agrees. Besides, if I had it to do over, I'd do the same thing. I felt I was right at the time, and I don't feel any different now. I regret the outcome of some of my actions, but I'd still fight for what I believe in. Even if it meant doing the same things again."

"Can we hunt for quail again?" asked Justin, oblivious to the direction the conversation was taking.

"Sure, this time we'll get enough to feed everybody."

Justin spied the rope attached to the cypress close to the river's edge. This time, he knew he would get an answer. "Beau, who swings from the rope?"

Beau pulled the shirt from his eyes and gave only a casual glance to the swing. "Anybody who wants to. You, if you want."

"Aren't you too old?"

"Hell, I hope not," and as though it was a challenge, he moved toward it. He gathered the rope in his hand, tested its strength, pulled it tight and with a yell much like Tarzan, swung to the middle of the river, released his hold doing a backwards flip, and landed feet first in the chilled waters of the Frio.

A moment later, his head broke the surface.

Justin stood on the rocks clapping. "Can I do it after I catch another fish?"

"Sure. Why not?" said Beau, pulling himself from the cool river.

"Aren't I too young?"

Slowly, Beau brought the towel over his wide shoulders, moving it back and forth. "You're never too young to learn."

"I thought so," Justin said coyly.

Neither noticed Krysti standing behind a tree watching and listening from the moment Beau had removed his shirt and lay on the rock. Her fears were for naught, and she remembered what Sunday said. "If Beau is alive they will return." Even Ted said Beau would return. And each time he did return. The past was the past, war was war. Feeling foolish at her unwarranted fears, she approached the pair.

Justin was the first to see her. "Hey, Mom, you want to see me on the swing?"

Krysti stepped carefully down the trail toward Beau who was now sitting erect. "Aren't you going to catch another fish first?"

"Oh, yeah," Justin said almost forgetting. Then he turned his attention to the river and the pole he held in his hands.

"Hi, Krysti. Wanta go for a swim?" Beau asked.

"I just might," she said, removing her shorts and T-shirt, revealing a one-piece swimsuit clinging to every curve. The simple black suit revealed the beauty of her slender figure.

Silently they stood before each other, both afraid they might say the wrong thing. Justin spoke first.

"Beau, I've caught another fish!"

Calmly Beau stood next to Krysti and continued to gaze hopefully into her green eyes. He wanted to take her in his arms and tell her how he felt, but instead he answered Justin. "Do as I showed you. You know what to do."

Both turned and watched as the young man wrestled with the fish, finally bringing it to shore. Krysti made an instinctive move to help, but Beau pulled her back. He shook his head at her. "Let him do it alone."

"But he—," Krysti said in desperation, only to have Beau interrupt. "He can do it."

So she watched as her son took the fish with the finger and thumb of one hand while the other hand wiggled the hook free.

The excitement in his eyes was indescribable. "Look," Justin said. He held the small trophy high, showing his conquest.

Krysti could no longer deny the fact Justin was growing up and growing up fast.

"Watch this," her son added.

Laying his catch aside, Justin walked straight for the rope. Again, Krysti made a move and again, Beau held her.

"Let him go," Beau said.

Justin swung to the middle of the river, released his hold, and plunged feet first to the waters below. Krysti had not comprehended her son's abilities until she watched him swing from the rope to the river. Pride filled her heart.

When Justin bobbed to the surface, Krysti yelled enthusiastically, "That was beautiful, son." He responded with a little laugh and a waving fist. "I wish he could stay like that forever," she sighed.

Beau picked up a flat stone and turned it over in his hand. "No, you don't. Soon he will grow into a man; then he'll break away from you and find another." He brought his left hand back and with a side arm motion, sent the flat stone skipping across the waters of the Frio until it hit the bank on the other side of the river.

"Cool!" said Justin as he watched the stone bounce across the water.

"Remember these moments forever," said Beau. "You can't change what will be."

"I know," Krysti sighed, remembering his changing height and size. "But I don't want him to change."

"One day, he'll make you proud, and you'll be happy he's a man."

"Don't rush it. He's growing up fast enough," Krysti laughed, and she gave Beau a playful push. She ran her hand through her long auburn hair at the same time throwing her head back to get the hair away from her face. "I just regret his growing up, at this time."

Beau nodded his head. "When things return to normal, maybe he'll do something most Americans have never done."

"What?"

"Appreciate his freedom."

"Then, you think we'll win?"

"I hope so."

Beau and Krysti were about to continue their conversation when Cozmo and Pickett interrupted them.

"Beau, we need you at the hangars. Robby wants to ask you some questions about those planes," said Pickett.

Cozmo turned in the opposite direction. "I need to head back. Admiral Garrett and I are going out to contact the Duck."

Beau nodded to Cozmo, turned to Krysti with a wistful smile, and then yelled to Justin, "Hey, Champ, would you pick up the area for me?"

"Sure," said Justin, crawling out of the water.

The two men made their way to the aircraft, leaving Krysti and her son alone. She helped him gather the gear. "He is a nice man. Don't you think?"

There was a sparkle in Justin's eyes, and a bit of frustration when he said, "That's what I've been telling you. There's nobody better."

The return to Cliff Palace was quiet—just what Krysti needed to clear her mind and organize her thoughts. The peace was short-lived. She heard someone running down the path in her direction. Deberg came to an abrupt stop in front of her. He was exhausted from running and unable to talk. The shock in his eyes alerted her to trouble.

She grabbed his arm and tried to calm him. "Cozmo, what's the matter?"

When he could breathe, he spoke. "The admiral! It's Garrett. Grabbed his chest. Fell to the ground. Hurry! He's next to the trucks."

"Take me to him," Krysti ordered. Then she turned to Justin. "Find Beau, find the others. Tell them to come to the trucks. Hurry!"

"Yes Ma'am!" Without hesitation Justin was off, running in the direction of the mesa where he knew he would find Beau.

Without as much as a glance back, she followed closely behind Deberg for what seemed an eternity, but in reality was only a few minutes. On the ground, beside the Jeep rigged for communications, lay Ted Garrett, unconscious.

Krysti was on the ground beside him in an instant. Already he was turning blue, and she could see he was not breathing. Deberg stood to the side helpless, as Krysti took full control.

"Damn," mumbled Deberg. "He was breathing when I left."

With the cool determination she'd learned from years of training, she checked his vital signs. No heartbeat. Swiftly, she straddled his body and with her thumbs locked together, she pressed firmly against Garrett's chest. He was having a heart attack.

"Is he dead?" Deberg asked faintly.

Krysti answered from between gritted teeth. "Not if I can help it!" Again and again, she pressed on his chest. She moved to Garrett's side, tilted his head back, cleared his mouth, pinched the nose, and tried to breathe life into his limp body. She struck his chest with her fist and then repeated everything again. If only she was in the hospital, she thought. In the hospital she could use the shock treatment and possibly bring his heart around. She stared at the car for an answer and gradually an idea evolved.

Ruben and Beau were the first on the scene. Soon the others arrived. Krysti ordered Beau to take her position and continue pressing on Garrett's chest.

Instantly, she was on her feet checking the Jeep. She raised the hood and yanked the wire from the coil. "Wire! Wire!" she demanded of anyone. "Any kind of wire, damn it!" Then her eyes locked on Donna. "Get water, towels, and a blanket!" Without hesitation Donna moved fast as a rabbit to get the items.

"What about this antenna cable?" Fitzhenry asked, as he picked up the cable attached to the communications radio.

"Perfect," she said, grabbing it.

Thinking only of himself, Larry James halted her. "That may be our only chance to escape. Besides, the old man is dead now." Larry was lucky Beau was unable to hear, but it made no difference.

"You can go to hell!" Krysti said savagely. With both hands, she knocked James to the ground and tore the cable from the radio. "You can fix it later." she added, moving immediately to where Beau still worked on Garrett.

"Knife," Krysti said snapping her fingers, while casting her eyes around the small group. "Quick!"

Daddy John responded, hastily removing a large pocketknife from his pants pocket. The others gathered and stood in stunned disbelief, unable to move.

Krysti peeled the rubber insulation from the antenna and shoved the end tightly into the coil of the Jeep. She found a roll of duct tape in the back of the vehicle and used it to attach the wire to the coil. Next, she stripped a large portion from the opposite end of the cable exposing a foot of metallic wire. Then she wrapped her hands with duct tape to try and limit the shock.

Krysti pointed at Fitz. "Try to start the car, and don't stop till I tell you!"

"It's not going to work," Marix said with a shake of his head. "Have you ever done this before?"

"Hell, no, I haven't!" Krysti yelled. She bent over and without a word she shoved Beau to the side. "But we'll know if it works pretty soon." She slapped the exposed wire down on Garrett's still chest and pressed both hands firmly against his body: one over his heart, the other on the left side of his ribcage. She looked straight at Fitz. "Now, Mark!"

The force of the current caused Krysti's whole body to shake, but she forced her mind to concentrate through the pain. She screamed out as the force of the voltage knocked her from Garrett's body and almost rendered her unconscious.

Krysti groaned, but managed to crawl back to Garrett and put her ear against his chest. Still, no heartbeat. Again, she took the cable and started to place it on Garrett's chest.

This time Marix grabbed her hand. "I won't let you do this."

"The hell you won't." Krysti tried to jerk her hands free. Again, she turned her eyes to Fitzhenry. "If he doesn't let go in two seconds, turn it on anyway!"

Marix glowered as Fitzhenry reached for the key. But her resolve was enough, and he released his hold on her. Beau made a move toward Marix, but halted when it became apparent that no action on his part was necessary.

Again, Krysti put herself through the pain of the torturous electrical currents the coil created, and once again she was thrown from Garrett's body. She put her ear to his chest and this time her efforts were rewarded with a faint sound within Ted's chest. His heart beat again!

His body convulsed and Krysti turned him to his side as he threw up. Donna arrived with the items Krysti requested.

"Let me help," said Donna, putting a hand on her friend's shoulder.

Exhausted from the incident, Krysti welcomed the relief. She crawled a few feet away and fell limply against the front tire of the Jeep mumbling to herself. "I'll be damned, it actually worked. That's a new one for the books." She turned to Donna saying, "Will you cover him and make him warm and put something under his head?"

"Sure." Beau jumped in. "I'll help."

Krysti leaned against the Jeep and slowly removed the duct tape from her hands.

The others were motionless as statues watching what had happened. No one moved or did anything until Daddy John spoke. "In all my days I have never . . . how 'bouts I get you a drink, girl?"

For the first time, she began to relax since the incident started, and a grin of success began to light up her face. She pointed at Daddy John and winked her eye. "Sounds wonderful."

"Well, come on."

"No, I'll wait here until he's out of danger."

"Sure. Be back in a minute." As Daddy John made his way back to Cliff Palace, half the group returned with him.

Beau came forward and put his hand on her shoulder. "Thanks."

"You don't need to thank me. I did it for him."

"Ted's like a father to me," Beau said. He rose to his feet and started clearing the area. He fixed the cable to the radio, staying near should he be needed.

A few hours later, Daddy John and Robby finished fabricating a makeshift stretcher to move Ted. Krysti kept a close vigil on him throughout the night until she was sure he was out of danger. A few times he woke and spoke incoherently, but for the most part he rested peacefully under the watchful eye of Dr. Socorro.

The next day, Garrett awoke complaining someone must have used his chest for a punching bag. After his complaints were aired unsuccessfully, Krysti fed him soup, then ordered him to bed for more rest with strict orders for no more cigarettes. He refused the last order, but Beau made it known he would back what the doctor said.

Ted mumbled mutiny, said he didn't need any rest, and promptly closed his eyes. He proceeded to sleep away the rest of the day.

Chapter 7
ON A WING AND A PRAYER

For a week they worked on the assorted aircraft. April was already upon them. The weather was unusually cold but still pleasant. If not for the war it would have been a perfect time for almost all of them. But there was a war, and there were things that needed to be done now.

Each of the men managed to find a compatible G-suit. The suits, although old, would accomplish the required task, along with parachutes for each pilot. Lead was melted and poured into molds to make bullets. The machine guns and the ammunition belts were checked, loaded, and set in place. They managed to make eleven of the fifteen fighters operational. All would have a fighting chance.

Beau and Ruben were already set with the matching P-51 Mustangs. The other P-51, painted all white, would be Fitzhenry's.

Mulholland, Sullivan and Cozmo picked the British Spitfire, a formidable aircraft with similar capabilities to the Mustang. Marix chose the P-38 Lightning, the only fighter with two engines. Blackman would fly the heavily armed and fortified P-47 Thunderbolt. Pickett, James, and Warren drew the famous P-40 Warhawks.

Daddy John said the one BJ flew had actually been salvaged from China after the war, and was one of the original Flying Tigers. The remaining aircraft, two more P-51 Mustangs, a British Spitfire, and another P-40, were not ready for combat.

With the task completed and the knowledge Garrett would fully recover, the group was jovial again. The admiral's recovery was a great relief to Beau, but he became a full time cantankerous load for Krysti. Ted's recovery was difficult since Krysti had to fight him every step of the way. She ordered him to rest and take it easy. Occasional pain helped him abide by the rules she set.

Beau called a meeting and told the men, "The toughest part is yet to come. Any attack we conduct against the enemy will be against overwhelming forces. Simply, the odds are against us. There *will be* casualties. Any man who decides not to fly will not be required to go on any of the missions. Flying these aircraft will be strictly voluntary. All of you are the best of the best, but each of you must decide if you will take the challenge."

James started to stand, but hesitated, waiting for someone else. When no one stood, he remained seated.

Marix stood, but not for fear of flying but to question Beau's authority. "I outrank you. I should be in charge of these operations."

"Colonel, sit down. You have a choice of going or staying. Right now these operations have nothing to do with the Navy, Air Force, the RAF, or your rank. We're a bunch of volunteers fighting for our lives. The invading forces have torn my country apart and stolen my freedom. I'm going to walk this land free, as I once did. Even if it means my death."

"You don't have the rank to run this operation. I don't think you're qualified," continued Marix.

Due to his condition, Ted had asked Beau to run the operation while he, himself, would keep control on the ground and in the communications. He promised to stay away from their meetings, but failed to keep the promise for two reasons: Krysti allowed him from his room and he wanted to taste the action again. Garrett was standing at the back of the room unnoticed. But no longer.

"Colonel," cracked the familiar voice of authority.

Everyone turned around to see the man from whom they had always taken orders.

Garrett continued. "I suggest you sit your butt down. Commander Gex is the leader of this group. He is familiar with the area, and he is the one best suited for tactics of this nature."

"I flew the Falklands and *Operation Iraqi Freedom*. I've accounted for four enemy aircraft," snapped Marix, still surprised at Admiral Garrett's visit.

"I don't give a damn if you flew to the Moon. Gex 'Aced' out over Iraq. While he was in Israel, he shot down seven of the Arab's jets. He is the only full-fledged Ace we have here. That's not even taking into account the two victories with the P-51 Mustang. Besides, I heard about the snake you shot," said Garrett.

The last comment brought a chuckle from a few of the men. Garrett continued. "We need somebody who can and will exhibit control. While I'm here, you take orders from me. If I'm unable to give orders, you will take orders from Commander Gex."

Pausing to stress the point, Garrett's eyes scanned the room. "This order is for everyone. Gex commands these missions. You disobey him— you disobey me." He aimed his next words at Marix. "Now, buster, if you don't like my decision, take it up with a higher authority. If you can find one!" He snapped his fingers and spoke to Robby. "You're in charge of communications. I don't want to hear you let Colonel Marix use our communications system in any way whatsoever. Do you understand?"

"Yes, sir," came Robby's instant reply and automatic salute.

"That's all, gentlemen. Don't let me interrupt your meeting. Carry on." Then Garrett turned around and walked casually from the room. Once outside he smiled to himself. He felt no pain in his chest but decided to rest before Krysti chided him for his unauthorized activity. He immediately went in search of Daddy John, in hopes of some good ol' fashioned reminiscing.

The meeting continued, with James standing. "This is suicide; maybe we should reconsider this mad scheme."

"Aw, hell," said Ruben with a laugh. "Why worry? We're probably all gonna get killed."

Looking rather pale, James swallowed hard.

"Excuse me," said Schmitt from the back of the room. He held a box with wires hanging over the side. He continued to talk as he walked to the front of the room. "I have an equalizer. I think I can give you an edge."

Beau waved his hands for Schmitt to come to the front. "What is it?"

As Schmitt walked he talked. "This." He reached into his box and pulled out a Bell automotive radar detector.

"A radar detector?" smirked Marix.

"This is insane," whined James.

"Let him speak," boomed the normally quiet Blackman.

The room was quiet when Schmitt reached the front and faced them.

"At Red Flag in Nevada, they had training missions for the Air Force much like Top Gun for the Navy. Well, thirty years ago the F-14 was unexpectedly having problems getting kills in practice. For a week, the sophisticated radar systems of the F-14s never got a kill on any of the A-4 Skyhawk enemy simulators. The General in command demanded an explanation, and after an inspection of the Skyhawks found the pilots had installed regular radar detectors from Radio Shack.

Seems when the F-14 radar goes on it sets off the detector. The time between the beeps will determine the distance. Fired rockets will give a continuous uninterrupted buzz or all five of the lights will light up. I'm trying to fix it so the first light flashes at radar detection, with four lights for lock on and all lights when a rocket has been fired.

"These detectors will also enable you to detect ground radar and help you elude detection. It's really simple. The first light indicates radar; as each light goes on, it means you're getting closer to either the plane or ground radar. Doing this, you can maneuver away or toward the radar. On the return flight, you can avoid detection.

"After I've finished the units, they will be able to detect infrared, microwaves—"

"Great for incoming ovens," Ruben mused aloud.

"They have laser rockets," added James.

"Good point," said Schmitt. "Remember, lasers are just another type of sound wave, just more intense. If you can make a wave, you can detect it. A few years ago, Texas lawmakers okayed laser radars for highway patrolmen." He held the Bell unit in the air. "Well, these guys anticipated that. This little unit can detect both."

The room was quiet. Robby held up two FM radios. "One is for communications between aircraft and the other is a scanner that will seek and lock on transmissions." He pulled a handful of wires from the box. "I want to install receivers in all your helmets."

He dropped the wires, reached in the box, grabbed a smaller box, removed the lid, poked his fingers inside, and then threw dozens of pieces of aluminum foil in the air, fluttering like confetti.

"Well, boys . . . this is the chaff. The women have been cutting foil into tiny squares. I have enough ejection tubes for all the planes. This will play hell on their radar-activated rockets." Next, he pulled out a short tube. "Flares! I think these will pull approaching rockets away. Those prop planes have no heat sign to pursue; the flares should do the trick."

"You must be jesting." Marix stated more than asked.

"No. I'm not. And it will work. Sure beats the hell outa what you have now!" Schmitt retorted rather angrily.

"Looks good to me, I'm ready," said Fitzhenry with his youthful enthusiasm.

"I think it's the edge we need," Ruben added.

Surprisingly, Blackman vocalized his opinion. "I'd rather die in those planes fighting than do nothing."

"Aye, mate. It beats waiting for them to find us."

Deberg added his views. "Whatever we can do to stall the invaders will give our country that much more time to regroup."

"Yeah, remember the Alamo," snickered Ruben.

"We lost at the Alamo," Beau noted.

Ruben snickered. "Depends on which side you were on."

Beau turned and slapped Robby on the shoulder. "Do it, Robby. We need everything we can get."

"I don't think we have much of a chance," Marix said sarcastically, "but I will still go."

Beau shook his head and laughed. "We have a better chance than you think." He caught the eye of each man. "This isn't like the jets you're familiar with. Feel your aircraft, be one with her. All of you have flown props before, so there is nothing to be afraid of. Preferably shoot a target straight on but if you can't, then sight the enemy and lead them like you were shooting skeet."

Ruben laughed and said, "It's time for the rabbits to leave the briar patch and attack the bear."

Kipp nodded. "Aye, mate, a bunch of *Thunder Bunnies* we be." The men laughed, but it was a name that would stick to the small group.

"We'll hit them first, hit them fast, and hit them hard," Beau added.

"Yeah, kinda like takin' a gun to a fistfight," chirped Ruben.

"Doesn't seem right," Marix remarked.

"Neither were the airliners they shot down!" snapped Sullivan, his thoughts on Natasha. "I say kill as many as we can."

"Where do we hit first?" Mulholland asked.

"Gentlemen," said Beau, "when Robby finishes installing his gadgets, we hit Laughlin Air Base in Del Rio."

* * *

The days seemed to drag for the men, and tension began to build. They were ready to fly, anxious to taste combat, but Beau refused to leave on a mission until all of the men were familiar with their machines.

First, Schmitt would show them how the radar detectors, chaff, and flares worked until they were familiar with the operation of those items. Secondly, if Schmitt felt any of the men did not understand the new system, that man would be grounded from combat.

Schmitt finally completed the installations in all the aircraft. Each plane was equipped with six canisters of chaff: enough for six attacking rockets. Also, installed in every aircraft were two diversionary flares, two series of radar detectors, FM radio, and an FM scanner to detect enemy radio broadcasts. The day after Schmitt finished, they made final preparations for the mission. Beau ordered all the men to rest the day before the mission. Nothing was to be done on the aircraft unless absolutely necessary.

The night before, they were treated to roasted quail on the mesa near the hangars. Tracy finished her handiwork on the airplanes, and they all admired her artistry. She had painted pictures on each of the planes that she felt best represented each pilot. Each picture had words lettered in calligraphy under the cartoon. The pictures were based on the stories Ruben had told her about each of the men.

James was called *Snake*, although no one in the group knew why. Actually, the name was derived because of his sneaky black market trading during *Operation Iraqi Freedom*. The action almost got him discharged from the service. The picture of a snake biting a plane was painted on the side of his P-40.

Because of the story related to Tracy about the dead doves and his family, Dean Blackman had the cartoon of a dove in the upside down position with 'X's where the eyes belonged. Below that in red letters, which looked like dripping blood, were the words *Dead Dove* painted on the side of his Thunderbolt.

Due to his strange cat-like eyes, Pickett was called *Catman*; therefore, the caricature of a man cat was fitting for his plane.

Sullivan's Spitfire had an upside down plane for *Flipper*.

The white P-51 Fitzhenry would fly had large black script letters with the words *White Lightning* and a large thunderbolt angled through the letters.

Cozmo's name was strange in its own right, but when Tracy was told the story of *Boink*, she painted the caricature of a plane rubbing a flat nose with its wing.

Deberg loved it. "I hope I don't do that again."

The men called Mulholland *The Gray Ghost* because of his gray hair and age. In the month confined to Cliff Palace, he let his beard grow, and it too was gray. Therefore, on the side of his black Spitfire . . . a cartoon of Casper the Ghost, in gray.

On the side of BJ's P-40 were painted two playing cards, the Jack of Spades and the Ace of Spades: *Black Jack*.

For Beau's black and gold P-51, Tracy had a beautiful rendition of *Rikki-Tikki-Tavi*, the *Mongoose*. She had seen the picture on Beau's old plane and had even seen the same cartoon show as had Ruben. The picture was done delicately with an airbrush, and it appeared like the vertical tail was shaking.

None could match the beauty of the work done on Ruben's black fighter. Tracy had grown up hearing the story of *Moon Shadow*. On the side of the Mustang was painted a beach scene with Indians and a Moon overhead. The Moon cast eerie shadows from the Indians, forming the word *Moon Shadow*.

Ruben was speechless when he saw the painstaking work of the picture on the side of his fighter. "It's beautiful," he finally managed.

The celebration continued late into the night. Most slept late the next day. The eleven pilots were all anxious, some were excited, and one was afraid.

Late that night the *Thunder Bunnies*, as they affectionately called themselves, struck out on their first mission. The attack went flawlessly, and the air base was severely crippled. They counted under their belts two F-14s, one F-15 and another F-16 along with scores of other jets and supplies. Again, the night had been overcast and afforded cover. During the attack, they noticed a fenced area filled with American prisoners cheering them on. The saddest part of the attack was their inability to help the prisoners.

Halfway back, Pick ran into trouble when his oil pressure dropped. "This is Catman, I need to pull out. Oil pressure dropping, I'm feathering the engine. Good luck." He banked left from the formation and dropped from view.

"Mongoose to Moon Shadow. We've lost a rabbit. I'm gonna find him and bring him back. Get the rest of our bunnies back to the Briar Patch," Beau ordered over the new radios.

"Roger," Ruben replied as Beau dropped from the formation to help Pickett.

Ruben and Mulholland guided the group to a safe return. The friendly Bell radar proved a lifesaver when it picked up ground radar. Watching the lights on the radar as Robby indicated, they were able to elude enemy contact and return safely to Cliff Palace.

Everyone waited anxiously for Pick and Beau. The hours passed and still they waited, but their comrades failed to return. Marix and James were the first to retreat to Cliff Palace. Soon others returned to the comfort of their temporary home. Only Ruben, Blackman, Schmitt, Daddy John, and Krysti remained behind.

"Krysti," said Ruben, as he put his arm around her shoulders. "There's nothing ya can do here. Why don't you go back with the rest?"

"I'm worried about him," Krysti said in all honesty.

"Beau's fine, he just needed to help Pick. You go on."

Krysti returned to Cliff Palace but couldn't sleep. Two hours later, she heard the approach of planes, and half an hour later, she heard the men talking as they came along the narrow trail to Cliff Palace. She listened as Pickett recanted his rescue.

"If it hadn't been for Beau, it would be my funeral you'd be going to now. When I landed, about a half dozen Jeeps with machine guns and lights converged on my Warhawk. They had a truck with about twenty or so men—all firing like hell. Shit, I was just one guy. Next thing you know, Beau here comes swooping out of the sky from nowhere, guns blazing. He wiped them out. One Jeep managed to hightail it outa there, but you can bet your ass they're still running. Let me tell ya, it's gotta be scarier than hell to see a plane belching fire from no more than twenty feet. Scared the hell outa me when you flew over. I swear his prop tore up the fabric on the roof of that personnel carrier."

Ruben laughed. "Yep, that's the *Mongoose*. You might say he was dusting some moving crops."

Beau laughed. "I was about ten feet over them. But I've never seen anything work better to scare ground troops at night than to fly a few feet off the ground shooting all your guns. They must have picked up the radio when you left the pack. We'll have to set a sequence next time and alternate frequencies. You're lucky it was a loose cable to the oil sending unit so you could fly back."

"Let's turn in," were the last words Krysti remembered hearing.

* * *

The Jeep pulled into headquarters; the driver was drenched in blood and spoke rapidly in Spanish.

"Tell him to speak English," said the Syrian leader.

After the soldier calmed down, he recited his story to Sharafan. Again, it was propeller driven planes giving the troops hell. More planes lost at Laughlin. This could not continue. Whoever they were, they had become a thorn in the operations. For some reason, Sharafan's thoughts again turned to Beau Gex. Could it be, Sharafan wondered?

Sharafan would personally send troops to cover the territory he felt most likely to conceal this small force. He would activate the troops in the morning and begin the search. He ordered al-Majid and Aziz to assist Ortega in the search, something both men eagerly accepted knowing it would once again put them back in the action and give them the opportunity to kill more Americans. Al-Majid tapped his faithful machete, eager to put it to use again.

His logic for the search did not include prop driven aircraft and the ease with which they landed or could be maintained. His mind could only conceive of jets as the problem, so the logical search started in the wrong direction.

As Sharafan prepared his men, a runner brought a message from General Navarro. Sharafan was to report to the Naval Air Station in Kingsville. Something had been found in one of the hangars and Navarro wanted Sharafan to investigate the discovery.

* * *

Beau felt it necessary that any radio contact be made away from Cliff Palace, at a distance of twenty miles or more. The danger the radio operators encountered would be far less than the consequences of having Cliff Palace discovered. After the raids, the invaders would be on the alert for radio transmissions of any kind. All were in agreement, and a rotation was set for a different pair to make each trip.

The enthusiasm of Duck Waddle had not diminished. He knew the attack was indeed World War II vintage aircraft. He didn't care how it was done, just as long as it continued. One day he made a request they attack the Naval Air Station in Kingsville. They had noticed an increase in aircraft and felt an offensive was about to begin.

Then Waddle pleaded. "Every day you delay them, you give us time to rebuild and mount an offensive of our own. What you are doing could be a key in our ability to strike back. We need whatever time you can give us. We have halted the spread of smallpox and the anthrax appears to be over."

The general from the north had requested a difficult mission on a heavily defended air base. For days, preparations were made for the next raid. The men were on edge. The excitement and anticipation were getting to them. They had finished another tedious day of work on their aircraft, and most were ready to retire to Cliff Palace and relax for the evening.

James was one of the first to return. In the living area he found Justin brooding over the box with the two mockingbirds. As he approached he could hear Justin crying ever so slightly.

"What's wrong, kid?"

The boy held the box so James could see inside. Both birds were now covered with feathers. One looked up at James expectantly. The other one did not move at all. "Buddy is dead," he said, while trying to hold back the tears.

With a shrug James said, "You probably killed the little bastard. You feed him so much he probably strangled." Then he turned and made his way to his room leaving Justin with the thought he had killed the small bird.

Before James reached his room, Beau, Ruben, Blackman, and Kipp came upon Justin and found him barely able to hold his sobs.

"What's wrong, Champ?" Beau asked. About that time Sunday, Krysti and Lindy walked into the room from the kitchen.

Justin showed them the mockingbird. "James said I killed it."

"Hey, Mate, the man's all wrong. You didn't kill the bird."

"You did your best. The bird was already sick," said Blackman.

The tears stopped flowing. "James said I fed it so much it strangled."

Krysti sat on one side of Justin and said, "It's not your fault."

Ruben put an arm around Justin. "If it was your fault they would both be dead."

Livid with anger, Beau said, "I'll show you what it looks like when someone strangles." And with those words he started to move towards James's room.

James probably owed his life to Blackman, Kipp, and Ruben. As much as they would have liked to see Beau strangle him, they forced him to stop and calm down. And it took all three men to stop him. Krysti had a new opinion of James and found she was a little sad when the three men stopped Beau.

Beau sat down next to Justin, took a deep breath and said, "You did what you could. Sometimes no matter what you do you can't save the ones you care for. Champ is still alive and he still needs you."

Softly, Beau picked up the motionless mockingbird. "Come on Justin; you and I will go to the river and bury Buddy."

* * *

Late in the afternoon of the fifth day into preparations for the raid, all was readied. The men were concerned about a daytime attack, but Beau explained the base would be prepared for a night flight. They would approach the base from the west as the sun was setting. When the mission was finished, the sun would be down and the escape could be completed with the aid of darkness.

Beau stood before the men. "Anyone who wants to stay, can." He paused but no one walked away. "I want you to know this will be a very difficult mission. In fact, each additional mission will be more dangerous than the previous."

"Why?" asked Deberg.

"Because they know we are real now, and you can bet your ass they will be watching for another attack. They'll be better prepared next time." Deberg and a few of the others nodded in agreement.

"You know your aircraft, but let me say this," Beau continued. "You haven't had to shoot at another moving aircraft yet. Everything has been stationary and on the ground. In the air, you must depend on marksmanship and deflection shots. Remember, lead the enemy aircraft and let them fly into your shots. Our fighters are not like the electronic jets you are accustomed to. Let me remind you, again, this is like shootin' skeet. Lead them or you'll miss. To make this mission successful, we need speed, teamwork, discipline, and surprise.

"We'll go in pairs. Stick with your wingman. Work together. Don't be caught napping. The radar unit will alert you to enemy aircraft. Should you be fired upon, remember that the radar detector will give a continuous signal so you can take evasive action to avoid the missiles. We return in fours and stay close because the return trip will be dark."

The men's faces revealed excitement and anticipation, but not fear. Beau could see they were ready.

"Let's do it."

The men crawled into their aircraft. A Three Musketeers bar placed strategically over Ruben's gauges was the first thing he saw—just like the one placed in his cockpit before the last mission. Beau had hung it there just like he had before each mission in *Operation Iraqi Freedom* and every flight the two had ever done together. Slowly, he tore the wrapper and threw it from the cockpit to the ground below, before he slid the canopy shut. He cursed his friend, but ate the small chocolate bar without a moment's hesitation.

The fighters were loaded and ready. Schmitt gave the signal, and the *Thunder Bunnies* rolled from the mesa in pairs. First off the mesa were Ruben and Beau, the leaders. Mulholland and Blackman followed, and close behind them came Marix and James, then Pickett and Deberg. Last off the mesa was the only trio with Warren, Sullivan, and Fitzhenry.

"The chief and ten little Indians," mused Blackman.

They were halfway to Kingsville when the trouble began.

They maintained an altitude of 200 feet. Enemy radar was ineffective below 300 feet and would not detect them. Then Beau got a reading on his radar.

"This is Mongoose. Listen up, Bunnies. Close in, the bears have come to play. We have company at six o'clock high."

"Roger, I've picked them up," came the identical answers from Deberg and Pickett.

Beau twisted his head. "About ten miles out." The radar detectors beeps were coming closer together. "Form a V, Flipper, break away and form the flat head of the formation with Moon Shadow and me. I'll take the lead. Black Jack and Lightning to Port, with Boink and Catman. Baron and Snake, starboard. Ghost and Dove behind them."

The others twisted about in the cockpit of their aircraft, hoping for a view of the attackers.

"I see a phantom," said Ruben.

"Mirage," came Mulholland.

"Mig-25," said Marix.

"A Tomcat," said James, his voice wavering when he recognized the F-14.

Beau watched the radar and crossed his fingers, hoping Robby was right about the radar detectors. Four jets chased them, a Mig-25, a Mirage, F-4 Phantom, and an F-14. The ones to watch would be the French Mirage and the F-14. As if the others weren't bad enough, Beau thought.

Warren suddenly yelled over the FM radio, "Get back in formation, Snake!"

"Pull back, Snake!" Marix demanded.

"Snake!" snapped Beau when he realized James was pulling away from the formation. "Close in!"

"You're crazy," cried James. "We've gotta get outta here; there's a Mirage and a Tomcat."

Calmly, Beau answered. "I guess the Mig and Phantom don't bother ya. Good, I like a man who shows bravery in adversity. This is Mongoose to Grey Ghost. Should any of the bunnies stray from the pack—roast 'em! Is that understood?"

"Aye mate, that I will. At this distance, I could hardly miss," mused Mulholland.

"Our success depends on everyone following my orders. Increase air speed to 350 mph. When I give the order, the three leaders will loop firing guns. The others bank sharply to your sides, come around, and open fire. We should catch them in a crossfire. Moon Shadow, when I give the order, I want you to—"

"Drop the tank. Roger. I suppose the missiles they fire will be attracted to the heat."

"Hopefully." Beau watched the fascinating new device as it tracked the incoming bandits. So far, it worked exactly as predicted. Then came the first sign they were spotted, when the Mirage and the F-14 surged ahead. The radar sounded—rockets locked on! The *Thunder Bunnies* were about to have their first real test. Instantly the continuous signal sounded.

"Now!" yelled Beau, instantly dropping his tank and jerking the stick back.

The turn exerted a tremendous G-force against his body: a sensation he had experienced many times before. The bladder suit worked by compressing against his legs and lower torso, keeping the blood up toward his brain. In the inverted position he saw a ball of flame roll skyward. The rapidly accelerating F-14 did not anticipate the trap created from the exploding tanks of homemade napalm. It was caught in the inferno, and erupted into a ball of flame. The Mirage pilot pulled back when he saw what happened to the F-14. This enabled Beau, still in an inverted position, to put the Mirage in his sights. Beau opened up with the 20-millimeter guns, and from an inverted position shoved the stick forward and made a half roll, so he could keep the Mirage in his sights.

Twelve 20-millimeter machine guns from two P-51 Mustangs struck the French-made Mirage from the underside as Ruben executed an identical maneuver. When the Mirage sputtered smoke, both Beau and Ruben rolled from the chase. The Mirage tumbled to earth.

The Mig closed in on Deberg. Pickett moved swiftly to assist. The Phantom turned away to chase Blackman, pounding the P-47 with all its guns. Blackman was taking a multitude of hits, and pieces peeled away from the slow moving Thunderbolt. Still, the heavy, rugged fighter held together.

The Phantom made a fatal mistake when it became too involved in its fight to notice Mulholland and the wide sweep he made. Mulholland waited until Blackman passed in front of his Spitfire, then he opened fire, leading the enemy. Bullets ripped across the canopy, and the Phantom began a wicked spiral toward the earth with a dead pilot.

Unable to elude the Mig, Deberg took an unmerciful beating, with Pickett unable to close in on the pursuing Mig behind him. Marix moved into position behind the Mig. He hesitated for a better shot before he fired, and that moment of hesitation was too much.

Smoke belched from Cozmo's Spitfire; it rolled over, started to come apart, and exploded before it hit the ground. Marix fired as the other nine planes swarmed the helpless Mig. It was hit with a hail of bullets from every conceivable direction and disintegrated in midair.

"Regroup, regroup!" snapped Beau. "We've a mission to complete."

"They're gonna kill us," whined James.

"Listen, Snake," came Ruben's voice over the radio. "I'm not too happy over losing Boink, but I don't think he'd be too happy if we just up and quit. I'm sure he'd want us to finish it for him. And in case you didn't notice, these obsolete buckets of bolts just kicked the shit out of a couple of the most formidable jets in the world."

Ruben was right. They succeeded in maneuvers no one would have dreamed possible. Now they knew they could fight and win.

"Regroup," Beau said again. "Flipper, join Catman."

Smoke puffed from Blackman's P-40 Warhawk.

Mulholland asked his wingman, "'Eh, mate you okay?"

Blackman fought with the controls. "Roger." He had anything but control.

They continued toward their destination in silence. A short distance ahead was Kingsville. Daddy John had said to dive on them from out of the sun, the same way American volunteers in their P-40 Flying Tigers had done to the Japanese over the jungles of China before World War II.

"There she is. Okay climb. Get the sun behind you, find a target and use your ammunition wisely," Beau ordered, as they rose quickly to over 400 feet. "Follow me."

With the safety of the setting sun behind their backs, they attacked. Beau nosed the sleek black and gold machine toward its destination of destruction. Ruben was hot on his tail.

Alarms sounded and men ran for their fighters. The *Thunder Bunnies* watched as the enemy searched in all directions, but from where they were coming. All eyes were up but they were unable to locate their attackers.

"Mongoose, looks like they expected company," said Ruben.

"Affirmative, Moon Shadow. But surprise is still on our side. How about we give them something they won't forget."

Beau started in the direction of the more superior jets. On these, Ruben and Beau concentrated their guns. They no longer had the napalm tanks, used to deceive the earlier attack. Behind them came the Spitfires and White Lightning in his P-51. Their tanks would accomplish the task.

The enemy managed to get six jets into the air. BJ was doing a barrel roll trying to evade a Vietnam War vintage F-4 Phantom. Bullets riddled the old P-40 that had once fought against the Japanese in China. Now a jet the P-40 was never designed to fight, attacked. Fitz, seeing his wingman in trouble, did a snap roll to bring his fighter about to help BJ.

BJ had drawn the jet in an ever tightening circle, pulled his flaps full down, pulled the stick back, and squeezed the trigger to his guns. They answered, and the old Warhawk shuddered as it neared stall speed. Instantly, the F-4 surged over the P-40, exposing its vulnerable underbelly. The machine gun fire formed a perfect line of perforations along the belly from front to rear, with nary a bullet missing its mark. Warren's actions took less than a second.

Staring at the perfect row of bullet holes, Warren mused to himself, "Tear along the dotted line." The F-4 burst into flames and split apart. BJ rolled his machine, and aimed for the ground to gain speed. He had defeated a jet with his old P-40 Warhawk.

Mulholland put his Spitfire into a loop, and the dive he came out of brought him to a speed more than 400 mph and directly over a runway from which an F-86 Sabre was accelerating to become airborne. Mulholland kept his sights just ahead of the jet, firing a burst from his cannon as he gave chase. The F-86 raced down the runway absorbing Kipp's pursuing shots. The Sabre never made an effort to lift, because the pilot was dead. At the end of the runway, the F-86 hit the soft sands of Oso Bay, then started to cartwheel across the water. The exploding fuel sent debris cascading in all directions.

The battle continued as though "Father Time" had accumulated all the best in flying machines into this one point in history for an ultimate rematch—the final battle to determine who would be King of the Sky. Could antiquated aircraft defeat jet age technology?

The men began to feel unbeatable, and with the element of surprise on their side, the enthusiasm carried over to their flying. The enemy had superior machines, but the attackers' ability far outweighed the equipment being used against them, and teamwork did the rest. This day against superior machines, they were the superior force.

BJ's P-40 began to smoke. So did the Jugs, as Daddy John fondly called Blackman's P-47.

"Mongoose to all bunnies, return to the Briar Patch," Beau ordered. Only moments earlier his guns jammed. Only two HVAR rockets remained for attack or defense.

During the battle, the enemy tuned in to the *Thunder Bunnies* and monitored their transmissions. From below came a familiar voice filling the airways. "Mongoose! I knew it would be you."

"Cobra!" sneered Beau. "Come on up, I'll wait for you."

"Coward, you have destroyed my aircraft as it sat on the ground," said Sharafan. "Next time, I will be ready and waiting. I will destroy you."

"You and who else? Allah? Tell Allah he eats pigs. In fact, why don't you and Allah go screw yourselves," snapped Beau.

To compare Sharafan to pigs was one of the worst insults Beau could make. Only Beau remained, slowly circling the field in a gentle bank. Where was Cobra? Beau had two rockets. He controlled his anger, knowing his men might need the defense. The gasp Beau detected over the radio as Sharafan spoke told him his comments raised the ire of the men in the room with him. Beau landed a blow to Cobra as surely as if he fired a rocket.

"You will die!" hissed Sharafan.

"This is Mongoose. Sorry, I've had all the fun I can stand for now. Try and keep our base a little cleaner, will ya boys? Because one day we're gonna take it back from you. Have a nice day, gotta go now." Beau laughed until his sides ached, making a point to keep his radio open so Cobra could hear. As he zoomed away, he did the victorious barrel roll just to rub the insult in, then added, "I'll be back, Cobra."

Beau put the double-staged, super-charged, Rolls Royce Merlin engine into full boost to catch the *Thunder Bunnies*. The black and gold P-51 responded superbly, as though it were a jet. Daddy John had done his work well. In a few moments, the Mustang was exceeding an unbelievable horizontal air speed of 550 mph. Just before him loomed the others, of which two smoked profusely. The mission was completed faster than expected, even with the advent of the attack and their first fatality, Cozmo. The last rays of sunlight were fading fast.

Calmly, on the radio Blackman said, "Going down. Losing control of rudder and stabilizers." The P-47 acted erratic, but somehow Blackman maintained a semblance of control. The ship continued to drop and headed directly for an area of rough rocky terrain covered with trees. The plane crashed violently and disappeared. Beau and Ruben cut from the group and circled the area.

"Grey Ghost, take 'em home. We'll follow," said Beau.

"Aye, mate . . . good luck," answered Mulholland.

The remnants of the group moved on while less than a half mile away, ground troops watching the derelict plane crash rushed to the area. Ruben and Beau could see no sign of life, and the surrounding area was too rough to land. With the arrival of the troops, it made any rescue impossible as darkness quickly squeezed away the remaining light.

"Guns jammed but I'll take care of their transportation," said Beau. He flew low firing one rocket, destroying two of the troop's vehicles.

"Damn, Mongoose. Move over and let me use my guns. If the Dove is alive, you'll kill him," demanded Ruben. He tipped the wing of the P-51, dropped above the treetops, and strafed the troops twice.

The final traces of daylight were flickering away when a lone figure stepped from the woods, waved a rifle in one hand, and held what looked like a small sword in the other.

"He's alive!" shouted Ruben.

Beau waved his wings in response. Then they watched as the small figure disappeared into the thick growth directly toward the advance of the enemy's ground troops.

Ruben's voice held a touch of sadness. "They'll kill him."

The tone in Beau's voice was just the opposite. "Heaven help the enemy. That wasn't Dean disappearing into those woods; it was the *Dead Dove*. He's on his own turf now."

Ruben understood, and immediately they raced to catch the others. Just as they arrived, they saw another casualty start to drift away from the Rat Pack. BJ was falling from the formation with Fitz close on his wing.

"Black Jack leaving formation, engine gone. Setting her down. Hey, Moon Shadow, you think you can get Scotty to beam me up? Like right now!" Warren begged. "Good luck to my black ass."

To see his friend, Warren, going down upset Ruben but he readied his best accent of Scotty. "Sorry, Cap'n, I'm afraid I'm havin' a wee bit of a problem with the transporter."

Fitz said, "This is White Lightning, I'll follow him down."

"Get outa here, kid. Unless you have a spare seat in that aircraft, there's no way I'm gonna make it back," said Warren.

Right behind BJ came Fitz, his wingman. The one who had become his friend and had beaten him at running. BJ found a level field and landed his wounded plane. When he climbed from the cockpit, he was startled to see Fitz's P-51 bouncing along the ground and pulling alongside him. The kid just stood in his aircraft smiling.

"Get the hell outa here," said BJ waving his arms frantically.

But the kid released his bulky parachute, which was also used as a seat, opened the pack, and dumped its contents to the ground below. Then he tried to sit in the cockpit and disappeared from view. He pulled himself to an erect position and stood in the seat within the cockpit.

"Well, if you're not going, I sure can't. I need you so I can see to fly," said Fitzhenry with a shrug of his shoulders.

"You stupid son-of-a-bitch, you're going to get us both killed with that stunt," mumbled Warren. He climbed from the old Warhawk and stomped across the soft earth toward Fitzhenry and his Mustang.

"Hurry," yelled Fitzhenry, pointing to the headlights of approaching vehicles. They had been spotted, which was all the incentive Warren needed as he quickened his pace and bolted across the remaining space. When he got to the aircraft, Fitzhenry was standing on the wing of the P-51. Warren hurriedly set himself in the seat, and Fitz nestled in his lap. Warren was larger than Fitz expected and the canopy would not close. Fitz removed his helmet but still the canopy could not be closed.

Rifle shots sounded and Fitz pushed the throttle forward. As the aircraft bounced down the rough field, Warren heard Fitzhenry groan, and slump in his arms. Blood oozed from Fitzhenry's forehead.

"Fitz!" yelled Warren. His yell was enough to bring the dazed Fitzhenry to his senses. "You been hit?" he asked in his sweet Bostonian accent.

"Shit, no," said Fitzhenry rubbing his forehead and embarrassed. His head had hit the canopy, almost rendering him unconscious. He pointed to where the skin and hair from his head still clung to the steel of the jet. Fitz tried to free his helmet but it was wedged between the seat and their bodies.

BJ could not restrain a laugh. "Hell, you're gonna kill us anyway."

"My helmet," said Fitzhenry, jerking at the object stuck in the seat.

"Damned be the helmet," said Warren, reaching around Fitzhenry, placing both hands on his forehead. "Go! Go!"

The sound of men yelling could be heard above the sounds of the engine. Bullets zinged into the sides of the fighter. The aircraft responded and gathered speed as it bounced down the earthen field.

A scream of pain escaped BJ's lips, when his fingers were jammed against the canopy leaving a piece of his black skin beside some of Fitz's scalp.

"Ooohhh ssshhhit!" yelled Warren as they became airborne.

Fitzhenry laughed. "What are you afraid of?"

"It's not so funny," snapped Warren. "I've never taken off being used as a seat." Again Fitz laughed, but this time BJ could not restrain himself and he laughed also.

"Back there when I was running toward your plane, I ran faster than you did that night at the beach," snickered BJ.

"Did not," snapped Fitz.

"Did too."

"Did not."

They were safely in the air and on their way to Cliff Palace, arguing all the way.

* * *

After the attack, Sharafan and Tahar Zahir made for one secluded hangar. They walked about and past destroyed hangars and planes, but even before Sharafan arrived he was relieved to see the hangar undamaged. They entered through a side door, where the men inside resumed their work on a strange plane whose appearance was more like an aircraft from outer space. The black jet remained poised as though waiting to climb to the far reaches of the universe.

One of the workers, Carlos Zapata, spied Sharafan and promptly presented himself for a report on the SR-71 Blackbird.

"Did the attack destroy anything?" Sharafan asked.

"Sir, we only lost power temporarily. There was no damage."

"Good."

"When will the craft be flight ready?" Zahir asked.

Carlos shrugged his shoulders. "It is hard to say." He pointed to the Blackbird. "This is not like any aircraft I have ever worked on."

"Hurry," Sharafan ordered, glaring directly at Zapata.

Zahir and Sharafan walked from the hangar and surveyed the damage.

Sharafan was consumed with thoughts of his enemy. Gex and his group had become a major liability for Sharafan and his men. The damage against the invading forces was enough to cause unexpected delays in supply movements and available aircraft. Valuable time was spent repairing fighting aircraft and military bases—time better used in continuing the assault against the remaining American forces. The attacks from Gex's small forces were giving the opposition time to regroup, something Sharafan wanted to prevent.

A search was desperately needed to find Beau Gex and his men. Sharafan was sure they were well hidden and within three hundred miles of the bases they attacked. When he finished surveying the damage, he would return to Corpus Christi where he would engage Juan Ortega in the task of searching and finding the men who continued to plague him and his attempts to advance the invasion.

Turning to Zahir, Sharafan asked, "Tahar, will you be ready to fly when the Blackbird is ready?"

"Yes!" Zahir responded with eager anticipation.

With a cold calculating smirk, Sharafan said, "When it is completed, we can be assured of the American's defeat. With the SR-71 we have the power to destroy the space station Starburst."

* * *

The sky was dark when the men landed at Cliff Palace. Now they waited for the last two.

Larry James, still angry and slightly afraid of Beau's order to shoot him down if he had pulled out of formation, kept his fear and anger well hidden. He wanted to confront Beau with the threat but he knew better. Maybe he would try to smooth over the incident and get himself on Beau's good side. He approached Beau, who waited with Sully, Kipp, Donna, and Ruben with Sunday wrapped under his arm.

"Excuse me, Commander Gex," said James, from behind him.

Searching the skies for his friends, Beau turned cold blue eyes on James. "Yes."

"I want to apologize for what I did up there. I . . . I didn't think."

Beau returned to watching the skies. "Forget it. I'm sure it won't happen again."

A moment later, James braved the question. "Would you really have shot me down?"

Just then the sound of an engine became distinct and they could see the outline of the white P-51 Mustang against the sky. No other aircraft returned, leaving everyone with a sinking feeling, except for James who cared little for anyone but himself. James continued to wait patiently for the answer.

For a moment Beau just stared at him before he answered. "No, I wouldn't have shot you down," he said with icy coldness. He turned and moved toward where the approaching aircraft would land. With his back turned to James, he continued in a voice, clear, distinct, and void of emotion, "Kipp would have shot you down. Just like I ordered!"

The white P-51 rumbled down the mesa. Beau and the others hurried toward the lone plane to learn what Fitz knew about Warren.

James grabbed Mulholland's arm. "You wouldn't have done as he said—would you?" James asked, trying to muster an artificial laugh.

Kipp just grinned and popped Donna on the rear with his hand. "Aye, mate, that I would. If ya had moved from formation, I'd of shot ya down just like one of the enemy."

Consumed unexpectedly with shock and fear, James started shaking and broke into a cold sweat. He thought he was going to throw up.

Before the aircraft came to a complete stop, Beau jumped on the wing but was not prepared for what he saw. Before him was Fitzhenry with no helmet, his face covered with blood and laughing uncontrollably. "Fitz, are you all right?" Beau asked, earnestly concerned. "What happened to BJ?"

An invisible voice came from below Fitz. "Get this heavy son-of-a-bitch off me."

The voice startled Beau, and he slipped on the wing. Yet without the slightest hesitation, Beau grabbed Fitz and helped him out.

Leaning over and peering into the confines of the deep cockpit, he spied his big friend and laughed. "You make just about the prettiest cushion I think I've ever seen."

"Damn it, I've had just about all the laughing at me I can stand for one evening. If you're going to laugh, go away," Warren snapped, with a wave of his hands.

Beau laughed, and now Ruben and Kipp were around the cockpit and also laughing at Warren.

"You should see yourself," said Ruben.

"Aye, a bloody mess, ya are." They all burst out laughing.

Fitz and BJ recanted their story as did Beau and Ruben of what befell Blackman. With heavy hearts, they returned to Cliff Palace. Everyone wondered how Dean would fare against the enemy. Their thoughts were of their dead friend Cozmo, knowing it could just have easily been any of them.

* * *

Two days after the attack, Sharafan and Ortega completed plans for the search. They took a map, located the three spots Beau Gex and his group attacked, and calculated their fuel range. Using a compass they scribed circles indicating their perimeter range. They would concentrate their efforts in the area of the three overlapping circles.

Ortega and three highly trained groups of his men would proceed to three points somewhere on the perimeter of that area, where they would lay in wait for more radio transmissions. They knew the group Beau Gex led occasionally contacted the American forces far to the north. Using three groups split in the different areas, they would use special equipment to home in on the transmissions. This triangulation method would form three straight lines to the point of transmission. Where they crossed would be the location of the signals. But it would take time. The first few intercepted transmissions would indicate a general area. They would have to spread out and catch the signals in between.

Sharafan explained the urgency of finding and eliminating the problem. Also, Sharafan ordered Ortega to capture Beau Gex alive and contact him when they did. The Cobra had some unfinished business with the Mongoose.

Chapter 8
THE ABDUCTION AND THE FURY

A week had passed since the disappearance of Blackman and the death of Deberg. Early May brought about a sullen attitude for the men. Five months had passed since the invasion of America. With the loss of the two men, Sunday, Krysti, Tracy, and even Lindy worked hard to make the atmosphere more home-like and tried to take the men's minds off the death of their friends. For May it was unusually cold, even freezing one day.

Krysti tried in vain to talk to Beau but he was rarely around. The only way to learn about him was through her son, because Justin still managed to find time to be with him. A strong bond had developed between the two and they seemed inseparable. And wherever Justin went, Champ was always nearby and usually mounted on his shoulder. The bird and the boy had the cutest ritual they had developed between themselves. Justin made sure that he always carried breadcrumbs or little berries in his shirt pocket. Champ leaned to rub Justin's neck with his beak and in turn Justin would take something out of his pocket and give it to the friendly little mockingbird.

Mike persisted in wanting Krysti to marry him but was still unsuccessful. Krysti no longer stayed with him. Their relationship had turned to ice. During this time of death and destruction, a new and budding romance developed between Fitz and Tracy. When there was free time it was hard to find Kipp and Donna apart.

For the first time anger overwhelmed discretion as Marix demanded Lindy be with him for part of the night. They found a secluded place not far from the river, and without the slightest bit of affection they became lost in each other's animal passions. Still no one suspected. Not even James, who assumed it must be Pickett since Deberg was dead. He found Pickett alone but could not find Lindy. He never gave a thought to finding Marix.

Daddy John and Schmitt along with Beau and Pickett spent much of their time repairing and making ready the aircraft in preparation for another raid. Even Daddy John did not have an unlimited supply of parts and weapons. Now the supplies were running low, which would limit their missions. At most they only had enough supplies for a few more attacks. Daddy John was surprised but also excited. He thought he had museum pieces and never thought he would run short of supplies for his beloved but ancient aircraft.

Larry James was occupied doing nothing and accomplished the task quite well. Ruben strutted like a peacock over his son. Even in the midst of the war, these were the most pleasant days Ruben and Sunday had ever experienced. Never did anyone hear a cross word or a voice raised in anger when they spoke to each other. There was a deep love and a bond between them that few people ever experience.

The only problem was Sully, who slipped back into a deep depression over the almost undeniable assumption his wife, Natasha, had been killed when the airliner she had been flying in had been shot down.

One day, while they prepared for the next attack, Fitzhenry took off in his P-51. Not until he arrived late in the afternoon, with a smoking P-40 Flying Tiger following close behind, did anyone piece together where he and BJ had gone.

The two men thought the adventure great fun. The enemy neither destroyed nor tampered with the P-40, which they found still intact. They used duct tape to seal one oil line and Vice-Grips to hold the throttle cable in place. Fitzhenry used a piece of bubble gum, wrapped with more duct tape, to seal a fuel line. After a few hours of patching lines and refilling the oil, they were ready to return. The old Warhawk managed to hobble home one more time.

The planes had taken a beating. Now constant maintenance and repairs were required to keep them air worthy.

Baby Paul was the new sensation and every time the women had a chance to baby-sit, they eagerly anticipated each opportunity. For Ruben and Sunday, the problem was finding time alone with their son.

One afternoon while the men worked on what Sunday called their *air toys*, both Sunday and Krysti drafted Tracy and Lindy to watch baby Paul. Without much arm-twisting, they agreed. The two women disappeared to hunt for berries, wild roots, and onions. They hoped to find enough berries to make pies for the men.

The women continued along the edge of a small tributary of the Frio, where the water was ankle-deep. They found a small spring nearby, feeding the river. They followed the spring until they came upon a large area of wild onions. They were shocked when they found the area disturbed.

"Strange," said Krysti. "Someone has been picking these, and recently."

They were filling a small pail when Krysti abruptly rushed to Sunday, who was on her hands and knees, and pushed her roughly under the brush.

Sunday was about to protest the obviously intentional action but before she could complain, she heard Krysti whisper, "Be quiet, don't say anything." Then Sunday heard a strange voice from the opposite side of the spring.

"Lookee, pretty lady. You want come wit Haun?" Slowly but surely, a wicked recognition registered on Haun's Neanderthal brain. "You!" he bellowed, remembering the auburn beauty from the incident at Shanghai Pete's.

"Go away! My friends are near," said Krysti defiantly. As she talked she slowly walked away from where Sunday lay hidden.

"Your friend put big hurt on Haun. Now, Red, you gonna pay for his mistake. You are mine," snapped Haun.

With a quickness and agility not evidenced that night in the seeming distant past at Shanghai Pete's, Haun bounded the spring and grabbed Krysti. She managed to let out with one ear-piercing shriek before he grabbed her. A large dirty hand swiftly covered her mouth.

Sunday made a move to help, but Krysti's eyes beseeched her to stay back. Sunday controlled her urge, knowing that not being discovered was the only chance to tell the men and possibly provide for Krysti's rescue.

At a signal from Haun, Monroe held Krysti's arms behind her body. Haun tore the blouse from her torso, and fondled her breasts roughly, pinching the nipple hard between his finger and thumb.

Defiantly, the brave woman stood before him. Tears came to Sunday's eyes as she watched in silent horror. A sadistic grin filled Haun's face. He tore the button and broke the zipper at the front of Krysti's jeans. He then slid his dirty hand down the front of her pants until he found what he desired. There his hand remained.

For the first time, Krysti showed signs of panic as she kicked and squirmed to free herself. But it was all for naught against powerful Monroe.

"You bastards! He will kill you," screamed Krysti with a heavier than usual accent. Somehow she truly believed Beau would appear as he had before.

"Not this time. He will not find us," Haun said confidently. He pressed his lips against hers, forcing his tongue brutally into her mouth. His breath still smelled like old wine and cigarettes. She bit savagely at his tongue and brought her knee up firmly.

A groan mixed with surprise, pain, and anger belched from his mouth. He slapped Krysti across the mouth hard, making blood trickle from her lips. His large dirty hand squeezed her right breast roughly. Blood from his tongue filled his mouth, which he spat on her chest. Then he brought his right fist behind his head, bringing it forward with such force against

Krysti's left breast she lost consciousness. Haun threw her body over his shoulder, and the three men left the area.

Crawling from the underbrush, Sunday quivered and sobbed uncontrollably. Regaining her footing, she cried out loudly. Then she heard someone approaching. They had returned!

* * *

Of all the men only Kipp, Beau, and Dean wore weapons at all times, and Dean was no longer around. Beau always wore the two knives and the revolver strapped to his side and his rifle was never far from his reach. Every man had a rifle and kept their weapons near.

With work on the planes finished for the day, Kipp, Donna, Ruben, and Beau were about to return to Cliff Palace when a distant scream of terror alerted them. Not too far away, James and Marix also heard the screams and grabbed their weapons.

"Where are the women?" snapped Beau.

Ruben answered with fear and concern in his voice. "Krysti and Sunday went to pick berries."

"Where?" ordered Beau.

Simultaneously, Ruben pointed and broke into a run with Beau. Kipp and Donna kept up the pace but far behind them trailed James and Marix.

Soon Beau, Ruben, and Mulholland detected sobbing and ran in the direction of the sound only to burst into a small opening where they frightened Sunday even more. Sunday saw Ruben, hesitated for a moment, then dropped to her knees and continued to cry.

"My God, Krysti!" Sunday moaned. "They have her! He hit her so hard! I . . . I think she's dead. She saved me."

"Who? How many?" Ruben hurriedly asked his wife.

"Three," then Sunday paused. "Ruben it's them—the same men we saw at Shanghai Pete's the night Beau returned."

The revelation stunned Kipp, Ruben, and Beau. They had seen Haun and his men in Hondo the day Chin was killed. Not only were invaders on American soil, now they had to contend with the treachery of their own kind. Renegade gangs of Americans stealing what they wanted and killing for pleasure.

"Sunday, which way did they take Krysti?" Beau asked gently. She pointed in the direction of the river.

Ruben turned to Donna. "Take Sunday back."

Before Ruben turned away, his wife grabbed his arm. "Ruben." Trembling with fear she stunned him when, with hate filling every fiber of her being, she said, "Kill them!"

An unusual chill filled the May air as five men, including Marix and James, worked their way through thorny mesquite, scrub oak, and thick brush and across the solid stone path toward the Frio River. They reached an impasse where the spring joined the solid rock base river. A thorough search revealed nothing of Krysti's abductors.

"Blimey bastards took to the center of the river," said Mulholland.

They searched in vain for signs. Finally, Mulholland pointed down the river. "There's a few roads. Musta gone this way, mates."

Beau shook his head. "I don't know. If you're wrong she'll be dead when we find her. I have a feeling. Ruben, you go with Kipp. I'll go upstream. Fire your rifle if you find anything." Beau never acknowledged Marix or James's presence.

"We'll go with you," Marix said to Beau. He despised and envied and hated Beau for his calm control. Marix was the senior officer and still felt he should be giving the orders. If Beau were dead, he would be the leader and Krysti would be his.

"I don't need you two to nursemaid," Beau said rudely. Then added, "Keep up. I won't wait!"

Immediately, Beau bolted upstream through the rushing, frigid, knee-deep waters of the Frio. He crisscrossed the crystal clear river trying to find signs of Krysti or her abductors. Marix and James trailed behind, but neither knew how to track, and both were having their problems just keeping pace with Beau's fleet, graceful, deer-like moves. Footing in the stony riverbed was precarious at best and moving fast only worsened the situation for Marix and James.

Beau continued over and around the sun-bleached rocks and boulders filling the river. With their feet wet and cold, Marix and James soon opted to use the worn stone bank and from there see where Beau went. Beau continued his quest ranging back and forth across the river, oblivious to fatigue or the icy water filling his boots.

A sparkling object beneath the water caught his eye bringing him to a sudden halt. Wedged between two rocks was a chain dangling in the current. He reached beneath the water and pulled free a cross with diamonds. Krysti's necklace! His rifle pointed skyward and a shot rang out. The unanticipated sound so stunned Marix, he stumbled into James who tripped and fell into the river.

In the distance Beau took note of a storm moving closer and gambled Haun and his men could not differentiate between thunder and the rifle. A gamble he had to take, knowing Kipp would hear and not be long in coming.

Momentarily turning about to check his support group, Beau leered at the helpless pair in the river. Before he resumed his urgent search for the woman he loved, he stuffed the cross in his pocket.

Both sides of the river rose sharply, creating a canyon through which the now waist-deep river flowed. The rushing waters deepened, forcing the three men to the narrow trail skirting the river at the base of the still rising cliffs. Farther into the canyon, the flowing waters appeared to stop as the river widened, creating a large, clear, deep pool, full of living creatures. Perch and minnows darted about the calm waters. A small perch, in search of food, broke the surface.

Shards of stone, the size of automobiles, broken from the sheer walls of rock above, filled the calm river. A portion of the cliff, fallen into the water thousands of years before, formed a natural arch. The three men continued beneath it. Still no signs, and yet this was the only possible direction Krysti's captors could go. Beau continued along the path with the other two men trying desperately to keep up the pace.

Large cypress trees lined both sides of the river providing abundant shade. The massive root systems wrapped like tentacles about the stone, and snaked into the river for additional support and nourishment. From the safety of a thick-leafed cypress, the inquisitive face of an owl turned around. The yellow trance-like eyes of the owl watched the intruders pass. A half-mile farther, the cliffs dropped away and the river again raced wildly among the rocks, forcing Beau into the water to continue his relentless search back and forth on both sides of the Frio River.

A small catfish darted between two rocks as the men neared. Surprised at the intruders passing, two doe and a buck, soon to start his new growth of antlers, stopped drinking. The three deer turned on their hooves, and silently melted into the rocky terrain.

Marix and James were exhausted from the desperate pace even though they had traveled only a small portion of the distance Beau covered, and with none of his intensity. They had observed none of the abundant life surrounding them during their painful attempt to maintain the frantic tempo. Beau had seen and heard everything.

Abruptly he came to a stop. He found what he sought: a sign where the men moved from the river! At the water's edge, something large and clumsy had disturbed an area of pebbles. Animals weren't clumsy. As though possessed by a demon, never uttering a sound, Beau continued his methodical search of every crack, every rock, and every bush along the path leading up and away from the river. Squatting, crawling, he searched, letting nothing escape his eyes. He seemed to glide across the rocks like a lizard.

Not far from the river along the sparse trail, Beau found a piece of Krysti's tattered and bloodied white blouse hanging from a thorny mesquite branch. His heart sank when he saw that her abductors had escaped in a vehicle, which he assumed was the truck he had seen when Haun passed through Hondo. In his mind he saw the image of the torn and twisted body of his murdered wife. He would not let Krysti die!

His controlled anger stirred him to still greater efforts, while two totally exhausted men barely managed to stay with the desperate hunter ahead of them. Fresh tire tracks, spotted with dripping oil, continued intermittently in the dirt filling the spaces between the large flat surfaces of stone. The tread marks came to an abrupt end on an asphalt road. The trail was lost.

Thunder from the north echoed Beau's anger. In the distance, dark clouds rolled ever closer as rain threatened to remove every sign of Haun and his men. Beau must hurry or Krysti would be lost to him forever. But which way should he go?

Bent halfway, holding his side and gasping for air, James whispered to Marix. "We can't go on. Tell him to stop."

"He won't stop!" said Marix, trying to catch his breath.

"He will stop!" said James with a sinister smile, tapping his rifle. Both men nodded, knowing they could force Beau to wait.

Unaware of their intention, Beau assessed the situation. He had seen Haun and his cohorts two weeks earlier. If they remained in the area, water would be their primary concern, so they would surely be camped on the river. The road west continued for fifteen miles before it crossed any river, while the road east wound to the southeast, crossing the Frio four times in a matter of miles. The sound of two rifles being cocked immediately diverted his attention.

Marix and James yelled in unison. "Stop! We have to rest."

Beau turned to confront his assailants and saw their rifles drawn on him.

"Krysti may be dying! I must go!" Beau pleaded.

"You'll wait for us," said James, assured he had finally gotten the best of Beau. "If you try to leave, we'll shoot you."

The response they unleashed was like coming suddenly upon a wild animal that was cornered. Beau's reaction to their threat was nothing like Marix or James expected. No longer could Beau restrain his rage, and with a quick motion of his wrist he cocked the lever action of his old 30.30 as it hung at his side. Simultaneously he flipped the cover from the deadly revolver.

Horrified, Marix and James watched Beau's eyes change to cold, steel gray. Marix felt the hair on his neck rise and James's knees quivered, almost buckling. They weren't looking upon Beau anymore but rather an animal bent on death and destruction. Death filled Beau's eyes. "People are gonna die today! Let it start here!" Beau snarled from between clenched teeth.

"You can't expect to get us both," said Marix, confused and now terrified the possessed man before him was serious.

"Maybe, maybe not. But guess who gets it first? I know how a coward reacts, so when ya move, the bullet will be waiting. Shootin' you two will be about as hard as shootin' a bottle off a fence. Only you're bigger."

Both men dropped the rifles to their sides. James said, "Hey, we're on the same side. We just want to rest."

Beau snickered at the cowards. "Yeah, I can tell we're on the same side. You wanta rest while Krysti might die." He spun about to take the easterly route along the road, firmly believing that was the direction the truck had gone. Momentarily he paused, and turned to face the two cowering men one more time. "If you ever pull a gun on me again you better shoot because the next time—I'll kill you! If Krysti is dead—I'm gonna kill both of you anyway."

"You can't be serious," said Marix.

"I'm dead serious. Pray she doesn't die!" With those last words, he turned and broke into a full run, continuing his quest.

Both men started to raise their rifles. They could kill him now and be rid of their problem forever. But what if they missed? They hesitated then let the rifles drop to their sides, leaving Beau to search alone.

Mile after mile he ran, with each successive mile faster than the previous. Beau covered five miles and crossed two bridges and checked every trail big enough for a car before he found a well-traveled path dotted with old and fresh oil. There was no guarantee what he found would lead to Haun but the path had been traveled often and very recently and it was the only sign he had found. He surmised they would be near the water, and the tracks did lead to another part of the Frio River.

Now he moved slowly because somewhere ahead would be a guard to signal if anyone approached. A few minutes later, he found that lone guard. Lightning flashed and thunder sounded. The storm was near but it mattered little now. Cautiously, Beau maneuvered for the kill.

* * *

Consciousness returned slowly. Krysti remembered the berries. Then the vision of Haun filled her throbbing head, and she forced her eyes open. She was nude and spread eagle on a table. Two men held each of her legs apart while a third held her tied hands stretched over her head. To her right, four men took turns raping the body of a slim woman with long wavy brown hair. In an instant, Krysti's trained mind told her the woman was dead but the men continued the ruthless onslaught on her motionless body. On the other side was another brown-haired woman, and she, too, was nude. Her terror-stricken brown eyes pleaded to Krysti for help. Krysti scanned the campsite, and instantly counted a dozen men.

"Put her in the truck. We'll use her later," said Haun. Monroe grabbed the brunette's hair roughly and half pulled and half carried her to the truck where he threw her in the bed.

Krysti had no doubt as to her fate. "She is awake," yelled the man holding her.

Haun walked over to Krysti's prone body, and put a hand between her legs. She tried to scream but one of the men held her mouth. He glared into her eyes determined to take both his revenge and pleasure with the helpless woman.

"Monroe," said Haun at the same time snapping his fingers. Instantly Monroe dropped his pants and violently raped Krysti.

In Krysti's terror, Haun talked to her calmly as he squeezed her breast. "First, Monroe, then Lawrence, and then you can have me." Haun laughed sadistically.

When Monroe finished, Lawrence took his brutal pleasure. Krysti knew she was going into shock but she continued to fight with all her might. The slimmest of all hopes kept her alert. Still she hung on and endured the horror and the humiliation. Krysti was angry, afraid, and she wanted to kill!

Haun dropped his pants and readied himself for his turn, "Lookey, girlee, you want Haun?" Again he laughed. He motioned the man pressing down on her mouth to release his hold. She promptly let out a terrified scream.

"No one can hear you. Scream again," Haun taunted, smiling in triumph.

Krysti needed no insistence and she continued to scream until Haun stuffed a pair of socks deep into her mouth. The socks were unexpected, and she sucked them in, wedging them against the back of her throat, blocking her windpipe. In the same instant, she felt Haun enter her body. Horrified, she was afraid, and not of Haun but the socks because she could no longer breathe. She was suffocating, and nothing or no one could help her.

Haun bent over as he repeatedly shoved his body against her. With his face inches from hers, he laughed hideously when he saw the fear in her eyes. Now he claimed this beauty for his own personal use. Haun was now the victor.

"Hey, girlee, your friends won't help you this time—you're mine!" he said. He continued his savage lustful rape, pushing his body against hers. Haun gloated at his conquest and started a laugh that turned to a roar of triumph.

Krysti's eyes were filled with tears when she realized death was near and she could do nothing to prevent it. She wanted to say goodbye to Justin. She would never see him again. Where were her parents? Would they ever know what happened to her? Poor Justin would never know what happened to his mother. She wanted to tell Beau she was sorry. Then she lost consciousness.

* * *

Beau came closer to the guard, but was still too far away. He waited for the man to turn so he could move within range. To shoot him would only reveal his position and possibly bring further harm to Krysti. He regretted not having the crossbow and prayed she was still alive. Thoughts of Krysti and the danger she was in tormented him. He was becoming impatient, but out of necessity he waited until he could execute his move.

He heard a scream that turned his blood cold. It was a woman's scream of terror mixed with a plea for help. The time to rush the guard was now, but instead he remained still in the brush. He used everything in his power not to reveal his position, because the guard was facing in his direction. Her life depended on it. Again the scream could be heard in the distance.

With the second scream, the guard turned in the direction of the sounds. Beau made his move with a lightning quick motion, sprinting across the opening toward the guard. The man turned, for some unknown reason, and faced the intruder with his rifle ready.

Beau's rifle found its mark first but not with a shot. In full stride, he swung his weapon from his waist in an arc with tremendous force. The long steel barrel caught the guard on the bridge of his nose and sent the lone sentinel crashing to the ground, dead before he landed.

The dead sentry had inadvertently helped Beau when he had glanced in the direction of the scream. Since the man knew the location where the scream came from, Beau moved rapidly over the trail in the same direction. The deadly .357 magnum was drawn and the bloodied rifle still cocked and ready.

Suddenly, he burst into the campsite, which reeked like an unkempt barn filled with cattle. The smell of urine and feces was staggering, and the stench of death filled the air. The river camp was a pocket of death in an area abundant with growth and life. To Beau's horror, he saw a dead woman with brown hair. Momentarily, he was relieved when he saw the woman was not Krysti. But the relief was temporary as he realized the same fate awaited her. Was he already too late?

"Where is she?" Beau bellowed half crazed. Instantly, his mind made an account of the area. Thirteen men: two near a pick-up truck, three with revolvers hanging at their side, another held a rifle, and the others clustered about a table where men laughed sadistically. The one with the rifle would be the most dangerous. Beau would eliminate him first. The ones with the guns would be next. Slowly, he rotated the barrel of his father's 30.30 around so it pointed in the direction of the man holding the rifle.

A hulking form, with his pants around his ankle, stood near a table with three men, who were partially concealing another body. Beau's unexpected entrance startled them. Those holding Krysti released her.

Haun, with his pants around his ankles, spun around. Instantly, both men recognized each other.

"So it is you. You come too late," said Haun triumphantly. "The girl is dead and now you will die." Then, Haun pointed to Beau while yelling to his men, "Kill him!"

Nothing Haun said registered on the man gone crazy before him. When the men released Krysti, the sudden shift of weight on the table caused it to tilt over, and her small, frail, battered, and bloodied body slid to the ground. Her face was ashen as in death. Beau saw the woman he loved, raped and beaten, lying before him dead. His mind snapped and he crossed that fine line to which some men hang so precariously close: from sanity and control to insane rage! He became an uncontrolled animal. Beau didn't see Haun and his men. Instead his mind was filled with a vision of men in turbans rising from the sand. The dream had become reality one more time. This time, they would not escape!

A primal guttural groan of rage and anguish escaped his chest, stirred from the dawn of man's savage beginnings—an eerie response to the site of death that could only be described as half crazy, half animal and with a foreboding of doom. Then a hideous growl escaped his lips. The savage, animal rumble momentarily halted all the men. Even Haun felt a chill run up his spine. Before them stood a human wraith with one thought—the blood lust of revenge!

Two shots rang out simultaneously. The man with the rifle dropped in his tracks, and Haun let out a scream of terror and pain as a bullet from the .357 magnum hit his right kneecap and blew a hole out the back, almost severing the lower portion of his leg from his body. He tumbled to the ground. The rifle snapped forward and back as Beau added a new shell to the chamber.

The three men with guns started to draw. But Beau reacted much faster with his magnum as he took out one of the three. With his rifle he shot another, then the magnum found the third. A fresh bullet was in the chamber of the 30.30 ready to send another messenger of death.

The camp became bedlam as men ran for cover and all went for their guns and rifles. Another man dropped before a shot was fired. In his crazed desire for revenge, Beau saw Haun rise to his good knee supporting himself with the aid of his rifle. Beau turned and with the .357 magnum, took aim, slowly, methodically, and deliberately, at Haun's manhood. With one shot he found his mark. Haun let out a blood-curdling scream of agony, clutched both hands to a hole where his mangled manhood dangled. He tumbled forward face-first in the sand.

A shot rang out hitting Beau in the thigh and dropping him to his knees. Another shot creased his shoulder. Beau dropped the gun and took aim with the rifle. Two more men dropped in rapid succession. Four of the five remaining men jumped in the pick-up to make their getaway. Beau took aim and shot, knocking one of them from the back of the truck. This time he took aim at the driver, but a bullet hit the dirt near his leg. He threw his body to the ground, rolled over twice, then concentrated on the present danger, rapidly disposing of the tenth man. He turned the sights of his rifle back to the truck as it disappeared from view. Three men escaped. Three too many, he thought.

Instantly Beau was on his feet, the hole in his leg forgotten. Quickly he ran to Krysti's aid.

It was not the crazed man who leaned over Krysti and cried, "No! I won't let you take her from me." In an effort to check her breathing, he noticed the obstruction. Pulling the socks from her throat, he yelled. "Not this time!"

Krysti had stopped breathing and her face and lips were blue. Afraid of what he would find, he touched his ear to her bare chest. He detected a faint heartbeat. A whimper came from his throat and tears clouded his eyes. Gently, he turned her head back and pinched her nose together, pressed his lips against hers, and blew life into her still lungs. He watched her chest rise. Firmly he pressed down on her chest and listened to the air release from her body.

"Breathe!" Beau begged, repeating it again and again. Again he repeated the steps. Four more times he did the lifesaving procedure.

"Breathe, God damn it!" Beau demanded.

In desperation, he yelled. "Don't leave me now. Come on Krysti, come back to me!" Again he pressed her chest down. As if answering his desperate plea, she gasped then coughed as her lungs took over and sucked the next breath. At first her breathing was ragged, then it fell into a slow natural rhythm and the color slowly returned to her face. Krysti remained unconscious, but she was alive!

Not until now had he seen the brutality Haun and his men administered upon her tiny body. Slowly, and with great intensity he surveyed the campsite for clothes, towels, and blankets. In a stockpile of stolen loot, he found a few fresh and clean items he needed. In the distance, he heard shots and turned in the direction the truck had disappeared. He saw nothing, and he had no intention of waiting to discover the perpetrators of the gunfire.

The desire for revenge was forgotten in his desperate attempt to save Krysti. He removed the torn and tattered remains of her clothes. Carefully he wrapped her in a blanket. To compound the problem, a brisk breeze blew across the camp of death, the air turned cold and swirling dust filled the air. The trees leaned toward the south.

In a camp where Haun and his men spread death and destruction not only to the people they encountered, but also to the areas where they stayed, Beau managed to gather a canteen, a towel to clean her body, and clothes for her. The storm would pass over before he could return to Cliff Palace.

Gunfire continued in the distance. To stay in the camp now would be putting Krysti's life in danger needlessly. He had no idea what was happening but he couldn't take time to wait and find out. Haun could have more men and they could be returning to camp. He moved swiftly to find cover from the storm as far away from the camp as possible.

Before Beau departed the death camp, he walked to where Haun lay. Near death, he shook and continued to clutch at his groin area, while blood oozed between his fingers. Lightning flashed in the blackened sky and thunder sounded instantly. Dust whirled in the air and the wind blew Beau's thick blond hair to the side. The distant gunfire stopped.

Beau grabbed Haun viciously by the hair on his neck. "You're lucky I'm not mad. You're gonna live," lied Beau. "Without these," he said, using the barrel of the rifle to tap Haun's missing parts, "you're not gonna be much of a man." Then he dropped his head to the sand.

He returned to Krysti, swinging the rifle over one shoulder and the canteen over the other. He placed towels and clothes within the blanket wrapping her, and tied a small rag around the wound in his thigh. For a brief moment, he paused at the sound of a single rifle shot.

Gently he lifted Krysti, and with a slight limp started for the cliffs he knew lined the river. Rain slowly pelted the campsite, creating puffs of dust with each droplet. Afraid for Krysti's safety and the fact the men might return, Beau made a quick escape from Haun's camp.

Not far from the site, in a short cliff on the north side of the river, Beau found a small crevice eaten away from the timeless passing of the river. The small cavern was large enough for the two of them and a small fire at the other end. The rock overhang would provide cover from the rain and wind.

Beau placed Krysti in a position to take advantage of the protection the overhang afforded. Hurriedly, he gathered an armful of wood before the rain increased in intensity. He cut some native cactus to use on the open wounds and scrapes covering her body. He found a spring, emptied the canteen, and filled it with fresh clean spring water.

Safely within the small hold of the cliff, Beau started a quick fire then tended to the wounds, wiping her body clean and applying the healing liquids squeezed from the cactus. The skies turned dark as night, lightning flashed, thunder boomed, and the rain turned to a torrential downpour.

His mind could not conceive the torment she had surely suffered. Her left eye was swollen shut. A large bruise appeared over the left part of her chest. Her face and hair were caked with blood and dirt; the thin, perfectly-formed lips were cut and swollen. Softly, he kissed the grotesquely-shaped lips. He took a cloth, wetted it, and carefully wiped the blood from her face and cleaned her mouth. He squeezed the cactus, forcing it to drip on her lips, thus forming a protective film over the broken and swollen skin. Next he put the oversized clothes on her small frame. All the while he worked on her small damaged body, he spoke to her whispering words of kindness and encouragement. She never regained consciousness.

Krysti shivered from the blowing chill of the Texas "Blue Norther." Beau rubbed her feet and hands and wrapped her feet with a dry cloth. Finally, he crawled beneath the blankets and used his body as a barricade from the elements.

Still, she shivered. Beau opened his shirt and rolled the back of hers up. Then he pressed his warm body against hers, wrapped his legs about her legs, and encircled his powerful arms around her shoulders. He held her hands in his and rubbed them. Calmly, he whispered in her ear, repeating the same soothing words over and over.

Minutes later, her shivers ceased and he could feel the slow rhythmic breathing. Holding her close, he relaxed for the first time since his search began. Fatigue began to set in and even with the torrential downpour and constant crack of thunder, he fell asleep with his arms wrapped around the woman he loved.

Chapter 9
"ANGEL EYES"

Marix and James walked dejectedly along the road filled with their own personal thoughts of revenge, anger, and embarrassment at their inept actions.

"The man's a lunatic just like they said all along," said Marix, angry he cowered down to Beau. His confidence mounted with every passing moment.

"He's fuckin' crazy. Did you see him pull his rifle on us when we were trying to help him?" said James. He had already convinced himself of his own good intentions.

In the distance, a Jeep approached. They hid to the side of the road, and when they recognized the occupants of the vehicle, Ruben and Kipp, they jumped from their hiding spot and waved them down.

After hearing Beau's signal, Kipp had felt it best to get the vehicle to pursue the kidnappers. All four went to the spot where Beau had continued his search alone. Ruben tried to get Marix to explain why Beau had continued without them, but he only got feeble excuses and mumbling from the two men.

The four continued along the road trying to find signs of Beau and the abductors. They drove about four miles when they saw a man, less than a quarter mile ahead, standing in the middle of the road waving a rifle.

"Look mate, there he is," said Mulholland accelerating the Jeep toward the distant figure. A tremor of fear crept through every fiber of the two dirty little cowards as they pondered Krysti's fate. Was she dead? And if she were, what fate lay ahead for them at the hands of this demon possessed man?

"That's not Beau," said Ruben, sure the man was someone else.

"It's a bloody ghost," shouted Mulholland only adding to the anguish of the two men.

Ruben recognized the man first. "It's Dean!"

Alone in the middle of the road, Dean waved his rifle and waited for the Jeep. They exchanged a joyous, but short-lived reunion. Ruben and Mulholland explained to Blackman the seriousness of the situation. Blackman jumped on the running board of the Jeep, grabbed the windshield, and they continued the search. Lightning flashed against the dark sky and a few seconds later thunder rumbled past.

They traveled less than a mile from where they found Blackman, when two shots rang out as one. He identified them as a revolver and a rifle. Could it be Beau? More shots were heard and they hastened in the direction of the gunfire, and what had sounded like a small war.

They turned from the road and moved cautiously toward the sounds of the escalating shootout. No sooner did they turn than they saw a body in their path. Then the sound of the battle stopped just as quickly as it had started. Almost immediately a pickup truck came barreling toward them, bouncing along the rocky dirt trail at a considerable rate of speed. The three men in the truck came to an abrupt stop, sliding sideways when they saw the Jeep.

Ruben, Mulholland, and Blackman were about to confront them when the three men pulled guns and started firing. Instantly they fell to the dirt and returned fire, while James and Marix took refuge behind the rear of the Jeep. In the midst of the gun battle, there was a mighty flash of lightning from the dark sky followed immediately with a crash of thunder. A few more shots and the short confrontation ended.

When the shooting stopped, Marix and James rose from behind the Jeep with weapons drawn. Three men lay dead attesting to the marksmanship of Mulholland and Blackman. Slowly, they approached the truck. Behind them came James and Marix, with their rifles ready.

As they approached the pickup, a rustling sound could be heard in the bed of the truck.

"Watch out, there's more in the back!" James yelled. Valiantly James charged to the front and leveled his rifle at the back of the truck and squeezed the trigger.

But the bullet he fired soared harmlessly into the air. Blackman moved like lightning, jerking the barrel of the rifle straight up at the last possible moment.

"Are you crazy," snapped James. "They might kill us."

Blackman just glared at James, who immediately hushed. "Never shoot unless you know what you are shooting." Blackman grabbed the rifle from him and handed it to Mulholland. "You're more dangerous to us than the enemy. If you knew anything, you could tell the noise was coming from somebody helpless in the bed of the pickup and not something to fear—and for some reason you seem to fear something."

Those were the most words anyone ever heard Blackman say at one time. He approached the truck slowly while Mulholland and Ruben held their rifles in readiness.

Silently he moved to the side and peered into the rear of the truck. He motioned the others to approach. Effortlessly, Blackman sprang into the bed, removed the flight jacket he still wore since being shot down, and knelt by the body.

A lovely shaped woman lay bruised, battered, and nude in the back of the truck. Her terrified eyes jumped at Dean's every move. He brought her to a sitting position and draped his jacket about her shivering shoulders. When he pulled his knife, she whined pitifully and cried hysterically at the sight of the blade. With a gentleness none of the men had ever witnessed in the Indian, he talked calmly to the beautiful woman with the long brown hair.

"I'm here to help you," he said softly. "The men that hurt you are dead." He touched the bonds wrapped tightly around her wrists with his knife. He felt her body quiver more in fear than exposure. "You have nothing to fear—I promise."

With a flick of his wrist, the knife cut the bonds and she was free. Terrified, she squirmed to the back of the truck bed and clutched desperately to the jacket, all the while letting out pitiful, little cries filled with fear. Dean tried to move closer but she moaned in sheer terror. Again, he spoke to her calmly and with authority. Then the Indian took his knife, and holding the blade in his hand, extended it, handle first, to the woman.

She grabbed the large knife and held it before her. Her eyes moved rapidly from man to man.

Again, Dean spoke. "A friend of ours may be in the same situation as you. We need to find her." A brief description of Krysti brought a light to her eyes. "You've seen her?" asked Dean, moving closer. She held the knife out touching Blackman on the chest. "If you must, then do it. I think you know we are here to help you and our friend." He held his arms to her as though to embrace her. "Come with us, you will be safe."

She dropped the knife and slumped into his arms. Sobbing uncontrollably, she pointed in the direction of the camp. "She is there. Hurry, they'll kill her!"

The four men raced on foot to the camp, leaving Blackman with the terrified young woman as she let go with a flood of sobs both from the terror and relief from her horrifying situation.

Dean put his hand under her chin and lifted her face so he could see into her eyes. "You have pretty eyes," he said with a reassuring smile. "What is your name?"

For the first time since the invasion, she felt safe. She sobbed, "Cindy."

Blackman squeezed her gently and patted her back. "I am Dean Blackman. You're safe now."

She believed him and for the first time in the weeks since Haun killed her husband, Bill, and took her prisoner for his pleasure, her body released all the tension and torment her captors had held over her.

* * *

Droplets of rain were falling when Ruben arrived in the camp. Mulholland followed closely with Marix and James bringing up the rear. Nothing moved except for smoke from the still smoldering fire. They could hardly believe the carnage of the campsite or the bodies littering the area. They could not believe all the death and destruction one man created.

"Looks like a war zone," whispered Mulholland.

"It's Beau, he's been here!" said Ruben.

There was a woman's body at the far end of the camp. She had brown hair. Mulholland went to see if the body belonged to Krysti.

"Is it Krysti?" yelled Ruben, his rifle still ready in his hand as he watched the area closely for intruders. Marix and James trembled in anticipation of Mulholland's response. James became nauseated with fear it might be her.

"No, it's not," said Mulholland, "but this lass has been badly beaten and raped." Horror filled Marix's eyes as he viewed the scene.

Mulholland pointed to tracks. "He went in this direction."

"He's found Krysti," sighed Ruben.

The rain had increased slightly when a groan attracted their attention. Cautiously, Ruben and Mulholland approached the body. Marix and James, behind them, moved even more cautiously and continued more out of curiosity than anything else. Ruben turned over the hulking mass, and instantly recognized the dying man to be the brute from the bar.

Mulholland looked up at Ruben. "The guy from Shanghai Pete's."

Ruben nodded. "Yeah, I think his name was Haun." Haun had turned ashen gray and still clutched the bloodied groin area with his dirty hands. One look at him and Ruben knew Sunday was about to get what she asked for. He was near death.

"He shot it off!" Haun groaned. "He is crazy! He said I will be like this the rest of my life." With those last words he died. His hands relaxed and released the area exposing the missing appendage.

"My God! He shot it off!" said Marix.

James turned around, fell to his knees, and threw up. He continued to gag, wondering if Krysti were dead and if the same fate awaited him. Mechanically he clutched his groin area as if by doing so he could save it.

Dean drove the pick-up into the camp. Cindy stayed in the front seat while Dean got out to see what the others had found.

"Well mate, looks like he got what he deserved. Best be gettin' back to Cliff Palace. The rain's coming."

James and Marix suggested the men be buried. Blackman told them to find a shovel and bury the bodies themselves if they felt it so important.

"Yeah, you can stay and return in the truck when you finish. I just hope they don't have any friends still around," said Mulholland with a wicked laugh.

The thought of more men coming back was enough to make James and Marix change their minds. The cascading sheets of water convinced them to return with the others.

They left behind thirteen bodies. The body of the dead woman was carefully wrapped in a blanket and then placed in the back of the truck so they could bury her when they returned to Cliff Palace. Marix and James rode in the back of the covered Jeep with Ruben and Mulholland. Dean and Cindy followed in the truck.

When they arrived, Sunday and Donna took Cindy and found clothes for her. They took her to the room Krysti used to treat the sick. There they tended her needs while explaining who they were and how they came to be in their present position.

Cindy told how she and Bill, along with another married couple, had left San Antonio three months after the invasion, to escape the invaders. The two men told the women they would be safer in the hills. Haun and his group found them on the river and during the night killed her husband and the other man. Then they raped the two women repeatedly over the weeks till Dean found them. Cindy told Sunday the woman Ruben and the others found was her friend. She held little hope for Sunday's friend Krysti against the likes of Haun and his men.

Sunday was impressed with Cindy, who through the ordeal had kept her sanity and survived. Cindy was shocked when Sunday explained they could not find Krysti, but Haun and nine of his friends were found dead around the campsite. Cindy wanted to know how many men it had taken to kill them and asked how the woman could have disappeared.

To this Sunday answered, it was only one man. She told Cindy about Beau and how he was the only logical answer to all of her questions.

* * *

The rain abated letting the pair sleep peacefully beneath the safety of the rock overhang. Beau awoke swiftly and alert, as was his nature. He guessed the time to be an hour before sunrise. Reaching across Krysti, he poured water from the canteen onto a rag, then wiped the feverish face of the helpless woman he held in his arms. He squeezed drops of the wet liquid to her dry lips and in her unconscious state, she responded mechanically, licking them.

"That's my girl," said Beau. Repeatedly, he put the liquid to her lips, knowing the need for her body to be replenished with fluids.

He pulled her close and kissed her neck. It would be better if she rested for a few hours more before he started the long trek to Cliff Palace. Best to wait for the warmth of the sun before returning.

Her face was swollen, cut, and bruised; the beautiful auburn hair was matted and dirty. None of this registered on his brain. He only cared that the woman he loved was alive, and he knew now that she was the most important thing in his life. For a moment, he rubbed her shoulders and whispered words of encouragement to her. Gently he pulled himself to her and carefully wrapped her in his arms.

Again, Beau kissed her on the neck and whispered in her ear, "Rest now." Then he repeated the same words he had said to her countless times throughout the night: "*Angel Eyes.*"

Chapter 10
ILLUSIONS OF TRUTH

Sunday stood near the head of the bed staring at Krysti's face. The swelling had gone down and she was resting. Two days had passed since Beau carried her to Cliff Palace. They had taken care checking her for any internal injuries. They were concerned for Krysti because of the unknown amount of time she had not been breathing before Beau found her. He said her heart had still been beating, which was a good sign, but the trauma of the brutal beating and the savage rape still left questions unanswered as to Krysti's mental condition.

The memory of Krysti's poor body after the ordeal was appalling to Sunday. When Beau returned, they managed to get her to the room before anyone saw her. Only Sunday, Donna, and Beau were aware of her condition. Beau had described the scene of the rape and his assumption Haun was not the only one to have his way with her. He hoped the information would help Sunday treat Krysti, if she knew all the physical abuse she had undergone. He told Sunday she looked great compared to her condition when he found her. Sunday took time to stitch the small wound in Beau's leg, then she concentrated her efforts on Krysti. Of the success of her recovery, only time would tell.

The two, along with Donna, concurred; keep the information of the rape silent. Cindy was having problems handling the situation. Krysti would have to come to grips with the same problem as best she could. Things were different now. Krysti would not be able to call a doctor for counseling or group therapy sessions. There would be no workshop, no professional help. This was a time of war and horror. Tragedy would be commonplace. The individual would have to cope with the problems on her own to survive. At least she was alive, and time would hopefully heal the rest.

Beau sat next to her bed, his hand clinging to the small gold necklace he had found in the river. The necklace her father gave her for her eighteenth birthday, the one Haun tore from her neck. The same necklace Beau intended to give her when she regained consciousness. He was the only one who believed she would have no ill physical or mental effects.

What concerned Sunday was Beau. He had kept his vigil at Krysti's side for two days, never leaving her bedside. Constantly, he talked to her. Sunday listened to Beau call Krysti *Angel Eyes,* a term she had not heard since before terrorists killed his wife Becky in Rome. *Angel Eyes* were words Sunday and Ruben knew very well. Sunday sensed his deep feelings for Krysti.

The only change in his attitude came when Marix made an effort to see her. He had barely entered the room before Beau issued a savage order for him to leave. Sunday asked why, and Beau just answered that Marix knew the reason. Marix uttered no complaint and exited from the room. He made no further effort to return while Beau remained in the room.

Ruben finally brought Beau to his senses, explaining to him it would terrify Krysti to awaken and find him watching over her in his condition.

"In case you haven't looked at yourself in the last few days," said Ruben slapping his friend on the back, "you look like shit. You'd scare the hell outa me if you were the first thing I saw if I'd been asleep for a few days."

Beau managed a feeble grin and agreed to go with Ruben.

"You take care of her for me, will ya?" Beau asked Sunday.

When she nodded, he laid the gold necklace on the nightstand next to the bed, took one last look at the woman he had saved from certain death, and gently touched her forehead. "She looks good, doesn't she?"

Ruben shook his head in disagreement and put his hand on Beau's shoulder. "I don't know how to say this nicely but she looks like shit."

"Ruben!" snapped Sunday.

"And you look worse, Beau!" Ruben finished. "Now, let's go eat."

One more time Beau bent over and whispered in Krysti's ear, "Rest, *Angel Eyes.* You're safe now."

In the kitchen, they rustled up some food and made themselves a meal. They talked about Haun and how his punishment fit the crime. A few minutes later, Beau managed to crawl into bed, falling into a deep sound sleep.

When Marix learned Beau was asleep, he made another effort to see Krysti. Sunday saw no reason to stop him. Near the bed he saw her for the first time. He couldn't restrain his feelings when he saw the hideous sight before him.

"My God, she looks terrible."

"You'd look terrible, too, if we dragged you behind a truck," snapped Sunday.

"She wasn't pulled behind any car. I thought she was beaten."

Angrily Sunday put a hand on her hip and with the other pointed to Krysti. "In case you've never seen it before, that is what a woman looks like when she's been beaten by a half dozen men. Not a pretty sight, is it?"

She wanted to tell him Krysti had also survived a gang rape. How would Marix handle the rape? That was something Krysti would have to tell him.

"I'm sorry, I never knew," Marix said solemnly.

For an intelligent man, Marix was surprisingly ignorant. Even the scene of chaos and the dead raped woman in Haun's camp didn't register the fact in his brain that it might have happened to Krysti. Since they had not found her in the camp, for him nothing had happened to her, even though Sunday had told him about the assault.

Sitting in the chair next to her bed, Marix noticed the small necklace and out of curiosity picked it up and held it in one of his hands. He admired the dainty piece of jewelry, not even remembering it was the same cross she always wore.

Suddenly, Krysti moaned, moved around in her bed and slowly regained consciousness. Dreams raced through the injured woman's mind. Images of three men raping her were vivid in her thoughts. Far removed from the hideous scene of her physical defeat were soft words of kindness and the words "*Angel Eyes*" that kept pulling her back from a black sinking hole. For some reason, she could see Beau just above that hole with his arms outstretched, reaching for her. She could not recognize the voice that continued to keep her hopes alive. She wanted her son. She must be dead. The socks.

"Justin," Krysti mumbled.

The word almost knocked Marix from his chair as he pushed back. "Sunday! She's awake. She's calling Justin. What do I do?"

"Here," said Sunday, handing him a wet cloth. "Rub her forehead." She pointed to a jug of water and a glass. "She will need water, but just give her a little. I'll get Justin and Donna. Just talk to her. She's been through a lot."

Sunday ran from the room to find Krysti's son, so he could see his mother. She also went in search of Donna so she could attend to Krysti.

Mike pulled the chair closer to the bed, sat back down, and watched helplessly. He took her hand in his as her eyes flickered open. He became angry when she mumbled her next word.

"Beau." When Krysti opened her eyes she thought she was lost. For some reason, she had not expected to see Michael. "Where am I?" she asked, her voice grating against her dry throat.

Mike offered her a glass of water, which she readily accepted. "You're safe now. Back at Cliff Palace."

"Justin?"

"Sunday went to get him. We were worried about you. Just rest."

"The woman? Is she alive?"

"Yes, she's alive. She was in the back of the truck but we found her," said Mike, who had already conveniently forgotten his own ineptness during the situation and how James had almost shot her.

"The socks, how did you . . ." Krysti didn't finish the statement. For some reason she had expected to see Beau. Was it really Michael and the others who saved her?

A light came on in Mike's head when he realized she didn't know anything or at least she didn't know much. He had just found a way to win her back. If she remembered nothing of the events leading to her rescue, and if he could just answer the questions properly, he could become the hero. "Forget the socks, what's important is you are safe. You know how much I care for you, Krysti. I still want to marry you."

Krysti was bewildered and confused. She wondered how he could want to marry her, after what had happened. How could this man, of such a fine bloodline, want a woman who had been used by God only knows how many men? Michael had found her and still he looked on her lovingly. He truly was a wonderful man. Beau had not even bothered to be here with her. "How can you want me after what has happened?"

"What happened is not important. You and I, the future, that's what is important. It is all I care about."

Instantly, she recognized the gold necklace in his hand and remembered it being torn from her neck when Haun dragged her down the river. She never thought she would see it again. "My necklace, you found it! You saved me?"

Marix remembered the necklace as the one Beau plucked from the river. As far as the question, he would work around it gently. "I must say, in all honesty, I could not have done it alone. Kipp, Ruben, Dean, James, and I managed to find the campsite. The necklace was lying in the river. We were lucky to have found it. We were more concerned about you."

How modest, she thought. Marix was giving credit to the others for her rescue. He could have found the necklace only if he had come in the right direction. Did Krysti hear him correctly? She asked, "Dean?"

"Yes, we found him while hunting for you. He's fine."

"How long have I been—" Krysti stopped, puzzled and unsure of things happening around her.

"You've been unconscious for two days."

"Two days," she whispered under her breath.

"You're safe. That's all I care about," Marix said reassuringly.

For some reason, Krysti blurted out, "Wasn't Beau there?"

This would be the ultimate coup for Mike. "No, he wasn't there when we found the camp," Marix said. As he spoke he hung his head and shook it slowly. He smiled with pleasure to himself because he hadn't lied. Beau was not there when they found the camp.

"I must tell you . . . no, I can't," he said feigning sorrow.

"No," said Krysti squeezing his hand. "Tell me."

Ironically, Krysti showed compassion for the one she believed had remained behind to give her comfort and attention for her near fatal ordeal.

Marix could barely repress a smile. "Don't tell anyone, especially Sunday and Ruben. You know how much Beau means to them. I think the situation is very hard for them to handle as it is. Promise?"

"Yes, I promise. I wouldn't hurt Sunday or Ruben for the world."

The plan was working better than Marix imagined. "Beau pulled a gun on James and me while we were searching for you. I'm afraid he cracked under the pressure. James and I went with the others and that's how we found the camp." Mike told the truth as he saw it. Even he began to believe his own twisted story. Now, if she just assumed he had found her.

In her condition, it was easy to believe the first one she saw. What Beau had done was more than she could take. How could he have abandoned her? "What happened to those men?"

"They put up quite a resistance. We had to kill them," Marix said in direct reference to the three men shot while he and James watched helplessly from the rear of the Jeep.

"And Haun?"

This one he knew because Ruben had called out the dying man's name. "I've never seen a man as big and mean as Haun. He's also dead."

"Good!" said Krysti. The vindictive retort surprised Mike.

Now there was no doubt in her mind. The facts were clear, beyond a shadow of a doubt—Michael had been her savior. Everything he told her fit together just as she last remembered.

Something still troubled her and she hoped Michael would have the answer to one last question to which the answer eluded her. "Michael, does *Angel Eyes* mean anything to you?"

This was one question he had no idea how to answer. What was *Angel Eyes*? This one, he would have to answer truthfully. "I'm sorry. I have no idea what you're talking about."

With a sigh, she said, "It's nothing. I think it was something I must have been dreaming the last two days. Forget it."

The time had come for Marix to change the subject before she asked a question he could not answer correctly. Now he could make his move.

"I love you, Krysti. You know I'll be there when you need me," he said and squeezed her hand.

"You're such a sweet man," said Krysti. "I never dreamed you were like this. How could I have doubted you?" Before Marix could respond, Justin came running into the room.

"Mom!" yelled Justin busting through the door with Champ trying to cling to his shoulder. Sunday came through the door just as Justin bounced on the bed and hugged his mother. Champ had already escaped and fluttered to the top of the lamp next to the bed.

"I'll leave you alone," said Mike, half-worried Beau might return.

After a brief reunion, Sunday brought soup so Krysti could regain her strength. Sunday ordered Justin out until his mother had eaten. As he walked from the room, Champ fluttered to his rightful position on the boy's shoulder.

Krysti sipped the warm fluid. "Isn't Michael a thoughtful man."

Sunday had no desire to argue with her. She did not want to talk about how Beau had saved her. "I suppose."

Krysti swallowed the soup. Yes, she thought, Michael was right. They were worried about Beau. She felt it best not to discuss him and upset her friends. A vision of Haun haunted her, more real than if he had been alive. She dropped the soup and began crying.

"Oh, Sunday," Krysti bawled. Sunday put her arms about her depressed friend

Krysti continued. "How can I face another man? I feel so dirty. Michael understands. Beau will think I'm such an awful person."

"There, there, Sugar. Don't worry. Anyone with any feelings will understand what happened," said Sunday, comforting her distraught friend. She wondered if Mike would understand when he learned the truth that Krysti was raped. "If they don't have the compassion to accept the situation, you don't want them. You didn't offer yourself to those men, they forced themselves on you. Don't worry about Beau, he will understand."

"Sunday, if you only knew . . . I'm . . . I'm pregnant!" cried Krysti, hiding her face within her hands.

Sunday was stunned at the revelation. "What?"

Krysti managed to pull her red-eyed, tear-drenched face from her hands. "The baby is Michael's. But I don't know if he wants me after what happened. I don't know if I love him. What will Beau think? Sunday, I'm so confused."

"But the rape? The baby couldn't be alive," said Sunday assuming the violent assault would have killed the baby.

"No, the baby is alive. I know it. I can feel it." Tears rolled down Krysti's cheeks. Sunday held her friend's chin up and wiped the tears from her eyes.

"If a man doesn't understand what has happened, then you don't need him around," Sunday said. She wondered how both men would handle the news of Krysti's pregnancy.

"I feel so awful."

"Listen, Krysti, I don't want to hear any more talk about this. You're a doctor. We need you and so does Justin. What happened has happened, and there's nothing you can do to change it. I know, it's rough. God knows I probably couldn't handle it. But you have to get a grip on this. Do you understand?"

Krysti managed a pitiful smile and wiped the tears with the back of her arm. "Yes ma'am. If you get me some more soup, I promise to be a good patient."

A smile of relief filled Sunday's face. "One more bowl of soup coming up." Just then the door to the room opened and a tall brunette dressed in a robe entered.

"You're the one," said Krysti pointing to Cindy, instantly recognizing the woman who was also Haun's prisoner.

Cindy nodded. "I'm glad you survived. I want you to know they'd been doing those terrible things to me for weeks. My girlfriend died just before you arrived. They were savage animals. I'm lucky your friends came along. Especially you." Unknown to Krysti, Cindy's last words were in reference to Beau's miraculous rescue that saved Krysti from death.

Naturally, Krysti assumed Cindy meant Michael and the others so she agreed. "Yes, I know."

"Dean is nice, don't you think?" asked Cindy.

"Of course he is," said Krysti. "I almost killed him."

"What?" asked Krysti.

Then Cindy told the story of how they found her. Her memory of the events were hazy since she had seen none of what happened from the bed of the truck. So as it turned out, the men she recalled coincided exactly with those in the story Michael told her.

Cindy found no reason to continue her story or go into great detail about the incident with Haun for two reasons. First, the less she talked about it, the more removed she became, and secondly, because Krysti obviously knew everything since Beau had saved her. She never said any more about the incident to Krysti, and likewise Krysti felt it better not to talk about the incident to Cindy unless she mentioned it first. Both felt the less said about Haun and his men the better it would be for each of them.

For the first time Krysti could see the other survivor of the trauma and terror Haun and his horde administered to everyone they came in contact with. A full-scale war, and their biggest dangers turned out to be Americans and not the invaders. This tough female, Cindy, was a survivor. Krysti would do all in her power to overcome what had befallen her. She would also try to please Michael, if he still wanted her after what happened. He had a much stronger character than she originally thought, and his modesty amazed her, but what she admired most was his straightforward honesty.

That night when she went to sleep she couldn't explain the recurring dream—not a nightmare but instead a pleasant dream. She could hear a strong, compelling, and gentle voice. A voice that inspired hope. The strength of his words brought her comfort, helping to heal the awful mental wounds. And always, he repeated to her the words, *"Angel Eyes."*

* * *

For a week neither Krysti nor Cindy wandered from the safety of Cliff Palace. Occasionally Cindy had nightmares, but each woman sought the other's company, and it seemed to cure the problems they faced concerning their rape and abduction. Cindy had done remarkably well considering Bill, her husband, and her two friends had been murdered. Seeing Cindy handle a more severe problem than hers enabled Krysti to recover much faster. And with the passing days, she never learned the truth about how she was actually saved.

The ruse Marix used worked to perfection. Cindy saw no reason to discuss the rescue, assuming Krysti already knew. Also, neither woman wanted to remind the other of the physical abuse both survived. Cindy was unaware Krysti had been unconscious through the whole ordeal. The truth was never revealed.

The day after Krysti regained consciousness, Beau managed to get a moment to express his pleasure at her recovery. What he couldn't understand was the coolness toward him. It no longer mattered she was spending her time with Marix, he told himself, because she was safe and alive. Although he wanted to warn Marix not to hurt her, he felt it better to say nothing. Actually, he was happy just talking to her even though she was almost cruel with him. At least, now, she would speak to him.

"You sure look a lot better than when we found ya," Beau said sincerely, taking into consideration the others who tried to find her.

Krysti couldn't believe what she was hearing. Beau was taking credit for her rescue. Well, she would just ask him a few questions. "When you found me," she asked smugly, "where was Cindy?"

"I didn't see Cindy. She was nowhere around."

"You weren't with the others when they found Haun?" she asked.

"No, I wasn't with them," Beau said not realizing the question was aimed at finding out if he had helped in the rescue.

Krysti had no way of knowing Beau had executed her rescue alone and that he had almost been killed trying to save her. His answers only verified Michael's story and the last things she remembered. Obviously, Beau lied to her. She thought a great deal of him and it hurt but it was best not to let her feelings keep favoring him. Surely, he was a better man. It hurt to think he would lie. His heroic actions in the air were common knowledge. But what changed him on the ground? Why couldn't he be a gentleman like Michael?

Why did he threaten Mike and James? If he had just not lied. Something was amiss, and she couldn't put her finger on it.

For the first time Krysti could remember, Beau walked from the room with sagging shoulders, as though defeated. She had never seen him so totally beaten before. She had intended to ask him about the socks and the words "*Angel eyes*" but she wanted no more lies so she didn't confront him with those questions, and it didn't matter because she knew he wouldn't know the answers. She decided not to ask any more questions, especially to Beau. There would be no more lies if there were no more questions.

Another thing Krysti knew nothing about was the strange on-again off-again relationship that had developed between Marix, the man she trusted, and Lindy. Once Marix thought he had Krysti back with him he had dropped Lindy like the proverbial hot potato. James didn't understand the sudden passion Lindy showered on him and he didn't care as long as it was there again. As to these things Krysti was clueless.

Cindy entered the room as Beau was leaving. "He's a brave man," she said. "I wouldn't want to be in his shoes making the decisions he has to make. He must have a lot on his mind."

"He's strong. He'll survive," said Krysti. She started to ask Cindy why he wasn't with the others when they found her, but her throat refused to let her voice continue. And why should she ask? After all, she knew the truth.

Chapter 11
WINGS OF DEATH

Using the triangulation method of finding the Americans proved to be more difficult than Juan Ortega first imagined. The men he hunted were clever in changing their locations when they transmitted, so he and his men continued the search.

He was concerned with what he accidentally stumbled upon when he and his group pulled from the highway to rest and get water from the river.

Juan Ortega walked through carnage and fourteen dead men. The evidence pointed to a fierce fight with a dozen rotting bodies attesting to the small war. At first, he wondered if it might have been the group he searched for, but none of the bodies resembled the men he had seen when he was placed in the Naval Air Station. They were more like the renegade groups of pathetic Americans he occasionally encountered. One man, a very large man, appeared to have been tortured.

The search continued, but they found nothing to suggest it was the group he hunted. No military weapons and absolutely no evidence of any aircraft. Still Ortega radioed Sharafan and told him of his find.

Sharafan was growing more and more impatient with every passing day, which was reflected in his anger toward Ortega. When Ortega finished with Sharafan, he resumed the search with more intensity than before. Not because of Sharafan's reaction, but because he was angry he had not found them. Ortega, more than ever, was determined his efforts would be rewarded with the capture of those he sought. Again, he checked with his radioman but still no transmissions. They moved farther down the river, set up camp, and waited.

* * *

The small fortress was buzzing. Duck Waddle had asked if they were capable of flying another mission, and when he received the affirmative, he told them the next target would be Bergstrom Air Force Base in Austin. Duck Waddle requested the men do what they could to destroy as many planes as possible.

When the request was presented to the men, they all agreed to attempt the attack. Work had progressed on the P-40 Warhawk Fitz and BJ had recovered, making it again operational. Another P-40 Warhawk had been commissioned from the pile of derelict planes and was also combat ready. Blackman would fly the new fighter added to their air circus of combat-ready relics.

On this mission, they would again attempt the attack near sundown, and hit Bergstrom from the west. All was in readiness for the attack to take place the next day. Everyone relaxed in Cliff Palace and drank Daddy John's magic elixir. Kipp and Donna disappeared early in the evening, while Ruben and Sunday were the center of attraction with Little Ruben. The friendship between Tracy and Fitz continued to grow with each passing day. One thing Lindy made sure of was that Marix was aware of her daytime meetings with James. Somehow it worked because Marix was jealous. He wanted both women.

For a week Beau had tried to see Krysti and talk to her, but she always found excuses to avoid a direct conversation.

The women worked at preparing a party before the next mission to take the edge off the tension before the attack. Beau watched and wondered who would be next. Would they lose another? Pilots were a strange lot, their motto: Be merry tonight for there may not be another. Who would ever have thought they would be attacking an enemy on American soil.

He watched Marix and Krysti. Suddenly, Cliff Palace was not to his liking so he wandered away to the mesa and his P-51 Mustang. There he would receive the attention he needed from the cold, black, steel bird he flew.

On the mesa, Ted, Daddy John, and Robby finished making last minute checks and changes. While they worked they bragged over old war stories. Ted had lost weight from the heart attack, and appeared no worse for the incident. They were all drinking Daddy John's concoction. Watching the three men, no one would have dreamed there was a war. The night air was cool and dry and a slight breeze blew in from the south.

"Well, well," snapped Daddy John rising from his chair. "If it isn't our Ace pilot." He poured his brew into a cup and handed it to Beau. "Hey, son, it looks like ya been to war already, and lost. What's troubling ya?"

"Women. Can't figure them out," Beau said taking a healthy swig of the burning drink. As he swallowed, the drink rolled a warm trail all the way to his stomach.

"Have you talked to her?" Garrett asked.

"Nope."

"Hell, a woman's like the enemy. Ya don't go run and hide. You attack. Go tell that woman what's bothering you. Make her listen. Nothing gets accomplished by moping around," said Garrett, feeling good from the drink. He felt no pain in his chest, and Krysti had given permission for him to regress for one night.

"Hell, if ya flew your fighter like you're doing with this girl, you'd crash and burn on your first mission," said Daddy John.

He saw Beau's glass was empty, so he promptly filled the cup again.

"I think I've already crashed and burned," mumbled Beau.

"It's never too late," Garrett added, remembering his own mistakes from the past. "You just have to move in and be persistent."

Schmitt interjected, "Aw, just jump her bones. What she needs is a good—"

"Robby, I don't think this is that kind of situation," interrupted Garrett.

"Yes sir."

"Look, son," said Daddy John as he put his arm around Beau's shoulder, while filling his cup with his free hand. "A woman's like a fine flying machine. Treat her right, and she'll respond." He picked up his cup and sipped the brew.

"I've tried. I'm sure the problem is what I've done in the past," said Beau. He chugged his drink.

Daddy John politely filled it again. "Give it time. Besides, what you did in the past is what heroes are made of."

"I don't want to be a hero. I just want to live in peace," Beau said, as he walked to his workbench. The small hand held tape player Beau listened to when he worked on his plane lay on the bench. He had managed to snatch it, along with some tapes, from a store in Hondo. But tonight, oblivious to Ted and Daddy John, he pushed play on the tape deck and started listening to one particular song like he had on numerous nights when he worked alone on his aircraft. To ease the pain he was feeling he took another drink. And then another.

When the music started to bother the others and they complained, he climbed into the cockpit of his black and gold machine. From the cockpit, they could hear him singing or more like yelling the words to the song.

Hours later, the three men begged him to return with them to Cliff Palace, but when he refused, they left him singing to himself and returned to the festivities within the cliff.

When they arrived, Daddy John found Donna and Kipp, with Sunday and Ruben, arguing about the invasion and where the blame lay. The argument had expanded to include Krysti and Marix.

Daddy John waited patiently and finally interrupted. "The damn government just gave away too much and sat on their butt and forgot to cover their asses. Just left the back door open and let them walk right in." Abruptly, he turned to Ruben. "Would you mind gettin' yer friend out of his plane and make him get some sleep? He keeps singing some damn song about there being no Heaven."

"Sure," said Ruben. He turned to Sunday, kissed her, and started for the mesa.

As Daddy John walked away, Krysti followed then stopped him and asked, "Daddy John, did you say he was singing something about Heaven?"

He paused and turned to Krysti. "Yep. He plays that damn song all the time, but tonight he played it over and over, till it almost drove me nuts. The boy's just drunk as can be. He stood in the cockpit of his plane, laughed at me and asked me, 'Imagine if there were no Heaven?' Heaven? Kiss my ass, he's going to hell if he doesn't get ready and get some sleep. I just hope he's okay for tomorrow's mission."

Before he finished saying the word "heaven," she was already moving in the direction of the mesa and far behind Ruben. As she retreated from Cliff Palace, Marix grabbed her.

"Don't grab me like that!" Krysti snapped. Fierce green tiger-eyes caught Marix unprepared as her accent became more pronounced. "I don't appreciate being treated like that after being raped by those men—especially Haun," she said bitterly.

"Hey, I was just wondering where you were going," Marix said. Already her words churned in his brain. "What do you mean raped?"

"You found me, Michael. Surely, you know," said Krysti taken aback at his statement.

"Yes . . . I didn't understand what you said," stammered Marix.

"I think I was pretty damn clear. I'm going to see if Ruben needs help." Then she left Marix standing alone on the mesa. Could he really have misunderstood her? She dismissed the idea and continued along the path.

Standing on the mesa with only his thoughts for company, Marix shook his head in dismay. "Raped? Raped! And Haun. I can't believe she didn't tell me."

Marix was shocked and disgusted. To him, Krysti had become a dirty creature. He must have time to clear his mind and his feelings. A few minutes later, he casually asked Sunday how bad the rape had been, telling her he was concerned for Krysti.

Marix's smooth-talking manner and the drinks helped loosen Sunday's tongue. Why would he ask, unless he already knew? So she told him the graphic details and failed to discern the disgust well hidden behind the chameleon exterior. Marix went in search of Lindy.

* * *

When Ruben arrived, he could hear the tape playing. The batteries were weakening, and the music was slowing. From above the cockpit echoed the sounds and the drunken voice of his friend trying to keep pace with the much slower version of the song.

"Hey, you stupid shit," said Ruben laughing. "Get outa there and let's go back." He could not see Beau who was sitting in the seat. Without his gear, it made him invisible to those on the ground. He stood and smiled, then tried to salute with his hand, but caught his lips instead of his forehead. His head bobbed and weaved, and he disappeared back into the cockpit with a thud.

The tape clicked off, and the singing stopped.

Krysti emerged from the shadows. Ruben motioned her to stay on the other side of the plane and put his finger to his lips for her to remain silent. Ruben laughed, which helped ease her mind. Ruben moved his lips forming the words, "He's okay."

"Ruben?" came a voice from deep within the cockpit.

"You got it. Now let's go."

There was a moment's silence before anything happened. "Grenade!" yelled Beau and he hurled a small object in the direction of his friend. Krysti did a stutter step, and her eyes grew large as she watched Ruben catch the small object.

"Damn it, Beau," said Ruben, glancing at the small Three Musketeers bar. "I'm trying to quit eating these."

Beau's face popped over the edge of the cockpit, and he shook his head. "I don't come down until you eat it." A grin crossed his face.

Ruben tore the wrapper and bit at the candy. With half the bar stuffed in his cheek like a chipmunk, Ruben pleaded, "Come on down, Beau."

Beau's face disappeared again. "Hey, Ruben, look up at the stars. Sure is pretty. No hate, no war up there."

Krysti walked from the side of the plane to stand beside Ruben. She spoke softly so Beau could not hear. "Does he do this very often?"

"Last time I remember him drinking to a point like this was when his wife was killed by terrorists. The same bomb killed his son. Shawn would have been about Justin's age now." He turned to Krysti. "He likes you. In fact, for the last five years, he's had nightmares about terrorists killing his wife and son. Recently, they started again, but this time—"

Krysti interrupted. "That's terrible. No wonder he's acted so strange."

"You didn't let me finish," snapped Ruben. "The dreams are the same except the woman is you and the boy is your son. He doesn't want anyone to know about the dreams. But since you don't give a damn about him, I don't imagine it would bother you hearing it."

Watching the pain and hurt in Krysti's eyes gave great gratification to Ruben. He was about to ask her how she could be so cold to the man who had saved her from death and Haun. He just wanted to see the expression on her face when he asked her.

She wanted to tell Ruben she didn't know all those things about Beau and that it didn't matter anymore that he wasn't there when she was rescued.

They were both about to say something to each other when Beau yelled from deep within the fighter.

"Hey, Ruben. Do you suppose those homeless people are still carrying their protest banners saying 'No homes. No Peace.' Can you see them telling the invaders that?" Beau could hear Ruben laugh. "I wonder if people are still picking up their welfare checks. Imagine the anti-abortionists walking down Main Street telling the invaders it's murder to kill an unborn fetus. Ya think they understand war yet? Those people are in deep shit now, aren't they?"

"Yeah, Beau, they're in deep shit. Now come on down, it's late," pleaded Ruben.

"Ya think the politicians and those protestors still wanta hang my ass?" Beau queried, laughing after he finished.

"No. They probably hope there's a thousand more like you," said Ruben.

"War! Rules of war!" Beau moaned. "Rules of war are made by men who never have to fight war except on paper. They don't see the ones they love die; they don't have to wonder if it was them that killed children. Only you and I have to worry about it, while they make Goddamn rules on how and where you and I are supposed to act. Kill this one, don't kill that one, kill these by the rules, and by all means, don't cross over the lines they set. Ruben, it really sucks. You know?"

Ruben sighed. "Yeah, buddy, I know."

"Ya know she hates me."

"Who hates you?" Ruben asked and frowned at Krysti.

"Krysti. I guess she's doing the right thing with Marix. Hell, the Baron has all that money and property. I sure don't have much to offer her— except maybe a bad past."

On the ground, tears were forming in her eyes, and she shook her head. "I didn't know," Krysti whispered so Beau couldn't hear.

"Beau, it's time to go."

"I know why she hates me. It was those kids they say I killed. I don't know if it's true, but . . . I die a little inside each time I think I might have killed kids."

"Beau, it doesn't matter. I understand," said Ruben.

"I know you understand. But she doesn't. She's like the protestors at the base. Hang him first and ask questions later."

In the silence of the mesa, Krysti and Ruben could hear Beau's voice break as he continued to speak. "Those kids . . . if you only knew how much it eats at me. Who was worse, the terrorists or me? Did I murder those kids? I'm sure Krysti is justified in what she thinks of me. I just wanted revenge for Becky and Shawn."

The muscles in Beau's cheeks quivered. "I've never told anyone this but after the explosion, I searched for them. Parts of bodies were everywhere. When I found Becky, a portion of her left side was blown away. As soon as I saw her, I knew she was going to die. But Shawn, all I found was . . . his . . . he had been . . ." Beau's voice trailed off, and he put his face in the palms of his hands and then rubbed his lips. His voice wavered. "All I found was his arm; it still held his toy plane. That's how I knew." With those words his voice trembled, and the words ceased as his throat tightened.

"Hey, man, stop. You don't have to tell me anymore," Ruben said, turning his head and frowning at Krysti.

"No. Let me finish." Still his voice faltered, and he tried to regain control of his emotions so he could finish his story. "Becky was still conscious. She was frightened and asked me to hold her. She asked me if Shawn was okay. I told her he was fine and already outside with the other survivors." Beau's voice cracked. The voice no longer sounded like it belonged to him. "Those were the last words she heard." Beau's eyes were red, and tears started slowly rolling from each eye as he finished. "I lied to her, Ruben. I lied to her."

Ruben detected Beau's sobs, and his eyes began to mist. He felt his throat constrict as he rubbed his eyes with his index finger and thumb. "What you told her was the only thing you could have said."

"I know, but you know what the worst part is?"

"No, what?"

"I don't mind Krysti hating me. Hell, I don't mind if the Baron gets her but what hurts most—she won't even talk to me. God, Ruben, it's killing me. If she would just talk to me. I really miss her silly little smile. I could watch her all day and be happy. If she'd just talk . . ."

The tape player started to play and they could hear him sing the words, *"Imagine there's no Heaven . . ."*

No longer able to restrain herself Krysti cried out, "Beau, I'm sorry." She was unable to hold the tears back. "I didn't understand."

The tape player clicked off. Beau stood erect in his machine, and his eyes flashed with anger. "What are you doing here? I don't need your sympathy. I don't need anyone. Get out of here!" Beau demanded almost viciously. "Ruben, get her out of here!"

"Okay Beau, I'll take her out of here. But you come on up later," begged Ruben.

Beau threw the tape player, slamming it to the floor of the mesa, shattering it into dozens of pieces. "Go!" he demanded. Ruben didn't hesitate in hurrying Krysti from the mesa.

"Why are you taking me away? He wouldn't do anything."

Ruben just shook his head. "You'd be safer with him than you are with me right now. Personally, you piss me off. He asked me to take you away, so I'm only doing as he asked." Then Ruben's voice faltered. "You broke his heart, and I'm just giving him some time to himself like he wants."

Far behind them in the shadows of the mesa, Beau's drunken sobs echoed from the black and gold Mustang. Only the antiquated fighter planes heard his sadness, and they all listened quietly.

* * *

Not long after they returned to Cliff Palace, almost everyone knew about the events on the mesa. Ruben failed to keep his tongue in check.

Krysti felt miserable and confused and vowed to talk to Beau in the morning. How could she explain to Ruben how she really felt about Beau? How could she talk to Ruben about his lies? For the first time she wanted to forget what she knew and forgive Beau and become his friend. What of Michael; did she love him or was she just lonely and he was available? Beau was the real man. No, Michael was the strong one, after all he had saved her. But Beau was so strong. Justin liked Beau. Kids were seldom wrong. Could Justin be so wrong this time? And the baby!

Sunday came to Krysti and tried to console her. "Forgive Ruben. Beau is his best friend."

"Aren't you mad at me?"

"I'm not happy with what has happened," said Sunday. "But this is a war and strange things are happening. You came closest to dying at the hands of men from your own country. The same country Beau and Ruben are risking their lives to protect."

"I'm sorry, Sunday. I promise to make it up to Beau."

"Just talk to him, Sugar. He never asked for much."

Krysti thought more about her rescue and wondered if the recurring words *"Angel Eyes"* meant anything to Sunday, then she asked, "Sunday do the words An—"

But Sunday interrupted when she saw Marix approaching. "Sorry, Mike is coming, I'd better go."

Krysti turned to greet Michael. "I'm sorry, I don't think I'll be good company tonight. I'm going to bed."

"Let me walk you to your room," said Marix. They walked to her room in silence. At the door she turned around to accept the kiss she had come to expect from Michael. He offered none, only a blank stare.

"What's the matter?" When she moved near him she felt him recoil at her touch.

"I've been thinking things over. With this war, I think it best we evaluate things and make sure we want to get married."

"I never said I would. You always said you wanted to. Something else is bothering you. What?"

"The things that happened to you," said Marix, who for the first time spoke truthfully. "I have to think about it for a while."

"My God, Michael. I was raped. I don't have a disease. You won't catch it from touching me. What did you expect?"

"No, that's not it," said Marix. "You should understand I need time just like you."

"It happened to me, not you!" snapped Krysti, at the same time opening the door to her room. "But if it's time you want it's time you've got!" Then Krysti slammed the door in his face.

Krysti tossed and turned most of the night, but early in the morning, she fell into a peaceful sleep and again dreamed of the elusive voice and the words "*Angel Eyes.*"

* * *

The next morning was cloudless and warm. Most everyone in Cliff Palace slept late. When Krysti managed to wrestle her body from bed, she found Justin's empty. The smell of coffee brought her to the kitchen where Sunday and Ruben were at the table eating and talking. BJ and Fitz were in the living area trying to draw Sully into conversation. She knew Sully was having bouts of depression over his wife Natasha. BJ and Fitz were always trying to find ways to lift his spirits.

Cindy had made a remarkable recovery, thanks to Dean's watchful eye. On the terrace of Cliff Palace high above the river, Kipp and Donna held hands. To their side were James, Marix, and Pickett sipping their morning coffee. The others were on the mesa with the aircraft.

Krysti approached Ruben and Sunday, who was holding baby Paul.

"May I sit here?" she asked.

"Sure," said Ruben, jumping from his chair. "Let me get you some coffee." Ruben brought the coffee back, and then took Paul from Sunday.

"I'm sorry about last night," said Krysti.

"Forget it," Ruben said. "I should apologize to you. It's just that Beau's my friend. I'd follow him into hell if he needed me."

After a moment's hesitation, she asked, "Do you think Beau is angry?"

Ruben laughed. "No. Maybe with himself. If you want to know what he's like when he's angry, ask James and Marix."

"What do you mean?"

"It's not important," said Ruben remembering what Beau had told him about the standoff with the guns when he was searching for Krysti. "They had a run in with him. He was angry then."

The doors to Cliff Palace opened letting Justin in, and when he joined them Champ glided down from the window where he had been patiently waiting and landed on the young boy's shoulder. Justin was in his swimsuit and was carrying a towel. "Have you been swimming?'" asked Krysti.

"Yes, ma'am. Beau took me this morning and taught me to do a flip off the rope. We saw a real water moccasin!" said Justin excitedly.

"You be careful."

"You're not mad I was with Beau?"

"No."

"Gee," came Justin's reply. Confused at the change of attitude, he almost forgot Beau's request, but he caught himself and turned to his mother. "Oh yeah, he said he was sorry for last night. He said he hoped he didn't embarrass anyone. Are you gonna be mad at him, Mom?"

Ruben and Sunday chuckled. Krysti smiled. "No Honey. I'm not mad at him."

"Whew!" Justin said, wiping his forehead in mock relief.

No one saw Beau the rest of the day. Late in the afternoon, everyone went to the mesa to make a final check before the mission.

A picture of contrast, the planes rested on the mesa in all their former glory. Ten space age pilots waited to fly outdated planes manufactured before they were ever born. Planes that had no right to be in the air, much less conducting the acts of war, yet ready to claim their rights in the sky. Much could be said for the tenacity of Daddy John and his determination to stick to details. No longer was it a question of whether or not they could hold their own. They had fought and won.

Ten relics of a war past, with wings spread proudly, waited for the next challenge. Yesterday's heroes, armed and ready to do battle against today's invincible forces once more.

Final checks were made. Prepared to fly by touch and skill, ten brave men climbed into their machines.

"Damn it," muttered Ruben, taking the familiar Three Musketeers candy bar suspended from the canopy, and tearing open the wrapper.

Beau had already climbed to the wing of his Mustang when he felt a tug on his pant leg. He turned to see Krysti standing beside the wing pulling at him. His smile was sheer relief to her.

"Sorry about last night. Hope I didn't make a fool of myself," he said as he bent closer to her.

Krysti shook her head and returned the smile. "I just want to wish you luck. And Beau, if you're not mad, I'd like to talk to you when you come back."

A smile filled his face, making the boyish blue eyes sparkle. "That's the best thing I've heard in a long time." He touched her face gently, and then moved back to his cockpit. He climbed in, paused and then turned to Krysti. "I'll be back. You can count on it . . . *Angel Eyes*."

Krysti couldn't believe her ears when she heard those two elusive words. The sound of them almost took her breath away. "What?" Shocked and stunned, she staggered back unable to utter another word. Instantly, she recognized the elusive voice in the dream.

"I'll be back," Beau repeated as he slid the cockpit closed.

"*Angel Eyes*," Krysti mumbled as she backed from the plane. Tears came to her eyes.

The roar of the engines filled the box canyon as they all came to life. First off the mesa was Beau. Following closely were Ruben and then the others. Sunday stood beside Krysti and together they watched as the men disappeared from view.

On the return to Cliff Palace, Krysti asked Sunday, "Does *Angel Eyes* mean anything to you?"

"That's what Beau used to call his wife Becky. I never thought I'd hear him say those words to anyone else. While he sat next to your bed, he never stopped talking to you. He always called you *Angel Eyes*," said Sunday.

"What do you mean, next to my bed?"

"Are you serious?" asked Sunday, but the response in her eyes told her Krysti knew nothing. "Beau sat beside you for two days. We couldn't drag him away. He never left your side. After he brought you back, he held your hand and clung to your necklace like it was a life preserver. He kept calling you *Angel Eyes* over and over. It was so sweet."

"But Michael found me. He found the necklace," said Krysti.

"Michael? Ha! Michael had a hard enough time finding the river," Sunday said. She shook her head. "Only Beau could have found your necklace in the river. He found you, he saved you."

"Why didn't he tell me?"

"Tell you? I thought you knew. I'm sure Beau thought you knew. Why should he say anything? Beau doesn't talk about the things he does. Having you alive was his reward. Why should he brag about finding you? Everybody knew. Well, I thought everybody knew. I think it's about time someone told you about Beau."

"Yes, tell me everything."

Sunday talked and it was like somebody had opened a floodgate of stories. In the next few hours Krysti knew all about Beau. Sunday told her all she knew about the rescue, the standoff between Marix and James, even the truth about the sniper, and the story behind *Angel Eyes*.

* * *

The *Thunder Bunnies* broke into five groups of two, with Ruben and Beau taking the lead. With the dependable radar detector on and engaged, they spread each pair at a distance of about 800 yards. Mulholland and Blackman brought up the rear of the ten old fighters.

"Mongoose to Gray Ghost, do you copy?"

"Roger, Mongoose."

"Shoot any stragglers that pull out of formation."

"Roger," came the response.

The others understood what he meant. On the previous mission James had left the formation under the pretense he was having problems with his aircraft. When they had returned, Beau personally test flew the P-40 and found it in perfect working order. Thus, the strange command needed no explanation.

They all knew their part in the raid on Bergstrom in Austin. The leaders would come in from the west and hit anything moving on the runways. Simultaneously, Fitz and BJ would approach from the south. Their main objective was to hit moving aircraft. Blackman and Mulholland would follow Beau and Ruben, eliminating any aircraft preparing for takeoff, while concentrating on parked aircraft. Pickett and Sullivan were to trail behind Fitz and BJ. Marix and James would watch for stragglers ready for flight.

After the first run, they would make passes on parked aircraft, radio towers, and munitions buildings.

The first pass went flawless, catching the base completely by surprise. Unable to find any moving aircraft on the ground, Beau dropped his tanks on a cluster of five jets near the end of one runway. The fighters erupted into a blazing inferno. As he pulled away and banked to the left, he failed to notice the approach of a Dassault Mirage from his rear—a jet with enough armament and rockets to eliminate the whole force of *Thunder Bunnies* single-handedly in a fight at Mach-1 and at 30,000 plus feet.

But the ceiling was less than 300 feet above an ever-changing terrain obstructed with buildings, shadows, hills, boulders, and trees, unlike the clear view and altitudes where it normally operated. The jet's electronic lock-on would be almost useless with the background echoes picked up from the terrain below. The Mirage was a formidable jet in any other circumstance, but now just another opponent against the old propeller driven aircraft.

Beau's radar registered the jet as it readied its rockets. Following at a distance, Ruben anticipated the craft just before it lifted skyward. He released two of his HVAARs, then pulled the stick back and executed a bank-roll to the right, so he could see the results of his shots. While in the inverted position, he saw his rockets slam into the sleek French fighter, sending a nova of fire and flame in all directions.

"That's one, Mongoose," laughed Ruben.

"Roger, Moon Shadow. I owe ya one," came Beau's reply.

Fitzhenry moved swiftly from the south, hitting a moving jet on the runway, then pursued an F-4 Phantom lifting from the same runway. Near

350 mph, the white P-51 crawled up the tail of the unsuspecting Phantom. A quick burst from the four 20-millimeter cannons finished the jet. The jet started to smoke, then burst into flames. The pilot bailed out of his crippled machine and floated slowly earthward as the F-4 crashed violently a half-mile from the end of the runway.

"Confirmed kill for White Lightning," said Warren as the machine guns from the P-40 wreaked havoc on the anchored aircraft below.

Marix came screaming past next with James not far behind. James maneuvered toward an F-86 Sabre as it slowly accelerated down the east-west runway. With all guns blasting from the P-40, the Sabre burst into flames, and James still poured lead into the disabled aircraft. A thunderous explosion followed, and he jerked the stick back and flew through the billowing smoke from the demolished fighter.

"I got one. Did you see it? Someone confirm the kill. I got one," said James excitedly.

"Kill confirmed," Sullivan said. Dropping extremely low in his Supermarine Spitfire, Sullivan lined his aircraft for a row of jets and squeezed down on the two 20-millimeter cannon and four .303 inch Browning machine guns. Sullivan was nearly over the ten jets, firing all his guns, aiming toward the end of the row, when he dropped the elevation of his aircraft. "This is for Natasha, you bastards!"

Anyone on the ground could have flung a stone in the air and hit Sully's aircraft. Men fired rifles and machine guns at the low flying aircraft.

"Pull-up Flipper! Pull-up!" ordered Beau. "You're too low!"

Smoke belched from the engine compartment and the Spitfire dropped a few feet. With all guns blazing, Sully's Spitfire grazed one of the parked jets. "Natasha!" were Sully's last words. The aircraft's right wing dipped sharply, sliced through an A-4 Skyhawk's fuselage, then broke apart in a spectacular death roll. The Spitfire cart-wheeled across the five remaining jets, engulfing them all in an orange ball of flame.

"Flipper!" screamed Ruben.

Sully was gone. With bombs and guns almost spent, Beau ordered them to return to base when the radar registered enemy aircraft. Three aircraft approached. One F-14 and two F-4s.

"Status report!" barked Beau.

"Catman, I have adequate fuel and firepower," said Pickett.

"Low on fuel, guns spent," said Marix, not using his despised call name of *Red Baron*.

"The Snake is out," lied James, "and the fuel is low."

"White Lightning, I'm used up," said Fitzhenry.

"Moon Shadow, I've got plenty," lied Ruben, anticipating his friend's heroics.

"How about you, Gray Ghost?" Beau asked, checking his radar again on the fast approaching jets.

"I'm in fair shape, mate," answered Mulholland.

"Gray Ghost, take them home. Moon Shadow, do you have enough fire power?" Beau quizzed.

"That's an affirmative."

"We'll pull them off. Ya'll head home."

"Roger. Good luck, mates. Let's go home," said Mulholland. They grouped in pairs, dropped closer to the ground, and headed for Cliff Palace.

"Moon Shadow, let's go up and let them know we're here," commanded Beau. He pointed the nose of his aircraft skyward and turned the P-51 at a 90-degree angle to his parting squadron. As he leveled out at 1000 feet and waited the arrival of the three jets, he caught the glimpse of another aircraft. What followed them was not a jet. Beau turned his head as far around in the teardrop canopy as he could, and dipped the wing. Instantly, he recognized Pick's familiar P-40 Warhawk.

"Catman, break away. Break away!" ordered Beau, but it was too late. The jets were within range. "Dive!"

The radar registered rockets fired from the F-4s but not from the F-14 Tomcat. Instantly, they dropped chaff and flares. The first rockets were easily avoided as the jets fired their heat-seeking Sparrows.

The three jets passed and as they turned to meet the three prop planes, Ruben, Beau, and Pickett pulled into a slow tight turn, drawing them in close. Ruben curled around behind one F-4 and opened up fire. He hit the jet, but only slightly damaged it before he ran out of firepower. One drew Ruben into his sights and fired a rocket. Ruben's radar detector signaled rockets fired. In one motion he dropped his chaff, banked sharply left, and rolled away. Beau and Pickett jumped the tail of the second F-14. Beau fired the last rounds of his ammunition.

Making an unexpected and foolish move, the F-14 flew through the crowded and confused aerial engagement or *furball*, and fired four rockets. A foolish move since the rockets could not differentiate between the aircraft for which they were intended. Beau and Ruben peeled away from the approaching rocket.

"Catman, dive!" Beau yelled.

The rocket scored a direct hit on Pick's old P-40 Warhawk, and the antiquated aircraft disintegrated in midair.

"Moon Shadow, I'm out of ammo," said Beau.

"Then we've got real problems, so am I."

The jets pulled in close, and the pair managed to avoid them. Beau let one F-4 draw in close behind, he slowed the Mustang, tipped the wing, and pulled into an ever-tightening turn. The unsuspecting jet continued his foolish pursuit. Beau watched his airspeed and craned his neck to watch the closing Phantom.

"That's it, baby, just a little closer," he said, trying to bring the jet closer. The Phantom began to shudder, the turbines stalled, and it went into a flat spin. The deadly plunge continued until it hit the ground and burst into flames.

The P-51s continued evasive action, but the two remaining jets clung tenaciously to their elusive quarry, refusing to fire, sensing the predicament of their enemy. Beau realized the enemy pilots knew their problem and were either going to follow them back or capture them when they ran out of fuel.

There was one way they could escape and Beau put his plan into action. "Moon Shadow, I'm out of fuel. Must land."

"You can't be—" But Ruben never finished

Beau interrupted. "You don't understand, we're out of fuel, check your gauges."

Ruben didn't understand but he guessed Beau had a reason. "You're right, Mongoose, so am I."

An unfamiliar voice, in clear English, burst into the radio. "We have out maneuvered you. You are our prisoners. Land—now!"

When the attacker spoke over the radio Beau spotted what he hoped would do the trick. Below and next to the highway were a small store and an abandoned automobile service station. "Follow me, Moon Shadow, and let's do as they say and land below. Stay close."

"Roger."

The same voice came over the radio again. "We will land behind you and take you as our prisoners until troops arrive. Do not try any tricks or we will shoot you down. We are armed and will not hesitate to kill you."

Beau landed and pulled his aircraft near the two buildings to watch the approaching jets. When he saw the direction in which they intended to land, he faced his aircraft in the same direction and slid the teardrop canopy back. Ruben pulled behind Beau, both aircraft still running. As the jets landed and rumbled past the two aircraft, Beau jumped from his cockpit and sprinted for the buildings, all the while waving his arms at Ruben to come with him.

Ruben responded and followed his old friend. "What the hell are you quittin' for? I'd rather die than surrender!"

Beau returned with his hands full of empty cans and sheet metal. He laughed and faced Ruben. "You may still get the chance to die if you wish. Hurry, grab all the scrap metal and light objects you can find and throw them in the road in front of our planes."

In understanding, a grin spread across Ruben's face. Swiftly, he grabbed everything in sight and threw it onto the road. In the midst of these irrational antics, the two men laughed like school kids playing a childish prank. Only this prank meant life or death.

"They're coming toward us," Ruben said, watching the F-14 and the F-4 as they taxied down the wide road nearing them and the debris now covering the road.

"Back into the plane and stand-up in the cockpit," yelled Beau. Sprinting to his fighter, he leaped upon the wing. "When I tell you to, cram that throttle and haul ass!"

"Roger!" answered Ruben and in full stride jumped to the wing and bounced into the cockpit.

As the two jets neared, Ruben and Beau stood in the seats of their aircraft and held their hands in the air. Both pilots in the jets slid their canopies back. The pilot of the F-4 started to exit his jet as did the pilot of the F-14. The pilot of the F-14 noticed the engines still running and remained in his jet and grabbed the switch to the radio within his helmet. From the radio blared the now familiar voice of the pilot in the F-14. "Shut your engines off."

"Now!" Beau yelled and both men dropped into the seats within their respective aircraft and shoved the throttle full forward. As they rolled past the unsuspecting captors, Beau shot them the universal three-finger salute known around the world. Ruben was brazen enough to stand in his cockpit, blow them a kiss, and then plopped back into the cockpit to face the problem at hand. Escape!

Both men weaved their aircraft back and forth as they increased their speed down the deserted four-lane highway. The radar indicated the rocket systems of the jets activated, but the safety on the limit switches prevented the firing of rockets until the jets were airborne.

"They still have guns, pull-up!" Beau barked.

"Too slow," Ruben answered.

"Moon Shadow, pull-up or let them shoot your ass off," he ordered.

The enemy pilots fired with their cannons, coming close but not hitting the old prop-driven aircraft. Instantly Ruben yanked on the stick, activated the superchargers, and dropped the left wing of the P-51, hoping to clear the road, avoid being shot down, and not crash. The cannon projectiles flew harmlessly past. The angry pilots below continued to fire in a futile outrage at the successful deception. The two Mustangs dropped and leveled out as the landing gear skipped across the soft earth once, twice, then lifted effortlessly into the air.

Banking slightly, in the darkening skies, both men watched the two enemy jets prepare to resume their pursuit. As they revved the turbines of their fighters to max, the debris spread across the highway sucked into the turbine fans. The F-4 flashed and caught fire but the F-14 was not so lucky. The fragments of metal sucked violently through the turbine busted a fuel line and the jet burst into a fountain of orange and yellow flames outlined in black smoke that billowed skyward.

"Now that was slick," Ruben said with a cocky tone in his voice. "Took out an F-14 with empty beer cans." He laughed and said, "This Bud's for you."

"Let's go home. Drop down. Let's hug the ground for a while. I just hope the others made it."

"You worry too much, Mongoose. They're probably back and waiting for us," said Ruben confidently.

The rest of the squadron had not run into the enemy, but they had problems of their own.

* * *

The six remaining planes continued toward Cliff Palace. None of them noticed as James slowed, dropped low, and unloaded his guns harmlessly into the ground. He congratulated himself at the ingeniousness of his scheme. Let Beau check his guns this time, and he would find them empty. James feared Beau more than the enemy. If he could only find a way to rid himself of Gex, his life would be much simpler. He shoved the throttle forward and closed in on the rest of the formation.

"Where did you go?" snapped Marix when he noticed his wingman approach.

"I thought I saw something on the ground. Wasn't sure so I checked it out."

"Snake, this is Gray Ghost. Don't leave again," came Mulholland's voice over the radio.

"Roger," said James, half-smiling at his successful deception.

Flames erupted from Blackman's engine. "Dead Dove, can you make it?"

"Negative. Gonna hit the silk," came Blackman's eerily calm response. They watched as he rolled the canopy back and with no sign of emotion in his voice said, "Ejection system won't work. Will execute manually."

The men watched as the P-40 Warhawk slowed to 150 mph. Orange flames flailed wildly from the engine showing Blackman clearly in the night sky. Calmly, the Choctaw Indian climbed from the cockpit as the engine froze and the nose started to dip into a dive. Blackman stood on the wing, bent back into the cockpit, and extracted his rifle, then jumped and was swallowed in the darkness below.

They traveled another fifteen minutes when BJ's engine sputtered. "Sorry guys, running out of fuel. Must have a leak. I need to land this baby before it's too late."

"I'll follow you, Black Jack," said Fitzhenry.

"No, White Lightnin'," ordered Warren as he rolled from the formation.

Not far behind came the white P-51 Mustang. "Let's find a place with gas and stop and go."

"I said, don't follow me."

"I'm going' down with ya whether ya like it or not. Besides, I could use some fuel too."

"You hard headed son . . . okay, let's get some gas." Two more pulled away. The three remaining aircraft reached the safety of Cliff Palace without incident. Only Mulholland waited for the return of the others.

* * *

Fitz and BJ hugged a nearby road hunting for a possible place with fuel. One advantage of their World War II vintage planes, the handiwork of Daddy John, was that if it became necessary, they could use regular or unleaded gas.

"You have your MasterCard," snapped Warren as he saw a building in the distance resembling a small food mart lined with gas service islands.

"What?"

"Never mind. Up ahead about a thousand yards on the left."

"Yeah, I see it."

"What if you and I stop and fill them up? Maybe get some chips and a few beers for the drive home. Make that order to go," said Warren cynically.

"Are you crazy?"

"Probably." BJ lowered the landing gear and gently touched down. He cruised near the food store and brought his fighter to a stop and killed the engine next to a gas pump. He climbed from the cockpit and stood on the wing reading the sign: "Please shut off engines before pumping gas. Pay cashier before fill-up." Warren jumped to the ground.

Fitz rolled up behind BJ's P-40 Flying Tiger and climbed from his craft. BJ took a few steps to read the name of the place, then started to laugh out loud.

"What's so funny?" asked Fitzhenry.

"This is a *Stop n Go*, how appropriate. I'll bet they never dreamed some old warplanes would actually use this place to refuel. Come on, let's see if we can find a pump and siphon some of the gas from the tanks below ground."

The store door was broken and most of the contents stolen or vandalized. Outside and behind the store, they found a barrel with a pump still attached. Warren unscrewed the two from each other and went to the front of the store where he cut the fuel line from two of the standing pumps. Fitzhenry found duct tape in the store next to the *Stop n Go*. While

Warren fabricated the new pump, Fitzhenry pilfered through the store. He found a box of doughnuts still wrapped and a bag of corn chips. In the large refrigerator room, he found a half dozen unopened hot beers scattered about. After he gathered his booty, he returned to Warren.

With the make shift pump, Warren began the tedious task of refueling both aircraft. First, he pumped some gas and sniffed for varnish. The fuel was still good and had not broken down.

Fitzhenry offered him a hot beer, which he readily accepted. He pulled the tab and took a long swig.

"Well, it's not the best, but it's the only thing we've got," he said. He reached into the bag for a handful of chips and shoved them into his mouth. The chips no longer had a crunchy texture; instead they were stale and chewy.

"Ya think they made it back?" Fitzhenry asked. He picked at the mold covered doughnuts. After little or no success trying to pinch away the mold, he finally decided to discard them in favor of the stale chips.

Warren pondered the question. "When Beau is around, you can almost count on making it back. They were low on fuel and firepower though."

An hour later with their fighters full of fuel and their stomachs full of chips and hot beer, they were ready again.

"Time to go, White Lightnin'. Better mount up. Let's go home."

A few minutes later they were in the air and safely on their way to Cliff Palace. The raid had cost them dearly and to the dead they added Sully and Pick. Lost again was Blackman. They were slowly dwindling in force.

* * *

The cabins were a mile from Concan on Ranch Road 127 where it crossed the Frio River. The cold running spring water was enticing but not to the men who operated the radio equipment or their leader, Juan Ortega. Two other groups waited patiently: one a few miles north of Garner State Park, and another eight miles east at Regan Wells.

Ortega was sure they would soon locate the transmissions. They continued to come closer and closer. It was only a matter of time before they could capture the ones who transmitted the messages. Another attack and Sharafan showed more anger than ever before. Personal reasons pushed Ortega at this game. He was determined to win.

Sharafan's last words still lingered: "If you find Beau Gex or any of the others, save them for me. I want them alive."

Ortega was determined to bring one back alive. And he was curious as to what Sharafan had waiting for the prisoner.

Chapter 12
PICNIC

Two days after Sullivan and Pickett were killed, the mood of the close-knit group was still rather tragically suppressed. Blackman had gone down in his Spitfire but no one could locate his aircraft to learn if he survived the crash. Many expected to see him reappear as he had before. He always took his rifle and deadly knife with him on every mission should he be forced to land. Those who managed to watch the descent of the Spitfire saw no parachute in the light of the flaming plane.

The fighting had been fierce, and they were lucky not to have sustained more casualties. Only Fitz and Ruben's heroics prevented more deaths.

Although they had not known each other long, Cindy took the loss of Dean, her savior, very hard. Her own cure for the loss of someone else close to her was working and helping in every activity with vehemence.

Krysti spent very little time with Marix. She had not forgotten what he said, nor had his feelings changed drastically. And she had not forgotten her promise to speak to Beau. She asked Ruben about talking to him, but he recommended she give him more time to deal with his loss of Sully. She could wait no longer.

In the two days since the air battle, Beau had not returned to Cliff Palace, but instead elected to remain in the hangar working on his ship and checking the airworthiness of the others personally. Each death seemed harder to take than the previous—and Sully was an old friend.

Ruben talked to Beau periodically and Justin managed to make him take time to swim in the river. Kipp and Donna would bring him food from Cliff Palace. Daddy John just worked quietly beside the man, watching, listening, and offering unwanted advice.

"Son, ya gotta carry on. Every one of those men knows what can happen each time they go up. You know that. Now, quit feeling sorry for yourself, and git on with your life," he said. "Now you need to head to the Jeeps. You and Ruben are due for a communications trip at noon. It's time to make contact with Duck, and it's your turn."

Beau stepped into the warmth of the sun. He knew Daddy John was right. After the trip he planned to talk to Krysti. He regretted not talking to her yet, but he had spoken to no one. With his rifle and crossbow, he made for the Jeeps. Ruben had the gear organized but was dressed in a swimsuit, attire not appropriate for the trip.

"You aren't ready," said Beau.

"Not going."

"Who is?" Beau asked.

"I am," came the soft voice from behind, "if you'll have me." Beau turned to see Krysti standing behind him. She held a picnic basket in one hand and a bottle of Daddy John's famous *Fix it All* in the other. Justin stood beside her.

"No you're not."

"Aw, come on Beau, have a heart. This beautiful lady has knocked herself out to fix you lunch. The least you could do is see what she made to eat. Hell, I'd at least do that."

"It's too dangerous."

"Please let us go with you," Krysti begged.

A smile started forming in his eyes, and he shook his head. "I know I'll regret this. All right, you win."

"Oh, boy!" shouted Justin.

"See, Krysti. I told you he wasn't such a bad guy," said Ruben.

Beau pointed his finger at his friend. "I'll have a talk with you later, but for now . . . thanks." Ruben watched the three load up the Jeep. The last items put into the rig were the rifle and the crossbow.

"Do you think you'll need those?" asked Krysti.

"I hope not," said Beau, pulling himself into the camouflaged Jeep. "But if I need them, they'll be there."

Since the communications call was to be made at a distance from Cliff Palace in order to prevent discovery, Beau suggested they go to Garner State Park, a once famous park in Texas located less than thirty miles north of Cliff Palace. They avoided the major highways, and for a short distance they skirted Highway 127 where it crossed the Frio River. Nestled near the bridge was a cluster of cabins, a resort known as Neal's Lodges, where more than sixty cabins dotted the hillside on both sides of the Frio.

As they crossed the bridge and headed the short distance north separating them from Garner State Park, they had no way of knowing the deserted tourist resort on their right was no longer deserted.

* * *

Inside the resort, thirty men and four trucks with extensive tracking gear waited patiently. They had come to locate the radio transmissions. For weeks, they had chased and hunted the elusive signal.

The sound of a vehicle passing alerted two of the men. One said, "I should tell Ortega someone has passed."

Another man shook his head. "Don't bother him. He is not happy today. Anyway, no one would pass here except our own men."

"You are right," conceded the one who first heard the vehicle passing. No one wanted to incur the wrath of Ortega, who would surely report it to his leader Sharafan.

* * *

Only the boldness of their passing saved their lives. Krysti had forgotten how much joy she derived from Beau's companionship and regretted the time they had lost because of her stubbornness. At last they could renew their friendship. The drive was refreshing and she felt safe.

They arrived in Garner State Park, without the slightest indication as to the close proximity of the enemy. They drove to a secluded area and stopped. The deserted park was both pleasant and strange. A park once filled with hundreds of festive vacationers now had only three. They ventured into Garner State Park cautiously. Beneath the peaceful shade of a massive oak they ate. The multitude of oaks conveyed a feeling of peace and safety to the unsuspecting visitors.

Justin loped off to explore the park and Krysti poured drinks; while Beau tuned the radio to make contact, he hesitated. He was about to turn the radio off and call after they ate, when he heard somebody on the frequency. He continued with the transmission. The message was brief and Duck outlined the next attack. For the first time ever Beau was careless. He was at peace, relaxed, and happy. When he finished the transmission he shut the radio off, but unlike every other time a transmission took place he did not return to Cliff Palace. Instead he walked casually over to Krysti and the picnic lunch she had prepared. He was very, very happy.

She poured a glass of wine and extended her hand to Beau. He took the drink and pulled a blanket beneath a tree, near a large boulder where he could view a vast portion of the park. He sat on the blanket and leaned against the rock. Krysti came near and sat beside him, stretched her legs, and yawned. Beau smiled and patted his leg. She accepted his invitation and laid her head in his lap and gazed happily into the peaceful trees. Gently, he rubbed her forehead with his free hand while he continued to sip the drink. The gentle motions on her temple put Krysti at ease. She was safe and nothing could harm her.

"You're beautiful when you smile," Beau said warmly.

"I'm sorry, there are so many things I didn't understand. Will you . . ."

"Forget it. Just promise to be my friend."

"I promise," said Krysti. Somehow she regretted all he wanted was her friendship. "You were there?"

"Where?"

"When I was . . . raped."

"Yes."

"Why didn't you tell me?"

"I did but it seemed to anger you. I didn't think you would want to talk about it. I figured if you ever wanted to talk about it I would be ready."

Krysti remembered the conversation and her assumption he had lied. Strange how the truth had appeared to be a lie.

"Did you see?"

"I don't think you want to know."

"No, please tell me."

"Yes, I saw. Haun was still on you when I arrived. I thought you were dead. After I removed the socks I was able to start your breathing again."

Beau was the only one to mention the socks. Now she could visualize the scene more clearly. Monroe and Lawrence had also had their way with her. Krysti covered her face.

"I'm so ashamed," she said and started to sob. "All of those men took turns with me."

"Krysti, it's okay," Beau said as he lifted her to him and held her in a tender embrace. "There's nothing you could do."

"How can you touch me after what happened?" Krysti asked, the shame evident in her voice.

Gently, he pulled her head from his chest and submerged himself deep into her green eyes and smiled softly. "Because you're very special to me, *Angel Eyes*." Then he kissed her gently on the lips. She responded and for a few minutes, they were lost in each other's gentle caress.

Krysti was happier than she could remember. She held him tightly and whispered, "Beau you mean so much to me. I know it now."

She could feel his heart beating rapidly, and she sensed a sigh from his strong chest. They clung to each other for a few minutes.

Beau sighed, "Krysti! Oh, Krysti . . . I lo—"

Yells of distress interrupted his words. Justin was in trouble! In less than a heartbeat Beau was on his feet, pulling Krysti to hers. He snatched the rifle and the crossbow from the back of the Jeep, and moved hurriedly in the direction of the screams, with Krysti close behind.

At the top of the ridge Beau stopped her. In the clearing ahead they saw Justin and two men. The men were dressed in the same army gear the invaders at the bases wore. This was closer than he wanted them. Beau cursed himself for not leaving after the radio transmissions. But it was too late now.

"My God!" whispered Krysti. "What do we do?"

"Do exactly as I say," said Beau. He pulled the rifle from his shoulder and slipped a round into the chamber. Then he took the crossbow from his shoulder and loaded it with a long steel shaft. "Do you understand what I'm about to do?"

Krysti understood his intentions were to kill the two men, "Yes."

"Go to the Jeep and start it. When you see us, be prepared to drive like crazy," said Beau. Krysti nodded that she understood. But as she turned to do as she was told, he grabbed her arm.

"One more thing. I've taken Justin with me many times. He knows what to do. Should I not be with him, leave anyway!"

"No, I won't!"

"Do as I say. These men won't be as nice as Haun. If I'm not with Justin, it's for a reason. You must leave!"

Krysti was reluctant but accepted his terms. As she moved for the vehicle, Beau found a point to his advantage. He laid the rifle to his side, then he put the crossbow to his shoulder and took careful aim on the man not holding Justin. The man was turned sideways from Beau. Carefully, he took aim behind the man's left ear. He pulled the trigger gently and sent the steel shaft on its deadly path and immediately picked up the rifle.

The soldier holding Justin heard his comrade moan in agony. For only an instant did he see a strange object protruding from his right eye. The dead soldier started to fall, and before the remaining soldier could comprehend what was happening, he heard someone yell and he looked away from Justin.

"Down!"

Instantly, Justin fell to the ground. The soldier temporarily released his hold on the small boy but before he recovered, Beau lined the man in his sights. The rifle shattered the silence of the park, and the soldier dropped in his tracks, a bullet through his heart.

Beau jumped down the ridge and met Justin halfway.

"Wow, what a shot!" the boy said excitedly.

Beau turned and held the crossbow toward him. "Can you use this if you have to?" Justin's eyes grew large. He understood and rapidly nodded his head up and down.

"Hurry, back to the Jeep!" Beau ordered. He gave the boy the loaded crossbow and slapped him on the rear.

They both started running, but no sooner did he utter the words than men swarmed from the opposite side of the clearing. They started firing their weapons at Beau and Justin. Beau stopped and turned to face the men that were now attacking them. He would need to give Krysti and Justin time to escape.

"Go!" yelled Beau. "Go!" he ordered in earnest.

At the opposite end of the clearing, Beau was instantly recognized and that recognition enabled Justin to reach safety. Juan Ortega saw Beau Gex and now concentrated his efforts to capture the man for Sharafan.

"Forget the boy!" said Ortega, barking orders. "I want the man. And I want him alive. Sharafan has unfinished business with him."

All the men, including Aziz and al-Majid, were ready to capture the lone American.

Neither did Beau hear the words nor did he see Ortega, or he would have remembered him as the painter that day at the Naval Air Station. If Beau had seen him, he would have taken careful aim and killed Ortega where he stood. He had no time to find cover so he spread himself in the dirt at the edge of the clearing. The most important thing to him was for Krysti and Justin to escape. To this, he would give his life if necessary. He studied the terrain surrounding him for a means of escape. He found none.

To his right, less than 150 feet away, Aziz moved along the edge of the trees. He did not hear the orders and was working his way to a position where he could chase down the boy.

Aziz darted across a ten-foot opening in the trees to put him clear of the man they intended to capture. Again, the rifle shattered the quiet of the once tourist-filled park. Halfway across the clearing, Aziz dropped in his tracks. Three men lay dead. Al-Majid watched his friend Aziz collapse and swore he would kill this American.

From the safety of the trees, soldiers fired with rifles and machine guns. Dirt jumped all around Beau. Two men darted across the clearing, weaving back and forth. He took careful aim on the man in the rear. When he made his cut, Beau led him slightly, squeezed the trigger, and dropped another soldier. The next man went down in the same fashion.

An hour passed and Beau continued to hold his position. It was only a matter of time before they caught him. Four men managed to circle behind, making his capture imminent. Again, gunfire ripped the ground before him. This time one of the dancing bullets knocked dirt in his eyes, temporarily blinding him. As he tried to rub the sand from his eyes, the soldiers instantly saw his predicament and immediately swarmed forward for the capture.

Beau stood and fired his rifle blindly in all directions hitting nothing but air. As the shadowy forms closed in about him, he used the empty rifle as a club. He felt the rifle impact a body. He swung in another direction and connected, all the while wondering why they didn't shoot. Then a heavy object hit his head. He tried to lift his arms, but they fell limply to his side and his legs buckled, sending him to the ground.

Still semiconscious, he felt his head jerked savagely from the ground. Revenge filled al-Majid's eyes as he brought back his machete ready to end Gex's life.

Ortega was quicker, stopping al-Majid from his actions.

"Alive!" barked Ortega. "Or have you forgotten what Sharafan demanded?"

Al-Majid lowered the machete. Beau heard the voice, but he couldn't open his eyes.

"Ah, Beau Gex. Now Sharafan will finish what he started with you," snickered Juan Ortega.

Those were the last words Beau remembered before he lost consciousness.

Chapter 13
TORTURE

Soldiers loaded Beau's limp body in an open military transport and returned to their temporary camp at Neal's Lodges resort. Once a hub for tourists, it now served as headquarters for the invaders and their leader. They would interrogate the man they captured until he revealed the location of the rebels. After all, wasn't Sharafan conducting the interrogation, or was it more accurate to call it torture. Never had a man survived the questions without revealing the information Sharafan wanted. In fact, no one had ever survived any of his sessions, except Beau, but he had not received the full treatment.

Beau regained consciousness just before they arrived at the old recreation area. He recognized it, and as they traveled down the hill toward the river he took his bearings.

Neal's Lodges were ten miles south of Garner State Park and twenty miles north of Daddy John's hideaway. The resort cabins were located to the northwest side of the bridge crossing the Frio River off old Highway 127. The main office, with a large dancing area, rested near the river. Apparently, the soldiers had waited in the cabins for days. A trailer once used for evening hayrides, lay abandoned between two empty cabins. Dozens of cabins dotted the hillside.

At the bottom of the hill they turned left and stopped at two cabins that were less than a hundred feet from the cold running waters of the Frio River. Into one of these cabins, with the number 27 above the door, Ortega and his men took Beau.

From a hill to the north of Highway 127 and east of the Frio River, a woman and a boy kept a close vigil. They were located on a ridge with an excellent view of Neal's Lodges. Just below them a dirt road skirted the ridge. A road where tourists, mainly children, would take summer hayrides along the river and were treated to drinks, watermelon and roasted marshmallows. The once joyous trail lay silent and deserted.

When the prisoner was pulled into one of the cottages on the hillside, the two distant figures returned to their vehicle and disappeared in all haste to the south.

The wooden slat floor creaked beneath the soldiers' weight. They took Beau to an old wooden table, threw him into a chair, and tied him to the ornate wooden spindles. The room was cozy and would have made a wonderful weekend retreat, were conditions different. Times had changed. Now the room was to be used for some type of grisly interrogation. Beau recognized one of the men leaving the room as the painter he had been suspicious of at the Naval Air Station in Corpus Christi during his Civilian Review Board interrogation. He was sure they waited for Sharafan.

He wondered if any of the Civilian Review Board had survived. If only he could have seen their faces when the invasion occurred. For a moment he thought of the *Five Horsemen of the Apocalypse*. Then his thoughts returned to Krysti and Justin, and he hoped they had escaped unharmed. Beau didn't need to see his captors to know what to expect. It was soon in coming.

He also recognized one of the men that watched him as one of those with Sharafan when they first encountered each other. Al-Majid stood guard, ready for Sharafan to do what only he did best. He smiled, eager for him to start.

Ortega returned with Sharafan, who held a small object no bigger than a cigar box—the same box he was unable to use in Lebanon. Sharafan laid it on the table in front of Beau. He held one of the knives taken from his prisoner. They had failed to find the identical blade Beau carried in his boot. The knife Sharafan held was the one he carried down the back of his neck. Sharafan ran his finger up and down the double-edged blade.

"Very nice."

"Yeah? Why don't you give it to me, and I'll show you how it works," Beau said casually.

Sharafan was ready to begin the questions. He prayed to Allah the answers would not come easily. Sharafan nodded to one soldier and al-Majid to untie Beau. Each held one of his arms with his palms up on the table.

"Come on, Sharafan. Not this shit again. Can't you do something different for a change?" said Beau. At least he was determined to give Sharafan a hard time before it was too late.

"Very funny. You will make it better for me. It's been a long time, but here we are again. This time, no one will save you."

Beau laughed. "You said that before. Don't you have any new lines?"

"You will reveal the location of your comrades before I finish."

"Over my dead body," snapped Beau.

"Most assuredly. We caught the boy," said Sharafan. The information almost devastated Beau, but he showed no outward sign of concern.

"I have already worked on the driver." Finally, a sign of desperation registered on Beau's face when he realized Krysti had been captured and was being tortured. "He will talk soon," Sharafan added. He did not understand the reason for the smile gradually filling Beau's face.

He? thought Beau. So Cobra had not captured Krysti. Beau said, "Kill him. It doesn't matter. Your words smell of pig dung as you do."

Instantly, Sharafan brought the back of his clenched fist across Beau's face, bringing forth a trickle of blood from his mouth. The comparison was the ultimate insult for the Syrian and Beau knew it.

"Is there anything else you would like to say?" Sharafan asked.

"Yeah. You can stick it up your ass," said Beau with a snicker.

Quick as a cat, Sharafan brought the knife down on Beau's right hand, penetrating the palm and imbedding the knife in the wood of the table. A groan of pain escaped Beau's lips and his head slumped to his chest. Sharafan grinned his approval. He pointed to the left hand of the prisoner. One soldier grabbed the hand, turned it palm up, and held it firmly against the wooden table.

Wrapping his fingers in Beau's hair, Sharafan jerked his head up viciously. "Don't pass out yet, you must watch my work." With a snap of the fingers, a guard placed a hand beneath Beau's chin and wound his fingers in the blond hair, holding the head erect.

Inside the small box were two razor-sharp knives and dozens of curious-looking, dull, black needles six inches in length. The barbs were thicker than a straight needle, and at the end was a hook similar to the point on a fishhook. They were like miniature spears.

Reaching in the box, Sharafan took out one of the small spears and admired it lovingly. "Isn't this beautiful? I have yet to use these and not have the person tell me what I want."

"Well, ya screwed up this time, asshole."

Sharafan ignored the comment. "Let's see how brave you are later. Watch this," said Sharafan as he took the needle in both hands and bent it in the middle. The small brittle shaft splintered, sending pieces in all directions. "You will see what it does soon. Oh, I almost forgot," he said gleefully as he took a razor-sharp knife from the box. He placed it to the end of the small finger on Beau's right hand. Then he peeled the skin off the end of the already half-missing finger with the expert ease of a butcher slicing steaks.

This was an action Beau fully expected and for which he was mentally prepared, refusing to give Sharafan any pleasure, so through the pain he showed no facial response.

"Unfinished business," came the sadistic remark. "And the classic battle of the Cobra and the Mongoose. I think your Rudyard Kipling underestimated the power of the Cobra."

The seemingly hopeless situation made Beau grin. He said, "Couldn't get me the last time. What makes you think you can now?"

Suddenly, Sharafan took the next digit from the small finger, nearly removing the finger from the right hand. Beau screamed out in agony. Blood started to form a small pool at the end of his hand. The final joint on the small finger still hung from a small portion of skin.

"Let's dispense with idle talk. Now let me show you these ingenious devices," said Sharafan, grabbing a half dozen of the sharp needles.

Sharafan put the hooked end against Beau's chest just below the collarbone, then shoved it deep into his chest. The small shaft continued to enter until it slid beneath the shoulder blade on his back, leaving an inch of the shaft protruding from his chest. The pain was almost unbearable. "Fascinating little things, don't you think?"

"You're a grand host," Beau grimaced, "but if it's all the same, I really need to be gettin' back. I have friends waiting for me. You know, friends? Something you don't have."

"I'm afraid I can't let you do that," Sharafan said, as he readied another needle. He placed the second needle on the right forearm and slowly worked it in and down near the joint of the elbow. Again, Beau tensed and groaned but refused to scream out in pain.

"Talk. Where are the aircraft? How can they beat us?"

"Can't tell you where, 'cause my friends would get real pissed off. As far as how . . . well, all we really needed was a couple of hang gliders, 'cause you guys really are a bunch of wimps," Beau said, trying to intentionally smile through the pain. The ploy must have worked, because a hand came crashing into his face.

"Now, we will get down to business," said Sharafan with fervor. He arranged the small spears one after the other. Carefully he chose one, and then started sliding it in the end of the index finger of the right hand, skimming along the bones and near the tendons until the needle had entered the palm.

"Watch this," Sharafan said excitedly, like a kid with a new toy. He slid the hand up the blade until it reached the hilt of the knife. Then he brought the index finger back slowly as if to touch the back of his wrist. Even Beau could not stand the pain as he yelled out. He felt the bones pop from the joints, one by one, and could sense the steel shaft splintering within. Sharafan managed to reach the wrist with the tip of the finger.

Beau lost consciousness. A pail of frigid river water thrown on his face revived him with a gasp. His right hand throbbed unmercifully, making even his temples ache.

"Don't go to sleep yet. We've just started to play. Remember the desert? The second secret?" Sharafan asked sadistically. "Tell me where your friends are, and I will tell you the other secret."

"Kiss my ass, pig shit!" Beau managed, showing anger through the pain.

His words brought immediate retaliation. A fist to his mid-section deflated his lungs, leaving him gasping for air. As his mind danced through the pain, on the edge of consciousness, he couldn't help but wonder about the secret Cobra held. What could be worse than the success of the invasion?

"Good. I would have hated for you to tell me so soon and spoil my fun. Let's continue," said Sharafan with a sadistic grin.

Next, he slid a needle slowly in the end of index finger on the left hand but this time he didn't dislocate the digit. After no response, he went on to the middle finger of the left hand. The finger next to the mutilated little finger of the right hand followed. Then came the thumb. Again, Beau lost consciousness but was revived immediately. Soon all the remaining fingers of the right hand were penetrated.

"I'm very proud of you. You will be much fun. You have gone farther than anyone else and only passed out twice. Some of those I have worked on died before this point, but they were old and feeble. Please let me know how it feels," Sharafan said, rather amused.

He placed a needle between the index and middle finger of the right hand, then slowly shoved the shaft through the center of the palm until it contacted bone in the wrist.

"How was that?"

The world was spinning around him and Beau knew he had to keep his senses, but the pain was prevailing. "F . . . fu . . . fuck you!"

"Good, you enjoyed it."

As his thoughts swam in pain, Beau probed his mind for a plan to delay the inevitable. How could he get Cobra to postpone the torture? How could he devise a means of escape against insurmountable odds?

The deadly adversary prepared another slim shaft of pain. Again, Beau lost consciousness.

* * *

The Jeep slid to a stop beneath the trees, throwing rocks and dirt over the other vehicles. Krysti and Justin jumped from the vehicle and ran for Cliff Palace.

"What are you gonna do, Mom?" asked Justin as they dashed along the narrow path toward the others.

"Get help and return for Beau," Krysti said. Fear and concern were evident in her words.

"All right!" At Cliff Palace they would find help to rescue the man Krysti knew she loved.

The first ones they found were Marix and James. After she explained the situation to both men, they refused to help saying it was too dangerous. They could not and would not help her. Krysti glared at Michael. She continued seeking help while Justin lingered outside. He stared at the two men. "Beau said never to count on you or to turn my back on you. I think you're chicken," Justin said sarcastically. Then backing up slowly and facing the two men as Beau had taught him, he followed his mother into Cliff Palace, leaving Marix and James to their own thoughts.

Inside, Krysti found Sunday and Donna. They told her Robby, Ted, and Daddy John were on the mesa working on the aircraft.

"We need Kipp, Ruben, BJ, and Fitz to rescue Beau."

Sunday shook her head. "They are hunting for deer but should be back soon."

"Not good enough. I'm going back, so you must tell them. I will leave Justin; he will be able to show you the way back."

"That's insane, you can't go alone," snapped Donna.

"She's right, you know," chimed Sunday.

"Probably, but I'm going anyway."

"You can't. It's foolish," said Sunday.

"If they catch you they will kill you," said Donna.

"I'd be dead now if it wasn't for what Beau did to Haun," Krysti said with a nervous laugh. "I owe him my life."

They tried to dissuade her but without success. She collected a rifle, loaded it, and swung it over her shoulder. She departed Cliff Palace and made her way down the trail to the vehicles, where she found Marix waiting.

"I won't let you risk your life like this," Marix said with an exhibition of concern.

"Help me or get out of the way!" Krysti snapped.

"It's foolish. You can't go."

Instantly, she slid the lever back on the M-1, allowing a live round to fill the chamber. Then she pointed the barrel at Marix. "Move!" she demanded.

He promptly obeyed the order and moved to the side, allowing her access to the Jeep. She climbed into the seat, while keeping the rifle aimed at him. With only a determination to gain Beau's freedom, she bounced down the rocky trail. She had no plans, but it didn't matter. Something would happen when she got there, she was sure of that.

* * *

The needle was about to enter the tip of the thumb on the left hand. Only the thumb and middle finger remained without a small shaft protruding from the end. The index finger of the right hand dangled in a foreign position. The knife still embedded prevented blood flowing from the wound Semiconscious Beau spoke. "When I die, you lose."

"What?" asked Sharafan. He hesitated, and pulled the shaft away.

"You'll never know," Beau mumbled.

Sharafan laid the steel needle on the table and shook the object of his torture. "Know what? Speak up."

To make his plan work Beau faked being unconscious. Sharafan shook him and again they threw water in his face to revive him. Beau coughed and acted delirious. Again, Sharafan shook him.

"I'll always be the best. I beat your jet with an old fighter. You lost. You never beat me, and you know it," Beau said using the last thing that might get him a temporary reprieve from his date with death.

Sharafan pounded his chest. "I'm the best. I have won!"

Even through the unbearable pain Beau said confidently, "But not in a jet. Get me a fighter. I can beat you even with my hands this way,"

Would Cobra take the bait? It was a wild scheme but it was his only chance, as slim as it might be. He faked unconsciousness and again they used more water. Most likely he would die for his effort. But he noticed Sharafan was upset, and Beau knew an arrogant man's ego would be his only hope. Making sure Sharafan heard, Beau mumbled, "The Cobra can't beat the Mongoose."

The idea of beating the man Sharafan hated most in the world pleased him. Destroying Beau in a jet fighter would vindicate Sharafan and his family. Those thoughts raced through his mind as he paced across the room. He grabbed Beau's blond locks and pulled his head back. "You will see who is best. I will let you die in the air before my guns. The Cobra will win." Bending over the table so their faces almost touched, he continued. "When I return, I will tell you the other secret."

Sharafan's laugh sent a chill up Beau's spine and made the hair straighten on his neck. Again, he wondered about the secret Cobra continued to dangle before him.

Standing erect, Sharafan motioned all but al-Majid to go with him, and to him, he gave an order. "Watch him till we return. We will make contact with the base, and tell them we are bringing back a prisoner." Reaching across the table, he wriggled the knife stuck through his captive's right palm. Sharafan snickered when Beau's face contorted with pain. "Do this, if he gives you any trouble."

With a laugh al-Majid nodded, all too ready to wriggle the knife. The men followed their commander from the room, leaving only al-Majid behind.

Escape lay with a bold plan to eliminate the guard. Beau let his head fall to the table. With every heartbeat, his right hand throbbed unmercifully. The groans continued as he moved his head, so his eyes could peer over the edge of the wooden table. The left hand drooped over his leg.

First, he would need to remove the needle protruding from his index finger. Secondly, he must distract al-Majid long enough to grab the knife, pull it from his palm, kill him and escape before Sharafan returned.

His hand felt heavy and unreal as he lifted it to his mouth and grasped the tiny steel shaft protruding from his index finger. With his teeth, he gripped the shaft and pulled. The pain was excruciating and the groan from his lips was not artificial. He was unable to remove the shaft. The hook was stuck on bone and tendons. He must remove it if he was to get the knife. Escape could be accomplished only if he could use his thumb and two fingers. As long as the shaft remained, he was unable to use either hand.

Beau put the tip of the index finger against the underside of the table then bent it back as far as he could stand and shoved the shaft deeper until he could discern a bulge in his palm, revealing the location of the shaft. The pain was excruciating but the shaft refused to break through the skin as he hoped. Instead, it was completely embedded in his hand. No longer did it extend from the tip of his finger. It was fully buried within the finger and palm.

Mentally, Beau marked the bulge on his palm. He had one last chance. Again he raised his heavy hand and the bulging point to his mouth. With his tongue he felt for the hardness of the shaft beneath the skin. When he located the spot he bit viciously, tasting his own blood. Beau searched with his teeth and tongue. He found the barb of the shaft, gripped it between his teeth, and pulled his hand away. Slowly he extracted the whole shaft. He spat the needle to the floor. Carefully he touched the finger to his uninjured thumb and pressed. The pain was tolerable and the finger strong enough to do what had to be done.

Al-Majid came around to Beau's left. It was time to make his move. One mistake and he would be dead. If he waited, he would be dead anyway. Beau sat up straight, moaned, and asked for water. AL-Majid came closer. Beau mumbled, and he moved within striking distance. His sadistic desires were his downfall as al-Majid, with a cold smile, reached across to wriggle the knife buried in Beau's hand.

The left knee came up with tremendous force catching al-Majid unaware and between the legs. He gasped with pain and doubled over. Beau reached around his neck, slamming his head into the table.

Instantly, Beau reached for the knife and jerked it from his hand, letting out a groan as he freed the impaled hand. He swung the knife in an arc toward the recovering guard, catching him across the neck. Al-Majid grasped the wound, staggered back, and reached for his machete, but to no avail as Beau moved forward and dealt a deathblow with the blade.

Through the excruciating pain he made his mind concentrate on only three things: running, the river, and freedom. He hesitated at the entry to the cabin. In the corner of the room was his rifle. He stuck the knife in the wall, moved swiftly to the rifle, and swung the 30.30 over his shoulder and around his neck. He tightened the strap as firmly as his left hand was capable of doing, and retrieved the knife from the wall. Quickly he darted from the cabin and ran for the river, never pausing to look back.

Like a hunted animal he bounded for the river. Quiet as a deer he made his way from stone to stone along the water's edge. Lest he be discovered, he hastened through the river giving thanks Sharafan had not touched his legs. The desperation of the situation made him temporarily oblivious to the pain in his hands, chest, and arm. A hundred yards down the river he came to a bridge. The river deepened; he hesitated, jumped into the frigid water, and let his body be pulled past the bridge and through the rushing torrent of the Frio River.

Swiftly the river carried him away. He reached with his right arm to stabilize his movements, but torrents of pain flowed from his elbow and the fingers with the small steel shafts. His heart pounded, and with every beat, he felt the shaft sticking from his chest. Still, he clung to the knife. The pain became intense, and he nearly lost consciousness. His strength faded as the cold rushing river pulled him beneath the water.

* * *

From Krysti's vantage point, on the hill across the road from the cabins, she could see the cabin into which she first saw Beau taken. Occasionally she thought she heard a scream. She continued to watch from the safety of the rocks.

Darkness settled and her mind froze when she thought Beau might have been moved and could very possibly be at another location. Fear for his safety filled her mind. She watched as three men left the cabin. They walked to another structure and disappeared inside.

Only a few minutes had passed when she decided to approach the cabin and see if Beau remained inside. Before she moved, another man dashed swiftly from the building running directly for the river. It was Beau! The way he ran, she could tell he was injured. She must help. Krysti scrambled to her feet, but before she turned, a hand reached around and clamped over her mouth. The arm of the intruder slipped around her body, holding her tight. Unable to scream, she was still able to act.

With all her strength, she brought her elbow back and into the intruder's midsection. Before he collapsed onto the rocks, Krysti spun about with her rifle ready. She would not be denied.

What she saw caught her unprepared and she lowered her rifle.
* * *

Slowly, Beau pulled his exhausted body from the cold water to the rocky riverbank. Somehow in the wild ride down the river he had managed to cling to the knife. He propped his injured body against the bank to rest before he continued the journey.

Both hands were swollen. The right hand was twice its normal size, and the only relief from the throbbing pain was to raise his hand above his head. His right hand was useless. The index finger hung in a grotesque manner. The digit of the small finger dangled . Blood still oozed from the wound and ran down his hand. With every breath his chest throbbed from the small shaft stuck deep inside. He removed the rifle from his shoulder and leaned it against the bank.

Chills and fever slowly overwhelmed him and blurred his vision. Gently he felt for the index finger and with a great deal of pain tried to set the joints back into their proper place. Trying to breathe was painful and exhausting. Toward the end of the fatiguing chore, he lost consciousness.

How long he remained unconscious he had no way of knowing, but when he came around, he continued the task of setting the finger. The hand was too swollen to put a splint around the injured digit. His teeth chattered as he cut off part of his undershirt using his knife and teeth. He raised his right hand to his mouth and grabbed the nearly severed portion of his small finger with his teeth, moved his hand to pull the finger taut, then used his knife to remove the useless dangling joint of his right hand. He spit the dead portion of his finger into the river. With portions of his shirt, he wrapped the hand to prevent it from being battered. The wrapping would enable him to keep dirt away from the wound and hopefully stop the small finger from bleeding. Shivering, he leaned against the rocks to regain his strength before he started for Cliff Palace, which now seemed so far, far away.

Beau rested and waited for his strength to return. Instead, it was replaced with fatigue, more chills, and fever. His whole body quivered. Faintly, he heard men approaching. They came closer with every passing moment. They searched for him! He crouched near the bank and waited with knife in hand. Unsuccessfully, he tried to keep his teeth from chattering and giving away his location.

A large figure dropped to the riverbed behind Beau. He heard someone mumble something. Semi-delirious, he could not comprehend the words; he only understood the danger of his position and feared he would not escape. In one motion he brought his elbow back with such force it caught the man unaware. Now was his chance, and even though the elbow with the small shaft sent a surge of pain through his body when he hit the man, he moved cat-like with the knife to finish his adversary.

The knife was near its target when two powerful hands gripped his wrist, stopping the knife from reaching its destination.

From behind, another antagonist grabbed the arm that Beau had tended and wrapped.

His determination refused to let him be defeated. He lifted both legs off the ground and kicked both of the men holding him. All three tumbled to the rocky riverbed.

Beau lost the knife. His remaining energy was exhausted. The captors yelled at him, but he was too feverish and exhausted to understand their words. Still, he rose to his knees and swung his left arm in a valiant effort to defend himself and prevent his recapture. Immediately the feeble attempt was thwarted and his arm stopped. He swung with the injured right arm, and a shadowy figure gripped the wrapped hand. Burning pain coursed through his body in his final effort. Escape was not to be. His doom was sealed. He passed out from the pain.

Chapter 14
THE HERO

With his senses returning, Beau refused to open his eyes until he absorbed his surroundings. He had been captured and was now lying in a bed with sheets. His body was stiff and sore and when he tried to move his hands, he could feel they were wrapped. Was he in a hospital? Yes, Cobra had found him and was going to fulfill the bargain. That could be the only reason he was still alive.

He opened his eyes slowly, but was shocked to find Ruben sitting beside his bed, and behind him in the corner of the room was Beau's rifle. He was back at Cliff Palace.

"Ruben?"

"Well, it's about time. While all of us are working, you spend your time lying around here sleeping. Some people just have all the luck," Ruben said with a laugh.

Raising one of his hands, Beau saw it wrapped in bandages. His friend was sporting a black eye. He tried to point with his heavily encased hand. "What happened?"

"This?" he said pointing to his own eye. "You did it, you stupid shit! I jumped down the riverbank and you leveled me. If it hadn't been for Dean, you'd have killed me. Shit, you didn't give us time to say a thing. As bad off as you were, it was us fighting to save our own skins from you. Hell, we should have shown them where ya were, and let you finish them off yourself. Ya didn't need us."

So it was Ruben who had saved him. And he said Dean, too. Had Dean returned one more time? "Dean?"

"Yeah. He found his way back again. Seems like we can't get rid of him. He found us while we were hunting. On the way back to camp, Justin told us you had been captured. So Kipp, Dean, Fitz, and me along with Justin, came hunting for ya."

"Krysti!"

"Calm down, she's fine. Tried to rescue you alone. Fitz found her just as she was about to start her own personal rescue mission. Damn, she can fight, too, nearly beat the shit outa Fitz. Woulda killed him, too, if she hadn't seen Justin first."

"How long have I been here? Where is Krysti?" he asked, while trying to sit up in bed.

Ruben forced Beau back down. "Whoa there! Not so fast, Hero. Krysti is over there," he said pointing to the side of the room where she lay on a bed curled up and sound asleep. "You've been delirious for three days. Had a hell of a fever that finally broke last night. Krysti operated on your hands. I don't need to tell you how bad they were. Just ugly as shit. Well, she made the neatest little incisions and I think she must have pulled dozens of pieces of metal from your hands. Shit, that shaft she pulled from your back must've just missed your lung. And here," said Ruben pointing to the right elbow, "she made a little incision and pulled the shaft right out the back. Those things were wicked. Cobra?"

Beau nodded his head. "His own overblown ego enabled me to escape."

"Nasty son-of-a-bitch. Since this thing happened to you, we've just kinda hung low and sent no radio messages. Not sure if they zero in on us or not, but no sense in taking chances. Jets have been spotted flying overhead and a few helicopters within a mile of Cliff Palace, but there's no way they can spot the mesa. Even if they do, they can't gain access to Cliff Palace. We post guards to the entrance at all times now."

"What about our planes?"

"Everybody worked real hard to make it appear abandoned. We put every piece of trash and debris we could find on our once beautiful runway. We piled a lot of dead trees and as much sand and dirt as we could find. We saw a helicopter start to put down, but I'm not sure if it was the dust and sand cloud or the fact there wasn't a clear place for it to land that made it pull up and leave. They returned again that night and I think they were using night vision. They came close to us but everyone was inside. They couldn't have seen anything."

"That's good," said Beau. "Smart move making it look like trash."

"Yeah, but it will take us at least two days of cleaning just so we can use it again."

Krysti was still asleep.

"How is Krysti?"

"She's a tough cookie. I have respect for the little darling. I don't think she slept for two days. You kept mumbling *Angel Eyes*, and every time you did, she'd get all teary-eyed. Sunday and Donna have been helping her take care of you."

"Thanks, Ruben." Beau felt a burning sensation on the lower part of his buttocks. "My butt hurts. What did I do?"

Ruben laughed. "Nothing. Krysti took a little of your ass to cover that God-awful looking finger."

Beau smiled and held up his right hand but the wrappings were so thick, both hands were more like boxer's gloves.

"She gave me strict orders to feed you soup when you came around. I'm gonna get some, and I'll be right back." Ruben headed for the kitchen to prepare the meal.

For what seemed only a moment, Beau watched Krysti while she slept. Ruben returned, and Beau ate the broth as ordered. He was already tired, and when he finished, Ruben left and he went back to sleep.

* * *

For three days Sharafan and his men searched the countryside for signs. He knew Beau Gex and his group were near. Again, Beau managed to escape from Cobra, but this time through trickery. It would not happen another time. He was angry with himself for allowing it to occur. More confusing was how Beau could have escaped with hands in that condition. Most men in his shape couldn't even maintain consciousness, and that was one thing Sharafan knew about.

The search had progressed to the north of where Beau had escaped: up the Frio River across to the Sabinal River, then down the Sabinal, and again up the Frio. Jets and helicopters found nothing. Sharafan continued the search with select ground troops.

His soldiers had seen signs of recent travel along the Frio River. The vehicles could have belonged to anyone, but it was a sign someone had passed through the area and done it recently. Possibly, even followed the river to set-up camp, hiding from men like Sharafan. One of his scouts had seen a log cabin at the top of a hill only a few miles away. Sharafan ordered his men to search along the river. They had night vision but could find no signs of the men they hunted.

One day Sharafan and his men came upon a cabin high on a bluff above the Frio. Sharafan had a feeling about the cabin. Ortega told him someone had been there as recently as a few weeks ago. They ransacked it but could find nothing. He knew he was close. Orders were given to Ortega to give the whole area a good search.

"Search along the river," Sharafan ordered. "See what you can find." Ortega and his men were ready to go when a call came over his radio. General Navarro demanded to speak to Sharafan.

"You must return immediately," he ordered.

Sharafan almost shook with rage. "I am close. I can feel it. Another day and I will have them."

"Three days are enough," grunted Navarro. "If you spent more time with our advance against the Americans you could do more harm to the American you hunt by completing the destruction of his own country, than by satisfying your own personal vendetta."

"I will take care of both," snapped Sharafan.

Navarro demanded, "You, Ortega, and all of his men are to return immediately."

Sharafan asked, "What is so important that we all must return?"

"The American's Blackbird is near completion. You will supervise the test. When it is ready, I want you to choose your best pilot. Then we will destroy the American space station. Also, you must protect the Blackbird from the men you so eagerly search for. They must not succeed in finding and destroying the Blackbird. Report to Kingsville, get the Blackbird, and bring it to Corpus Christi at once. When the American space station is destroyed, then you can find your American pilot."

With the space station Starburst destroyed, the Americans would have no hope of challenging the invaders. As much as he regretted it, Sharafan halted the search and started for his new destination—Kingsville and the SR-71 Blackbird.

* * *

For a week, Krysti cared for her patient, carefully nursing him. When the bandages were changed, the hands revealed single stitches where she had made a small cut to remove the broken fragments of steel or to find the wicked hook so the steel shaft could be pulled through and removed from the hand. The index finger had been carefully set in a splint. The healing process was progressing extremely fast. The right hand was only slightly swollen. The small finger was missing completely. Krysti had grafted skin from Beau's buttocks to cover the end of the missing little finger.

As part of his convalescence, Krysti would take Beau to the river. She learned a great deal about the man she had thought to be a murderer of children. During his recovery from the wounds she found him to be sensitive, kind, and humorous—everything he appeared to be when she first met him. Her heart was saddened that she had been suspicious and had wasted the chance of such premium time with the man she truly loved. He wouldn't talk about the rape, unless she wanted to, and he avoided no question she would ask.

Sunday and Ruben told Krysti the story surrounding her rescue. Kipp told her about the scene with Haun when they had first run into him at Shanghai Pete's. The stories made more sense now. She learned from Ruben how James and Marix had threatened Beau when he was attempting her rescue, which was one part about which even Beau did not go into great detail. The only reason she knew was because she asked Ruben, and he set the story straight.

Krysti found it hard to believe Marix would do such a thing. As she evaluated the information, it became clear Marix did not lie. He conveniently left out parts or did not tell the whole story to make it best benefit him. The pieces of the puzzle now fit into all their proper places. How foolish she had been, and now she intended to do whatever she could to make it up to this kind, caring, and loving man. And Justin, for lack of a better word, simply idolized Beau. That was the best sign.

One afternoon while Krysti and Beau were in her examining room, they were interrupted when Marix entered the room unannounced.

"Excuse me," he said as he entered. He glared at Beau but said to Krysti, "I'd like to talk to you in private." With an arrogant tone in his voice, he showed more confidence with Beau injured. Even if Beau tried something this time, he was ready to confront him. After all, what could a man do who had lost the use of his hands?

Beau stood and raised his covered hands in the air. "Hey, I'll go and leave you two alone." He left the room carrying a hurt little boy look in his eyes, but he also carried with him the confidence of a man who understood the situation and his position with Krysti.

"What do you want?" Krysti snapped.

"I don't want you seeing him. You're mine," ordered Marix. He was determined to have what someone else appeared to want. Even if he didn't want her in marriage, he still needed her for his physical pleasures. He had become bored with Lindy.

Aghast at the brazen statement, and finding it hard to comprehend how Marix had the audacity to approach her after what he had done, her true feelings almost slipped out of her mouth, but instead she said, "I belong to no one, especially you. You're the one who wanted time, or have you forgotten."

"I've changed my mind."

With Beau around, he had become jealous: jealousy rising to the point he was willing to overlook the fact Krysti had been raped, as long as he could take her away from Beau. Since there was no one else in the camp for him except Lindy, he would take Krysti back. He was willing to try and put from his mind what had happened to her—a consideration he thought was big of him, since he reasoned most men would not be able to put behind them what she had done. "He has nothing to offer you. I have everything."

Krysti recalled Justin's words, remembering what he had said about Michael and Beau. Her son had been right all along.

"What I need, you can't give me," she snapped. "And you lied!"

"I never lied!"

Krysti laughed and placed her hands on her hips. "Call it a trickery of words, a convenient omission, or whatever else you want. To put it simply, I don't trust you. Nor do I feel safe with you." Contentedly she smiled. "Beau can give me more than you can ever give: kindness, love and tenderness. If you were only half the man he is you might be worth something, but I could never be interested in you Michael, ever!"

Marix failed to control his anger and he let it get the best of him.

"Haun didn't give you enough," he snickered, sarcastically piercing through her raw emotions of the gang rape. "You want to let Beau Gex have his way with you too."

"That's what terrifies me about you, Michael. You are so many different people I never know who I'm talking to or who will respond to me. Get out!" she fumed, angered at accusations that she might have wanted Haun's advances. "Go!" she yelled.

Defiantly they faced off, neither giving an inch to the other. They stood confronting each other when the door unexpectedly opened.

In stepped Beau. "Did you need anything?"

"No, Michael was just leaving." Marix took himself from the room, intentionally bumping Beau as he departed. On the receiving end, Beau refused to give ground.

"Are you okay?" he asked, sincerely concerned. He watched as tears formed in her eyes.

"Haun, why did it happen?" she asked, holding back the tears as she remembered the terrible event: the event in which she had mistakenly thought Michael to be her savior. She trembled with anger and the memories of being defiled at the hands of Haun and his hideous cohorts.

"It's okay," Beau whispered, wrapping his heavily bandaged hands over her small shoulders. "I'm here."

The green eyes gazed up into his smiling face and she wiped the tears away. "You are an amazing man, Mr. Beau Gex."

With a smile he said, "Beau. My friends call me Beau."

She laughed and wiped the tears from her eyes. "How did you get into the room with those?" she asked, touching his hands.

He pulled away, turned sideways, and rubbed his forearms together. "I heard you yell at him, and I thought I oughta come on back in."

Stretching on her toes, she reached up and kissed Beau on the cheek. "You're so sweet and thoughtful. Come, let me take the bandages off. Today, I'm going to remove the stitches."

Soon the bandages were removed and the stitches plucked from the hands one by one. Krysti was careful with the index finger of the right hand. After she removed the stitches, she fabricated a small splint the length of the finger and into the palm. Then she wrapped the injured finger to limit its movement. Only a slight bump remained of the small finger, and it was healing rapidly. All the stitches except four were removed. The injured area was again wrapped with gauze.

"Kinda ugly, huh?" asked Beau.

She laughed. "I've seen worse. But, I must say you heal quickly. When I fixed your dislocated finger, I checked the tendons. They were stretched but I believe the finger will be functional. You need to work on it."

Krysti tossed him a small, black rubber ball like the ones used in hand ball, which he snatched in mid-air with his left hand.

"After the splint is removed, use this every day to build strength in the finger and to shrink the tendons."

"Yes, Doctor," said Beau. He watched his left hand as he squeezed the ball, testing the hand he had not used for more than a week. "Let me tell you, this feels a hell of a lot better than it did a week ago."

"You look better, too. Let me see that hand," Krysti said. She took it and examined each finger.

Playfully, Beau pulled her near and kissed her forehead. "Thanks, Doc."

Krysti blushed. "Be a good patient and let me finish."

After she checked him over, Beau walked to the mesa. On the way, he worked the two good fingers and the thumb on his right hand, surprised at how much strength he still had. She had done a spectacular job of removing the steel splinters and mending him. With his left hand, he grabbed a small branch stretching across the trail and broke it from the bush. The left hand, although stiff and sore, felt fine.

Marix watched Beau walk along the narrow trail of the mesa, and hurried along the same trail at a distance, waiting to confront him alone. Seeing an opportunity, he hurried to catch up.

"I want you to stay away from Krysti!" Marix ordered.

Beau turned to face him. Disgust filled his face. "I think we've already had this conversation. Once was enough. Go play with yourself, Marix."

Marix felt bold. Beau had none of his weapons and his hands were injured. He knew from the conversation of the others what had happened. Marix crouched in the manner of hand-to-hand combat. "I will teach you some manners now. You think you can stop me?" Then, he moved toward Beau.

Shaking his head like the situation was only a minor nuisance, Beau waited until Marix was within range. Marix swung with his right hand, which he easily dodged. Then Beau swung his left hand to Marix's groin area, firmly grasping him by his balls. A slight groan came from the helpless man's lips. "Let's get something straight," Beau said, pulling up and slightly twisting Marix's manhood. He held Marix's balls and then paused for effect. "You're a pain in the ass. Now my hands are really bothering me or I would've already castrated ya." He gave a little twist and Marix groaned. "If ya don't believe me, just ask ol' Haun. He's a ball-less wonder much like you. Get the drift?"

The vision of Haun returned to Marix, and he let out an affirmative groan. "Uh, huh."

Good boy. One more thing Marix; don't fuck with me anymore!" Beau gave Marix an added squeeze, and released him. Without waiting, Marix backed away, turned and promptly retraced his steps to Cliff Palace.

A chuckle from behind made Beau turn around. Coming up the trail were Schmitt and Daddy John.

"Now, I'd say you got the man's attention," laughed Schmitt.

"Well, the boy's not as stupid as I thought. I didn't think he knew when to quit pressing, but he sure proved me wrong. He does know when to back down. Now doesn't he?" said Daddy John, chuckling to Robby.

"Sorry ya'll saw that."

"Hell, Marix's been asking for it," said Schmitt.

"I wouldn't have wanted to miss that for the world," said Daddy John. "I'll say this for you, Beau, you can really squeeze an answer from a guy when you want." They all started to laugh. "What say we go clean up and eat?"

After dinner, Cliff Palace quieted down early. Somewhere outside along the path of the mesa walked three couples, Donna and Kipp, Fitz and Tracy, and Dean and Cindy.

Ruben and Beau played with Little Ruben while Krysti and Sunday exchanged motherly advice and laughed at the two men's childish antics.

At a secret place on the river Marix found Lindy.

Everyone had settled in for the evening. Donna and Kipp delayed their eventual return to Cliff Palace. Finally, Sunday, Ruben, and their son turned in for the evening. Beau and Krysti walked to the ledge of Cliff Palace and gazed into the small peaceful canyon. She stood next to him holding his arm.

"It's so beautiful," she said.

"Yes, it is. Gonna be a full moon soon," he said peering up to the starlit sky.

"Moon Shadow?" queried Krysti.

"Yes," he said and melted into her eyes. "How about we test your handiwork," he said extending his hand in her direction. "Take my hand . . . walk with me."

She took his hand and together they strolled along the narrow trail to the top of the ridge over Cliff Palace. From the south came a brisk breeze, stirring the trees in the cool night air. Not far away, the Frio could be heard rushing across the rocks on its way to the Gulf of Mexico.

"In the past I was so unfair to you, Beau. You've come to mean more to me than I thought possible. But there is something I haven't told you. Something I must tell you now."

"You're upset. What could be so bad?"

No longer could she face him as she dropped her head in the darkness. "I'm pregnant. The baby is Michael's. Please, don't hate me."

Krysti shivered and noticed Beau's grip on her hand never faltered. He moved behind her to block the breeze and wrapped his arms about her. She moved her fingers softly up and down his strong arms. The gentle touch and sweet smell of Krysti's hair excited him. "As long as I have you nothing else matters," Beau said sincerely. "The baby is yours and that is all that matters to me. When the baby is born, she will be mine."

A smile of relief combined with contentment revealed her happiness. "She?"

Bending down, he kissed her on the neck. "I always wanted a little girl." She turned to meet his mouth and melted into his arms. Together they clung and kissed with a passion they could avoid no longer.

Gently pulling Krysti's head away with his hands, Beau kissed her on the forehead and embraced her to him as he whispered in her ear, "I love you, *Angel Eyes* . . . more than you can imagine. But—"

"What, Beau?" she asked, gazing into his face with tears of happiness.

"I have nothing to give you. My past will haunt me the rest of my life," Beau said dejectedly.

Krysti laughed and pulled away, momentarily thinking of Marix and what he had offered. "My precious sweetheart. You have everything. And as far as your past is concerned . . . *we* will handle whatever comes—*together*. Beau, what I want can't be measured with the material things you can give me. You have given me all I need. Everything I want is here," she said, touching the left side of his chest. Tears came to her eyes and ran down her cheeks, glistening in the night-light. "You're my hero. I love you, Beau."

Again, they became lost in each other's arms. There was no war, no hate, only love and peace. The love they felt for each other, the peace and tranquility of the moment, consumed them.

Together they remained in each other's embrace. At the sound of Kipp and Donna approaching, they hid in the shadows, until the pair disappeared down the trail to Cliff Palace. No one was near. The night was theirs.

"Can we be alone, just you and I tonight?" asked Krysti.

"Yes. Come with me," Beau said

Taking Krysti's hand, he led her to the old cabin where they had first met Daddy John. Inside, Beau walked to the small oak table where he lit two candles standing in identical brass holders. Krysti moved across the room and sat on the edge of the oversized bed. A moment later, Beau moved across the room and sat beside her. With his left hand, he gently brushed the auburn hair from her face, then slid his right hand behind her head, and pulled her willingly to him, where their parted lips met. Krysti pulled Beau to her, falling back onto the bed. He kissed her softly on the face, the neck, and below the chin, all the while rubbing her side and slowly moving his hand to the small of her back.

Krysti could resist no longer. "I want you," she whispered.

To her delight Beau responded softly, "I thought I would never hear you say those words to me."

Within the sanctity of the room, they made love as shadows danced on the walls. His touch was as tender and gentle as his kiss. She wound her fingers in the long locks of his blond hair as he ran his hand down her smooth bare back. Never had he been so loved. If there was a Heaven—this was it. He had never felt so complete.

Each marveled at the touch of the other. They discovered each other in a way they had not imagined possible. Never had Krysti felt this way. He touched her and loved her like no one had ever done.

Never before had Krysti been kissed and held so passionately with such tenderness and love. A man with his strength and size could have held her helpless in his grasp if he demanded. Instead she received soft and gentle caresses that were so unexpected from a man of such power. Lovingly, he fulfilled her every need and desire.

Darkness cloaked the old log cabin, securing the two from the outside world with its war and problems. Sealed safely inside were the discoveries of new love and dreams of the future. There they remained until the new day dawned.

What cruel twists the future held.

Chapter 15
TO FIND A BLACKBIRD!

The week after the removal of the bandages on Beau's injured hands showed a marked contrast in Krysti and Beau toward each other. The two acted like high school sweethearts, and none were happier with what they saw than Ruben and Sunday. Peace prevailed over Cliff Palace for all but two people: James and Marix.

The peace and tranquility were about to end. Early one morning in the middle of June, they finally felt safe enough to contact General Waddle. What they received from him was an urgent request. Large numbers of fighters were being stockpiled at the air base in Corpus Christi.

More frightening was the information that the Coalition had made the captured SR-71 flight ready. Now the same jet Beau had flown was a symbol of potential defeat for America. The enemy had not even tried to conceal their plans. After all what could catch the Blackbird? Nothing. What could defeat the Blackbird? Nothing. The Blackbird could outrun any fighter and any rocket.

Rumors abounded that the Coalition had already test flown the SR-71. Men were prepared to fly the Blackbird on a suicide mission to destroy the nearly completed laser system installed in the space station Starburst. The *Aurora Project* was now a dismal sign of ultimate defeat for the United States. The northern remnants of the United States forces tried to push through but without success. Duck Waddle had tried to raise Admiral Garret's small fighting force but failed, and came to the conclusion they had been defeated by the invading forces.

The request was for one more mission—an urgent mission that Duck devised. He wanted their renegade group of antiquated fighters to destroy the SR-71 before it could successfully launch into space and destroy the space station Starburst. Time was a critical factor because the enemy was nearing the end of preparations and they were about ready to send out the Blackbird.

"We are not strong enough for a counter attack. They have a defensive line we cannot penetrate," Duck said. "If they launch the Blackbird, they will destroy the space station. *Aurora* is almost complete. All we need is time. Without Starburst, America's fate is sealed. Your men are the only ones even capable of an attack. Our future depends on you destroying the SR-71. It must be destroyed *at all costs*." Those were the last words spoken as Duck signed off.

The plan was suicidal. The odds for success were slim, and those for survival even less. Duck explained if they did nothing at all, the result would be the same as trying and failing. Eventually, the United States would be defeated and they would be captured.

The old relics, the *Devil's Angels,* as many in the close-knit group referred to them, were to destroy the SR-71. Immediately they started preparations for the seemingly suicidal mission. But this time the Coalition would be ready for Beau and his renegade band of old warbirds.

Beau saw little chance of survival and wondered who, if any, would survive. Yet, what other choice did they have? They discussed the plan of attack, deciding to leave in two nights. The attack would take place under the added protection of darkness. A full moon would help locate the target, but would also make them more visible to the enemy. As dangerous as it might be, they knew a daytime raid would be expected and even more suicidal.

The group worked furiously making preparations for the mission. The last Spitfire was readied for Blackman. Tracy did her work and decorated the side of the plane with the familiar cartoon of the "Dead Dove." Lindy earnestly did all she could to help.

No one noticed the sincere effort Larry James put forth. He loaded the belts soon to be mounted for the machine guns on the fighters. Extra belts of 20-millimeter ammunition lay in front of the sleek black P-51 with the insignia of a Mongoose. The belts were loaded and ready. It was impossible to notice the oversized rounds mounted part way down. When the guns reached those specific rounds, they would jam, making the guns of the fighter useless.

Carefully, James planned the death of his enemy, Beau Gex. The treachery would never be discovered. With his plane readied and his cowardly task accomplished, James moved away from the area. He sought out Marix, who was putting the final touches on his P-38.

Breathless, Larry pulled Marix to the side. "Beau's finished! Our problems are over. He'll never bother us again!"

"What do you mean?" asked Marix as he wiped the grease from his hands.

"I fixed his ammo belts so the guns will jam. He's not coming back on this one," James said, his body trembling with excited anticipation.

"That's murder!" Marix retorted, shocked at James' actions.

"Murder? Beau would have let Kipp shoot me down. That's murder. I'm just protecting myself. No! I'm protecting the others too," James rationalized. "Besides, he's crazy to be taking us up against them." Then Larry laughed almost hysterically. "He won't ever do it again."

Marix hesitated. "I don't know about this."

"You don't know?" he asked incredulously. "Don't you remember when we were trying to find Krysti? How he threatened to kill us for no reason? I tell you, he's crazy. We tried to save Krysti, and he wanted to kill us."

Marix digested the information and realized this was a chance to rid himself of his challenger once and for all. Then again, he had nothing to do with James's actions, so they couldn't blame him. And Krysti would be his.

Anger in James' voice was evident when he became annoyed at Marix's reluctance to answer. "I'm going back to Cliff Palace. Just think about it for a while."

"Yes . . . I will," said Marix. Larry turned and slithered away on the narrow trail.

Marix thought long and hard. Maybe he should warn Beau. No. Larry was right. Beau did seem possessed. He was not like any normal man. He had tried to murder Larry. Wasn't it Beau who had taken Krysti from him? He should rightfully be leading the group. And he wanted her back. Beau was a threat to the whole group. Yes, Larry was doing the proper thing. Beau should be done away with. With him gone, Marix would be the leader, and he was sane enough to stop the crazy raids. Marix would be their savior. After all, Beau had been responsible for the deaths of Pickett, Deberg, and Sullivan. It was Marix's obligation to assure the safety of the group before others died. Beau should be eliminated!

Before he returned to Cliff Palace, Marix glanced toward Beau's sleek P-51 Mustang. He hesitated. Fear gripped him for a moment. Beau had saved his life on three separate occasions. What if Beau was shot down and he was in a situation like before? Gex always seemed to show up at the last moment. Suppose someone was in trouble when Beau's guns jammed. However, had Marix not improved tremendously in his own P-38? He felt confident enough in his own ability. He would not need Beau's assistance.

Fear for his own life almost made him warn Beau. In the end, it was his desire to be leader, have Krysti, and see Beau dead that justified James' actions to him. Even if the sabotage were discovered, no one would suspect him. A sly grin crossed his face as he finished the work. A few minutes later, he followed Larry's path, a path of certain death.

Oblivious to the cowardly actions of a few of their own, the others continued their work on the aircraft.

Schmitt worked rapidly on Moon Shadow preparing her for her final mission. "Ruben, you have any ammo belts loaded and ready?"

"Not yet. See if Daddy John has any loaded." Schmitt turned and spied the loaded and waiting belts located near Beau's ship. He approached Beau, who was making a final check of his guns. "Hey, Beau, ya need help loading the belts?"

Beau glanced in the direction of the waiting ammunition belts. "Someone went to a lot of work for nothing. I loaded mine and mounted them a few days ago. I kinda like to load mine personally."

"You mind if I use them on Moon Shadow?" Schmitt asked, jerking a thumb in the direction of Ruben's aircraft. He always called each plane by the name the pilots used when they were in the air.

Beau waved to Robby. "Sure, use them all if you need them. Just make sure he's loaded to the hilt. We're gonna need all we can get."

Schmitt formed an okay sign with his finger and thumb. "You got it. He'll be ready when I'm finished."

Carefully, Robby loaded Moon Shadow with the sabotaged ammunition belts, oblivious to the deadly results of his actions. Intended for Beau, instead the belts of useless ammunition were given to Ruben.

The work was finished early and as usual none of the pilots talked about the mission. The time was for celebration. For some, it would be their last.

Unknown to anyone, Marix demanded Lindy's attention. They found each other at the same place they had always met for their illicit rendezvous. The only difference was when Marix tried to embrace her she pushed him away gently.

"What's wrong?"

Lindy tried to smile. "I believe there is more to love and life than you have to offer. I want more and you can't provide me with what I need. I'm sorry but you lack tenderness and affection."

Marix huffed. "You can't tell me you didn't like it."

"Oh, I liked it for what it was but I know now it's not the way it should be."

Angrily he snorted. "I suppose you want Beau."

She sighed and frowned at Marix. "Beau is a good man. He loves Krysti and I respect that. I hope I can find half of what Krysti has found in Beau."

"You bitch."

With a laugh Lindy said, "I think it's time you know that I'm only fifteen."

Like a man staggered by a punch, Marix's legs buckled and he managed to stammer, "You said you were nineteen." He caught himself and spat out, "You lying bitch."

A mischievous laugh escaped her lips. "We aren't too much different from each other you and I. I have listened to you and watched you and I hope I never become like you. But in a way I am like you. I lie by omission, yes. But I told you the truth. I said I was going on twenty, and in your mind you heard I was nineteen." Lindy laughed uncontrollably.

"And next year I will be going on twenty." She turned and started to walk away from Marix but continued to talk as she went. "Then the year after that I will still be going on twenty, and the year after that."

Marix could no longer hear Lindy as she disappeared into the darkness.

* * *

In Cliff Palace few noticed Lindy when she came into the door and then went into the kitchen to get a drink of water. Only Krysti noticed her singing as she too was going to the kitchen for a few things. Leaning against the kitchen counter, Lindy chugged the water. She was still humming.

Krysti smiled. "You sure seem happy, young lady."

Pausing from the drink Lindy said, "Yes I am. I want to thank you for everything you have done for me. I truly wish you and Beau the very best life can give you."

Sincerely, Krysti said, "Thank you Lindy. I hope the best for you."

For a moment she hesitated. "I'm not a very good girl. There are things I have done I think you should know about but I also don't think I should tell you, but I would like to try and be a better person." She thought about telling Krysti about James, Marix, and Deberg. But she had deceived them. No, she should say nothing of her encounters with those men.

"Lindy, keep your secrets. The fact you are telling me this is all that counts from this moment forward."

"I want you to know that I'm really only fifteen and not nineteen like everyone else thinks."

Also with a glass of water in her hand, Krysti held it high almost like a toast. "Good for you, Lindy." They touched glasses.

"You don't act surprised," said Lindy.

"I'm not."

"Did my mother tell you?"

"No. She happened to mention you started school early and that next year you would be a junior. The math was simple from there."

"Of course. Well, I feel better now."

"And so do I, Lindy. So do I. You are going to be just fine now."

Together they walked into the living area, more like a mother and daughter than friends.

Early in the evening, Donna disappeared with Kipp. Soon after, Tracy and Fitz followed, their relationship progressing unusually fast. Also, not surprisingly, a relationship other than friendship had developed between Dean and Cindy.

James approached Lindy, but she politely refused and told him there would be no more between them. Krysti watched. After James walked away Lindy caught Krysti's eye. They both smiled knowingly at each other.

Ruben spent his evening with Sunday and little Paul. They walked along the river for a while, then disappeared into the privacy of their room to enjoy each other's company for the night.

In the living area of Cliff Palace, Daddy John, Robby, and Ted were spinning yarns from the past while their enchanted audience of Justin, BJ, Dean, and Cindy listened to every word. Lindy took time to be a little girl and enjoy the stories with the others. And as usual Champ, now full grown with beautiful greys in his feathers and a pale belly, was perched on Justin's shoulder and actually appeared like he was also listening to the stories, although he took time to rub Justin's neck and get his expected surprise.

During one of those stories, Krysti and Beau eluded the attention of those gathered. A short time later found them near the log cabin in which they had sealed their personal promise of love and devotion.

Together they stood on the rock ridge overlooking the serene canyon and the river below. In the distance, they spied Fitz and Tracy embracing. Moon shadows surrounded them, watching their secret passions.

A time for love and building, not for war and destruction. In the heat of war some found time for love. Beau and Krysti held hands as they watched the couple in the distance. Krysti lifted his hand with both of hers and softly kissed the back of his nearly healed right hand.

"I love you," she whispered.

The soft passionate green eyes made his heart race as he responded. "I love you, Krysti."

Tears filled her eyes. "I was so confused; I doubted you for so long. Forgive me."

"How could I do otherwise?" They smiled at each other, and embraced.

Softly Krysti asked, "When you fly are you ever afraid?"

Beau pulled away, and with a half-smile creasing his lips said, "Yes, I feel fear. The fear prepares me and protects me."

"How can you keep doing it if you feel fear?"

"You have to understand it's not something I look forward to. It's something that must be done." Then he pointed to Fitz in the distance. "He's the best pilot of the bunch. He still knows no fear and fights with natural ability. What I'm trying to say is, once I climb into the cockpit and start the engine, the fear disappears. It's hard to tell you what happens to me up there, but when I leave the ground, I'm one with my aircraft. I can't be beaten. I truly feel I am unbeatable. A strange thing happens to me. It's like I can sense the next move of the other aircraft before it happens. Defeat and fear never enter my mind once I'm in the air. I think only of victory."

"Would you be mad if I told you I'm afraid?"

Again, he pulled her near and kissed her soft responsive lips. "No, I wouldn't be mad," he said, and then added confidently, "I can also tell you I will return. I promise!" He gazed lazily at the stars and squeezed her hand.

"What are you thinking?"

"Remember the mission I flew after we first met? Now I must destroy that same aircraft. When I flew the Blackbird, I felt alive. Like I could touch the stars. I've always loved flying more than anything."

"Oh?"

Beau pulled Krysti's hands to his chest and smiled down on her. "I can't explain how I feel inside. But as much as I love it . . . I love you more." He saw the sparkle in her eyes. "Don't be afraid. You will never be alone. I will be there when you need me. I will protect you and keep you from harm. And love you always!" Softly he kissed both of her hands.

"Another time, another place, we might be planning a life together . . . thinking of marriage. I'm sorry, that was presumptuous on my part," Krysti said and turned her head down.

"No, I don't think so," Beau answered. He lifted her head and smiled into her eyes. "The time and the place are in the heart."

With those words he reached to the ring hanging from his neck, and with a jerk broke the leather cord. He tossed the cord to the side, then took her left hand and slid the ring on her finger. A gift from a woman halfway around the world was now a perfect match around Krysti's ring finger.

Krysti held her hand in front of her face. "It's beautiful."

"The inscription reads: Love Eternal," Beau said. "With this I pledge my love. To take away your fears. To be there always."

Krysti smiled and a tear fell from her eye. She reached around her neck and removed the necklace her father had given her. Engraved on the cross were the words, "With all my love."

"I want you to have this." Krysti took the necklace in both her hands and reached up as he bent over. She fastened it about his neck. "I will always love you. You've shown me love is real. Let me take away the pain and make you happy when you're sad."

Feeling at peace Beau said, "You'll never be alone anymore. I will love you forever and ever."

"You make me feel special," Krysti said and her eyes sparkled. "You've given me something I never thought I would have. No matter what you do, or where you go, I will always be with you." Tears of happiness rolled down her cheeks. "I've never been loved like this. It's the way I always dreamed it would be! Tonight, I want to be with you."

This time she pulled him to her and kissed him passionately about the face and neck. "I will always love you."

They disappeared into their private haven, the old log cabin, to spend their final night together.

* * *

The next day found most of the group performing final checks. While Beau looked over a few things in preparation for the mission that was now only a few hours away, Krysti and Justin brought down two baskets full of sandwiches and drinks.

Champ now ventured outside and was perched in his normal position on top of Justin's shoulder. The little mockingbird rubbed its beak against Justin's neck. Almost mechanically, Justin reached in his shirt pocket for one of the many breadcrumbs he kept, and held it toward his little feathered friend. Each time Champ would peck at it and then take it and eat the tiny morsel.

Everyone took a moment from their work to get a sandwich and a drink. Ruben, Sunday, Beau, Krysti, and Justin were talking and eating when a nearby bird singing a beautiful song distracted them. But none of them were as interested in the song the female mockingbird sang as Champ. The bird jumped up and down on Justin's shoulder and was obviously excited. Somehow the little pet bird managed to sing to the intruder clinging to a low branch of a nearby tree.

Now the other mockingbird seemed just as interested in Champ as Champ was in her. Fear of creatures and humans kept the other bird away although now both birds squawked and screamed at each other incessantly. It was obvious both birds were trying to invite the other over for a visit. The intruder would not budge. Champ was like a pinball in a game gone wild as he bounced all around. Jumping to the table, he looked to Justin and then to the mockingbird in the tree, as though asking Justin to follow. And then Champ flew into the tree and landed next to the other mockingbird. They made noises and Champ fluffed his wings and raised and lowered them as though to impress his new little lady friend.

"Do you think that's a girlfriend?" Justin asked.

"No," said Beau. "They can't mate for a year. But he obviously is very interested."

"Maybe not his girlfriend yet," laughed Ruben.

Champ flew down to the table and appeared to be begging the other bird to follow, but she wouldn't budge. This went on for half an hour. Frustrated and tired, Champ was thoroughly confused. But each time he returned to the mockingbird in the tree he stayed a little longer.

"Poor bird," said Krysti. "He doesn't know what to do."

"Yeah," said Justin. "He doesn't know whether to stay with me or go with her." He turned to his mother. "What do I do, Mom? I want to keep Champ but he needs to go off and be with his kind and have his own family."

For a moment Krysti was stunned. She turned to Beau who smiled and nodded. Then she turned to her son, with tears in her eyes. "Justin, you need to do what is in your heart. Whatever you decide will be right."

This time Champ did not land on Justin's shoulder but rather landed on the table in front of him and looked straight up into the boy's face almost pleading for help.

Justin pointed to the tree and motioned with his hand. "Go Champ. Go. It's time to go away."

Turning to look at the other mockingbird, Champ appeared to be thinking. He turned back to Justin, turned his head to the boy, and spread his wings almost as if to say he was sorry. The bird stood as motionless as a statue as Justin tried to tell him to leave and the other mockingbird begged him to return. Finally, Champ flew to the tree and perched next to the other bird. The female mockingbird took off. Champ spread his wings ready to fly but he hesitated and turned his head to Justin.

"Goodbye Champ," said Justin.

Champ squawked, and took off after his new feathered friend.

* * *

Late in the afternoon Daddy John, Robby, and the others made their final checks before the mission. Beau and Ruben would approach the Naval Air Station from the land side to the south while Mulholland and Blackman would hit simultaneously from the west. Fitzhenry and Warren were to cross the bay and come in from the east. Marix and James would approach from the north. The success of the mission depended on a swift accurate attack. On the first run, they were to take out any combat ready jets on the runways. At the same time, they were to watch for the SR-71. If the Blackbird was not located after the initial pass, each man had been given a specified hangar to hit. If all worked as planned, the Blackbird might be destroyed while it lay at rest in one of the hangars. To assure success, they had to spot the Blackbird on the first pass.

With the briefing complete, the men drew themselves within the antiquated planes. Donna and Tracy waved a tearful farewell as they watched Kipp and Fitz each close their canopy and start their engines.

What astonished and pleased everyone was when the mighty Blackman squeezed Cindy gently and kissed her passionately, and she responded with the same for him. Content with herself now, Lindy watched and smiled.

Ruben kissed Sunday and Paul. "Now, don't you worry. Everything will be just fine. I love ya."

"Ruben, please be careful."

"Hey, I got Beau watching over me. What could go wrong?"

"I love you," said Sunday.

Ruben climbed into the high sheen black P-51 Mustang with the words "Moon Shadow" emblazoned on the side. Inside he found the familiar candy bar he expected. He made short work of it, and wondered if Beau would ever run out of the treats.

Tears rolled down Krysti's cheeks as she bid Beau farewell. With his hand, he lifted her head. "Chin up girl. I wanta see a smile." The words brought a temporary smile to her face. "I won't lose you now, *Angel Eyes*."

"I love you," Krysti said, her voice cracking.

Beau bent over and kissed her on the forehead. "And I, you." The wing groaned with the weight of his body as he climbed into the cockpit.

Krysti yelled to Beau. "Promise me you'll come back!"

Holding his hand in the air and giving the thumbs up, he smiled and responded. "I promise!"

Soon all the engines were rumbling and ready for the seemingly impossible mission. One at a time they dropped from the mesa, lifted up in the twilight sky, and disappeared for the last time.

If all went according to plan, they would be on the return trip to Cliff Palace beneath a full moon.

* * *

The full moon brightened the night sky, while the fighters flew slow and low, clinging to their own shadows. The Bell radar detectors were in place. More than once, they had given prior warning of the enemy's approach. The FM radios and scanners were set and all the chaff tubes and flares filled.

Beau scanned the peaceful, starlit skies from within the teardrop canopy of the P-51 as the group warily approached the target. How quickly things had changed. Less than six months earlier, he had taken the SR-71 on a mission, at a time when the base was a peaceful place of military activities. Now a foreign invader controlled the Naval Air Station, one of the most vital bases in the Northern Hemisphere: the military base where they had trained and worked—a base they were now ordered to attack. The same military facility that contained the same SR-71 now prepared to strike a deathblow to end the United States' slim hopes of victory. The Blackbird had to be destroyed, regardless of the losses!

And they were to accomplish the mission with outdated equipment: obsolete planes from a war long past. None of the men flying the aircraft were born when their machines had been in their glory days. Most were not even born when their aircraft were mothballed for the jet age.

Now jet age pilots flew the old aircraft with a tenacity and ability never expected or believed. To this point, they had defeated insurmountable odds, coming out victors against aircraft faster and more deadly than theirs.

Calmly, Beau gave instructions over the radio and the men split into four pairs going different directions. Another reason for dividing into four pairs was to throw the enemy off guard should they encounter resistance. This would leave the others free to complete the mission. Beau doubted the enemy would expect an attack from four different points. The strategy would assure better odds for the success of the mission.

The mission was impossible! It was insane and he knew it! But they had done the impossible before. Beau watched as the three pairs of fighter aircraft disappeared, taking with them six brave men with determination and insanity equal to his own. Eight antiquated World War II aircraft against an unbeatable opponent. This would not be a hit and run mission as before, because the enemy would be expecting them, and the enemy would be prepared this time.

Beau could still hear General Waddle's words: "Destroy the SR-71 Blackbird before it destroys Starburst. You must succeed *at all costs*!" They were expendable!

Beau glanced at the radar detectors: still no indication of enemy aircraft. He had expected an encounter, but he was more than content to finish the mission without any contact. Somehow he felt Cobra was near. He spoke into the small microphone within his helmet. "Moon Shadow, are you ready to burn them?"

"Aye, Cap'n, the dilithium crystals are charged. Warp drive, Cap'n?" asked Ruben in his best Scottish accent.

Beau grinned. "Yeah, Moon Shadow, warp drive."

"Ahh, Cap'n Kirk would be proud," Ruben continued in the exaggerated accent. "'Ere's one fer the Enterprise."

"Here's one for freedom!" said Beau as he fully engaged the throttle.

Enemy radar would alert the base, but not before they started their first pass. Should the radar tower not be alert, they would make the first pass before a warning sounded.

The two black P-51 Mustangs were at the southeastern edge of Corpus Christi, hugging the ground at over 200 mph. Under cover of darkness, aided only by the full moon, Beau and Ruben accelerated rapidly to just under 400 mph and started to ascend. They were ten miles out, less than ninety seconds, from the heavily fortified naval air station. If things went as planned, Mulholland and Blackman would come from the west, Fitz and BJ would arrive from the east, while Marix and James penetrated from the north. Hopefully each pair would be a little staggered to give the best coverage. After that each pilot would attack their selected site.

Two miles from the base, ground lights suddenly flooded the sky. The base was prepared and waiting. The alarm sounded, and for the first time anti-aircraft fire lit the sky. At their current speed, they would reach the outskirts of the base in sixteen seconds.

"Mud-mover!" barked Beau into the headset.

With those words, they forced their aircraft lower to avoid flak, and put the old planes within mere feet of the ground. Ruben responded immediately, dropping behind and to the left of Beau. Extended landing gear would have hit the ground so close did they hug the terrain, a maneuver that would handicap the anti-aircraft artillery.

Ground fire pounded the aircraft as they came in low. Bullets pierced the skin of both aircraft. One came through the cockpit of Beau's fighter and exited harmlessly out the other side. Marix and James approached on a parallel course from the opposite direction, a thousand yards to the right. At the same time, Beau caught the blur of Kipp's ship on his left, and Fitz closing in on his right. Ruben and Beau separated, lining up on two rows of jets sitting idle on the runway. A half dozen aircraft burst into flames from the intense 20-millimeter cannon fire.

On the initial pass Beau spied the SR-71 and his heart almost stopped. The Blackbird was flight ready and had already been pushed from the hangar in an effort to get it aloft to elude the attack. The pilot was being assisted into the cockpit. Once airborne, nothing could stop the SR-71 and its mission to destroy the laser space station Starburst. They were using the SR-71, a part of the *Aurora Project*, against America. Again, General Waddle's orders echoed clear in Beau's mind: "Destroy the SR-71. *At all costs!*"

Beau yelled into the radio. "I've spotted Blackbird at the northeast hangar. She's ready for flight. Take her out now! Repeat! Disregard your targets. Take out the Blackbird, now!"

Time was running out. The four pair of outdated planes completed the first attack run unscathed and made a quick turn for another pass.

The enemy expected to down them as easily as shooting ducks from the sky, but it was more like trying to rid oneself of pesky mosquitoes using a handgun. Trained for decades against fast moving, high flying jets, it became impossible to hit the slow moving, low flying targets.

Pilots from World War II would have been aghast at the tactics and speed of their former craft, but they would also have been impressed, since they had never flown at speeds exceeding sound, while Beau and the seven others had exceeded more than Mach-2. The speeds were relative to the experience. Not so much the machines as the men who flew them.

As the next pass started, the perfectly laid plans fell apart.

"Mongoose, bandits are filling the sky," said Ruben. "Jesus! Kinda gives you an idea of how those guys felt at the Alamo," he quipped, finding humor in the deathly situation.

"Moon Shadow, this is not the Alamo. We're not dead—yet!" laughed Beau. "Besides, if anything happens this low, think of it as a jump start to Heaven!"

"Thanks!" Ruben said, laughing to himself. The chatter of cannons and machine guns and the incessant boom of flak filled the night sky and turned it into day.

The enemy had prepared a counterattack of their own. They were ready to deal with the intruders. The *Devil's Angels* had no way of knowing that in the distance coming in low, under radar detection, were a pair of A-4 Skyhawks, an F-104 Starfighter, two F-4 Phantoms, a Mig 23, an F-14 Eagle, an F-86, and a Dassault Mirage.

The *Devil's Angels'* current problems were two F-4s and one F-86.

"Two Phantoms and a Sabre coming in."

It was too late for concern; they had a mission to complete. None except for one hesitated as they prepared for the second run. To him, death seemed the only logical outcome.

The enemy threw air history at the night stalkers, while they used air antiquity. Turning his head as far as he could in all directions, Beau scanned the skies and wondered where they found the old F-86 Sabre.

Ruben echoed his thoughts over the radio. "Where the hell did they get that old Sabre?"

For an instant, Beau forgot the much older aircraft he flew. His only thoughts were of the attacking jets and destroying the Blackbird. Never did the thought of his inferior fighter enter his mind.

"Forget them, take care of the Blackbird!" Beau barked instructions over the radio. "Okay, you *Thunder Bunnies*! Grey Ghost and Dead Dove, hit any aircraft moving on the runways!" he snapped to Kipp and Dean. "Red Baron and Snake, follow them. Check six!" he ordered Marix and James, the last words making them alert to an attack from the rear. Then he gave final instructions to BJ and Fitz: "Black Jack and White Lightning, follow us. If we miss, you must finish! If we score, take out the movers, wreck the runways, then get the hell out! Hurry, because you can bet more bogies are coming and coming fast. Let's do it!"

"Roger," replied Fitz and BJ, who had finished their run and were now making a 180 degree turn and aiming their machines in the direction of the hangar containing the reason for the deadly mission.

The Blackbird's engines had been started and men were clearing away.

As Beau and Ruben made their run, Marix engaged the F-86 and Mulholland pulled up to grapple with both F-4s. Mulholland's task was made easier when ground fire dispatched the second F-4.

Machine gun encampments opened fire on the lead black and gold Mustang as it roared toward the hangar which moments earlier housed the SR-71 Blackbird. Machine gun fire twice hit the clear teardrop canopy of the P-51 Mustang. Oblivious to the gunfire, Beau continued his deadly path with Ruben close behind. The radar detectors came to life indicating rockets fired from surface installations.

Waiting until the last possible instant, Beau held his course. The radar sounded for evasive action. He pulled two canisters of chaff and popped a flare. Simultaneously, he pulled back violently on the stick and jettisoned the two tanks of napalm Daddy John had so ingeniously manufactured. Miraculously, the SAMs missed Beau and Ruben. Their loads had been dropped toward the SR-71 Blackbird.

"Come back, you coward!" screamed Marix after shooting down the F-86. No one had to be told who it was leaving the scene of carnage. All knew the identity of the pilot being accused of cowardice: Marix's wingman, Larry James, the Snake.

"Snake, return now!" Marix demanded.

James was a brave man and he knew it. They were crazy! They were going to die! Fools ask to die and he was no fool. They could die, but he would not. Larry James continued his cowardly retreat.

In a vertical climb with superchargers fully engaged on the Merlin engine, Beau heard Marix's futile demand. In the same instant the aircraft was jolted from the explosions below. He rolled slightly and saw the SR-71 engulfed in flames. Their mission was complete; now to return home if it was at all possible. A ball of flames and smoke reached high in the sky, and Beau mumbled between gritted teeth, "Bye, Bye, Blackbird!"

"One Rhino in bloody flames," echoed Mulholland after his kill.

"Clear and on your tail," responded Ruben. "We have a Whiskey Delta," he said referring to Larry James.

"Bingo!" said Fitzhenry. "Aircraft destroyed. Making run to drop tanks." Then he aimed his white British Spitfire Hurricane at another target.

From behind came BJ in the old P-40 Flying Tiger. "That coward's going to get shot down."

"Forget him," said Beau. "Finish the run, and let's go home."

With awe in his voice, Kipp said, "Hey, mate, we got trouble! The damn thing's alive!"

All the pilots, regardless of the point of their attack, took a moment to tilt their wings so they could get a better view of the SR-71 Blackbird.

Slowly from out of the flames it crept—a demon, alive and creeping from hell's inferno to do her work. The Devil reincarnated with napalm dripping from the chine and wings. The SR-71 Blackbird crawled from the fire, pulling the protective covers away and clearing the burning napalm from the exposed tires. Flames rose from the canopy giving it a strangely alive and hellish apparition: a flaming bird determined to complete her mission. Slowly at first, the modified Blackbird accelerated down the runway.

"She can't make it," ushered Warren, an uncertain tone in his voice. The sight was eerie for all, as they watched the burning plane continue its acceleration.

Screaming over the radio Beau warned, "Negative! Pursue and destroy! Repeat, pursue and destroy! It's designed to tolerate far more heat!" He knew the outer skin of the Blackbird reached more than 1100 degrees during flight.

Already Mulholland and Ruben were in pursuit, with Fitzhenry close behind and closing in. However, as Ruben and Mulholland fired with what they had, the Blackbird made an abrupt turn for an open runway, with flames streaming behind. Fitzhenry closed the gap, but the Blackbird pulled away. The flaming plane was lifting from the ground, and about to engage the full force of the jets and streak safely into space.

Beau had anticipated the escape, guessing the strategy and running a near perpendicular course to the anticipated liftoff spot should the other three fail. Who better to anticipate than one who flew the Blackbird. A moment later, he found himself slightly ahead and leading the Blackbird, as it lifted from the ground.

An unrelenting burst from the 20-millimeter cannons fired across the path of the oncoming aircraft, as though awaiting the eerie apparition's arrival. The three-quarter inch bullets stitched their way down the black flaming skin, tearing at the wondrous Pratt-Whitney jet engine and rupturing a fuel line used as protective coolant. Momentum and power shot the Blackbird toward the heavens at a steep angle. First smoke belched from one of the jet engines, then flames erupted. The Blackbird burst into a thunderous ball of orange fire, and appeared more like a meteor taking off from earth. Creating a large sweeping arc spreading in all directions equally, the Blackbird fell back to earth. The small P-51 Mustang barely managed to clear the falling and burning debris.

Mission accomplished! Yet the real danger still lay ahead. Could they escape?

The radar detectors beeped, indicating jets approaching in the distance and radar engaged. The infrequent beeps increased as the enemy closed in. They grouped into pairs and set on a bearing that would take them due south and away from the approaching aircraft.

"Warp drive," said Beau. "Stay low, there is still a chance they may lose us in darkness."

A short distance ahead they saw the P-40 with James at the controls. Their hearts stopped when they saw his location. He was flying at one o'clock high. It was too late to avoid the enemy. At his height radar would detect his aircraft. Escape was in their grasp except for the one errant mistake James committed.

The enemy aircraft already had his location pinpointed and were on their way. A conflict loomed ahead because of the foolish actions of one man.

"Snake, drop your elevation, or I'll personally drop you out of the sky myself!" yelled Beau.

"Too late," said Ruben as the Bell radar detector's beep became more frequent. "They'll be here in a few seconds."

They were only a few miles from the Naval Air Station. The inferno created from the raid turned the night sky into day. They now had visual contact with the enemy.

James rejoined the group and was behind Marix, whining over the radio. "They're going to kill us," he said whimpering and on the edge of tears.

"If they don't kill you—I will," Beau said calmly. James gave no response.

"Okay, you *Thunder Bunnies*, pair off! Think clear! Stay low, force them down," Beau yelled. "Now bring the bears to the briar patch."

A chilling and all too familiar voice sounded over their radio frequency. "Twice you have gotten away, Beau Gex, but not this time. As you Americans say . . . third time is the charm. The third time will be your death!"

Rasht Sharafan led the attacking fighters. Would Beau now have a chance to fight Cobra? He gave little thought to his inferior P-51 Mustang or Cobra's F-14.

Waiting and hunting for an edge, Beau baited his old nemesis. "The Israelis told me your mother is a pig. They say you have sex with pigs?"

The response was lost as the two groups made contact, breaking into separate battles. A huge melee erupted as pilots moved for an advantage. The dogfight filled the night sky. An eerie orange glow, from the fires to the north, lit the deadly aerial engagement.

The strict training and discipline of the men flying the antiquated prop aircraft paid dividends. In pairs, Daddy John's *Devil's Angels* clustered together to provide protection from the enemy. The group of fighter jets overtaking them flew with experience, but they flew without organization or desire. Why should they worry? They were flying superior aircraft. So they chased their quarry into the "Briar Patch." Two enemy aircraft were shot from the sky as they flew past.

"Get me outa this furball!" yelled Warren. A Sabre, Phantom, and Mirage pursued closely behind.

Fitzhenry fired a leading salvo into the skin of the Mirage, rupturing hydraulic lines. When smoke belched from the crippled aircraft, Fitz moved to help his wingman as did Beau and Ruben.

In another desperate attempt to escape, James broke from the pack. As he peeled away from the dogfight, Sharafan in his F-14 spotted the lone fighter and executed a fast half loop, rolling out with the P-40 in his sights.

The Bell radar detector screamed at James when Cobra fired his missile. Only James's training and quick response saved him.

"Bandit on my tail! Bandit on my tail!" he whined.

Ruben spotted the problem and broke from the chase, letting Fitz and Beau take control of the jets pursuing BJ. He executed a split-S and rolled out at a slight angle to Cobra, who was closing swiftly on James. Ruben shoved the throttle forward to meet his friend's old nemesis. He led the unsuspecting jet, and when he felt it was in sight, he squeezed the button on the stick. The Mustang vibrated from the force of the four 20-millimeter cannons. Just as the F-14 reached a point where he would intercept the deadly projectiles, the guns stopped abruptly. Ruben's guns had jammed.

Sharafan was about to abort when he saw the guns fire. Why they stopped, he didn't understand. The F-14 computer locked on the rear of the P-40 and opened up with the 20-millimeter rotary cannon. Three-quarter inch projectiles ripped the cockpit unmercifully and entered through the back of Larry James blowing gaping holes out his chest and splattering his innards against the shattered instruments. The cannon penetrated the engine and smoke belched from the front of the aircraft, leaving a ghostly gray trail against the moonlit sky. Sharafan continued firing his guns.

The rudder disintegrated and half the left wing splintered apart. Smoking profusely, the P-40 rolled to the left and began a death dive to earth. Sharafan pulled away.

In his attempt to destroy Beau Gex, James had managed to arrange his own death. Inside the cockpit of the smoking aircraft he stared in shocked disbelief. In his hands he held the entrails from his body. In a last futile effort, as though believing he could save himself, he tried to shove the parts he held back into one of the three holes in his chest.

"I'm dead!" Snake mumbled. And he was.

Instantly, Sharafan did a half roll, and while in the inverted position turned the F-14, bringing it to the rear of his attacker. He sighted on the black aircraft before him, listened for the tone, and fired a rocket. Ruben's agile though obsolete aircraft avoided the missile.

Warren's P-40 was getting riddled from pursuing aircraft. "Hey, get these guys off my back!" For the first time ever, there was a twinge of fear in the eloquent Bostonian accent.

Bullets continued to hit BJ and pieces came off the old plane, while Fitz and Beau tried to maneuver into position, but it was too late.

"Hey, uuuhhhnnn—!" groaned BJ.

"No!" yelled Fitz, his guns taking down the Sabre.

"BJ!" screamed Beau.

The old Warhawk started to split apart, then disintegrated in a bright orange fireball. Immediately, Fitz closed on the rear of the Mirage, while Beau took the Phantom.

Concentrating on their quarry, they had forgotten Ruben who was sure he could elude his pursuer, but he was unable to do so, again barely eluding another missile.

"This is Moon Shadow, if you guys could take a break for a minute, I could use some help!" he snapped. Nimbly, he maneuvered his old Mustang away from the pursuit, avoiding yet another missile. "I've got a Gomer on my tail, and this asshole is really trying to ruin my day. I'm at your three o'clock, and my day's going to shit fast."

Ruben's strained voice stunned Beau. He had thought Ruben to be close on their tail. Beau twisted his head to Check Six and his heart almost stopped when he recognized the attacker. He halted his attack, and immediately did a chandelle, a reversal of course doing a climbing turn, and closed in on the two.

Another rocket fired, but, again, Ruben avoided the shot. He went into a split-s dive, then a quick climbing turn. At this point, he avoided another rocket. He tried to maneuver into a deliberate stall, but he failed to elude his adversary. The 20-millimeter cannons fired, hitting the aircraft.

"Hurry, Mongoose—I need you!" begged Ruben.

"Hold on, Ruben, I'm coming."

For the first time ever, Beau called Ruben something other than *Moon Shadow* in combat. Beau closed in quickly. He engaged the superchargers and exceeded 500 mph, leaving Fitzhenry far behind. He fired a round to distract Cobra, but still the F-14 clung to the tail of Ruben's P-51.

Sharafan fired another burst from his cannon, but again the ship eluded his shots. He had the Mustang lined up when he felt a burst from the 20-millimeter cannon of Beau's Mustang penetrate his aircraft. Gradually the oil pressure dropped. Beau fired again, but Cobra eluded the shots. Cobra had time for one more run at the fighter in front of his sights, before he would have to abort and take his injured aircraft home. He sighted the small ship and let go with a long burst, then broke away with Beau hot on his tail.

Beau got in a short fast burst hitting the injured F-14. It failed to bring the jet down, but the direct hits damaged it enough to prevent it from achieving supersonic speeds, and kept it within the speed of the P-51

Mustang. Slowly he closed the gap. In a few seconds, Cobra would be within his sights.

Without warning, something happened to make Beau stop his pursuit.

"Oh, shit! Mongoose, I'm hit! Damn, it's bad," said Ruben with a twinge of fear so unlike him. "I'm going down!"

Immediately, Beau broke away from his attack, letting Cobra hobble away to safety. The remainder of the enemy aircraft that had not already been shot down by the *Devil's Angels* had dispersed and were retreating with Cobra.

Beau came around hurriedly pulling alongside Moon Shadow's crippled aircraft.

Chapter 16
WHEN MOON SHADOWS FALL

"I'm going down!" screamed Ruben.

"Where's the plane hit?" Beau yelled.

This time when Ruben spoke, he took a breath between every couple of words. "No, you don't understand . . . it's not the ship . . . it's me . . . I've been hit . . . It's bad, Mongoose."

This time Beau's quick mind failed him as it filled with anguish over Ruben's predicament. Kipp's voice brought him back to reality.

"Hey, mate, we're low on fuel and heading back. Do you want help?" asked Mulholland.

For a moment, Beau scanned the night skies lit only with the full moon and the now disappearing orange glow of the Naval Air Station in the distance. The dogfight had taken them south along the shore of Texas. A few miles to the east lay Padre Island; to the northwest was Cliff Palace, safety, and Krysti waiting for him. A glance at his wounded squadron revealed Dean smoking heavily. Portions of the tail on Marix's P-38 had been shot away and he was having control problems with the rudders and the ailerons. Only Kipp and Fitz had sustained no damage.

"Ruben, let's go home. Can you make it?" Beau asked.

"Negative, Mongoose," Ruben moaned, pain apparent in his voice. "Beau, I've gotta set down now!"

"Okay, okay, I'm with you. Grey Ghost, take the *Thunder Bunnies* home. I'll stay with Moon Shadow and when we can, we'll return to base. Good luck!" Beau moved his aircraft after Ruben's faltering P-51 Mustang.

"Aye, Mongoose, and good luck to ya, mate!" said Mulholland.

The four aircraft turned slowly and began their trip to Cliff Palace and safety while their two friends continued to plod slowly to the southeast.

"Ruben, listen to me. If we land on the highway, they may find us. Change your heading to the east and set down on Padre. I doubt if troops are on the Island. Do you understand?"

"Roger," came the faint reply. The majestic but injured fighter turned slowly to the east.

"Hang in there. I can see the Island."

"I see it too," groaned Ruben.

"Now turn slowly to the right and continue along the shoreline. Slowly! That's it."

"Beau, I feel like shit."

"It's okay. You're lined up. Lower the landing gear." Beau watched for the gear to lower from the belly of the aircraft and lock in place. When he observed Ruben's P-51 wheels unfolding, he lowered his wheels.

"Hey buddy . . . I can't land it."

"Of course you can. Remember the crop duster. This is a cake walk. You can do it with your eyes closed."

"God, those were good times. I wish we were back there. We had more fun and got into more trouble. You could get us outa anything."

"And I'm gonna get us outa this," snapped Beau.

"That Cobra," Ruben coughed, then finished, "just isn't human."

"Shut up and land."

Ruben touched down on the sandy shoreline, but the aircraft lurched back into the air. Two more times he did this until he settled the aircraft onto the soft sandy beach. As the aircraft slowed, the left tire caught, spun the plane about, and came to rest pointing out to the Gulf of Mexico.

Beau stopped his fighter, jumped from the plane, and discarded the cumbersome parachute as he ran to his injured friend. The engine was still running when he hurled himself upon the wing and shoved the canopy back. Ruben sat motionless inside, shot twice through the back. One bullet had exited out through the front of his stomach, the other one out his side through his ribs. Carefully, Beau pulled his friend from the cramped quarters of the P-51.

A scream of pain escaped Ruben's lips, but he managed a grin as glazed eyes peered into Beau's worried blue eyes. "Damn, if these bullets don't kill me you will."

Anguish filled Beau's face. "Hey, I'm trying to be careful."

"I know," said Ruben shaking his head. "It already feels better having you beside me." He screamed out in pain. "God, it hurts. Stop! Put me down," Ruben begged.

They had reached the edge of the dunes, and Beau eased Ruben to the sand, removed the parachute, and gently turned his friend so he faced the sea. Beau emptied the bag containing the parachute and folded it in such a manner as to create a pillow. He leaned Ruben's head back against the soft white fabric.

When Beau checked the wounds, he didn't have to be a doctor to know they were fatal. Ruben coughed and spit blood. A vital organ had been hit and only a short time remained.

Ruben rolled his eyes toward Beau and managed a painful smile. "Say, I wonder if my life insurance will cover this?" he asked, forcing both men to laugh, then he coughed up more blood and tried to spit it out onto the sand, but instead it only rolled down his chin. "Shit, I'm dying!"

Beau took a piece of the parachute and wiped Ruben's chin. "No, you're not. Not as long as I'm with you."

"I can feel it . . . it's over . . . shit, I'm gonna miss you," and with those words his body convulsed in pain. "Don't leave me, okay?"

"I'm not gonna leave you." Beau could feel the life of his friend flow out from between his fingers holding a compress against the wound in Ruben's stomach.

"My buddy. I knew you wouldn't leave me." Tears filled Ruben's eyes. "God, I'm gonna miss not being able to see my son grow up. I can't go yet, it's just not fair."

"You're okay, Ruben," lied Beau, barely restraining the tears from overflowing his eyes.

Again, Ruben's body tensed to the sharp pain created from the 20-millimeter slugs he caught from Cobra's guns. "Bullshit, you liar! Let me talk while I can. You have to watch my son for me. Promise me you will."

"I promise."

Ruben's body wrenched in pain. "Remember when we met, and you took me up in that crop duster? God that was fun. Maybe, someday we can do it again."

"Sure, you bet."

"If you see Cobra . . . kill him for me, will you?"

"That's a promise."

"After all you are the Cobra killer. Remember?"

Beau smiled and nodded.

For a moment, Ruben faded off then returned. "You were the best football player I ever saw. Did you know I tried to break your leg . . . but you were just too darn good."

"I remember. Next to the goal line. Hell, I thought you had broken it. You hit harder than anyone I ever played against."

"I did?" asked Ruben, surprised at the admission.

"You bet your ass. In fact, if it had been anyone else, I'd have scored."

"Really?" Ruben said, pleased with the revelation. Then he coughed and grimaced with pain.

A grin stretched across Beau's face. "No doubt you were the best," he answered in all sincerity. Smiling on the outside, while inside he was in agony, knowing his friend was dying, he knew he could do nothing.

A feeble smile came to Ruben's face. "I'm glad I didn't break your leg."

"Yeah, me, too."

"Tell Sunday I love her." Beau just nodded his head but his mouth was unable to answer.

Foaming blood made a continuous stream down Ruben's mouth. "Hey Beau . . . it doesn't hurt."

"You stupid shit; you talk too much," said Beau through the tears.

Ruben tried to smile through the pain. "Hey, you got any of my candy bars?"

Beau wiped the tears from his face and reached into his chest pocket where he had two Three Musketeers bars. "Sure," he said. He tore the wrapper away and handed it to him.

Ruben bit into the candy and chewed it. When he swallowed, he grimaced in pain, but he bit another piece out of the bar and chewed on it. He offered it to Beau. "Want a bite?"

Beau took it, bit off a piece, and gave it back to Ruben.

"I knew you'd come through when I needed ya."

"I'll always be there, Ruben."

Tears ran down Ruben's cheeks. "Would you think I was a coward if I told you I'm afraid to die?"

"Hell, no, of course not."

"I'm afraid . . . God, I'm gonna miss you and the good times we had," he said through the pain. He reached up for Beau and they clasped hands that in some unseen way seemed to give Ruben a sense of comfort and security. "Beau, promise you won't bury me?"

"You're not gonna die," lied Beau.

Ruben reached to his neck and squeezed the small leathery pouch that hung about his neck. The same pouch his Grandfather Grandy had given him. "I'm Moon Shadow! Promise!"

Again his body was seized with pain from the wounds. His eyes rolled up and then closed, and froth surged from his mouth. Still, he clung onto life. Weakly his eyes fluttered open.

"Hang on, Ruben."

The sound of his friend's voice was reassuring. Feebly, Ruben squeezed Beau's hand. His voice came in a mere whisper, forcing Beau to bend near his mouth to catch the words. "Tell Sunday I'm sorry I didn't come back home . . .and . . . and I'll always love her!" The pain seemed to ease and Ruben smiled at Beau. "My buddy . . . you're the best friend a guy could have!"

As the final breath of life surrendered his body, he relaxed in Beau's arms. He seemed to smile back in the peaceful liberation of death.

Ruben was gone. Unbelieving, Beau tried to shake life into the limp body he held in his hands. "No! You son-of-a-bitch, don't do this to me! Don't leave now. Come back!" Then Beau clutched Ruben tightly to his body. "Aw, Ruben, Ruben . . . why?"

Grief overwhelmed Beau as he rocked his friend back and forth. The deep pain from within immersed every fiber of his being—a pain that could neither be tended nor removed. Inwardly his mind screamed out to be released from the torment gripping him like a human vice from which there was no escape. He held his beloved friend to his chest and cried.

After what seemed an eternity, Beau laid Ruben gently in the sand, stood erect and backed away. He stared disbelieving at the lifeless form. Any moment he expected Ruben to sit up, take another bite of his candy bar, frown, then with his big happy grin say, "My buddy." In vain, he tried to push the harsh reality from his mind, but he knew Ruben was dead. A low continuous moan came from his lips as he buried his face in his hands and dropped to his knees.

Clenching both hands in fists of anger, he raised his head and screamed to the heavens above. "God, damn you! God damn you! Why must you take every one I love?" Defiantly, he stretched his arms upward and with whitened knuckles yelled out his threats. "Take me! If you want someone, take me—I'm ready!"

Slowly, his defiant attitude changed and his thoughts returned to Ruben's words: "I'm Moon Shadow!" Beau stared at Ruben's P-51 Mustang facing toward the Gulf of Mexico. He heard Ruben's words and recalled the legend of Moon Shadow—a story he had listened to a hundred times before. One he never grew tired of hearing.

Beau didn't see the P-51 Mustang. Instead he saw the tribe of Karankawa Indians roaming freely along the coast of Texas centuries before, performing their ancient rituals the length of Padre Island. The same island where he now stood. The ritual of the spirit, the Legend of Moon Shadow. The release of a fallen Karankawa warrior's spirit from the Moon Shadow through fire. The ceremony where a dead warrior was burned beneath the full moon in the belief when the body turned to ashes, and the shadow created from the full moon vanished, the spirit was set free. Beau saw flames around the wooden ceremonial funeral pyre and the body of an Indian lying peacefully on top. But it wasn't an Indian—it was Ruben.

Beau understood. What better way to use Ruben's aircraft than as a funeral pyre.

He wrapped his friend's blood soaked body in the white silken material of his parachute and gently placed him within the cockpit. Only his head protruded from the fabric. Beau took the leather pouch from Ruben's neck and placed it about his own.

Before Beau continued with Ruben's last wish, he stripped the plane of useful items. As he removed the unspent ammunition, he was stunned to find oversized shells jammed in the 20-millimeter guns. Ruben's death had been no accident. His death had been deliberate! Immediately his thoughts turned to James and Marix, but James was dead. Somehow he felt Marix was involved, and he couldn't shake the feeling it had been intended for him.

Thoughts of revenge were temporarily abandoned as he started to search the sand dunes for a container to hold the gas he would drain from the plane. He found an empty plastic five-gallon paint container on the beach and worked hurriedly draining the unspent fuel and filling his aircraft. He took the rockets he could use and set them beside the Mustang, leaving two still attached to the aircraft serving Ruben's ultimate dream. He filled the container for the last time, leaving the tanks open to allow the aircraft to burn.

Then he carried the fuel to the cockpit, where he paused over Ruben's body. In death it seemed a slight smile lit his peaceful face. Did Ruben know? He reached for the flare gun attached to the side of the seat and pulled it free.

Beau took the pouch from his neck, opened it, and poured the contents into his hand. He took the smaller pouch and poured a portion of the sand on Ruben, took a hawk feather and placed it on the fabric wrapping Ruben's body along with two pieces of flint. Then he kissed the molten moon rock that looked like a face.

"Earth, wind, and fire," Beau mumbled. With his empty hand he squeezed the tears from his eyes as he murmured, "Here's your Moon Shadow." Beau put the remaining pieces back in the leather pouch, including the moon rock, and placed it back around his neck next to the cross Krysti had given him.

After he wiped his cheek on his sleeve, he reached deep in his pocket and pulled from it the last Three Musketeers candy bar, Ruben's favorite. Carefully he slid it into Ruben's shirt pocket and snapped the flap shut over the candy.

"You might need this on your trip," Beau said and managed a slight smile.

Still he continued to watch Ruben, hoping he would rise, believing the whole thing to be a cruel dream. But Ruben, Moon Shadow, failed to rise. Beau took a deep breath and sighed.

"My best friend," Beau managed through a hoarse, choked voice. He kissed his friend on the forehead. "I'm gonna miss ya."

Beau poured a portion of the fuel into the cockpit, and jumped to the sand where he splashed the remaining fuel on the wings and fuselage. He threw the empty can under the plane, ran a short distance from the aircraft, and turned. The Moon had moved to the western sky, but its brilliance was undiminished. Only an hour remained until sunrise; the night was still clear and crisp, filled with stars surrounding the Moon. He aimed the flare gun at the P-51 Mustang and pulled the trigger.

The aircraft burst into a glorious ball of orange flames, turning blue and red. Slowly, he backed away from the intense heat. Arms hanging limply at his side, Beau watched the inferno. The fuel tank erupted, sending flames skyward. One of the two remaining rockets ignited and soared into the sky, exploding over the water in a final tribute.

"For you and Grandy," Beau sighed.

In his mind, Ruben was the last of the vanished tribe of Karankawas. Beau repeated the words Ruben would say when he told the story of the Karankawa Indians and the Legend of Moon Shadow:

"When Moon Shadows fall,
Come footsteps in the sand
Where no one follows.
From brave warriors far away.

In flames! The spirits recall,
Memories by the sea.
They dance the land of Moon Shadows,
Eternal rest from the warriors' earthly stay!"

He stood rigid and saluted. "There'll be no shadow this night. Your spirit's free!" The second rocket blasted away and shot into the sky and erupted into a ball of flame.

A lonely tear rolled down Beau's cheek. Silently, he watched Ruben's funeral pyre burn, where centuries before similar ceremonies had been performed. With a heavy heart he moved toward his plane and watched the blaze while he loaded his aircraft with the plundered arsenal from Ruben's ship.

The first rays of sunlight crawled from the gulf extending their golden fingers over the sky as he finished loading his P-51. The full moon dropped low in the west. Dying flames still flickered over Ruben's craft.

Beau stood on the wing of his Mustang and turned toward the burned out shell of Ruben's aircraft and saluted stiffly. A sigh came from his chest, and he tried to blink away the mist filling his eyes.

"Till we meet again, my friend," Beau mumbled. He turned and climbed into his cockpit.

The engine coughed to life. Everything was normal on the gauges. He slid the canopy shut and increased the rpm's of the Merlin engine. The aircraft moved to the water's edge and Beau shoved the throttle forward. The Mustang rumbled down the sandy beach. He pulled the stick back, and the fighter responded immediately, lifting effortlessly. Beau turned out to sea and circled back to the still burning aircraft. He tipped his wing and made one last circle, all the while saluting. Tears rolled down his cheeks as he paid a final tribute to his fallen wingman . . . his best friend—Moon Shadow!

The aircraft climbed to an altitude of 1000 feet. At this elevation, Beau was sure he would be detected. He knew this, he was ready, and he was fighting mad!

Chapter 17
THE UNTOLD SECRET

The aircraft climbed steadily higher. Beau fully expected an encounter and hoped it would be with Cobra. Still, he aimed the P-51 in the general direction of Cliff Palace, safety, and Krysti.

After only a few minutes, the dependable Bell radar detector picked-up another aircraft with radar activated. Could it be? The Nueces River lay below and he was halfway to Cliff Palace: only forty miles to the lower part of the Frio River.

The encounter would take place over the Nueces River. He pushed the stick forward and watched the needle on the altimeter drop. There was no reason to give the approaching aircraft any unfair advantage. The radio was tuned to the same channel as the day before. If the pilot was Sharafan, and Beau thought it might be, then the radio would come to life soon.

The enemy and his rockets were within range, but no rockets fired. After all, the F-14 could destroy the small prop plane whenever Sharafan so desired. Already he had forgotten the tenacious fight the same plane had put up the night before.

"So it is you," came the excited voice over the radio. "Now I will kill you," Sharafan added confidently.

"Why do you think I waited for you. So you could kill me?" Beau taunted.

Sharafan knew Beau had intentionally waited for him to arrive but he didn't know why and he didn't care. Time for the *fatwa* to end and finish the revenge for his beautiful mother.

The cat had been lured to the mousetrap, with the intention of the trap being used on the cat.

They were within range and Beau could see both men in the two-seater F-14. The navigator glanced around somewhat nervously. Sharafan laughed into the radio. "Your plane is obsolete. You cannot possibly win."

"We've done damn well so far. You couldn't stop our raids; what makes you think you can stop me now?"

"What makes your aircraft so superior to mine?" asked Sharafan, intrigued with Beau's brash statement.

"I've got a sling and a stone that say you're wrong," Beau said, remembering Daddy John's conversation about David and Goliath.

"You talk in riddles," Sharafan laughed sarcastically. "How is your hand? You can't possibly use it well enough yet."

Beau laughed into the radio. "The hand is doing fine, but you made a fatal error. You ruined my right hand. You would call me an unclean infidel. You know why? I'm left-handed!"

A slight bit of nervousness could be detected in Sharafan's voice. "You will die anyway."

Thoughts of Ruben filled Beau's mind. He spoke the words he knew his friend would say. "Seeing as how I'm the underdog, maybe you could give me a handicap. Like say a free shot with one of my rockets before we start?" A smile creased his lips. He had become part of Moon Shadow.

"You must take me for a fool!"

"Why do you think I asked? Oh, well. How about an old-fashioned dogfight? No rockets."

"If that's how you want to die, so be it. But before you die, let me tell you the second secret."

Finally, Beau would learn what Cobra had so long kept hidden.

"Your wife and child? It was I who planted the bomb. You were to die also. I killed your family!" he gloated.

But Sharafan was not prepared for the quickness with which Beau responded. Instantly the little P-51 did a rolling dive, and part way through the drop, the 20-millimeter cannons opened up on the unsuspecting F-14. Bullets stitched across the wing.

Immediately, the jet responded as Sharafan put his plane into a roll to pursue the prop plane. "I want you to know who's going to kill you," snapped Sharafan.

"Can't be you. You're a weak woman with a coward's veil and ya got no balls, Cobra."

Beau laughed in controlled rage, and he was momentarily dumbfounded at having found his wife and son's murderer. Beau was fighting mad. Their murderer still lived, and he was excited at the prospect of revenge!

The F-14 was fast but Beau was quicker. The better man against the better machine. Although Cobra was an excellent pilot—and one of the very best—as long as he refused to use the rockets, Beau had a better than average chance, because the bear had been drawn into the briar patch thus balancing the scales. Skill against skill. Cobra had no experience in leading his target. His 20-millimeter cannon fired harmlessly into the air. Beau's Bell radar detector would register if Cobra changed his mind and activated his rockets. So far, the detector remained silent and Cobra kept his word. Beau wondered how much longer Cobra would do so. When the scales of battle tilted in Beau's favor, he knew Cobra would use his rockets.

"Your father?" Sharafan said more than asked.

"He's dead."

"I know," Sharafan laughed. "I killed him and the other pilot also."

The Mustang went into a split-s dive coming out near tall power lines. Beau was enraged as he weaved the craft between the thin deadly steel cables, then craned his neck to catch a view of the F-14. Sharafan saw the lines not a second too soon, and yanked on the stick barely missing the cables.

Anticipating Sharafan's evasive move, Beau sent the Mustang into a tight half-loop with a half turn bringing the aircraft into a position under the belly of the F-14. The cannons chattered to life shaking the P-51 as it fired at the vulnerable underbelly of the jet.

Projectiles crashed through the wing and into the cockpit. Two rounds hit the navigator: one in the neck severing the jugular, the other entering his chest and rupturing his right lung. The navigator choked on his own blood, and orange foam poured from his mouth. He lost consciousness, coughed spasmodically, and died.

Sharafan shoved the throttle and the stick forward and did an inverted half loop. He touched the afterburner and was instantly on the tail of the antiquated prop. Beau was in his sights. Victory would be easier than he imagined.

"Has fear set in?" He barked, simultaneously pulling the trigger on the rotary cannons, hoping to kill Beau Gex as he had killed Moon Shadow.

"Not really. No reason to be afraid of watching you die," Beau said. The words were almost as startling to Sharafan as the move Beau made. The cannons hit thin air, not the aircraft in his sights.

In one motion Beau pulled the flaps and throttle, hesitated for an instant, then shoved the throttle forward, pulled the stick back, and engaged the supercharger. The surge of raw power was tremendous. The F-14 was doing a slow loop, enabling Beau to line up the fighter in his sights.

Sharafan was unaware he was being chased. He never anticipated the aircraft to be so quick. The jet was still subsonic. But as Sharafan started his dive to finish his enemy, he was, for the first time, aware the enemy was nowhere to be seen. He twisted his neck from side to side. The bullets whizzing past his cockpit told Cobra the location of the small tenacious fighter. He was shocked to see the tiny fighter pursuing his tail with the persistence of a killer bee ready to sting. He tried to shake the pest, but it remained on his tail. The pursuit had brought them up and over 5,000 feet—something Cobra hoped would happen.

"You believe in Allah?" asked Beau as he sighted him in and fired. Again, the bullets found their target. The heavy fire struck and started to take a toll on the advanced fighter jet.

"Yes, what of it?" Sharafan did a barrel roll and hit supersonic, pulling away from the diving Mustang at nearly 600 mph.

"In a few minutes, you're gonna get to see him—forever! 'Cause I'm sending you straight to hell!"

Sharafan was sure the fighter pursuing him would be unable to pull out of the speeding dive, but again he underestimated the gritty, antiquated aircraft and the man at the controls who was the leader of the *Devil's Angels*.

The airspeed needle quivered against the peg because the P-51 Mustang was near the 600-mph mark—something the propeller driven aircraft was never designed for. Beau could feel it. To use the stick now, in such a dive, would inflict severe frame damage on the faithful old fighter. Without hesitation, Beau regulated the rudder and tab to pull out of the dive—the same thing he did with his old crop duster when he had experimented with its capabilities. The Mustang responded magnificently, and when he pulled past the critical portion of the dive, he pulled back on the stick and none too soon. He had less than fifty feet to the ground. He was now charging the oncoming F-14.

The Tomcat had gone subsonic to duel with the old Mustang. Like two airborne knights in armor determined to joust to the end, they charged each other, only the lances belched fire and steel. Two sophisticated aircraft from two separate eras in time, shooting hundreds of bullets per minute at each other, with each bullet almost an inch in diameter and capable of penetrating thick steel. As they neared each other, Beau's radar detector screamed its deadly warning, indicating rockets activated in the F-14. The little Bell detector had proven extremely helpful. Now it told Beau the time for guns had ended. He knew Cobra would not fire on this pass. At such speeds, the rocket would only work in a direct path and not react to its directional radar in time. To fire the rockets now would also mean possible death for Cobra. On the next pass, Beau knew he would use the rockets.

The 20-millimeter slugs from both aircraft ripped each plane apart as they passed. The Mustang started to smoke, and the F-14 lost fuel pressure as it made a wide sweeping turn. It too began to smoke.

Just ahead lay the Nueces River. Toward this river Beau aimed his faithful P-51 Mustang. A plan had already formulated in his mind to defeat Sharafan. Tall cypress and water oaks lining the riverbank would afford the protection and the diversion he needed.

Making a wide swing, the little P-51 dropped to the treetops, parallel and over the river, at a speed of more than 450 mph. Beau peered through the teardrop canopy and spotted Cobra more than two miles away. The F-14 was damaged and still traveling at subsonic speed. Still, the radar detector indicated the jet to have rockets engaged. When Cobra completed his turn and was on a return intersect line with the Mustang, and after Beau was sure Cobra sighted him, he dropped his plane below the tree line and out of view.

When he disappeared from view he pulled violently back on the throttle, dropped his flaps and landing gear, and wondered if the trick would work twice. The fighter shuddered violently and chattered to the sudden forces exerted on it at such high velocity.

Beau pulled up on the stick to keep the craft level. In but a few seconds, he had almost reached stall speed. Now for Cobra to do what he expected. The Bell radar detector became one continuous bleep indicating multiple rockets fired. Beau guessed four rockets fired to form a pattern stretching across his projected path. Instantly, Beau fired two of his HVAAR rockets straight down the river to where he would have been if he had not slowed his aircraft so drastically. He was holding the shaking P-51 steady at 120 mph.

Only four hundred yards ahead, the bank of the river exploded as a rocket from the F-14 smashed through the trees clearing the path for the three that followed. Another rocket crashed through the trees. One rocket from the Mustang was intercepted as it collided with one from the F-14. A tremendous explosion resulted. The second rocket from the P-51 crashed 100 yards beyond the original explosion. The fourth rocket from the F-14 crashed harmlessly into the trees on the other side of the river.

For an observer from the air, it would have appeared as if Cobra had scored a direct hit. Beau smiled.

To Sharafan, he was sure he had destroyed the fighter after he saw one of his rockets explode. He looked at the photo of his mother in the cockpit, touched it gently, and smiled. "It is over, Mother. They are all dead. We have beaten them."

The wing of his F-14 Tomcat dipped to the right so he could view his work. The first thing he noticed was no debris from the aircraft he had just destroyed. Quickly, he glanced out the canopy and too late saw the P-51 Mustang rising from the top of the water with all four 20-millimeter cannons blazing.

"Welcome to hell! This is for Moon Shadow!" snapped Beau as his bullets shattered the canopy of the F-14. Then he released his last two rockets. "Here, suck on these!"

Helpless, Sharafan watched the rockets speed on their deadly path toward his superior jet. "Nooo!!" he shrieked.

The rockets flew an accurate and deadly path for Cobra's F-14. When Beau released them, he pulled hard on the stick, shoved the throttle forward, and did a half roll turn to the left. The explosion of the F-14 rocked the Mustang, but Beau regained control almost immediately. He tipped the wing of the P-51 for a better view. Debris littered the flowing water. While on the opposite side of the river, fragments from the F-14 continued to fall from the sky.

Twice he circled the area to confirm the kill and make sure in his mind there had been no way for Cobra to escape. Cobra was dead.

Nagging pain in Beau's right leg alerted him to another problem. A quick inspection revealed a wound in his thigh. Hit by a shot from Cobra during the fight, he saw blood now pulsed from the open wound. Beau tried to tend to his leg as best he could. He opened his flight suit and tore a piece from his shirt to use as a tourniquet.

Now another problem as the oil pressure started dropping. Time to set the aircraft down and tend to his gallant and victorious fighter. The Mustang would not fly much longer. The loss of blood began to make him feel dizzy. Things started to spin around him, and before he could set the speed and trim properly, he lost consciousness.

The nose of the Mustang dipped slightly, and the aircraft slowly pointed earthward, in a gentle dive toward death. The cockpit was filled with a pleasant, friendly voice.

"My buddy! I appreciate the concern for your wanting to come visit, but you promised to take care of my family for me," came the familiar voice. *"Now, pull the stick back, you stupid shit!"* the voice ordered.

There was the strangest sensation someone was shaking his shoulder. Just as the voice demanded, Beau responded and pulled back on the stick. His eyes fluttered open in time to come out of the dive mere yards from the ground.

"Moon Shadow? Ruben, Ruben?" he called out, glancing in all directions around the small cockpit of the P-51 Mustang, expecting to find his friend. Subconsciously he tried to set the trim and speed. "Yes . . . don't worry. I promise to watch Sunday and Little Ruben."

His head started to droop, then he heard the voice again. *"Paul, you dummy. Don't forget or Sunday will kill you."*

Instantly his head was erect. "Yes, Paul, I remember . . . Ruben? Ruben! Come back." Beau pleaded, almost begging.

The oil pressure unexpectedly stabilized. Slowly and with great care Beau set the trim and balance on his wounded bird so it would fly straight and level. He must find a place to land.

Once the adrenaline rush wore off, he started to lose consciousness again. But now he was secure in the knowledge his best friend Ruben watched over him. There was no danger as long as his wingman, Moon Shadow, was with him. And that he was sure of now. Before his senses left him, he heard the reassuring voice again.

"I'll let you know when I need you again. Go ahead and rest now. "

Chapter 18
INTREPID SPECTER

Mulholland and Fitzhenry had flown many sorties and found only a burned out shell of a P-51 on the beach of Padre Island, near where they last saw Beau and Ruben, but the aircraft was burned beyond recognition. Another sad note was the discovery of a lone aircraft near the Nueces River. They could not identify the debris but thought from the direction, it could have been Beau or Ruben.

Mulholland and Fitzhenry flew whenever possible, continuing their search, as they were the only ones able. Blackman had been hit with enemy fire in the raid, and Marix had been shot in the shoulder and was getting around, but neither of the men were flight-worthy. Marix did manage to talk with Krysti again, although she remained cold and aloof.

Hearts were heavy indeed. Larry James, BJ Warren, Ruben Alonzo, and Beau Gex were all presumed dead. Their casualties could be added to those of Chin Tang, Barry Picket, Fred Deberg, and Tom Sullivan. Gone forever were Boink, Snake, Flipper, Catman, and Black Jack. But what of Mongoose and Moon Shadow? Had they met with the same fate?

For a week, Krysti kept her vigil on the mesa for the man she loved. Sunday remained in a state of shock when she realized Ruben was most assuredly dead, a victim of the raid on Corpus Christi.

Only Justin believed Beau still lived. Most thought it to be a foolish child's fantasy. A dream that would never come true. One night, Justin found his mother kneeling next to her bed crying and repeating the same words: "You promised."

Justin patted his mother on the back. "It's okay, Mom. Beau will come back." Krysti only cried more.

A homing instinct consumed her. She had a burning desire to return home to her parents in El Paso. She could do nothing about that when the invasion started. Now, more than before, she worried about the safety of her parents. Were they alive? Her father had been an ornery cuss. Surely, he had known what to do. What of Beau's brothers? They would want to know about Beau's death. Once Beau had described the place, going into great detail and even as far as to the location from the highway. She was sure she could find his brothers and their home Big Rock at the eastern edge of Big Bend on the Rio Grande, easier than she might find her own parents. She wanted to return home, but feared the dangers such a trip would entail. Could she escape detection? After all, the country was still in the control of the invaders.

Michael had changed, becoming more patient with her and Justin. No one understood how happy he was that his greatest tormentor was gone forever. He actually became a rather nice person to be around.

A week passed. Still, Fitzhenry, and Mulholland found nothing. Hope turned into despair. One night when everyone had fallen asleep no one noticed Krysti leave the safety of Cliff Palace. She followed the trail to the small quiet lonely log cabin above the cliff.

She opened the squeaky door and crept in. The private sanctuary where she and Beau had spent so few, and yet wonderful nights in the privacy of each other's love. The small cabin in which they had shared such joy and intimate moments and talked about the future and the dreams they hoped to live one day. She lit a single candle in one of the brass candleholders. Slowly she approached the bed and wrapped the covers about her. She held a pillow in her hands. She could sense Beau. It was the smell unique to him she could elicit from the pillow she held. With the cover and pillow clutched tightly in her arms, she paced about aimlessly within the lonely cabin. In silence she stood alone and closed her eyes. Beau was as clear in her mind as if he were standing beside her.

Tears finally came from behind tightly closed lids and ran down her cheeks. Krysti started to cry. "Beau . . . why? I love you . . . come back to me!"

She fell to her knees, wrapped her arms around her small frame, and rocked back and forth. "You promised!"

The pain of the lost love tore at her heart. The anguish of the truth was too much for her to bear. No longer could she control her emotions, and she burst into uncontrolled weeping. The sounds of her sobs could be heard even outside the thick walls of the log cabin. Again and again, she uttered the words: "You promised!"

Clutching the pillow, she fell to the cold wooden floor where she continued lamenting the death of the first man she had ever truly loved. Sadness filled the cabin that so shortly before had been filled with laughter and the spirit of life. Krysti crushed the pillow to her as though it would bring Beau back. Relief finally came to her tired and weary mind, as she could deny sleep no longer. Alone and despondent, she slept.

* * *

In Krysti's emotional condition, it was easy for Marix to rekindle some type of friendship and get close to her again. He had learned she was pregnant and the baby was his. She had not wanted him to know, but it no longer mattered. He was ecstatic and more than ever determined to take her away from Cliff Palace. His superficial wounds were of no consequence, and now he tried more than ever to convince her to go with him to find her parents, using them as an excuse to fulfill his physical desires. Krysti continued to deny him.

Although he told her Beau was dead, he feared the man still lived and would return, exacting a punishment on him for the death of Ruben. He was afraid that somehow Beau would know of his part in Ruben's death. For that reason, he must escape with Krysti as soon as possible. Yet as much as she desired to find her parents, she would not go.

Marix became insanely angered at her refusal to leave with him. She tried to explain it was too dangerous a trek, even though she wanted to find her parents. Such a trip would be suicidal and dangerous for her and Justin. She had no way of knowing Marix had no intention of taking Justin with them. His plans involved her and no one else. Marix swore an oath to himself he would have her again. Slowly, a plan evolved in his mind of how he could steal Krysti away without anyone knowing, until it was too late. When the time was right, he would take her and nobody could stop him.

Ten days had passed since the battle. All agreed to a requiem for the loss of Beau, Ruben, and the others—a special occasion to celebrate the life of the two men, not their deaths. For the first time in almost two weeks, there was a festive mood in Cliff Palace.

They moved to the mesa where they ate, drank, and remembered the finer moments. Sunday told stories and laughed at the memories of the outrageous antics of the man she loved and his best friend. Ted told everything he knew about Beau and Ruben and the past antics they had done together. Even Tracy had touching and hilarious stories to tell about Ruben and Beau. Those three were Krysti's only link to the man she loved. She even began to ask them to repeat some of the stories they told. And Justin had humorous and loveable stories about Beau although they had spent but a few months together.

Tears rolled down the cheeks of Sunday and Krysti as they would alternate between fits of laughter and moments of sorrow. Cindy and Tracy were thankful for Beau saving them. Lindy realized how lucky Krysti had been even for the short time she and Beau had been together. Dean, Fitz, and Kipp regretted not being able to know the men longer. Robby and Daddy John listened intently to the wonderful stories. They all regretted that they had only been able to have such a short time together. The two leaders had fought so valiantly and given their lives not only for them, but also for their country.

Krysti confided in Sunday and told of her and Beau's time in the old cabin above the river. She said, "You were right, I never dreamed it could be the way it was with Beau. He was so special."

Sunday nodded and with a small rag wiped tears from her eyes. "So was Ruben. I loved him so much."

Both women hugged each other for they knew each had had a special person in their lives that few ever experience. They laughed and continued to talk of their fond memories. Sunday told more about the two men and their past than anyone else.

In the midst of the celebration, they all became silent. From the distance came a familiar sound. A prop plane was coming down the canyon toward the mesa! Shocked and astonished, they watched the smoking approach of the P-51 Mustang. It was definitely Beau's aircraft. Like immobile statues they stood in silence as it landed. All except Krysti, who alone rushed to the slowly moving aircraft as it taxied its way back toward the group. Excitedly then, they all rushed the wounded plane.

Krysti jumped to the wing as the canopy slid back. She reached the cockpit as Beau stood erect. He hadn't even removed his helmet before she wrapped her warm arms about his neck and smothered his oily, dirty face with kisses, all the while crying and saying, "I love you! I thought you were dead!"

Beau was dirty and dried blood caked his uniform. For her he was a wonderful sight. He reached over her arms and managed to remove his helmet. Then he pulled himself from the cockpit. All the while, Krysti clung to him. Standing on the wing, he crushed her to him, and kissed her passionately. "I love you, *Angel Eyes*," Beau whispered in her ear. He could feel her heart beat faster at the sound of the words.

Pulling away, he reached into the cockpit and pulled out a dozen small wild flowers making for a rainbow of colors. They were half crushed and covered with grease. He gave them to Krysti.

"Beau, they're beautiful," she said, touching them to her nose to take in the dainty flowers' sweet fragrance. When she pulled them away, her nose was covered with grease.

"I saw them covering a nearby field and I thought I'd get ya some," Beau said, as he gently pinched the smudge of grease from her nose. "They sure were a lot prettier when I saw them."

"Nonsense. I love them," said Krysti, still clinging to the small wilted flowers.

Hand in hand, they made their way from the wing, when Krysti noticed Beau limping. She saw the blood caked on his leg. "Your leg, it's hurt!"

The leg of the flight suit was covered with blood and torn where Beau had tended to his injury. "Let me tell you, it feels a lot better now that I'm home." He slid to the ground and landed on his good leg, then turned, and gently lifted Krysti from the wing.

Everyone gathered around the small plane, except Marix, who watched from a distance. The first to greet Beau was Fitz, while Dean gave him a smile and a nod. Tracy grabbed a quick hug.

"I'm glad you're safe," said Ted, as moisture welled up in his eyes. At the back of the group, Robby, Lindy, and Cindy watched. Robby gave a thumbs up.

Kipp greeted Beau and Krysti as they walked away from the wing of the crippled P-51. "Hey, mate, we thought you was a goner."

"Me, too."

"We were giving you a requiem," smiled Mulholland.

"Sorry to disappoint ya," said Beau with a weak smile and a slight limp. He put his arm around Krysti's shoulders, and she responded, slipping her arm around his waist.

"Ruben?" asked Mulholland.

Abruptly, Beau became solemn and shook his head. Beau sought Sunday with his eyes and when he found her, he moved in her direction. Sunday stood away from the joyous gathering.

Tears were in his eyes. "Sunday, forgive me. I couldn't bring Ruben home."

Tiny droplets fell from her eyes. She put her hand on his shoulder. "The men told me what happened. If Ruben had known he was going to die, he would still have flown beside you."

"I was with him when he died." Beau's voice cracked and he could barely talk. "He said he would always love you."

Sunday started to sob and buried her face in his chest. He hugged her as tears covered his cheeks.

"I'm glad you're home," Sunday said, regaining her composure. "Ruben had always said if he died, he wanted you to be Moon Shadow!"

Beau shook his head in disbelief. "No, no . . . Sunday, I cannot be Moon Shadow."

She managed to smile at Beau. "It was his wish."

"Yes," chorused some of the others.

Sunday repeated, "It was Ruben's wish." Slowly, Beau nodded his head and tried to smile between the tight set lips.

Fitz turned to Tracy. "You've got to paint Moon Shadow on Beau's plane." Tracy shook her head yes and acknowledged the request.

Beau said to Fitz, "I think our flying days are over."

And so the legend lived on. No longer would Beau be the Mongoose. From that day forward, he would be Moon Shadow!

Justin ran to Beau's unoccupied side and wrapped another arm about his waist.

"Hey, Champ," Beau said as he ruffled Justin's hair.

"I told them you'd come back," said Justin with hero worship in his eyes. "But they didn't believe me. And guess what?"

"What?"

"Champ has visited me a few times!"

"I'm not surprised. That little mockingbird will never forget you."

Justin moved aside as Beau motioned Sunday near. Putting his arm around her shoulders, he wiped her eyes, and she clung to him.

Directly in front of Beau stood Daddy John. "They say you can't teach old dogs new tricks. But I say, you can't teach young dogs old tricks." Then he pointed to the fighter that had brought him home: *"The Devil's Angel."*

Behind them the sleek black P-51 Mustang rested, wings spread proudly—considered obsolete for almost fifty years, a relic from a past war, cast aside for the jet age. Now the sleek little aircraft had stepped through time to save a country from its own space age inventions. A country that had rejected her usefulness for technology. She had come from the past to defeat an enemy from the present to save the future. The *Devil's Angel* lay wounded but not slain.

Man and machine, a unique bond words couldn't describe. He gazed at the aircraft almost lovingly. "No, Daddy John. I'd call her an Angel. Along with some friendly help, she brought me home."

"Son, ya did one hell of a job," said Daddy John. "But you're one hell of a mess. I suggest we return to Cliff Palace and get you cleaned up. You can tell us the story after a little rest."

With those words of wisdom, they all returned to Cliff Palace. Beau told the detailed story to Sunday. Later, he recited the story to the others and went into detail about the death of Rasht Sharafan, the Syrian called Cobra.

The obvious question was where had he been, and what had taken so long for him to return? Beau explained how he had passed out twice but recovered and managed to land his ailing aircraft. After he landed, he knew he was lost. He managed to hide the plane, but had lost so much blood it had taken him four days of resting before he was able to try repairs on his aircraft. Roots, small birds, and animals were his source of food. Luckily a small stream had been near. A busted oil hose had allowed all the oil to leak from the engine. There had been no way to fly the Mustang.

He had searched the area trying to find tools and equipment to repair the aircraft. It had taken ten days to recover from his wounds and locate the much-needed, numerous abandoned cars. With tools he found, he constructed the pieces required to repair the Mustang. He found enough oil from derelict cars to fill the P-51. Although not the best way, he managed to nurse the aircraft home. Tired and weary from his ordeal, Beau stayed alert long enough to finish his story.

All had retired for the night except Krysti and Justin. With his head on Beau's lap, Justin was already asleep.

Krysti said, "I have a surprise for you. Give me ten minutes and I'll be back."

"While you do that I'll take care of Justin," said Beau. While Krysti went to prepare the surprise, Beau bundled up Justin, carried him carefully to his room and then tucked him into bed.

Now Beau sought out Marix to set a few things straight. Marix had remained apart from the others but Beau had watched him. Moments later, Beau found him standing alone on the mesa of Cliff Palace looking down at the river. Beau's presence obviously made Marix uneasy.

"I have something to tell you."

"I have nothing to say to you," snapped Marix.

"What I have to say is only for you." Unexpectedly, Beau took his clenched fist and hit Marix in the side of his face, knocking him to the ground. Still conscious, Marix rolled over on his back rubbing his right cheek and pulling his legs back to use his knees in a defensive maneuver, while trying to crawl away from his attacker on his back, using his elbows.

"Are you crazy!" Marix cried.

From between clenched teeth Beau bent over Marix and snarled, "Shut up and listen." Without saying another word Marix nodded. Terror filled his heart. He was afraid of this thing crouching over him.

Beau continued. "Ruben's guns were jammed. I'm sure it was James. Only I think he intended it for me. I don't know how," Beau hesitated before he continued, "but I think you had something to do with it. I think you knew."

Finished with his mission, Beau turned and started to walk away but had only taken a few steps when he stopped and turned back to Marix.

Once again Marix saw the same intense hatred and anger in Beau's eyes as when he and James had tried to stop him from searching for Krysti. Death in the cold steel blue eyes bored through Marix like knives. He cringed and slid away from the apparition before him.

From between gritted teeth, Beau added, "If I ever prove you had anything to do with Ruben's death—I'm going to kill you!" Slowly Beau relaxed; a smile gradually filled his face and he spun about to find Krysti.

Behind him was a terrified mass of what only some would call a man. Marix trembled in horror and could not quit his shaking.

At that moment something inside Marix's mind snapped, and he swore he would get revenge on Beau and make Krysti his. Breaching the thin line of sanity, Marix had finally been pushed across to the unstable tormented, dangerous other side.

* * *

Krysti found Beau. In one hand she held the stems of two empty wineglasses, and in the other, a bottle of Daddy John's wine. Together they made their way to the private sanctuary afforded them in the log cabin. Inside, on a small table near the bed, burned two candles. Next to the candles stood a clump of crushed and oil covered wild flowers resurrected with the water filling the glass container in which they now rested. Krysti poured the wine and offered a toast to the future.

"You said some friendly help brought you home?" Krysti asked.

Then Beau confided to her how he had almost lost his life. "If it hadn't been for Ruben, I'd be dead now."

"But Ruben was dead before you got shot."

"That's what I'm trying to tell you. I had passed out when I heard him warn me. Ruben saved me. The plane was about to crash when I heard him warn me a second time."

"You're safe now. If it was Ruben, be thankful," Krysti said. It hurt to see the sadness in his eyes. She knew. "You miss him?"

He tried to talk but the words would not come. With a great deal of effort, he answered. "More than you know."

Krysti squeezed his hand understandingly. "I'm just glad I have you back again." Her eyes sparkled, and she took his other hand in hers.

"I love you, *Angel Eyes*," Beau whispered.

"And I, you." She kissed him gently on the ear and whispered, "Be mine tonight!" She pulled him willingly toward the bed. Hours later Krysti fell asleep in the first peaceful night's sleep since Beau's disappearance.

He rubbed her temple gently with his fingers. Bending near her face, he kissed her tenderly on the neck. He gazed lovingly at the woman who was sleeping peacefully next to him. His mind drifted away and reflected on the strange events that had brought them together. She was strong and brave. As he watched her he knew the strange events life had dealt them had not ended but had just begun.

There was a war. Later he knew he would have to deal with Marix. How could he make Krysti and Justin safe? Again he looked at her. He smiled and tears of happiness filled his eyes. He loved her with all his heart. The short time with her, knowing she loved him, was worth an eternity. All he could do was take things a day at a time. It would be years before life returned to any semblance of normalcy. Maybe never. Today he had his love and that was all that mattered.

Love was almost all that mattered. Quietly, lest he wake Krysti, Beau rose from the bed and made his way from the cabin.

Outside, he thought about the others who had been lost. All that remained were Fitz, Kipp, and Dean. His mind refused to acknowledge Marix as one of them.

Gone was the old group, all but one. He was the only one who remained. War had taken Galloway, Sully, BJ, and his best friend Ruben.

In the peaceful darkness of the night, he peered into the heavens. No longer full, the Moon cast no more shadows. The Moon was gone, but not the memory of the man.

The tightness in his throat made it almost impossible to talk. But he found the words to speak to the heavens. "Ruben, I don't know how you did what you did, but I wanta thank you. If it's okay with you, I think I'll stay here with Krysti for a while."

For a moment, he thought he heard words in the distance. Words or was it the whistling wind? In the distance, faint but clear. A smile slowly filled his face when he thought he recognized the voice that said, *"My buddy! Take care."*

"Moon Shadow," Beau answered. He squeezed the leather pouch about his neck, the one that once belonged to Grandy, then Ruben, and now him. The pouch filled with the spirit of earth, wind, and fire.

The night was quiet except for the creatures in the shadows and the cold running water of the Frio River. A small animal rummaged the brush for food, and insects sang their eternal songs.

Alone, Beau stood with his thoughts and memories. With the memories of the dead friend who had saved his life, he said a prayer. A prayer for Moon Shadow.

GLOSSARY

Ace - Fighter pilot with five or more victories
ACM - Air Combat Maneuvering, or dog fighting.
Bag - Flight suit
Bat Turn - A tight, high-G change of heading. A reference to the rapid 180-degree Batmobile maneuver in the old "Batman" television series.
Bogey - Unidentified and potentially hostile aircraft.
Bandits - Identified hostile craft.
Barrel Roll - Medium-speed roll, course remaining constant.
Bounce, Tap - Unexpected attack on another aircraft.
Check Six - Visual observation to the rear of an aircraft from which most air-to-air attacks can be expected. This is in reference to the clock system of scanning the circular area around the aircraft: 12 o'clock is straight ahead, 6 o'clock is dead aft. Also a common salutation and greeting among tactical pilots.
Chandelle - Reversal of course by climbing turn.
CIA – Central Intelligence Agency
Double Ugly - Nickname for the enormous but less than beautiful F-4 Phantom. Also called Rhino.
Electric Jet - The F-16 Fighting Falcon, nicknamed because of its fly-by-wire controls.
Fox One, Two, Three - Radio calls indicating the firing of a Sparrow, Sidewinder, or Phoenix air-to-air missile, respectively.
Furball - A confused aerial engagement with many combatants.
G-suit - Nylon trousers that wrap around the legs and abdomen. Filled automatically with compressed air in high-G maneuvers, the G-suit helps prevent the pooling of blood in the lower extremities, thus retarding the tendency to lose consciousness.
Gomer - Slang for a dogfight adversary, the usage presumably stemming from the old Gomer Pyle television show.
Gouge, the poop, the skinny - The latest inside information.
Hummer, puppy or bad boy - Any ingenious machine-plane, car, weapon

whose actual name can't be recalled.
HVAR – High Velocity Aircraft Rocket
Immelman - A reversal of course by half loop and roll out.
Jock, Driver - Pilot.
Knife Fight - Close-in low-speed aerial dogfight.
Mach - The speed of sound is relative to the altitude and temperature. At sea level the speed of sound is approximately 750 mph. At 40,000 feet it is 650 mph.
MP – Military Police
Mud-mover or Ground-pounder - Low-level attack aircraft.
Rhino - Nickname for the F-4
SAM - Surface-to-air missile.
Scooter - Nickname for the A-4 Skyhawk.
Speed Jeans - G-suit
Speed of Heat, Warp One - Very, very fast.
Split-S - To half-roll and dive vertically.
Three-Nine Line - Imaginary line across the aircraft's wings. The adversary is to be kept in front of the three-nine-line.
Tits Machine - A good airplane. A favorite. Nostalgic term referring to great aircraft.
Tits-up - Broken, non-functioning.
Tomcat - F-14
Trim - to adjust control tabs for proper flying attitude.
Turkey - Nickname for the F-14 Tomcat.
Viper Jet - Nickname for the F-16.
Whiskey Delta - "Weak dick," a pilot who can't cut it.

REASONS FOR THE COLLAPSE OF THE ROMAN EMPIRE

Military – the military was spread so thin around the known world that the Empire could not defend its own borders. Military forces expanded and so did the pay. The Empire conquered distant but wealthy provinces but were unable to continue holding the territories. The burden to support the military became so great that the financial collapse from within began. Slowly the Empire pulled the military away from conquered and controlled territories. Gradually other countries took over these territories.

Taxes - the emperors were forced to raise taxes to pay for the huge military spending.

Health and the Environment – these declined as the wealthy kept the money and the government lacked the money to help the people. Alcohol was abused.

Corruption – the corruption of political and business leaders became rampant as they rewarded themselves and their followers.

Unemployment - increased as the small farmer virtually vanished when they were bought up and run by a few of the wealthy who lowered pay and expected more.

Inflation – lack of work hurt the poor as the wealthy horded most of the gold coins forcing the people to barter or steal for their needs.

Language – numerous dialects and languages were allowed. Communications became increasingly difficult. Eventually the various languages prevailed, ending communications with the Empire.

Urban Decay – became more prevalent as the poor were unable to afford rent, forcing many to crime for survival.

Technology – arrogant about their own abilities leaders let the technology lag behind other countries.

Chemicals – lead in pipes made the Romans sick and many died.

*Values and Morals – declined as leaders wasted money on lavish extravagances to please themselves and the people.

Islam - some even point to the rise of Islam as a reason.

Where does the United States stand today?

*During the reign of the Roman Empire, the leaders would give things to the people to keep them happy. The Coliseum with gladiators was created just for that purpose to keep peace among the people and make them happy. Today we have the gladiators perform in something called the Super Bowl. Now our politicians deem it necessary to give away high tech receivers so the poor will still be able to watch the Super Bowl on their antiquated television sets. Even now Congress is quickly approving an additional billion dollars so all the poor will be equipped with the new television receivers so they can be entertained at government expense or in reality the taxpayers' dollars.

NATIONAL DEBT, THE DEFICIT AND SPENDING

"The budget should be balanced; the treasury should be refilled; public debt should be reduced; and the arrogance of public officials should be controlled." -Cicero. 106-43 B.C.

 For my novel *Moon Shadow* to be credible, I had to come up with a reasonable way the United States could be invaded. I looked at Russia, Mexico, and other countries that had collapsed previously. All had gone bankrupt. I wondered if the same thing could happen to the United States.
 Let me clarify the National Debt and the deficit. The National <u>Debt</u> is the total amount of money owed by the government. The federal budget <u>deficit</u> is the yearly amount by which spending exceeds revenue. When you add up all the deficits and surpluses (of which there are very few) for the past 200 years, you will come up with the current National Debt. Our politicians love to brag about how "The deficit is down!" like it's a great accomplishment. Don't let them fool you. Here is an example: Let's say the amount of taxes collected is 2.3 trillion but the budget is 2.8 trillion, which will give us a 500 billion deficit already figured into the budget for the year. Suppose they only spend 2.7 trillion. Now they can brag about how they cut the deficit by 100 billion dollars when in reality they still added 400 billion to the debt. All smoking guns. Surely you will remember how under Clinton they continually bragged about the large surplus. Not true. Every year the National Debt increased under Clinton, but by using the example above they tell us we had a surplus. At the bottom of this article are the yearly increases in National Debt since 1978. Not since 1960 did the government spend less than the money it took in, which is something it should try to do every year.
 The National Debt is huge and climbing at the rate of around $75 million an hour, but as long as the economy is strong there is no fear. The government and almost all politicians assume it will stay strong, hence the

National Debt continues to rise—at an alarming rate. The best comparison is you as an individual. You make enough money to pay all of your debts and there is really no problem. In thirty years the house is paid and most of your bills are gone. But suppose you were laid off or injured and out of work for six months without any other source of income. What happens? You go bankrupt. Here is another scenario that is happening to our own government. Currently our government is spending thirty percent more than it takes in each year. Suppose you did the same. As an example if you made $100,000 per year and added thirty percent to your debt each year along with interest it would take fifteen years to reach a point where you owed one million dollars. At this point the interest you owed would exceed what you make. You would be bankrupt.

Our government is not immune to the same problem. In 2003 the interest on the National Debt exceeded $322 billion. Only two departments in the government exceed that spending: the military is one of them.

During 2004 the Federal Government took in 2.5 trillion dollars but spent approximately 3.1 trillion for a 600 billion dollar deficit.

Here are some other interesting figures. Currently the National Debt stands at $8,003,104,666,539.23. To pay this amount off, each and every American would need to come up with $25,000 today. From 1980, when Reagan took office, until 1992 when Bush left office, the debt went from less than one trillion dollars to over four trillion dollars. From 2000 to 2004 the National Debt under our current President Bush has increased more than two trillion dollars to its current level. At this rate when President Bush's second term is finished we will have a debt of nearly ten trillion dollars. The interest on that debt at five percent interest will be $500 billion. But suppose inflation hits. At ten percent the interest is one trillion dollars. At fifteen percent the interest would be a staggering 1.5 trillion dollars. Think of those numbers. The interest alone would be more than the money required to run the government.

I know that sounds like heavy inflation and more like a depression, which surely won't happen. They probably thought the same thing in 1929. Still, interest did hit double digits as recently as the 1990s. It can and will happen again. But when? How safe are we?

Another sad note is that Social Security is treated like any other tax and has already been spent. Social Security is part of the deficit and really doesn't exist anymore. Social Security is not part of the Federal Budget Fund. It is supposed to be a separate account with its own source of income and its own separate trust fund. Social Security payments do not go into the general fund, and should NOT be counted as general revenue. The trust fund is supposed to be used to pay benefits. But Congress ordered the Treasury Department to use the money in the Social Security Trust Fund as though it were general revenue, promising to pay it back. Now that promise is part of the National Debt. In reality Social Security is just another very large tax collection tool.

The Social Security Trust Fund is simply a meaningless record of taxes that have been collected for future needs, spent for current desires, and then recorded and counted as an asset. Fraud is a better description.

If something severe ever occurred in the next eight years like a combination of double digit inflation along with double digit unemployment, then the United States of America could possibly reach its darkest hour. The possibility exists for the United States to be bankrupt before the year 2015.

What you will see in the next few years is loss of government benefits to the people, not government employees, and a severe rise in the taxes.

That is exactly what happens in my novel *Moon Shadow*.

If you are interested in the National Debt go to these websites:

www.brillig.com/debt_clock/www.toptips.com/debtclock.html
www.treasurydirect.gov/NP/debt/current

I went to the "toptips" site and found the National Debt increased approximately $20,000 a second. In four seconds the National Debt increases enough to pay my salary for a year. Only four seconds! On November 19, 2004 our Congress had to pass a last minute bill that enabled our government to borrow 8.18 trillion dollars. On average the National Debt is increasing more than 1.6 billion dollars a day.

Sometime on October 18, 2005, our National Debt surpassed $8,000,000,000,000.00 (that is eight trillion). Go to the websites above and see how much the National Debt has increased since this was written.

I'm neither for nor against our presidents. I'm against the debt and the potential problems such a huge debt will bring our country. Did you ever wonder if our representatives have ever told us the truth? They never actually told us a lie but what they said could be classified as lies by omission. Note the years under Clinton and the supposed "surplus." There never was a surplus. The last year Clinton was in office the National Debt only increased 18 billion dollars. Not bad, but definitely no surplus. Under Bush's administration the National Debt has accelerated at an alarming rate. From November, 2004 to November, 2005 the National Debt increased in eleven of those months. Of particular interest are nine of those months. The debt in "each" of those nine months exceeded the total added to the National Debt during Clinton's last year as President. Even more shocking is that on October 5, 2005, the next 24 hours found the National Debt increasing almost as much as the last year of Clinton's administration.

During the month of October, 2005 the National Debt increased almost 100 billion dollars.

On Sunday, October 16, 2005 at approximately 7:58:03 PM, Central Standard Time, the National Debt exceeded 8 trillion dollars for the first time ever.

Below are the years and the National Debt back to 1959.

10/17/2005 $8,003,897,406,911.24
09/30/2005 $7,932,709,661,723.50
09/30/2004 $7,379,052,696,330.32
09/30/2003 $6,783,231,062,743.62
09/30/2002 $6,228,235,965,597.16
09/28/2001 $5,807,463,412,200.06
09/29/2000 $5,674,178,209,886.86
09/30/1999 $5,656,270,901,615.43
09/30/1998 $5,526,193,008,897.62
09/30/1997 $5,413,146,011,397.34
09/30/1996 $5,224,810,939,135.73
09/29/1995 $4,973,982,900,709.39
09/30/1994 $4,692,749,910,013.32
09/30/1993 $4,411,488,883,139.38
09/30/1992 $4,064,620,655,521.66
09/30/1991 $3,665,303,351,697.03
09/28/1990 $3,233,313,451,777.25
09/29/1989 $2,857,430,960,187.32
09/30/1988 $2,602,337,712,041.16
09/30/1987 $2,350,276,890,953.00
09/30/1986 $2,125,302,616,658.42
09/30/1985 $1,945,941,616,459.88
09/30/1984 $1,662,966,000,000.00
09/30/1983 $1,410,702,000,000.00
09/30/1982 $1,197,073,000,000.00
09/30/1981 $1,028,729,000,000.00
09/30/1980 $ 930,210,000,000.00
09/30/1979 $ 845,116,000,000.00
09/30/1978 $ 789,207,000,000.00
09/30/1977 $ 718,943,000,000.00
09/30/1976 $ 653,544,000,000.00
09/30/1975 $ 576,649,000,000.00
09/30/1974 $ 492,665,000,000.00
09/30/1973 $ 469,898,039,554.70

09/30/1972 $ 449,298,066,119.00
09/30/1971 $ 424,130,961,959.95
09/30/1970 $ 389,158,403,690.26
09/30/1969 $ 368,225,581,254.41
09/30/1968 $ 358,028,625,002.91
09/30/1967 $ 344,663,009,745.18
09/30/1966 $ 329,319,249,366.68
09/30/1965 $ 320,904,110,042.04
09/30/1964 $ 317,940,472,718.38
09/30/1963 $ 309,346,845,059.17
09/30/1962 $ 303,470,080,489.27
09/30/1961 $ 296,168,761,214.92
09/30/1960 $ 290,216,815,241.68 * (The last surplus)
09/30/1959 $ 290,797,771,717.63

One final thought. Could the National Debt reach ten trillion dollars by 2008? If so, what will happen to the economy? Remember I said earlier that our government collects about 2.1 trillion dollars but needs 2.7 trillion to run the government? Let's say we reach a 10 trillion dollar debt in three more years and suppose interest is say ten percent, then the interest on the National Debt will be one trillion dollars leaving only 1.3 trillion to run a government that is spending close to 2.8 trillion per years. This simply won't work.

Unless they do something very soon our government will be unable to pay off the National Debt. Financially our government is rapidly reaching a "point of no return." At the rate the debt is increasing we could reach a debt of $20 trillion by the end of 2012. The same time the Mayan calendar predicts the end of the world. A $20 trillion debt with ten percent interest would mean that in 2012 the interest on the debt would equal the taxes collected. In other words the end of the world for America.

April 1, 2009:

The above was added to in 2005 and has played out almost precisely as I predicted. This is no April fool's joke.

National Debt
04/01/2009 $11,208,076,192,300.55

When Bush left office the debt was 10.5 trillion. Currently, China, Japan and Saudi Arabia owns about four trillion of our debt in bonds they purchase each year. I want to give you some new numbers to think about. President Obama has been in office a hundred days and I'm ready to predict his outcome in less than four years. Obama and Congress have established a budget of 3.9 trillion or about 1.8 trillion more than our government brings in. I truly believe more than this will be spent; closer to two trillion over budget the next four years. If Congress and the president continue to spend like this we will owe nearly twenty trillion at the end of Obama's first term in 2012. At that time China, Japan and Saudi Arabia will probably own close to ten trillion of that debt. Suppose the interest rate in ten percent. After all selling bonds on a debt ridden country is very difficult unless you raise the interest and make it more appealing. Remember we collect 2.1 trillion in taxes. In 2012 the interest on the debt will be two trillion. Do you see where this is going? Now just suppose the three countries that buy the majority of our bonds refuse to buy them any longer. Do you know what happens? The United States of America will be bankrupt and become a third world country. You might say our dollar won't be worth a peso.

September 11, 2013

I understand why Boston has so many problems. Seems a teacher decided to replace the "Pledge of Allegiance" with a Muslim prayer. We've come a long way since Obama took over as President of the United States of America. We are now able dismiss the word "united."

How much has Obama cost us? Under Obama the debt increases almost 150 billion per month. For 120 days the debt has not increased from 16.8 trillion, but it is going up more than 150 billion per month. This is called a Ponzi scheme, where you steal from Peter to pay Paul. Madoff went to prison for doing the same thing; so too should Congress and the President. Ironically those who u loudest are government employees or those on welfare. Detroit is bankrupt and will soon stop paying retirement for government employees. The same thing will soon happen to the federal government. They are spending 4 trillion per year but only collection 2.5 trillion in taxes. Same thing happened to Russia in 1988. Obama has added 6 trillion to the debt in his first four years. Most of the money has gone to banks and programs to satisfy his desire. To put this in perspective, Obama could have given 30 million of the poorest Americans fifty thousand dollars a year for each of his first four years. That would have spurred the economy. Instead the Nobel Peace Prize winner spent in on incompetence, gun running, killer drones and war after war.

But America has more problems. Christians are now classified as

terrorists. You can't say anything against gays but they can say bad things about Christians. But the scary thing is what Obama has done for Muslims. They cannot be criticized or even watched as terrorists but 95 percent of the terror comes from six percent of our population. For the gays and lesbians I would like to say that Christians bear you no ill will; no thoughts of death or reprisal. On the other hand Obama calls America a Muslim nation. He has even said if he must he will side with Muslims. It is known that Muslims will force Christians to convert or be beheaded. Do you know how Muslims feel about gays and lesbians? If you don't you should. Now what do you suppose Muslims do to gays and lesbians? You might want to brush up on these religions. I don't think Obama and Liberals have your best interests at heart. Speaking of heart Obama wants to give a billion dollars to the Syrian rebel who cut the heart and liver out of his enemy and ate it. If you don't believe me just check it out:
https://www.youtube.com/watch?v=GfHSPLW63Gg

Who did 911? Who did Boston? Who murdered 13 people at Fort Hood? The Muslim Brotherhood offers them all of their support. Obama offers the Muslim Brotherhood all of his support; Libya, Egypt and Syria. Obama refuses to help Christians in any of those countries. To be honest you can count on one hand all of people in Congress and the Supreme Court who support Christians or Americans. I don't want to slay the Democrats because it appears the Republicans are no better. There are no Christian Conservatives that I see. They all want a socialist communist government and the way to attain that is to destroy Christian values. The American way of life as we know it may be gone forever.

If Obama has his way we may soon be greeting people with, "Allahu Akbar."

COMMENTS FROM THE AUTHOR

Moon Shadow was intended to be a piece of fiction for enjoyment, but after I finished, I realized it had become much more. The original idea behind *Moon Shadow* was to grapple with the collapse of the United States and a following invasion. For a long time I worked over and over in my mind how such a scenario could actually happen and play out. I began *Moon Shadow* in 1987 and had been working on the manuscript for three years when President George H. W. Bush invaded Iraq. At the same time, American companies were going bankrupt while the corporate officers were being arrested and put in jail. Many wealthy political contributors managed to elude prosecution while the national debt skyrocketed by more than a trillion dollars.

I first completed *Moon Shadow* in 1990, but I've since updated the story to reveal a repeat performance by many of the same misguided and greedy people involved in the first fiasco. I asked myself, "How could a fictional scenario such as the collapse of the United States and a following invasion actually happen and play out?" Greed and corruption were my answers.

Much like raising a child, I have reworked *Moon Shadow* by pouring my life into the story. For this I have watched *Moon Shadow* grow, and at times I have been surprised by what it has given me in return.

Nostradamus I'm not, but many strange things described in my novel have come to pass. The first version of *Moon Shadow*—written from 1987 to 1990—opened with the United States sending forces to the Middle East to protect our interests. This slice of fiction ended up being very similar to Desert Storm; in fact, I had described Desert Storm in alarmingly accurate detail. But my fictional account was completed in 1990, a year before Desert Storm actually happened.

Another piece of history foreshadowed in *Moon Shadow* was the *Aurora Project*, a top-secret government project to make a plane that could fly directly into space. I wrote in detail about this project—by name—years before it was made public in 1996.

My novel also describes torture and the use of chemical and biological weapons. Most disturbingly, in 1995 I added a section to the original manuscript that detailed how invaders hijacked passenger airliners and killed the president. In my 1995 revision, the man behind the hijacking was Osama bin Laden.

Originally, *Moon Shadow* focused on the actions of the first President Bush. With each passing year up until the present time and the George W. Bush presidency, I molded the novel and added sections to keep up with current events. The events described in *Moon Shadow* have played out with shocking accuracy and similarities that are terrifying.

On September 11, 2001, I was on a flight from Seattle to Houston when word reached us about the World Trade Center and the Pentagon. Less than thirty minutes out, the captain made an announcement saying a plane had hit one of the World Trade Center towers. At first people laughed—including me—as we all wondered how a small plane might have hit one of the towers. Then, a few minutes later the captain made another announcement.

"We have terrible news," he said. "Another commercial airliner has hit the other Twin Tower in New York. We're sorry but when we land in Houston this flight will not continue and you will need to reschedule your flight."

I can still remember the shock, horror and terror on the faces of many of the passengers on that flight. Speculation ran rampant on the plane as to who had done this terrible thing. We still knew nothing. One of the passengers thought China had attacked us, another thought it might be Russia, while a few guessed it to be drug dealers from Colombia since we had just arrested the leader from one of their major cartels.

I assured them it wasn't Russia or China since they depended on our business to help their countries. There was also no way it could have been Colombia because whoever had done such a thing committed suicide and no drug dealer was willing to sacrifice his life.

"Then who could have done this?" someone asked me.

I responded with my own thoughts. "Whoever did this was someone who was willing to die for what he wanted. I'm probably wrong because the last time something like this happened it was Oklahoma City and many thought it was someone from the Middle East when it actually turned out to be an American. But I think I know who might have been involved. I've been reading and writing about a man, Osama bin Laden. His dream has been to destroy the World Trade Center. It is said he was associated with the Twin Towers bombing a few years ago. I'm probably wrong, but if I were to pick someone who was responsible for what has happened, Osama bin Laden would be my first choice."

Most of those listening looked at me like I was crazy.

Again the captain made an announcement that sent fear and chills through everyone. "Ladies and Gentlemen, another airliner has crashed into the Pentagon. President Bush has ordered all aircraft to return to their points of origin. We are to return to Seattle immediately. You will need to make arrangements for your connecting flights."

Everyone was talking, all were scared, and each time the plane hit a bump in the sky, some of the passengers would scream.

To me it was obvious there would be no more flights. I spoke loudly to those around me, "Think about this. The president has ordered us to return. Whatever has happened, it's very serious. Before there can be any more flights they must first figure out who did it, how they did it and how do we stop it? There won't be any flights today, tomorrow or for days. When I get back to Seattle I'm driving back to Houston. Who wants to go with me?"

Again they looked at me like I was some kind of nut, but many were lost in their own chaotic thoughts and fears. Something tragic and terrible had happened and we only knew what we had heard from the captain.

I added, "And when the flights do start again do you really want to be the first to test the airways? I don't. I'm driving back to Houston."

The flight returned to Seattle and when we disembarked it looked like the people were running from a fire. Fear and terror showed in all their faces. Everyone was deserting the airport. I went to the closest phone and started dialing. Two people, Rich and Maggie Pyle, approached me and asked if I was really driving back to Houston. I assured them I was. They also started calling for a car. In less than thirty minutes we were getting into one of the last rentals. It was so strange to see the rental garage void of all but two cars. It was empty. Never in my life have I ever seen an airport so deserted. We started our journey to Houston.

Upon arriving in Houston I contacted the FBI and told them what I had written and that I believed there were plans to do even more hideous things to America. They never returned my call. The reason I contacted them was simple. For more than fourteen years I had been putting together my novel *Moon Shadow*, studying the minds of terrorists and what they might do. In my book I had detailed numerous terrorist acts against our country.

There are things described in *Moon Shadow* that have not yet occurred. Will some of these events be like Desert Storm, the *Aurora Project* and the September 11, 2001, attacks? Will they too come to pass?

Our American military marches to victory not much differently than did the British troops in their bright red uniforms more than two hundred years ago. At that time the British were unbeatable, but they lost. Now

America is unbeatable but has exposed its Achilles' heel. There is still time to correct it before it's too late. Not unlike the British Empire, George W. Bush and his American Empire are headed for the same fate.

You say, "Impossible! You are wrong!" I hope so. After all, *Moon Shadow* is only a work of fiction, but it is said truth is stranger than fiction. And don't forget what we were taught when we were in school: History repeats itself.

I have always believed history repeats. Man is an intelligent animal but he refuses to learn from his mistakes. What truly terrifies me are not the terrorists but the political and business leaders of our country. They have lost their honor and integrity.

Two and two is four, always has been and always will be. But that is not true for the politicians that run our country. You can pay them to make two and two equal something else. Our congressmen can look us in the face and swear two and two is five and we'll believe them, while at the same time another congressman will tell us two and two is three, and we'll believe him. Because of this, unless our leaders change their ways, our country is doomed. I believe we are now looking at a president that is capable of destroying our country.

Abraham Lincoln could see this and summed it up best when he said, "America will never be destroyed from the outside. If we falter and lose our freedoms, it will be because we destroyed ourselves."

I finished the original version of *Moon Shadow* in 1990 and continued to update the manuscript to stay true to current events. As the years passed, I watched with amazement as many of the fictional scenarios I'd created became true events. Today, my old novel *Moon Shadow* is as fresh and true as if it had been written only yesterday. In a terrifying way this only reinforces the old adage, "History repeats itself." Today we see our leaders at a point in time where they can learn from their mistakes and change history, but instead they continue to repeat the same mistakes. Has anything really changed?

From the beginning of time every empire has collapsed. There have been no exceptions.

THE MOON SHADOW SERIES:

An excerpt from Book 1:
MOON SHADOW THE LEGEND

Chapter 1
DESERT SECRETS

The full moon rose majestically over the dark shimmering Mediterranean Sea, while waves pounded against the desert sands surrounding the dead city. More than twenty-three years had passed since the *Desert Storm* operation of 1991. Two more wars had completed the devastation. Previously a beacon to tourists from around the world, the burned and bombed buildings stood like skeletons: a grim reminder of an elegant past. The once proud Lebanese city was a testimony to the destructive might of the United States of America. The destruction had come about to make the world safe from aggression and to protect the Jewish country of Israel, bordering to the south. A *New World Order* had been created to protect freedom and humanity—and to prevent wars. Still, men killed each other for God and country. The Muslims had succumbed, but had not forgotten and now their rapid rise to power terrified the world. While the United States became divided the Muslim world had united and ironically received their financial support from the President of America.

Beneath the Moon's glow a silver, ghostly whirlwind twirled about the cool, dark, desert floor, filling with thousands of timeless moonstruck grains of sand that frolicked freely through the changing spiral. Slowly it crept across the desert, toward the empty decaying resort. Moon shadows guarded the dead city. Desert winds howled their delight.

This night the desert rats were not the only ones stirring. The decaying structures of once beautiful architectural masterpieces were now a gathering place for Iraqi and Lebanese terrorists carrying out missions of retaliation, death, and torture. Inside the shell of a past ornate and exquisitely decorated hotel where people had once gathered to celebrate and dance, a lone lantern sent shadows dancing against the scarred stone walls and dusty, rock-strewn floor. Three men came to do their truculent work, while their captive waited for a death that would be long in coming.

In a far corner of the room, a lantern rested on an old, broken table. A rusted and bent metal barrel served as a leg for the warped and peeling desk. The prisoner was tied firmly to a worn out feeble chair. Two of the men held their intended victim's arms firmly against the tabletop, while the third watched.

The third man seemed out of place, like a person wearing formal attire to a mud-wrestling match. Impeccably dressed in a pilot's uniform, not a button was out of position. Even in the dust of the old building, his black boots retained their shine. Clean shaven, with a square jaw and a straight nose set in light skin, and with hair perfectly groomed, few would have guessed him to be Syrian. Except for the cruel eyes, he might have gone unnoticed in America. His heavy cologne presented a stark match to the pungent odor of his two companions. Carefully, he laid a small, dark green, metallic box on the table. Next to this, he placed a long slender knife, razor sharp on both sides.

The captured man's right eye was swollen shut with dirt caked in the wound above. Blood oozed from his nose, running down his chin and dripping to the cut stone floor. The impact of each droplet raised a tiny cloud of dust. An open cut above his left eye flowed crimson, making him turn his head sideways, move his cheek, and squeeze his good eye shut to clear his vision. Occasionally, he spit red from his injured mouth. He wore the uniform of an Israeli fighter pilot. The blood-soaked, matted blond hair, straight nose, and one visible blue eye were not that unusual for an Israeli, but he was not. The American pilot, dressed in an Israeli uniform, watched while showing no emotion.

The Syrian leader spoke. "I am Rasht Sharafan. They call me Cobra. You have heard of me, yes?"

"No," lied the prisoner. He had heard of Cobra, Syria's best pilot, who received his nickname from his exploits with and against the agile F-14 Tomcat. In combat, the F-14 was always his first choice. It was rumored that just for the opportunity to shoot down American pilots, he had flown for Iraq in the War of 2003. When not flying he would commit terrorist acts, exploiting the enemy through torture and terror. Cobra approached these abuses with the same vigor and excitement as a normal person anticipated sex.

"You any relation to Mickey Mouse? No, that must be your operations here. You must be Goofy," said the American fighter pilot. He paused to spit blood on the floor. Yes, he had heard of Cobra. Even during the second *Desert Storm*, or *Operation Iraqi Freedom* as it was called in 2003, his wing command specifically sought out the terrorist.

"Ahhh!" exclaimed Cobra with delight, when he finally recognized the elusive accent. His captive was American. Immediately he broke into English. "So you are an American! You did not look like an Israeli, but you speak their language well. So very few Americans come to our sacred lands except to steal our oil. Such a fine sense of humor—but it will not last long," he said, with a sly grin.

Sharafan took the knife from the table and slid his finger gently along the sharp edge, bringing his own blood. He smiled and licked it.

"Now you will tell me where the general's son is."

"Go to hell. Your men couldn't get me to talk; neither will you and your toys."

"No, no, you misunderstand me," Sharafan said, waving the knife almost apologetically. He pointed to his tool of torture and continued. "This is just the appetizer." Then he tapped the green metal container. "Inside here is what I call my box of pain. With it you will surely talk."

"I'll die first."

"Oh, you will die," he said casually, "and you will also tell me all I want to know." With those words, he pointed to the American's right hand. The man holding the prisoner's arm spread the hand flat and held it tightly against the table.

"You can't do this, the Geneva—"

Before he finished, Sharafan slapped his hand over the man's mouth, preventing another word from escaping. His face reflected his anger and bitterness as he finished the words.

"Geneva Convention?" he uttered with contempt. He moved his face until he was almost nose-to-nose with his prisoner. "Don't preach rules of war to me." With each word Sharafan became angrier. "While we fight with sticks and stones, America and Israel use rockets, jets, and tanks. We fight with honor; you fight the coward's war." He smiled down on his victim. "We will triumph. You will lose. Mark my words, they are the truth." He intentionally turned toward his men and raised his voice, "Allahu Akbar!"

In unison the other two men almost screamed the words that meant God is great: "Allah Akbar!"

A wicked smile filled Sharafan's face. "I will give you the same Geneva Conference you gave the prisoners at Abu Ghraib." He smiled at each of his companions. "Maybe we should strip and violate him like the Americans did our captured friends?"

With those words the anger of Aziz and al-Majid reached emotional highs that threatened to become explosive and deadly actions. Aziz chanted, "Allahu Akbar."

Al-Majid hit the prisoner on the head and pulled out his machete. "Let us take his head and show it to all."

In an effort to restrain his companions, Sharafan held his hand up to stop them. "The machete is swift and holds too much compassion."

The two hesitated and listened to the words. Ready to take instant action with the large, heavy blade, al-Majid lowered his weapon. Sharafan released the prisoner's mouth and tapped the deadly knife in his hand. His comrades watched and responded with grim smiles of sadistic understanding.

Hours earlier the American prisoner, Beau Gex, had been flying a retaliatory mission against Syria. His fighter group was ordered to intercept a bus of kidnapped Israeli children, which also included a top Israeli general's son. The bus was spotted on a road just inside Lebanon. Beau's fighter group responded quickly, finding the bus and making every effort to impede its progress. Low on fuel, all the airplanes returned—except for the American's. Somehow he forced the kidnappers into a ditch.

He waited for the children to run from the bus, and then, using the guns of his aircraft, killed their pursuers. Like the Israelis, the Arabs were also alerted and dozens more of the Arab kidnappers had joined in the pursuit of the children. Soon Beau ran out of fuel, and in an effort to delay the children's capture he aimed his plane toward their attackers. At the last second, he ejected, letting his jet score a direct hit.

Somehow Beau managed to gather the eleven children, including General Mosat's son Beginn, and reached the city in which the terrorists now held him captive. A few buildings away the children hid quietly like good little soldiers. Beau had used himself as a decoy to save them, giving Beginn orders to escape in the safety of darkness. Even in the face of death, the full moon gave Beau reason to worry about the children's safety.

Pain shot through his right hand as Sharafan sliced the tip of the small finger to the bone. He jerked and let out with a stunned groan. Smiling, Cobra slid the razor sharp blade down, then beneath the fingernail of the digit, and with a quick twist of his hand, removed it effortlessly. Puffs of dust rose from the floor as blood dripped through a large crack in the wooden table. Cobra aligned the blade with the first joint, rocking the knife gently back and forth, careful not to cut the skin. Unexpectedly, he snapped the sharp steel through the joint. Beau cried out in pain and caught his breath in short gasps. The small finger was neatly severed at the first knuckle. Cobra took a rag and wiped the wicked blade clean.

An excerpt from Book 3:
MOON SHADOW'S REVENGE
(Coming in 2014)

Betrayal

Darkness shielded the intruder crouching at the foot of the bed. He clutched a steel pipe firmly in his hand. Before him lay a man and a woman sleeping peacefully.

Determined to carry out his wanton act of treachery, Mike Marix was no longer the English gentleman or the pilot who had risked his life unsuccessfully to drive the invaders from the United States. Instead, he had become instrumental in killing Beau Gex's best friend, Ruben Alonzo. Beau had been suspicious and threatened Marix. He had also taken Krysti Socorro from him.

Sleeping in the security of their room, neither Beau nor Krysti were aware of the deadly act about to be enacted.

Now Marix saw an opportunity to take Krysti back and rid himself of Beau forever. Quietly, he crept to the side of the bed where Beau lay unsuspecting. The desire to smash him with all his strength consumed him. As he stood with trembling hands, his desire to kill Beau and be rid of him forever was tempered with the fear it might wake Krysti before he could seize her. When Marix brought the pipe down against Beau's head, he held back ever so slightly. Confident when he saw no movement come from his hated adversary, he moved to the other side of the bed where Krysti lay undisturbed. A surreal peace surrounded her.

Quickly and tightly, his hand clasped about Krysti's mouth rousing her with terrifying effect from her peaceful sleep. The more she tried to struggle, the more she became entwined in the sheets wrapped snugly about her lithe frame. So tight was his hand, she was unable to scream for help.

Only now was Krysti able to catch a glimpse of Beau through her auburn curls. He appeared to lay peacefully beside her, oblivious to Marix's actions. Blood trickled through his blond hair and onto the bed from a wound at the back of his head. This time he was unable to come to her aid.

A familiar voice, crazed with revenge, whispered his demands into her ear. "If you want him to live, come with me and don't make a sound." The cold harsh words came with a calculating confidence. Marix added, "If you struggle he will die."

Gone was the British officer and gentleman Krysti thought she knew. Michael Marix had become a mad man bent on possessing her.

"You know I love you. I will prove it to you." With disgust he pointed to the motionless body of Beau Gex. "I'm going to save you from him." Marix added, "I'm taking you home."

Panic consumed Krysti when she understood Marix's intentions. He intended to take her across hostile country. The invading forces of the Coalition still occupied and controlled all of Texas and the area stretching from the hill country near San Antonio where they were to El Paso, where her parents lived. To attempt crossing this part of controlled America would be suicidal, or most assuredly lead to capture.

Marix dragged her from the room, out of Cliff Palace, their cliff hideaway, to the ledge overlooking the Frio River. Once on the ledge, Marix paused and told her something that sent a cold chill up her spine.

"You have nothing to worry about. I brought Justin along. He's in the back of the Jeep waiting for us now."

Krysti couldn't move stricken not only with the sobering thought Marix would try to take her across Texas, but now the frightening revelation her son was also a hostage. As long as her son remained in Cliff Palace with the others, he had a chance to survive.

"No, please leave Justin!" Krysti begged. Her pleas fell on deaf ears as Marix swung her over his shoulders and started down the trail leading to the hidden Jeeps.

To add to her horror, Marix laughed. "Justin thinks you want this." Suddenly, his eyes changed and it frightened Krysti. "If you say otherwise, I can't even describe what will happen to him."

OTHER BOOKS BY JOE BARFIELD AVAILABLE IN PRINT

AND AS EBOOKS
Link to eBooks:
https://www.smashwords.com/profile/view/thecajun

 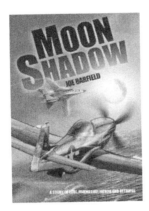 

MOON SHADOW THE LEGEND - (Book 1)
MOON SHADOW – (Book 2)
MOON SHADOW'S REVENGE – (Book 3) Available in July

Action-adventure - by Joe Barfield

In 2016 the Muslim Brotherhood has infiltrated America rising in numbers from three million in 2008 to over twelve million in 2016. They have established more than 45 jihadist camps across America determined to take over America and install Sharia law. Members of the Brotherhood attain key spots in the government and military. Hundreds of thousands are granted amnesty, while tens of thousands walk freely across the border of Mexico with the help of America's liberal adminiistration, the Department of Justice and the President of the United States. Unmolested they roam freely across America doing Allah's work. Muslims control the Department of Homeland Security with unlimited weapons and billions of rounds of ammunition. With men in key positions, Christians have been labeled traitors and the debt is given no limit with the express intent of bankrupting America. The United States is destroyed, not so much from outside forces, but rather from the greed within. Unable to pay what remains of the military they simply go home. Along with the President, the Department of Homeland Security and the Muslim Brotherhood control America. The invasion that began in 2008 takes America down. But the Coalition as they call themselves run up against American Civilians armed and deadly. A handful of pilots try desperately to take back America. Against insurmountable odds the future of America depends on its best pilot defeating an F-14 at night but all he has is an antiquated P-51 Mustang and an old Indian Legend; Moon Shadow.

Written in 1996, **Moon Shadow** has become eerily historical with each passing year.

Moon Shadow, the Legend

Considered a traitor and murderer, Beaux Gex, with the help of military friends, is determined to return to America and warn her leaders, but he soon learns they are the problem. Could America's top secret, Aurora Project save or destroy America? Will he be too late? Will the old Indian legend, Moon Shadow, save him or destroy him?

Moon Shadow

Trapped behind enemy lines, a handful of America's best jet pilots, led by ace Beau Gex, discover a dozen old World War II aircraft that they can use in guerrilla-type warfare against the invaders—their enemy. But when the invaders find one of the SR-71 Blackbirds—and intend to use it to destroy the space station, Starburst—Beau and his men are forced to fly one last deadly mission.

Now America's future depends on Beau, its best pilot, defeating an F-14 Tomcat at night. But all he has is an antiquated P-51 Mustang and an old Indian Legend, Moon Shadow.

Moon Shadow's Revenge

America has collapsed but Beau Gex, and Krysti Socorro have found love and they are safe. Their peace is destroyed when Krysti is kidnapped. Beau swears revenge even if he must kill them all to find her. But before he can rescue her it will be a long journey and he will need to deal with the "Crazies," and the Sand People."

For the not-faint-at-heart, *Moon Shadow* begins with one of the edgiest torture scenes since *Marathon Man*. And for those looking for love mixed in with their adventure, *Moon Shadow* satisfies as a tender romance between Beau and Krysti Socorro, an exquisite doctor. Will the betrayal of another tear them apart forever? Can a child save their love or is it too late?

THE CAJUN
(action-adventure) by Joe Barfield

A little Crocodile Dundee and a little Rambo. With a million dollar reward on her head, Kelli Parsons hides in the treacherous Atchafalaya Swamp where living or dying depends on one man--the Cajun!

FORMULA 2000, *the DREAM*
(action – based on a true story) by Joe Barfield

Hoosiers on Wheels.
Keeping a promise, a father enters his son, Shannon Kelly, in the Formula 2000 race series with only a dream and a prayer. When things go from bad to worse it takes a crusty old mechanic, Charlie Pepper, to show them how to win. They soon learn that with Pepper almost anything is possible.

URBAN KILL

(detective thriller) by Joe Barfield

Ex-policemen are taking wealthy men on the hunt of their lives—human prey! The only two witnesses have already been murdered. To solve the case, the lead detective must find a pimp called The Rat and the drug addict Pinky, because they have the answers. But the Rat and Pinky are trying to kill each other. The only people who can help him are a gay bar owner, a hyper, absent-minded forensics expert from India, and his one-eyed, three-legged dog, Lucky.

CHEM STORM

(action – chemical disaster) by Joe Barfield

A reporter and an engineer race to save Houston from a disaster worse than a nuclear explosion—a chemical storm!

Jean Alexander, a reporter for <u>The Houston Post,</u> is young and inquisitive and has gained unauthorized access to an area, where she finds five dead bodies. She wants to know why but a spectator alerts the guards to her presence and she is removed.

The following day a Civil/Chemical Engineer, Travis Selkirk, approaches Jean. She learns he is the spectator from the day before that alerted the guards. He points out the foolishness of her adventure and how the chemicals could have killed her. Jean baits Travis and gets him to agree to show her the dangers that exist on the Houston Ship Channel.

WORDS THAT DON'T OFFEND LIBERALS
(Satirical humor) by Joe Barfield

A humorous look at words that don't offend Liberals. The book will probably offend Liberals. This is meant for the entertainment of open minded people. This a book to keep notes. Check it out before you purchase your printed copy. Fun gift for your Liberal friends. They may never forgive you.

PALABRAS QUE NO OFENDEN LIBERALES
(humor satírico) Joe Barfield

Una mirada chistosa en palabras que no ofendan liberales. El libro probablemente ofender a los liberales. Esto es para el entretenimiento de personas de mente abierta. Este es un libro para guardar notas.
Compruébelo usted mismo antes de comprar su copia impresa. Regalo de la diversión para sus amigos liberales. Es posible que nunca perdonará.

The Single Male Parent's Cookbook and Short Stories
by Joe Barfield

The Single Male Parents' Cookbook, is a delightful combination of food and humor, two subjects everyone will enjoy. As a single parent, the author raised his children from the time they were four and six, and soon became an expert in the kitchen. As he said, "My cooking must have been good, because both are adults now and still alive, which only attests to culinary skills... or luck!"

The Single Male Parents' Cookbook combines recipes with humorous anecdotes of things that did and didn't work in the kitchen (and in the author's life). Joe includes lots of fun cooking ideas along with some that were not so good, and even a few you don't ever want to try at home! He shares everything from his Friday Night Special to his Motel Doggy (the electric hotdog). And let's not forget the ROC (Roaches on Chocolate).

Each recipe is followed by a short story about his childhood antics or raising his children. Not everything always ran smoothly. There was that time his boiled eggs blew up all over the ceiling. Oh, and that grease fire... don't ever pour water on a grease fire! But they say experience is the best teacher, and they are right. It wasn't always easy in those years, but Joe managed to retain his sense of humor.

He once heard George Carlin say that although he's over sixty, he never stopped being ten. That describes the author perfectly. In fact, Joe says, "I've been ten six times over, and my life is as fun as ever."

His final comments are, "Are you curious about my recipes for rattlesnake, rabbit, squirrel, and armadillo? I think you'd enjoy the rattlesnake. Can you picture me cooking the Roaches on Chocolate (ROC) on Rachel Ray's show?"

Don't let the cookbook confuse you. Joe is just a normal type of guy. Well, maybe except for the time he got married at midnight in a jail in Mexico. But that has nothing to do with cooking. Neither does the time he almost got kidnapped in the mountains of Colombia when he met his second wife. He's just a wild and crazy guy from Texas.

A Life in Time, My Story – non-fiction
by Joe Barfield

Remember lying on the grass in your front yard and watching the stars? Your best friend was beside you, and neither one of you uttered a word. Then a meteor flashed across the sky and both of you got excited and pointed to the sky.

Our lives are like a flashing meteorite. Often the moments go unnoticed, but we do manage to brighten and touch the lives of those around us. Although we are not all famous or well-known, our stories are important. Each of us has a life in time. These are a series of short stories about my life. From the past comes comparison I'm sure you have heard before, so let me ask you again: Who won the Super Bowl last year? Who won the Indy 500? Who won the last game of the World Series? Who were the Best Actor and Actress at the last Academy Awards? You might remember one, but you probably don't know the others.

Now ask yourself these questions: Do you remember the names of some of your teachers? What teacher helped you in high school? What valuable lessons did your mother and father teach you? And who was your best friend? They may not be famous, but they brightened your life just like that flashing meteorite. I believe life has been an adventure and that we learn from all the things that have happened to us.

The one thing I try to do is look at things in a humorous way. As a child I was called Tiger because I was always into things. I thought I was just curious. As a teenager the death of my father weighed heavily on me. We began to move around. I became angry—a "Rebel," as some of my close friends called me. I had conflicts with religion. When my children were four and six I became a single parent. I learned a lot from them. Most of the stories, I hope, will keep you laughing. There are some that are sad, but that is life. And that is what *A Life in Time* is all about.

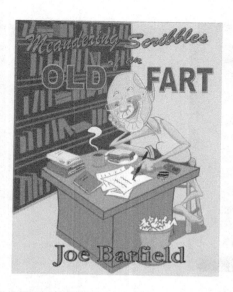

MEANDERING SCRIBBLES OF AN OLD FART – (Political essays) by Joe Barfield

People need to look at their government. I have written articles for over 20 years; from the first Bush to Obama. We have problems we need to face and quit sticking our head in the sand. It's okay to be a liberal or a conservative, but neither exists in our government today. Our politicians do everything but what they were elected to do: Represent the People.

If you are open minded you will enjoy this. If you've only voted one party all of your life then don't download this book. Stop to look at what our politicians are doing today. If you are an open minded Christian you might enjoy this. And if you are you must admit God is probably not too happy. Atheists are offended. Everyone should be offended that they are offended. When talking about being Christian in the military becomes an act of "treason," then we have bigger problems.

America has spent so much time protecting each individual's rights that no one has any rights. Throughout history every great empire has collapsed; there have been no exceptions.

WARNING!

This is for mature audiences so if you're a Democrat or Republican who always voted the same ticket, this is not for you, because it means you are incapable of thinking on your own, so I'd rather you not buy it. If you are a frustrated American upset with the current administrations then you may find these scribbles quit enjoyable.

Should I Forget

A simple reminder, since I might forget. These are scribbles of an Old Fart and you may find repetitions. This is due to "Oldheimers."

DISCLAIMER

Any resemblance to political persons in office is purely intentional.

FOR PETA'S SAKE!
For your peace of mind let it be known that NO animals were injured during the making of these meandering scribbles.
GIVE ME A BREAK!
I'm not a racist, and I'm not a terrorist, I'm just trying to be funny and open your eyes to other solutions. If you have better ideas then you write a book.
FINAL WARNING!
Before you read this I must remind you that you have three choices. You can only pick one so be careful. You are a Democrat, a Republican or an American.

If you picked one of the first two then don't get this book and if you do then don't complain. Americans tell the truth, the other two don't.

Offended yet? You will be; unless you're an American.
FOR OBAMA I'M AMERICA'S BIGGEST THREAT
I'm a white, Christian, heterosexual, and I believe in traditional marriage.
I am America's Biggest Threat.
Get Over It!

A Short Story Collection – fiction
by Joe Barfield

These short stories are based on actual events, and parts from some of my novels, and children's stories. *Sebring, the Rainman* is based on a race my son, Beaux, actually competed. What a race it was!

Night of the Virgin is a combination of events that happened to me in high school. I eventually married her in a jail, in Mexico at midnight. Some of the dialog from *Flight 223* actually occurred. You see I was on flight 223 from Seattle to Houston during the 911 attack. A very strange and chaotic event I will never forget.

I hope you enjoy these as much as I did bringing them to you.

ABOUT THE AUTHOR

The author, Joe Barfield, has led an interesting life, scuba diving, racing cars with his son Beaux Barfield, lifting weights and playing a variety of sports. He met his wife Lucia in Cali, Colombia while on a trip. One time she took him on a trip in the mountains of Colombia and at one point they thought they had entered a guerrilla camp and he would be kidnapped. It turned out to be a group of the Colombian military looking for kidnappers. He spent a few days with them and even has a picture of him holding a 50 caliber machine gun with one of the Colombian soldiers. Showing his tenacity, once he was determined to win a Halloween contest and went as far as making an eight-foot monster with moving fingers. He won the contest. For him racing has always been an exciting endeavor, winning his very first race and two years later winning his first professional race at Sebring. His son went on to be Race Director for IndyCar. Barfield said there were as many adventures off the track as there were on. A quote from Jim Fitzgerald sums it all up, "When you do it and do it right it is the greatest turn on in the world. A collage of pictures shows some of his adventures and cars he and his son have raced.

You might say I have led an adventurous life. I was married at midnight in a jail in Mexico when I was eighteen. Raising my children has proved helpful in my writing. My other activities include scuba diving, weightlifting, building houses, and even racing cars professionally; winning the 6-Hours of Sebring. On a wild adventure to Cali, Colombia, twelve years ago, I met my wife Lucia. She is one of the best things that ever happened in my life. While in the mountains of Colombia, I thought guerrillas had captured me but it was the military. I still remember my first thoughts when I saw their 50 caliber machine guns, "Oh my God I'm going to be kidnapped." To reassure my thoughts, Lucia turned to me and said, "Don't say anything I don't want them to hear your accent." Do you know what my next thought was? "OH Boy! I'm going to become a bestseller!"

For me writing has solved all the problems I couldn't in real life.

Connect With Me Online

My Webpage
www.jbarfield.com

SMASHWORDS
www.smashwords.com/profile/view/thecajun

AMAZON
www:amazon.com/author/joebarfield

See the Live For Today Trailer
http://goo.gl/Oesoxd

See the Moon Shadow Trailer
http://goo.gl/NSN4Ho